A WEDDING MISMATCH

KAYLEE BALDWIN

SWEETLY US PRESS

CHAPTER 1

ELIANA

"I don't believe I shall ever marry; I'm happy as I am, and love my liberty too well to be in any hurry to give it up for any mortal man." —Louisa May Alcott

"LET'S PLAY A GAME," Eliana said into the camera. It was the way she began every livestream, and already she could see the number of watchers ticking steadily upward into the hundreds.

"What game?" Dad yelled from the kitchen, suddenly clank ing dishes around like he was a one-man pot-and-pan band. "I'm up for cards."

"Uno! Uno! Uno!" her younger brother, Cameron, yelled out, using his talking device, as he streaked behind her wearing nothing but bright yellow swim trunks.

Eliana stared at the chaos behind her, streaming live to her seven hundred viewers. Nope, now it was eight hundred.

"I cannot play one more game of Uno." Mom groaned. "Maybe Grandpa will want to play with you. Should I call him?"

"Hey, guys?" Eliana called over her shoulder in her kindest, sweetest tone. "Remember how you all said right now would be a good time for me to start a livestream?"

"It is," her mom assured her. "Go right ahead. You're not bothering us."

1

She gritted her teeth but tried to smile through it, as she knew over nine hundred people were now watching her every move. Comments streamed in:

Where are you?
Is that your family?
Who's the teenager? He's hilarious!

She glanced up from her notes to see Cameron making faces at himself in the camera. He carefully held Louisa May Alcott, Eliana's adorably tiny desert tortoise, beside his cheek so she could look into the camera too. *Oh, Cameron.* He was her seventeen-year-old brother with Down syndrome.

Comments careened down her screen, most of them turtle emojis and hearts. Everyone loved Louisa May Alcott, and partnering that cuteness with Cameron was enough to make the internet explode.

Eliana ran a finger down her livestream outline, but everyone was going to be too distracted for her to go through her bullet-pointed list of why being single was better than being in a relationship. She flipped her notebook over. "Actually, let's save the game for another time."

She'd come up with a really cute version of two truths and a lie where she'd reveal her big news. Oh well. "As you may have noticed, I'm not in my usual recording space. My sister is getting married at the end of the summer, so I came home to Florida to help plan the wedding."

Speaking of Eliana's sister ... Julia walked into the tiny apartment and threw her bag down on the couch with the heavy sigh of someone who'd just turned in their grades at the very last minute. "I'm done," she said dramatically.

"Your sister is doing a livestream," Mom whispered loud enough for the camera to pick up the sound.

Eliana closed her eyes. There was no way to salvage this.

Julia yelped when she realized she was in the frame, being streamed out to over two thousand people now. She threw herself on the floor and army-crawled behind the couch—still on display. "I hate being on camera!" she hissed. "Why didn't you tell me?"

Time to land this plane, though both wings were on fire and it was heading straight toward crash-and-burn. Her numbers continued to tick upward. For someone usually so in control of what she put out into the world, this was very off-brand for her.

"I'm going to make this quick," she said.

More comments rolled in about how they loved seeing her family. She loved seeing them too, just not in the background of her recordings.

"My parents' plumbing pipes burst a few days ago, and they have to rip out the flooring and replace it all. So we're all staying in my sister's two-bedroom apartment together!" Was that enough enthusiasm in her voice? Enough excitement?

Dad grumbled something about paying for burst pipes and new flooring and a wedding. Eliana had only been staying with her parents for two days when the pipes burst in spectacular and disgusting fashion, driving them all out of the house immediately and changing everyone's plans.

"I want to tell you the big news I've been teasing all week ... Are you ready?"

"Yes!" Cameron's talker blasted right beside her ear. He rested his chin on her shoulder and stuck out his tongue at himself. She took Louisa May Alcott from him and kissed his cheek, feeling the scruff of a beard on his face. When had her baby brother started growing facial hair?

"I'm excited to announce that I'm under contract to write a book! The working title is *Happily Single*, and I can't wait to share it with you."

Cameron grinned, his chin still on her shoulder. Her heart warmed until he let out the longest, loudest burp he could muster for her 2,500 live viewers to see.

Her smile tilted but held strong. *If you pretend everything's fine, it'll actually be fine.* That mantra had worked for her to this point.

"Okay, bye!" she said quickly, and she logged off before things got worse.

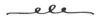

There he goes again.

Eliana lounged on a beach chair at the edge of The Palms Retirement Community's pool, where she kept an eye on Cameron swimming.

A scowling, scruffy-looking man, who most definitely did not fit in with The Palms' age demographic or well-kempt aesthetic, stalked through the lobby and past the pool for the fourth time in the last fifteen minutes. He looked like a cross between a Marvel hero and a villain, with his huge muscles and dark eyes that had a stay-back glint to them.

She breathed in the scent of chlorine and salt and pushed away the longing to jump in and cool off. She didn't want to risk streaking her makeup. Besides, when her hair got wet, it frizzed out like a lion's mane, and no one wanted to see that.

She opened her phone and flipped to her profile page. It had been two days since she'd filmed her livestream at Julia's apartment, and it was shaping up to be her second-most watched video. She wanted to believe it was because of her exciting book announcement and not because of her family's antics. But had she ever seen so many comments containing the word burp?

Not on her platform.

Cameron grabbed at her toes with his wet hands. She squealed in surprise and yanked her feet under her, and he laughed as he pushed away from the edge of the pool. A ripple of water cascaded away from him and toward where Grandpa Horace and his friend, Smitty, waded in the pool. Apparently, Grandpa and Smitty had become enemies after a bad business situation when they were younger. But when their grandchildren fell in love, they'd let the past go and had rekindled their friendship. The two men splashed around with Cameron, droplets hitting her legs and offering cool relief.

"How's the book coming along?" Grandma Winnie approached Eliana, holding two summery, yellowish-red drinks that matched her sleeveless floral blouse. Eliana gratefully accepted the tall glass of icy strawberry lemonade. Grandma Winnie's normally perfectly coiffed short gray hair had gone limp from the heat, as had Eliana's long blond hair she'd attempted to curl that morning. No hairstyles stood a chance today. It wasn't that Eliana had forgotten how muggy Florida could be in June—it was more that she'd selectively disremembered.

Her family was tripping over each other at Julia's, so they took every available opportunity to escape. Since they could technically live in the house during repairs—though no one wanted to—insurance wouldn't cover a rental. And due to The Palms' bylaws, they couldn't stay with

Grandma and Grandpa for the two months it would take to fix the pipes. But they could use the amenities with their grandparents.

"I'm struggling to concentrate on my book," she admitted. With Julia and Logan, Smitty's grandson, getting engaged and married within three months, Eliana didn't have a lot of time to pull off the perfect wedding. But Logan had just been accepted into a four-month extended learning program in Africa that he'd applied for nearly six months ago, and they wanted to get married before he left. Before *they* left, actually, since Julia had decided to go with him.

"You're welcome to work at our place," Grandma said.

"Thank you." Maybe she'd actually get some work done there.

"You know I love a good self-help book," she continued. It was a love they shared. "But *Happily Single*?"

Eliana was used to skeptics picking at her concept. Everyone seemed to believe you had to be in a romantic relationship to be happy and truly fulfilled. Eliana had married someone who'd made her feel the opposite, and she never wanted to feel that way again. She'd learned in the five years since they'd divorced that she was so much happier single than she had been in a relationship, and she wanted to share that wisdom.

"I'm not trying to convince people they should be single." Most of the time she thought they *should*, but that wouldn't earn her any points with Grandma. "But if that's the message they get, then I'm okay with that."

Based on Grandma's cloudy expression, that hadn't earned her any points either.

"Most of the people I know who are in relationships aren't happy," Eliana said gently.

"I am." Grandma sat in a beach lounger and watched Grandpa almost ... wistfully.

"You guys are different."

"Julia's happy."

"Is she?" That was another reason Eliana wanted to come to Diamond Cove months before the wedding. She barely knew her sister's fiancé, and she needed to make sure he was a good guy before this wedding went through.

"Happier than I've ever seen her," Grandma Winnie said.

Eliana hoped that was true. So far, Julia mostly acted stressed, but it *was* the end of the school year, and she was planning a wedding, and her newest picture book just released, and four people plus a tiny desert tortoise had unexpectedly moved into her nine-hundred-square-foot space.

Eliana sighed. She had to figure out another living situation. She did livestreams at least once a week, plus she filmed and edited long- and short-form videos that kept her platform engaged and coming back for more.

The handsome superhero/villain rushed past the pool for a fifth time, slightly less scowly. He spoke with an older man with a military haircut and biceps bigger than her head. When they separated, the older man paused to chat with Cameron for a moment, and then he approached her and Grandma.

"This is my friend, Don," Winnie said to Eliana.

"Hello," Don said with a sharp nod.

"Is everything okay?" Winnie asked. Grandpa Horace and Smitty swam over to join the conversation.

"Someone parked in Asher's spot, so I arranged to have the car towed."

"It's the out-of-towners coming to use the beach," Smitty complained. "They think they can park anywhere they want."

"They're entitled," Grandpa said.

Eliana shared an amused glance with Grandma. They all sounded a lot like grumpy old men.

Grandpa and Smitty left with Don soon after to make their tee time, and Grandma followed as soon as her lemonade was gone.

Eliana sat at the edge of the pool and stuck her feet in. No amount of Cameron's tugging on her legs and feet would get her in that pool. Cameron's cheeks looked a little too pink. "It's time to go home, bud."

He kicked his way over to the other side of the pool instead of getting out.

"Cameron!"

He closed his eyes and splashed around, making happy noises. She let out an exasperated huff. His shoulders had gotten too much sun as well. She should have made him wear his swim shirt.

She stood and walked to the side of the pool where he floated. "Cam, please. We need to go home."

His eyes had a mischievous glint as he kicked off the wall and glided to the middle of the pool. He wore a life vest, so he could float at any depth. He kicked back and floated on his back, his face tilted toward the sun as if soaking in as much of the rays as he could.

That little stinker. He knew exactly what she wanted him to do. And he knew how to pretend he didn't understand.

"I don't want to get in!"

He continued to float, easily ignoring her.

"Cam!"

He covered his mouth as he laughed.

"You're getting sunburned!" she tried again, but he only laughed harder, his shoulders shaking. He understood most of what was said to him, but he might not understand what she meant by sunburn, or the fact that it would sting later.

Amusement warred with annoyance as she kicked off her shoes and pulled off her sundress to reveal her black, high-waisted, two-piece swimsuit she never intended to get wet. She walked to the stairs and dipped her feet in. She held her hair up so it wouldn't dip into the pool as the water climbed her body.

Okay, this was still salvageable.

Cam's eyes glinted with excitement when he saw her coming, and he ducked his head into the water. When she got close enough to take his hand, he sprang out of the water like a dolphin and spit out a mouthful of water straight into her face.

"Ew!" She dropped her hair into the pool as she swiped at the spit-water on her face. Her fingers came away dark with makeup. *Great.* "Cameron, that was not nice."

Cameron slung his arm around her shoulders, hanging from her like she was a ledge. Her wet hair tangled under his dripping arm. "Sorry, sorry," he signed. He brought his face close to hers. "Love you."

She still remembered the first time she'd heard him say "I love you" when they were kids. She still felt that swell of happiness whenever he said it to her, despite her annoyance. "Love you too."

She wrapped her arm around his waist and used the water's buoyancy to carry him to the stairs. This time, he climbed out like that had been his plan all along, and found his towel. She hadn't brought a towel, so she waited to use his damp one. She tried to wipe off as much makeup as she could, but her liquid eyeliner wasn't doing her any favors.

Cameron carried his life vest and the swim bag while she put her sundress back on, and they headed toward her car. She took his hand, not wanting him to get any ideas about darting off after Sweetie, the ridiculous alligator dressed like Belle from *Beauty and the Beast*. Grandma said Sweetie was harmless, but no thank you.

A huge tow truck was in the parking lot. She recognized her car strapped to the back of it as it headed toward the parking lot exit.

CHAPTER 2

ASHER

A SHER PULLED OFF HIS helmet and set it on his motorcycle seat as a waterlogged woman in impractical tourist sandals raced past him, chasing after the tow truck. It served her right for parking in his reserved spot. At least, that's what Don had said when he'd convinced Asher to call a tow truck. It was the third time that summer someone had stolen his parking spot.

Someone shuffled behind him, and he turned to find Cameron Peters standing close enough for his wet swim trunks to drip onto Asher's shoes.

"Hi. How are you?" Cameron asked, using the talker.

Asher loved seeing Cameron use his talker so deftly. He'd only just started working with him a few months ago, when his old speech therapist had moved, and it was a fun change of pace to work with someone so young again.

"I'm good, man." He held out his hand for Cameron to high-five and then fist-bump. It was a handshake they'd developed a few weeks ago. He looked around for Cameron's mom or grandma. "Who are you here with?"

Cam didn't respond, so Asher tried to think of a different way to ask his question. Cameron watched the woman who had stopped the tow truck and was chatting with the driver using wild hand movements.

Uh-oh. "Who's that?"

"Elly," Cameron answered.

"Who's Elly?"

Again, no response. There were multiple reasons for someone not to respond. In Cameron's case, it usually came down to three reasons: Cameron didn't understand him, he didn't know how to navigate his talker to find the answer, or he just didn't want to communicate. Based on his sunburned face indicating that he'd already had a full day and was probably exhausted, and considering Cameron's general disinterest in answering questions, it was probably the latter.

"Can I use your talker?"

Cam allowed him to take it, and Asher navigated to the family page. There, he saw a button labeled Eliana.

He pointed to it. "Is this Elly?"

Cameron pushed the button. "Eliana is my oldest sister. She lives in Boston. Eliana makes videos."

Her picture on the button was small and blurry, but he saw some family resemblance in the hair color. He hadn't heard about Eliana—only Julia, who occasionally brought Cameron to his sessions. "I didn't know you had two sisters!"

Cameron snatched his talker back and navigated to his favorite pre-programmed phrase. "I am a man of mystery."

"You sure are."

Eliana stalked toward them, her dark eyes a thundercloud blue. "You'd better not park there! My car was just towed," she called to Asher, fuming. "You would think if the speech therapist isn't here by one, their spot is fair game."

He took her in: her cheeks were pink with both sun and heightened emotion. A few freckles also broke through, the wholesome and sweet look at odds with the daggers in her glare. Her hair was mostly straight but fell into a natural wave toward the tips. Yep, the quintessential entitled, beautiful tourist.

Even if she was related to one of his favorite people in the world.

"I went home for lunch," he said. He enjoyed going home for lunch. He didn't know how much longer he'd actually be able to secretly live in his late grandpa's bungalow at The Palms—he was shocked he'd made it this long already with no one finding out. But it's where he felt closest to his grandpa, and he was missing him more than ever.

10

"You're the speech therapist?" She huffed as she took him in from head to toe with folded arms. "You don't look like a speech therapist."

"How is an SLP supposed to look?" He clipped his helmet onto the bike and turned to face her fully.

"First of all, you're not wearing scrubs," she said.

He looked down at his favorite black T-shirt and jeans. "I don't always wear scrubs to work."

"And you're too ..." She waved her hand as if fanning smoke away. "Rugged and frowny." Her gaze lingered on his lips for a beat, and his mouth twitched as if it could physically feel her stare. "And your eyes are green," she finished, folding her arms.

"My eyes are green," he repeated slowly.

"Like *arrestingly* green," she said, accusatorily.

"I must have missed that question on the SLP exam," he mumbled as he glanced at his watch. He was already running late, thanks to not having a parking spot and needing to tow her car.

He waved to Cam and then jogged off without a backward glance at Eliana. She must be in town for Julia's wedding. Their paths shouldn't have to cross again.

He paused at the front desk, where Misty, with new lime-green streaks in her hair, sat on her stool at the computer. "Can you call a ride for Cameron and his sister?" He nodded toward them as they paused just outside the doors to pet Bear, the golden retriever leashed to Sweetie. Eliana leveled Sweetie with the same glare she'd given Asher earlier. "Charge it to me."

"Sure," Misty said. "Oh, wait! Harry is looking for you."

"Okay, thanks." Harry was helping him find a goose-shaped saltshaker to match the one his grandma had always used—and that Asher had broken last week. Maybe he'd located one.

Asher hurried off before Eliana could catch up to him.

Asher set out to find Harry after his last appointment.

"Asher. How's cleaning out the bungalow going?" Mr. Richardson, the manager of The Palms, wore a suit every day he actually came in to work,

11

even when it was over ninety degrees and humid outside. Based on the scent that followed him everywhere he went, he was sweating through the fabric.

"Good. Grandpa was a bit of a hoarder." He attempted to walk past, but Mr. Richardson took his arm to stop him. Asher lifted his brows.

Mr. Richardson dropped his hand and swallowed hard. "I need a time-line. We've been more than generous—"

"Give him a break!" Marilyn Detrix hobbled over to them with her cane—a cane she wasn't afraid to use in a variety of ways. She was one of the wealthier residents of The Palms. Asher had worked with her following her stroke last year. She never failed to notice when he was having a rough day, and she brought him his favorite candy bar every session, no matter how often he told her she didn't have to. Plus, he swore he'd seen her trip Mr. Richardson with her cane last week when he was trying to catch Asher in the dining hall. "Asher is grieving. He'll get to it when he gets to it."

"I understand." Mr. Richardson wiped at his sweaty forehead with a handkerchief he pulled from his pocket. "Maybe we can help you. Hire a professional crew."

"No. I'll handle it," Asher said.

Mr. Richardson looked sideways at Marilyn. It was clear he wanted to say more, be more firm, but he wouldn't want to risk making Marilyn angry.

"I need to go," Asher said. "Someone's looking for me."

He walked away with long, purposeful strides he knew Mr. Richardson would have to jog to keep up with, and Asher would guess that he'd never jogged a day in his life. Most of the time, Mr. Richardson passed his responsibilities on to Samantha, but ever since he'd learned he could rent out Asher's grandpa's bungalow at a higher rate than Asher was paying, he came more often to pressure Asher to finish cleaning it out. It was only by the grace of The Palms' owners, Adam and Belle Moreau, that he'd been able to hold on to it for this long.

Ty, one of the physical therapists, told Asher he saw Harry go into one of the conference rooms down the hall with the offices by the front entrance, so Asher poked his head into each of them until he finally got to the one at the end. He pushed it open to find a group of Palms residents in the middle of a meeting.

This really was an interesting group of people: Walt, Harry, Winnie, Polly, Nancy, Rosa, and Don. He saw them all hanging out together often but hadn't realized they had an entire meeting place of sorts. There was a standing whiteboard, but before he could see what was on it, Polly turned it to face the wall.

They were up to something. His grandpa had always hated secrets, said they only led to headaches and heartaches. He'd told him that when he'd caught Asher sneaking out to run away after his parents had died and Grandpa became his guardian. Asher had lied at first about where he was going, and then he'd broken down and confessed the truth. He'd planned to secretly live in his parents' house until he graduated high school.

Grandpa had reminded him they only had each other. Every other family member was gone.

He missed his grandpa. Some days were worse than others—especially the days when he wondered what his grandpa would think of the big secret he was currently keeping.

"I'm looking for Harry," he said abruptly. Did they all have to stare at him like that?

Harry headed toward him. Asher spotted Winnie, and a twinge of guilt pricked him for her granddaughter's car towed. Eliana might have rubbed him the wrong way, but Winnie had never been anything but kind to him. Especially after Grandpa died. He'd had to work to keep her—and her ability to sweet-talk conversation out of him—at a distance. He never talked to anyone like that, and her skills were uncanny. He couldn't let anyone close. It wasn't worth the risk.

"Are you dating anyone, Asher?" Nancy asked.

"Nancy!" Polly admonished, but Nancy waved for her to be quiet.

He squared his jaw. "No, ma'am."

"Why not? You're young and muy guapo!" Rosa said.

Walt chimed in. "You need to find a good young lady."

How could Asher explain to them that losing people was just too hard? He couldn't go through that again. He wasn't close to anyone, and that's the way he wanted it to remain. Safe.

"I have at least twenty ladies in my life." He winked subtly at Polly, who blushed and fanned herself. "And that's more than enough for me."

"Palms residents don't count," Don said.

Harry ushered him out, but Asher heard someone say his name on the other side of the closed door. Harry took him by the elbow and walked him away a few steps. "I think I found a saltshaker that looks pretty close," Harry said. "Do you want to come by later and see it?"

"Can you bring it by my office tomorrow?" If he went by Harry's house, Virginia would convince him to stay for dinner and then ask questions about his life, and he didn't want to have to dodge that all evening.

"Are you sure? Virginia is making her famous roast beef."

Yep, he was right. "I'll look for you tomorrow."

Harry agreed, and Asher left him to his meeting.

Asher rode his bike around town as the sun set, stopping to grab a burger, and then took his usual route through a small neighborhood with an unmaintained road that jutted off toward the beach. Most people didn't know about the road, since the cracks in the asphalt made it impractical for driving ... and it didn't lead anywhere except the beach. He drove almost to the end and tucked his bike between two overgrown trees.

He stayed close to the tree line until The Palms came into sight, and with it, his grandpa's bungalow. It sat at the edge of the beach, the very last bungalow in the row before the private beach turned public. The Palms allowed him to continue to rent it while he cleaned out his late grandfather's many, many belongings.

What they didn't know was that he'd been secretly living there for the past year. The Palms' resident flamingos—John, Paul, George, and Ringo—had wandered toward his grandpa's bungalow in a row as if steadily moving forward in an amusement park line. He couldn't tell the four of them apart, but some of his patients could, and they loved to regale him with stories of the flamingos' antics.

He made sure no one—no human, at least—on the beach could spot him, and then he raced across the sand to his grandpa's bungalow. It didn't matter if anyone saw him there—he was supposed to be there cleaning. The problem came when they never saw him leaving, so it was better to stay completely under the radar.

The familiar musty scent of his grandpa's bungalow greeted him as he walked inside. Something about his house—whether it was Grandpa's seventies-aesthetic decorating choices, the large stacks of boxes pushed to every corner, or the brown blinds that remained closed no matter what time of day it was—exuded a dull-golden feel. Like an old sepia-toned photograph found at the bottom of a dusty box. Or the set of John Wayne VHS tapes his grandpa loved and probably still had stored in one of those boxes.

Brownish-yellow and dusty could also describe Asher's life. The vibrant colors that came with experiencing a range of emotions or activities had leeched away, and he didn't have the desire—or energy—to get them back.

Except for blue. Specifically, the blue of the ocean—not the stormy blue of Eliana's eyes when she'd realized he'd had her car towed.

What had he been thinking, letting Don convince him it was the best course of action? Asher needed to lie low, not make waves, and stay off people's radar. Not start a fight when he was perfectly capable of walking.

Tonight called for swimming, so he changed into his trunks. He loved any and all water sports—surfing, snorkeling, scuba diving, windsurfing, swimming, whatever he had time for. He appreciated the wildness and beauty of the ocean, but also her rhythmic dependability. The tide always came in. The waves always crashed. The water that inevitably found its way into his mouth always tasted like fish and salt.

He tried to vary which beaches he swam at, but The Palms' was his favorite. As long as no one noticed him there too often, they wouldn't question his presence. A lot of employees stayed late to use the amenities, one of the perks of working at The Palms.

His entire body relaxed the moment he stepped into the ocean. Meter by meter, as his arms cut through the water, he was able to pack each of his worries tighter into the box in his mind, not unlike the boxes in his grandpa's house. He had every intention of going through them at some point, but "some point" never came, so they stayed taped shut and pushed aside. But always present, unfortunately.

After he swam so hard his arms and legs were jelly and his lungs burned with exertion, he lay on the sandy beach and stared up at the darkening sky. The very edge of the moon glistened, and he continued to watch as star after star poked through the sky, defying the sunlight still clinging to the edges of night with the kind of tenacity he admired but couldn't emulate.

He dug his fingers deep into the damp sand to ground himself. He was eventually going to have to leave his grandpa's bungalow. He couldn't live there forever, shouldn't even be living there now. But he wasn't ready for anything to change. Not yet.

Sometimes it felt like he was a shooting star hurtling toward earth, and no matter what he did, there were only two options available: burn out or crash. So he did nothing at all while he waited to see which fate was in store for him.

CHAPTER 3

WINNIE

WINNIE PULLED BACK FROM her sewing machine and grabbed her phone when it beeped with an incoming message. Was it Horace? She felt like a teenager again, hoping the dreamiest boy in school, Gerard Hammond, would notice her.

And just like when she was a teenager and Gerard would walk by without saying hello, her heart dropped when it wasn't Horace's name lighting up her phone.

Walt: Are we in agreement that Asher is the target?

This was good. This would give her something to focus on, other than the fact that Horace didn't have time for her anymore.

She was glad he and Smitty were best friends now. It was much better than them being enemies. She didn't have to hear Horace complain non-stop about Smitty. Or watch their terrible plans go awry.

No, instead, she was just ... lonely.

Between their tee times and lunch meetings and the trips they took to Arizona for the Super Bowl and the numerous car shows in Scottsdale, she felt like she rarely saw Horace anymore. And when she did, he was always telling her about this or that thing Smitty had said.

She'd be happy to never hear the name Smitty again. And to have her husband back. Some of the women at The Palms told her she was lucky to offload her husband so often, but she didn't feel lucky. Winnie was a shy person by nature, and without Horace there, she was spending entirely too much time in her own head.

Polly: I like him. He's always been kind to me.

Don: He towed someone's car a few days ago. That shows a strong backbone.

Winnie winced. She'd heard about that from Eliana, who had been none too happy to learn she was going to have to drive across town to retrieve her car.

Nancy: That was Eliana's car!

Walt: So they're off to a rocky start. It's not the first time.

Rosa: It's a thin line between hate and love!

Don: I've always liked a challenge.

Winnie: I'm glad you like a challenge, Don, because a towed car is the least of our worries.

Don: Operation Unhappily Single.

Polly: I'm sure Winnie doesn't want her granddaughter to be unhappy, even if she chooses to stay single.

How could Winnie convince Eliana to give relationships a second chance? Her friends needed to understand Eliana's past so they could help brainstorm how to get her to trust relationships again.

Winnie: Can you video chat?

All but Harry and Nancy could video chat, so the other five of them popped onto the link Nancy had set up. Winnie didn't know how it worked, but as long as she clicked on the link, the option for video chat with the Secret Seven—her matchmaking group of friends—always came up.

Polly had her large headphones on her ears, while behind her, geriatrics were doing downward dog on yoga mats in front of Paradise Lake. "Can you hear me?" she shouted.

"We can," Walt said, gruffly. "How do you turn the sound down on these phones again?"

"There's a button on the side," Don said. "Okay, what did you need to talk to us about?" He sat on a weight bench at the empty gym with his phone propped up where they could watch him do bicep curls. At least he wasn't on the toilet, like Harry that one time when he'd forgotten they could see—and hear—him. She shuddered.

"I wanted to tell you a little more about Eliana," she said. After Asher had interrupted their meeting, they'd all gotten a little spooked and had dismissed early.

"Can you speak up, dear?" Polly shouted.

Winnie put her mouth closer to the phone's mic, knowing it brought her face uncomfortably close to the screen. "Eliana was married five years ago to a man who turned out to be a frog."

"A frog?" Walt bellowed.

"Like the princess and the frog, Walt. Keep up," Rosa said. She was making dinner, and Winnie could almost smell sautéing onions and garlic through the screen. Her mouth watered.

"But didn't the frog turn into a prince?" Walt asked.

"Not this one," Winnie said grimly. "None of us were sad when she left him."

"Did he abuse her?" Don set his weight down, though his muscle remained flexed. She had no doubt that if she asked, Don would hunt Eliana's ex down and make him pay.

"Mentally and emotionally. He killed her self-confidence. Played into her insecurities that she has to be perfect to be loved. And since no one is perfect ..."

"It's better to not be loved," Walt finished quietly.

Winnie nodded. "She's writing a book called *Happily Single*. And if I believed she was actually happy, then I would support her fully and help her live her best life."

"But she's not happy!" Polly yelled.

"Exactly."

Don moved closer to the phone. "Let me summarize. We need to convince Eliana that she's not happily single."

That wasn't right, either. "I want to show her what it looks like to be happily in love. It's something she doesn't believe is possible for herself. And unless she can let her guard down, she's never going to let anyone in."

"Especially Asher," Rosa said with a sigh. "Why would he tow her car? It's so unlike him."

Don cleared his throat. "I may have had something to do with it."

"Don," Walt groaned.

"I didn't realize it was her car. Winnie, you need to teach her not to park in reserved spots."

Winnie closed her eyes for patience.

"Not helpful, Don!" Polly yelled. "Remember, step one is proximity. I've got to go, but I'll brainstorm some ideas."

When Polly hung up, she somehow ended the call for everyone. Winnie needed another distraction. She tapped out Eliana's number. Maybe hearing her granddaughter's voice could dispel this overwhelming silence.

"Eliana, what are you up to?"

"Trying to record content for my channel."

"Oh good." She breathed out in relief. "You have some time, then."

Was it her imagination, or did Eliana huff?

"I need you to try on your sister's dress for me." And she'd start dropping hints about how happy she and Horace were in their relationship while she was at it. Plant the seeds, and they'd start to grow.

CHAPTER 4
ELIANA

"I could never love anyone as I love my sisters." —Louisa May Alcott

J ULIA'S SNEEZE RACKED HER entire body the moment they walked into the florist's shop. Eliana fished a tissue packet out of her purse and handed it to her sniffling sister.

Natural light shone in through the tall windows surrounding the shop. It highlighted the colorful bursts of flower arrangements from every color in the rainbow. Logan had planned to come with Julia to pick out wedding flowers, but he had cancelled last minute to help his sister, Willow, with her two kids.

Eliana tried not to think of her own elegant wedding as she spotted a bouquet of white roses. Corbin's mom had insisted on a classic color scheme of black, white, and red. When the roses had arrived wilted, she should have taken that as a sign.

Julia sneezed again.

"Are you allergic to flowers?" the florist, Carrie, asked with a frown.

"Just some of them," Julia said, her nose sounding even stuffier than before. "Roses and lilies for sure. And sometimes I react around carnations." Julia blew her nose loudly, and her eyes were rimmed in red. The entire shop brimmed with a kaleidoscope of roses and carnations.

The phone rang, and Carrie led them to a table with stacks of photo albums to browse before she hurried off.

"Do you have any ideas?" Eliana asked Julia.

Julia blew her red nose. "I'd love to carry a bouquet filled with flowers indigenous to southern Florida."

"Let's see what they have." Eliana riffled through the albums until she found a bouquet with white gardenia and jasmine.

"Perfect," Julia said, her eyes teary.

"Are those crying tears or allergy tears?" Eliana asked suspiciously.

"Both. I just can't believe this is happening," Julia said, sniffle-laughing and wiping her eyes.

"Are you sure you want to get married so quickly? There's no reason you can't wait until after Logan goes to Africa to—"

"Yes, I want to marry Logan now. That's the fun part. Not this."

Eliana tried not to let her skepticism show on her face. She must have done a good enough job—or Julia was too distracted by her allergies to notice. "Why don't you wait outside, and I'll finish this up."

Julia hugged Eliana gratefully. "Thank you!"

Eliana finalized the details with Carrie and headed outside. She paused to watch Julia, who was texting someone—probably Logan, based on the sweet smile on her face. Eliana hoped with her whole soul that Julia really would be happy with Logan, but what if they weren't?

They could at least start with an amazing wedding. Eliana got into the car and turned to her sister. "What do we need to do next for the wedding?"

"I don't know."

"You don't have a checklist?"

"Not yet."

"Julia." Eliana would not allow her sister to have a wedding disaster. Wedding disasters led to marriage disasters, which led to a long, hard path to being happily single. "Give me your phone. I'll make a checklist while you drive."

—ele—

Grandma Winnie worked on Julia's wedding dress while Eliana edited her latest video at her grandparents' bungalow. This time, she'd opted not to do her weekly live, and instead attempted to put out three longer-form videos.

So far, this video was proving to be uneditable. First, the background noise in the recording was so loud, it was difficult to hear Eliana. The laundry was going—with five people in the apartment, the laundry was always going—and even though her family had sworn to be quiet, she could hear them knocking things around in the kitchen and TV area.

So she'd moved to the quietest room in her sister's apartment ... the master closet. Which led to the second major problem: the lighting. Her sister's apartment was wedged in a corner of the complex, which meant it never got any direct sunlight. This was great for keeping the apartment cool, but not so great for filming with natural light. The closet had cast her in shadows reminiscent of a horror movie.

When Eliana got to the part of the recording when Julia had forgotten Eliana was filming, walked into the closet wrapped in a towel to grab her clothes, and screamed ... well, that was that.

She deleted the entire video from her hard drive. Usually, she liked to save the things she filmed, but even the words coming out of her mouth were aimless and unscripted in a way that made it seem like she didn't know what she was talking about.

She slammed her fingers on the keys a little too hard, and Grandma Winnie looked over at her with raised eyebrows. "You okay over there?"

"Just frustrated."

"Maybe you need a break from whatever you're doing."

"Probably," she muttered. But instead, she checked her notifications and found an email from her agent and a video message from another content creator named Giselle.

She clicked on Giselle's message first. Giselle was the kind of gossip who could never truly be your friend, because nothing you said to her would remain private. The minute she got news, she immediately emailed and texted everyone she had contact info for. Eliana prepared herself for Giselle's overemphasis on words.

Giselle curled her hair while she recorded. "Elly. You'll never guess what I just heard. Remember Sienna, from Never Drinks Caffeine? Someone just posted a picture of her drinking an espresso. AN ESPRESSO. I thought it might be hot chocolate, because you know how much she loves it, but nope, ESPRESSO is written RIGHT ON THE SIDE OF THE CUP. And then someone ELSE released a series of photos of her ordering a DIET DR. PEPPER at the drive-through. And NO ONE knows this part yet, but you know that sponsorship she had with Fitness Meals? They've dropped her. I haven't heard any news about her new caffeine-free energy drinks brand deal. I'll keep you posted. Loves." She made a kissy face and logged off.

Eliana frowned. She didn't know Sienna well, but they'd met a few times on panels at various conferences. She sent a quick text to Sienna.

> **Eliana:** How are you? I just heard about the pictures. Those websites are ruthless. I'm sorry.

She'd known more than a few people who'd lost advertising contracts due to rumors. It was something she hated having to be mindful of, yet with the announcement of her book, she knew there were plenty of people who would get a twisted amount of pleasure by knocking her down a peg—forgetting that she was a real person, just like them.

She flipped over to her agent's email and skimmed it. Eliana's first advance payment for her book had been sent to her account. A nudge for Eliana to send the other book ideas she'd been theoretically working on. A reminder to have her first draft of the book to her editor by the end of August.

The last paragraph made her pause.

Please remember the terms of your contract with Big House Publishing:

- *Post on social media a minimum of five times a week*

- *One livestream a week*

- *Two content video releases per week*

Additionally, your followers are used to a certain level of professionalism and quality from you. One off week is totally understandable, and allowable in your contract. But any more than that may cause problems. We need to keep up our efforts with pre-publication buzz and capitalize on the momentum you currently have. Please be more consistent going forward. Let me know if there is anything I can do to aid you in this.

Best wishes,

Regina

Eliana cringed. It was already Friday, and though she'd kept up on her posting, she hadn't done a livestream or uploaded her two weekly videos yet. It was proving to be impossible with so many people around. And she hadn't worked any more on her book either. Her deadline was fast approaching, and it was absolutely vital she give it attention.

She needed quiet. Quiet to film. Quiet to write and think. But between planning the wedding and her family all being in her space, quiet was rare.

"What's the scowl for?" Grandma Winnie asked. She sat next to Eliana on the couch and handed her a slice of almond coffee cake set on a porcelain tea plate.

"I have more to do than time to do it in." She took a bite of the cake, and the sugar immediately made her feel better. When was the last time she'd eaten? She checked the clock and realized she'd blown right past lunch while editing. Her stomach growled as she ate another bite. "Thank you, Grandma."

"I'm worried about you, Elly." Grandma gently scratched her back. "You're too young to be so stressed."

"I don't think stress cares what age you are."

Grandma nodded in acknowledgment. "True. But you're young and healthy and on a beach. And that is an equation that doesn't equal stress."

"And eating cake," Eliana added through a full mouth. Speaking of ... "Grandma, can you take my picture?"

"Sure." Everyone in her family was used to taking pictures of her for social media. And she was grateful no one ever gave her grief for it or lectured her about being fully in a moment. They understood this was her job, and in return, she tried not to interrupt meaningful moments for content opportunities. Though she wasn't always great at it, especially when she was desperate for content—like, say, after her agent sent a message telling her to step it up.

Feeling overwhelmed? Stop whatever you're doing. Take a deep breath. Release it. And look at the clock. When is the last time you ate? Sometimes a piece of cake can change your entire perspective.

She posted a picture of her taking a bite of cake, along with the caption, and posted. She knew the comments would be a mix of people agreeing with her and sharing their own hangry stories, and raking her over the coals for suggesting that people eat sugar as a method for solving a problem. She'd learned over the years she couldn't please everyone. And some people would take anything she said to an extreme—like her eating a piece of cake meant she was sending the message that all people, no matter their unique dietary needs, should also eat cake.

She tried to ignore the negativity and had given her family strict instructions to ignore it too.

Grandma waited for her to post and put her phone away before she handed Eliana a baggie of almonds and a cheese stick. Eliana laughed as she took the snacks, feeling like she was in elementary school again. "Thank you, Grandma."

"Can you do me a favor?"

"Oh, so all this food was just buttering me up to get a favor?" Eliana teased.

"Of course not." Grandma Winnie placed a very offended hand on her chest. "One of my greatest pleasures in life is to feed my loved ones."

It was true. One of the ways Grandma Winnie showed her love was by making sure they'd all eaten more than enough.

"But," she continued, a teasing spark in her eye, "your mom and Cameron are up at The Palms' clinic doing speech therapy. Cam left his spiky ball here last time he visited. Can you run it over to him? If you leave now, you'll catch them just as they're leaving." Grandma held out Cameron's silicone ball with floppy spikes. He had at least three at Julia's apartment, so it didn't seem necessary to make sure he got this one too, but Grandma dropped it in Eliana's lap. "His session ends in ten minutes. If you hurry, you can get there in time to see him—I mean, them."

Eliana stood, and Grandma pushed gently on her lower back as she directed her toward the door. Maybe Grandma wanted alone time or needed space. Eliana knew exactly how that felt.

"Okay, I'm going." She laughed and turned to hug Grandma Winnie. She breathed in her grandma's familiar gardenia-scented perfume. It was one of the most comforting scents in Eliana's life. In Boston, if someone walked by wearing it, she was immediately transported to her after-school snacks in Grandma's kitchen, telling her about her friend drama of the week. "See you tomorrow?"

"Yes. Now go." She pushed Eliana over the threshold and shut the door behind her.

Eliana inhaled the salty ocean air and slipped off her shoes to walk through the sand toward The Palms. There was a sidewalk, but she loved the feel of sand pressing into the arches of her feet while the sun shone down on her face. Though some distant clouds loomed, it was a gorgeous day in southern Florida, the kind that made her want to lie out on a towel and forget every responsibility.

But that wasn't going to happen until she found a way to record and edit two videos. One of them could be short, but the other needed to be at least twenty minutes long.

She put her sandals back on and went into The Palms' clinic. Her mom had explained that since some of the therapists rented space in the clinic, they were allowed to schedule private patients in addition to their Palms resident patients.

She sat in the waiting room of the rehabilitation arm of the clinic for only a couple of minutes before Cameron walked down the hall toward her. Her mom was a few steps behind, chatting with Asher—the speech therapist who didn't look like a speech therapist.

He hadn't noticed her yet, and she took a moment to study him. The last time she'd seen him, he'd been all sexy scowls and furrowed brows, but with her mom and Cameron, his face was less surly. He didn't look like the kind of person who spent his entire day in a clinic. His skin had the sun-touched tone of a man who spent hours outside. The black scrubs he wore hugged his biceps, and she could see the barest tip of a tattoo peeking from beneath his sleeve. Just enough to spark her curiosity.

Eliana had never thought she'd get a tattoo—it was such a huge commitment—but on the year anniversary of her divorce, she'd found herself searching online for tattoo artists, and two weeks later, she had the outline of Louisa May Alcott resting above her hip bone.

She'd never posted about it on her social media, and though it wasn't a secret, she wasn't sure if her family even knew about it. It was something she'd done just for herself, a way to have Lou with her everywhere she went.

"Elly!" Mom gave her a hug while Cameron did some sort of high-five handshake with Asher. Her heart softened. She was still bugged with Asher for towing her car, but having a good relationship with Cameron went a long way with Eliana. "I didn't expect to see you here. I thought you were working this afternoon."

"I was trying to, but Grandma said Cam forgot his ball at their place and you'd be missing it."

Mom took the spiky ball with a raised eyebrow. "He has at least three of these at home. Pretty sure he's not missing this one—"

Cameron yanked it from her hands and held it to his cheek like he was giving it a hug after a long reunion.

"Or maybe not," Mom said wryly. "Thank you, hon."

"Anytime." Eliana gave Cam a quick kiss on the side of his head, but he was so involved in squishing the spiky ball he didn't acknowledge her.

She felt someone's gaze on her and looked to see Asher watching her carefully.

"I owe you for the ride share," she said.

He just looked at her for another beat, before he turned back to Mom and Cam. "See you next week." With that, he turned without a backward glance. Rude.

"What did I do to him?" Besides parking in his spot, but he'd towed her car, so they should be even. She watched his retreating back—and despite everything, she had to appreciate how good he made those scrubs look.

"That's just how he is." Mom shrugged as they headed out the clinic door, toward the parking lot. "Not much for conversation."

"Seems odd for someone who specializes in speech."

29

"Maybe." She lowered her voice into what Eliana recognized as the gossip tone, and Eliana leaned closer. "From what I hear, he used to be a lot more personable, but after his grandpa died, he changed."

Eliana frowned and considered the man through a lens of recognizing that he was changed by grief. The gruffness, keeping people at a distance, lack of caring for his hair and beard, even the black scrubs ... she could definitely see it.

Still, her bank account was smarting from having to retrieve her car. It was a myth that content creators made a ton of money. She made enough to live off of, but Boston wasn't cheap.

"Is your car back at Grandma's?" her mom asked.

"Yeah."

"Want a ride over there? We're going to stop by and say hi."

"It seemed like Grandma wanted some alone time. She couldn't get me out of there fast enough to give Cam his ball."

Mom laughed again. "Yeah, sounds like it. Maybe we'll just head home." She checked her watch. "It's getting close to dinnertime anyway."

Eliana hugged her mom. "I'm going to walk on the beach for a bit, try to get the creative juices flowing." She knew herself well enough to recognize when the best thing she could do to create content was a long, peaceful walk to work through all her thoughts.

A motorcycle engine started, and she saw Asher straddling the seat and putting on his helmet. He'd changed into dark jeans and a T-shirt, one of those soft ones that screamed for someone to snuggle up to it. He leaned forward to grip the handlebars, and for some reason, the movement left her mesmerized.

Eliana blinked and tore her gaze away. Whoa. Major zone-out on the grumpy speech therapist. Maybe she needed to stop and get a sandwich first and get her brain right.

Eliana paid for a turkey sandwich to go in the dining hall, and then she walked along the beach, determined to make the most of the few hours of quiet time.

She pulled out the notes app on her phone, hoping ideas for her first chapter would come to her. She knew what the topic was: introducing the concept of *Happily Single*. She needed to give a brief overview of her own story. But jotting down those one-sentence prompts and knowing exactly what stories to tell was different from putting those into paragraphs. There needed to be a narrative arc. Yet it couldn't all be about her; it had to relate to every reader.

She walked to the end of the private beach of The Palms, where a huge copse of trees reached out from a residential area toward the ocean. A low-to-the-ground wooden bridge spanned the marshy gap from tree land to sand. She drew close to investigate, an idea sparking, though she couldn't quite put her finger on how it might work. A bridge metaphor? Or the gap between how you expected to feel when you were single, versus how you felt, and her book as an empowering bridge between the two?

Her thoughts came faster than her fingers could type them into her phone. She took a few pictures of the bridge and then sat on the railing as more thoughts came to her. Sometimes it was like this. One image could spark inspiration. Her final version of the chapter might not even have a bridge in it, but that didn't matter. It got her brain moving creatively, and she could work with that.

She heard a noise that made her pause. It sounded like a motorcycle engine. It was far enough past the thick trees and foliage that she couldn't see it. She tried to get back to her thought process, but that one little moment of distraction killed it.

Really, it wasn't the motorcycle, but the immediate thought of Asher that had done it, which reminded her of the money she'd paid out for her car, which suddenly made her think of the money put in her account from her publisher.

She opened her bank app, and there it was. Several thousand dollars. Her stomach flopped. The fact that they'd paid her before the book was written was sobering. This was only part of the payment—another third would come when she delivered the book to the publisher, and the final third when it released.

Movement caught her eye, and she spotted Asher at the edge of the trees, his head swinging back and forth. He glanced in her direction, but the tree's shadows hid her. He carried at least six completely full bags, three in each hand. Grocery bags?

She ducked down as he scanned the area again, almost as if he was hiding something. Then he took off across the sand. He got close enough for her to see that the bags were indeed filled with fresh food—apples, bananas, oats, pasta, and tomatoes were some of the things she spotted before he approached the final bungalow in the row.

He stepped inside and shut the door behind him. All of the blinds were closed, so she couldn't see inside, even to see if he'd turned the lights on.

Curiouser and curiouser.

CHAPTER 5

ASHER

ALL ASHER WANTED WAS to eat his homemade pork taco leftovers in peace. One peek through the break room window, though, and he saw Mr. Richardson chatting with Timothy, one of the doctors. Asher had never liked Timothy—he couldn't speak without sounding condescending—and luckily their paths didn't cross often. Dealing with one of them was bad enough, but both?

Plus he didn't want to spend his entire lunch break dodging questions about when he was going to get his grandpa's bungalow cleaned up. *Never, Mr. Richardson.* The thought of going through all those boxes was too overwhelming, but he couldn't give them all away either. They were all Asher had left.

Mr. Richardson approached the door, so Asher hurriedly turned the corner. But not hurriedly enough, because Mr. Richardson spotted him.

A plump, wrinkled arm slid through his, and he was surprised to look down and find himself suddenly walking arm in arm with Winnie. "Have lunch with me," she said.

"Asher, a word, please?" Mr. Richardson called out.

Winnie picked up her pace. "We're in the middle of a *delicate* conversation, Glen. Whatever you need will have to wait."

Mr. Richardson stopped suddenly, his face red.

Relief flooded Asher. Thank goodness for Winnie and her impeccable timing.

Winnie leaned close as if continuing a confidential conversation. "Bruno has thick potato soup with slices of fresh-baked sourdough on the menu, and it's going fast."

Asher, still feeling Mr. Richardson's eyes on them, gave her a solemn look he reserved for patients telling him difficult health news, and nodded seriously. "That does sound delicious. Did he make lemonade today?"

"No, but he's doing Italian sodas with fresh cream. He says it complements the soup better than lemonade. Horace loves it."

"Doesn't Horace have high cholesterol?" he said, a little louder when he realized Mr. Richardson was still listening. He huffed then, and finally went down another hallway to his office. Was it lying to lead him to believe they were having a private medical conversation? Lie of omission, maybe, but Winnie had started it, and he didn't regret going with it.

"Yes, so he only drinks a little bit. The soup is made with two options: a sad dairy-free option that Bruno somehow manages to make taste good, and a full-dairy, full-cream, fully-transported-to-heaven-with-one-bite option."

"I'll take the heaven option, please."

They got a table and placed their order. "Is Horace joining us as well?" he asked. Horace had always been particularly close to his grandpa, and he had been the first person to come check on Asher after his grandpa had passed.

"He's busy today." Was it his imagination, or did she look a little deflated? "He and Smitty are taking a helicopter ride to some amazing golf island south of here. He'll be gone until Monday."

Asher whistled lightly. "That's a full week."

The waitress brought by their Italian sodas—raspberry for him, peach for Winnie. She sipped hers while he drank half of his in one long draw.

He didn't just stress cook—he liked to stress eat and stress work out. Did he have any hobbies that weren't stress induced? Not since Grandpa died. All the things they'd done together didn't seem as appealing anymore. Like golfing, garage-sale-ing, and whittling. Asher couldn't remember the last time he'd picked up his whittling knife.

"They were on a six-month waiting list for a tee time. As it is, they have to share a room to go this early."

That explained why she stayed home.

"They've been spending a lot of time together lately," she said almost absently as she swirled her straw around in her cup.

He never knew quite what to say when someone looked sad and vulnerable. "Sounds lonely," he said too gruffly.

Winnie didn't seem to notice or mind. "It is. Horace is gone all the time, everyone is planning Julia's wedding or working or making content videos, and I'm kind of forgotten." A beat passed while Asher figured out the right thing to say, but his mind was blank. Winnie shook her head with a self-deprecating laugh. "Listen to me, going on and feeling sorry for myself when I'm having lunch with a handsome man."

Asher's cheeks warmed. "Handsome may be overstating things." Maybe once, he could have been called that, but he was several months' of skipped shaving past that descriptor now.

"You, my dear, are the kind of handsome that the young people would call foxy."

Asher was positive young people never called anything foxy.

"Like a tougher version of Captain America."

He snorted. If he squinted and looked sideways and grew his imagination a thousand percent, *maybe* he could pass for a homeless version of him.

Winnie patted his hand. He could sometimes go days without being touched, but Winnie was always a hugger, arm holder, and hand or cheek patter. It reminded him of his grandma, who had been like that too. She'd died in the same accident his parents had, when he was in high school, but he could still recall the tightness of her hugs, how she'd held on like she'd never let go. And she'd never broken a hug first. She'd hug you until you were done with it and stepped away. Sometimes he'd tease her that he was going to hug her until she moved first, and she'd tell him they'd be hugging forever then, because she was never moving.

Man, he missed them.

His chest ached, and he drank the rest of his soda, fast enough for his throat to burn with the carbonation. This was why he didn't let himself think about his family too much.

The waitress delivered their soup, and he dug in right away. Bruno was an amazing chef, but his soups were legendary.

"I heard you met my granddaughter, Eliana."

Again, his cheeks felt ruddy. Was this the moment Winnie was going to lecture him on treating her visiting granddaughter poorly? He'd deserve it. "I'm sorry I had her car towed—"

"She parked in a reserved spot," Winnie said, shaking her head, but smiling.

"I could have parked on the street and—"

"There aren't street spots this time of year." Winnie was not going to let him apologize. "She could have parked in my driveway. And from what I heard, you paid for her ride home."

He shifted, uncomfortable. "Still, I shouldn't have done it."

"She's okay. It all worked out. And you got to meet her, which is fun."

Fun wouldn't be how he'd describe their first encounter. But he also wouldn't call himself foxy. They were in Winnie's world now, and he was along for the ride.

"Have you followed her on social media yet? She's at *Happily Single.*"

"No." He didn't do social media.

"Let me show you one of her videos." She found it and held her phone out to Asher. He realized then that he'd already finished his soup, while Winnie had barely touched hers.

A caption beside the video said it had previously been recorded live. He watched Eliana as she attempted to announce her book deal in the midst of her family making noise and attempting to talk to her. He smiled when Cameron came on screen and made faces at himself.

When Asher had done telemed calls for speech during COVID-19 quarantines, his younger clients had spent an equal amount of time making faces at the screen and playing with filters as they had practicing their words. He'd done more than one session with his client looking like a cat in outer space.

Eliana's grace and patience was apparent, though she had thrown more than one incredulous look at the camera, mostly when someone started banging around in the kitchen.

The video suddenly ended, and he handed the phone back to Winnie. "*Happily Single?*" Maybe it was a book he needed to read.

"Yes. But here's the thing." She leaned forward and whispered, "I don't know how happy she really is."

He got a lot of this. Loving grandparents who were worried about their grandchildren and wanted to talk things through with him during sessions or in the hallways. He didn't know if it was because he didn't talk much, but for some reason, people seemed to open up to him.

"She's lucky to have you, then," he said, meaning every word. If everyone could have a grandma like Winnie, the world would be a better place.

"I hope so," she murmured, staring past his shoulder at a framed acrylic painting of Sweetie and Bear on the wall. They were wearing a lion costume and a Dorothy costume. "Tell me, Asher. Do you think it's possible to ever truly let go of the mistakes in our past?"

"I hope so," he said, repeating her earlier phrasing. "Or else we're all in a lot of trouble."

"Well," she said as if pulling herself out of her reverie, "I'll stop talking your ear off and let you get back to work." Then she bustled away like a woman on a mission.

He thought about his conversation with Winnie for the rest of the afternoon while he worked with his patients. What mistakes could she be talking about? In his estimation, Winnie was the kindest, sweetest person at The Palms, and if she was worried about past mistakes, then none of the rest of them had any hope.

Unless she was talking about his mistake of calling a tow truck on Eliana. That had to be it. He didn't know how forgiving Eliana was, but if the heated glare she'd directed at him was evidence, then, well ... hopefully they wouldn't run into each other too often.

By the time he pulled his motorcycle into his usual spot, he was almost too tired to check and make sure the coast was clear. If anyone spotted him, he'd tell them he was cleaning. It was a legitimate excuse. Something he really should be doing.

He hadn't been able to shake the feeling all week that someone was following him, probably paranoia over Mr. Richardson. He peered deeply into the trees, near the old bridge, but no one was there. He was losing his mind. He wasn't made for keeping secrets like this. Grandpa would have been very disappointed in him.

He cut through the break in the trees and headed toward the bungalow, but something made him pause. A noise? A creaking.

He squinted in the quickly dimming light, and his heart stopped when he realized someone sat on the porch swing at his grandpa's bungalow, slowing swaying back and forth.

And not just someone. Eliana Peters.

CHAPTER 6

ELIANA

*"She is too fond of books and it has turned her brain." —Louisa
May Alcott*

W AS THIS HOW THE Grinch felt right before he stole Christmas? Or
Snape every time he gave Harry Potter detention? Should she feel
uncomfortable that she was relating to villains?

Eliana saw the moment Asher recognized her sitting on the swing at
his late grandfather's bungalow. The stutter in his confident stride, then
the determined line of his mouth as he stalked toward her like a sleek lion
approaching prey.

She swallowed. It wasn't too late to stop this plan before it even started.
Had desperation led her to fall so far?

Yes. The answer was yes. Because the more she thought about that
advance payment in her account, all those zeros linking like chains around
her wrists, the more she knew she had to do something.

Desperate times called for desperate measures. That was the saying,
right? And the fact that she'd come up with this idea while she'd lain awake
last night, Cameron's snoring in her ear ... Well, didn't all the best ideas
come in the middle of the night, after a lot of stress and sleep deprivation?

A newsletter topic started to form: "Five Ways to Make Sleep Deprivation Work for You."

First, those ideas that are mostly illegal when you're awake? They seem absolutely reasonable and justifiable when you're going on three hours of sleep.

"What are you doing here?" he growled as he placed his foot on the uneven wooden slats of the porch. The bungalow had fallen into some disrepair, unlike the other well-kept ones along the beach. She knew The Palms' maintenance center handled the upkeep of the bungalows, but for some reason, this one had been neglected.

He glared at her as he waited for her answer, and her throat suddenly felt thick. This close, he was more imposing than she remembered. Even though he stood at least six feet away, his presence took up the entire porch. It wasn't fear that made her pause—well, maybe a little, though something told her he'd never hurt her—but it was a tingling awareness along the top of her scalp. Like that feeling you get when someone runs their fingers through your hair.

Weird.

She stuck her foot on the ground to halt her gentle swinging, but she remained seated, trying to pull off an air of confidence. Of belonging. "You live here," she said.

"No," he ground out. He folded his arms, putting those biceps on display and teasing her yet again with just the barest glimpse of his tattoo. "My grandfather did. I'm here to go through his boxes."

"Interesting." She kicked off the ground to rock the swing again. It really was peaceful out here at the edge of The Palms. Quiet. Private. Nearly deserted. And the lighting that would come in through those back windows in the middle of the day? Absolutely perfect.

"If you don't mind ..." He walked up the steps and headed to the door, coming close enough for her to smell him—sunscreen and a hint of outside, as if the pollen and leaves had attached themselves to him while he rode.

"Not at all," she replied, continuing to swing.

He paused in the doorway, and she wondered if he'd go inside. But if she'd guessed his personality right—there was a whole lot of decency behind that growly exterior—he wouldn't leave her out there. "Can I help you with something?"

"Actually, yes. You can." She stood and approached him, realizing her mistake the moment she did. While on the swing, she felt like she'd had the advantage of looking casual, without a care in the world. The distance gave her courage.

Standing close to him, her heart couldn't remember how it was supposed to beat. Too fast, then too slow, and suddenly she was breathless. But if she stepped back, he'd know he affected her, and she couldn't let him see that he might have any upper hand in this.

"I need a quiet place to stay to create my videos and work on my book."

"And you're telling me this because ..."

"I've been following you for the last week." That came out a little darker and more stalkery than she intended. "From a distance." Nope, that was worse. His eyebrows winged upward. She hurried past it. "You come here every evening."

"It's when I have time to pack and clean."

"With bags of groceries," she continued. "And you change here to go swimming. And you leave here in the morning, walk toward those trees, and take your motorcycle to work."

His eyes took on a steely glint, but he didn't say anything.

"I know you're living here, and it's against The Palms' bylaws for someone your age to live here, so they must not know."

His jaw ticked, and she knew she was right.

She took a deep breath. Here was the point of no return. She'd already admitted to following him to a creepy degree (thank you, choices made while sleep deprived). Might as well continue on with the one-two punch of stalking followed by blackmail. "Let me stay here with you in the spare bedroom, and I won't tell anyone that you're here."

Her words dropped into the silence between them. They stretched out, growing heavier and more ominous, like an overfilled water balloon on the verge of exploding. She resisted the urge to squirm by holding her back even straighter.

The stakes were too high for her to get squeamish now. She needed this, or she'd never finish her book. Or the videos she needed to hype up her book.

He suddenly stilled. She turned to see someone walking a little dog along the beach.

"Come inside," he ordered, and he ushered her into the house, his hand almost, but not quite, touching the small of her back. Heat radiated from it, and a part of her wanted to lean back into it. The part of her not getting enough sleep and that thought it was a good idea to blackmail this man, obviously.

She nearly rethought the whole plan when her eyes adjusted to the darkness of the bungalow. It was the same floor plan as her grandparents', but having walls in the same places was where the similarities ended.

Where her grandparents' bungalow was light and airy and beachy in every sense of the word—with their sheer drapes that fluttered from the breeze of the open windows, their subtle tan and turquoise decorations to imitate the sand and ocean views outside, and the scents of coconut and ocean spray throughout—Asher's bungalow was dimly lit and stuffy. Even if the windows were open, the dark wood blinds and heavy drapes would not flutter in the wind. Almost no natural light worked its way into the house. And the stuff ... oh, the stuff. One might think that with so many boxes, the bungalow would appear empty, but not so. Belongings filled every nook and cranny and available space in the bungalow—everything from wooden tiki men to coconut carvings to stacks and stacks of leather-bound books.

Uncertainty swept through her, and when she looked back at Asher, he must have realized it. This was his trump card. He had a satisfied smirk on his face. One that only solidified her decision to do this. Because despite all ... *this*, it was quiet. And that was enough.

"You can't stay here," he said.

"I have to." She leaned against the back of a damask couch that looked at least thirty years old. Her grandparents had one like it when she was a kid. "I'll spend most of my time in the guest room. You won't even know I'm here."

"Doubtful," he grumbled. "There's no bed in the guest room."

"Then I'll sleep on the floor. Or I'll buy an air mattress."

He rubbed at his head, the first indication she had that she was stressing him out. "Is this because I had your car towed?"

"No. But it makes me feel less guilty about it."

"So if I don't agree to let you sleep on the floor of my grandpa's guest bedroom for the next—how long?"

"Two months."

His eyes narrowed. "For the next two months, you'll tell Mr. Richardson that I've been living here."

She shrugged. "That pretty much sums it up."

He closed his eyes and muttered, "I need a drink," before he headed toward the kitchen.

"So is that a yes?" she asked, following him. She leaned against the counter while he pulled out a cold water bottle from the fridge. In every way the rest of the house was dark and depressing, this room was very much the opposite. The lemon-yellow towels looked freshly laundered, the surfaces were spotless, and a plate of white chocolate macadamia nut cookies were stacked on a fancy glass-covered platter.

"I don't have a choice." He took the lid off the cookies, and she inhaled the scent of fresh-baked treats. He grabbed two, but then very pointedly took a bite out of each.

Petty to the extreme. She could respect that.

He *did* have a choice. He could kick her out right now, and she wasn't fully convinced she'd actually tell Mr. Richardson that Asher was living here. It was one thing to tow someone's car; it was another to get them kicked out of their house.

But again, desperate times. In the end, she had the upper hand, and they both knew it.

"I'll move in tomorrow," she told him. "Thanks, roomie."

"Don't call me that." He pushed off from the counter and went back to the master bedroom with a slam of the door. But she was too relieved to take it personally. It had worked. She'd never intended to become the villain in anyone's story, but here she was, and it actually didn't feel so bad.

She peeked at the bedroom door to make sure it was firmly closed before sneaking a cookie from the platter. She took a bite and closed her eyes. Holy cow, these were divine. Had he made them? This kitchen looked too spotless to have ever been baked in.

Good food. Quiet atmosphere. A beach right outside the back patio door. Yes, she could get used to this indeed.

Eliana banged on the door at six in the morning. She had been up all night again, solidifying her decision to follow through with this plan. "This is our only option," she said to Louisa May Alcott, who continued to sleep despite her habitat being jostled about.

Asher opened the door, looking very much like she'd woken him up. His hair stuck out in all directions, his shirt had been put on inside out, and his scowl would have been enough to make her take a step back if she didn't have the hope of a quiet day ahead of her.

"Good morning," she said quietly. One didn't want to startle a bear.

He blinked. "I'd hoped it was a nightmare."

"You're such a flirt."

"I am not flirting." He bit the words out one by one. Okay, time to pull back from the teasing. She didn't want to aggravate him so badly he changed his mind and decided to call her blackmail bluff.

She shifted, her bag heavy, Louisa May Alcott's habitat even heavier. He did a double take as he stepped back. Then, without a word or glance in her direction, he shut the front door and went back into the master bedroom. A moment later, the shower turned on.

She set Louisa's home on the table, dragged her bag into the guest bedroom, and attempted to push the door open. It snagged on something, but it was so dark inside, she couldn't see what. She pushed her shoulder against it, and something tumbled and crashed inside.

Oops.

She reached her hand in and moved it up and down the wall until she found the light switch. When she clicked it on, she peeked through the foot of the open door to see that the room was filled with boxes.

How much stuff had Asher's grandpa owned? No wonder he hadn't finished going through all of this yet.

She'd knocked over a stack of boxes that had been set too close to the door. She pushed the door open slowly this time, shifting the boxes carefully, until it was open enough for her to step inside.

Her heart sank. She was going to have to buy a baby-sized air mattress. *Better than being squeezed into Julia's apartment.*

Asher left without a word while she moved boxes around in an attempt to open up enough space for an air mattress. It was so dusty and hot, she felt like she was going to pass out. She cracked the bedroom window for fresh air and changed the thermostat from eighty—what in the world? Who kept it that hot?—to seventy-four. She'd cover the cost difference. It was worth it.

She cleaned up a small section of the room for Louisa May Alcott, but she wouldn't be able to keep her in here all day. Not with how dusty everything was.

After a break for her own shower, she managed to film and edit an entire video before Asher got home. She'd closed the windows and blinds after filming so the house could be his secure little bear cave when he got home.

"It's cold," he growled as he passed the kitchen where she made a grilled cheese using some of his many groceries. He had a well-stocked pantry—and she'd replace everything she used tomorrow.

"I'm in here all day, Asher. I'll pay the difference in your electric bill."

He didn't say anything else, just came out of his bedroom a few minutes later—wearing a wet suit that was zipped up to his neck—and left.

"How was your day?" she asked herself in a low voice as she flipped her sandwich on the skillet.

"Wonderful. I got so much done," she replied on a sigh. They weren't friends.

But this would be so much easier if they were.

CHAPTER 7
ELIANA

"I am lonely, sometimes, but I dare say it's good for me ..."
—*Louisa May Alcott*

B Y THE END OF the week, Eliana could count on one hand how many words Asher had said to her. It shouldn't bug her. This was exactly what she wanted.

Quiet served on a fancy platter, with a side of peace and inspiration.

The inspiration was flowing. She'd written an entire chapter since moving into Asher's bungalow. With the window open, facing the ocean, she could write and think and highlight her many saved research articles to her heart's content.

But after almost seven days straight, she was starting to feel antsy. Even on the weekend, he made himself scarce. For someone who was supposed to be going through boxes, there was a significant lack of going through boxes happening.

"When does he eat, Louisa? When does he relax?"

She was starting to suspect he waited for her to leave to help Julia with the wedding to do any of those things. And that bothered her. She hadn't meant to kick him out of his space. Only to share it with him.

"Should we go for a walk, Lou?"

She searched through Asher's kitchen cupboards until she found a plastic Tupperware to hold Louisa in for their walk, and they headed toward Grandma Winnie's house. The fresh air was exceptionally nice after being in the stuffy house. The box situation was a problem—nearly overwhelmingly so.

Eliana heard talking as she approached Grandma Winnie's door. She knocked, but after a moment, she let herself in, surprised to find several people sitting around Grandma's kitchen table. She recognized them all from The Palms.

Cameron sat at the table as well, playing a game on his tablet.

"Eliana!" Grandma Winnie stood. Did she look guilty? For what? Eliana took in the group around the table, the plate of cookies in the middle with large glasses of milk or lemonade in front of everyone. "What are you up to?"

"Just taking Louisa for a walk," she said, still feeling like she'd interrupted something. "If this is a bad time ..."

One of Grandma's friends turned the notebook they'd been writing on face down. *Okay.*

"I've got a minute to chat," Grandma said.

"I don't want to interrupt."

"I've been meaning to reach out to you." She took Eliana by the arm and pulled her a few feet away from the table. "Your mom says you temporarily moved in with a friend. Where at?"

"Not too far from here," she said, somewhat evasively.

"Is it a friend I've met before?"

"Maybe." She didn't want to lie, so she changed the subject. "Want me to take Cam for a walk while you chat with your friends?"

"Oh, I'm sure he'd love that. He's been on that tablet for almost an hour."

Eliana was sure he'd much rather stay on the tablet, but it was good for him to get up and move around. She knelt beside Cameron while her grandma introduced her to her friends.

"Everyone, this is my granddaughter. Eliana, you know Don. And this is Polly, Walt, Rosa, Nancy, and Harry," she said, pointing to each of them as she said their name. They all waved, and their names swam together into one big mush.

"Nice to meet you," she said. She held up a plastic bin. "And this is Louisa, my desert tortoise."

"What's the difference between a turtle and a tortoise?" Don asked.

"There are several, but it's easiest to remember that a turtle's habitat is generally in the water, while a tortoise's is on land. But I use the terms interchangeably, for the most part," she assured him. Most people didn't seem to mind one way or the other.

"He's adorable," said the one she was pretty sure was Polly.

"It's a she," Harry or Walt said. Wait, Walt had the hat, so it had to be Harry. "Her name is Louisa."

"How can you even tell with turtles?" Polly countered. "Plus, I once had a boy dog named Daisy."

Eliana whispered to her grandma, "Should I jump in or ..."

Grandma shook her head and whispered, "They can ask Logan about how to determine turtle—or tortoise—gender next time they see him, if they really care to know."

"Cam." She crouched beside her brother's chair. "Want to come with me to take Louisa for a walk?"

He blinked his vision away from the tablet and locked eyes on Louisa. He loved Louisa. He stuck two of his fingers into the container, just like she'd taught him, and Louisa scooched toward his hand until her nose touched his finger. He giggled.

"I'm just saying that you can name an animal whatever you want. A friend of mine had a cat named Blender," Harry said.

"That's a terrible name," said Don—the strong-looking one. Cameron was sitting right beside him and repeated "name" after Don said it.

"Have you talked to Julia?" Grandma asked Eliana as the argument continued. "Your mom said she was panicking about the cake earlier."

"What happened with the cake?" Eliana's fingers turned white against the edge of the table.

"I don't know. Something about the bakery being closed for appliance updates the week of the wedding ..."

Great. Planning a last-minute wedding was proving to be a major challenge, and it had been tricky to find a baker willing to squeeze them in with so little notice. "I'll message her." After she did a search of other local bakeries so they could have a backup plan in place. "Ready?" she asked Cameron.

"Let's go!" he said.

She squirted some hand sanitizer into his palms, and he rubbed it in, knowing the drill after touching Louisa.

He held her hand as they walked slowly down the beach. It was one of those perfect summer days, with a light wind coming off the ocean. Waves crashed around their feet and ankles.

Diamond Cove had to be one of the most gorgeous places on the planet. And this beach? Divine.

"Bathroom?" Cameron said suddenly, signing to her.

Uh-oh. When Cameron said he needed to go to the bathroom, that generally meant you didn't have very long to find him one before it became an emergency.

They'd wandered nearly to the edge of The Palms' private beach, and Asher's bungalow was only twenty feet away. She debated for only a moment before she tugged Cameron toward the bungalow, looking both ways first. No one in sight. "You can't tell anyone we were here," she warned him.

He was more concerned with getting to a bathroom than promising to keep secrets, which told her they needed to walk even faster.

She opened the door and showed him to the bathroom, then continued down the hallway to her bedroom. She pulled Louisa out of the plastic container and put her into her home, set on a stack of boxes that were functioning as a nightstand, and gently scratched her shell. She'd been surprised to learn that tortoises have nerves on their shells, and Louisa loved a good shell scratch.

Cameron could sometimes take a while in the bathroom, so Eliana headed to the kitchen to wash her hands and the container thoroughly. Tortoises could carry salmonella, and though the risk was minimal, she never wanted to take any chances.

She rapped her knuckles on the bathroom door when she finished. "You okay in there?"

He laughed, which usually meant yes. Or it meant he was getting into something he shouldn't. She opted to believe the first and went into her bedroom to sit on her newly acquired air mattress and check her email.

She heard the bath water turn on, and she groaned. "Cammmm!" she yelled. "We need to head back to Grandma's house in a minute." He loved taking baths and didn't care whose house he was at.

She returned a couple of texts, one from Giselle.

Giselle: HER DRINK BRAND WAS PULLED.

Eliana's stomach sank. Sienna had worked so hard to make her energy drink a reality, and now she was losing it due to one impulsive decision. Was drinking one caffeinated drink so bad? Only if your entire platform is about how you don't, she supposed. No one liked a hypocrite.

But Sienna wasn't a hypocrite. She was a genuine and loving person. Eliana opened her video message app.

"Sienna, I just heard about your new drink brand. I'm so sorry! I don't have words, but if there's something I can do to help, I want to do it. Let's do a collaboration video, whenever you're free. We'll do a silly game—like how many marshmallows we can fit into our mouths or something. Get everyone laughing and remembering that you're more than just one drink additive. Let me know."

She was getting that antsy feeling she sometimes got when her brain was spinning away from her, so she opened a downloaded article she'd saved for her book. It was a study on the mating patterns of tree swallows. Just interesting enough to distract her, and boring enough to calm her down.

Huh. While ninety percent of birds are monogamous, there are 10% that are not, including the tree swallow.

"Corbin must have belonged to the tree swallow family," she muttered.

"Who's in the bathroom?"

She shrieked and scrambled to catch her phone before it crashed to the ground. Asher stood in her doorway, in perfectly worn jeans and a T-shirt, his hair windswept, most likely from being on his motorcycle.

He wore his ever-present scowl like a mask he donned in her presence. She should *not* want to see him smile at her. But these constant glares were wearing on her. She was only human.

"I didn't hear you come in." The bath water or Cam's splashing about must have covered up the sound of him coming in the door.

He let out a short, stressed breath, and she realized he was imagining the worst—that she'd told his secret to someone.

"It's Cameron," she quickly said. "We were walking on the beach together, and he needed to use the bathroom."

"And take a bath?" he deadpanned.

"Apparently." She shrugged. "I'll clean up any messes he makes."

"I'm not worried about the mess."

"He doesn't know I'm living here, or that you are, for that matter. All he knows is that we came into a random house to use the bathroom. And take a bath." They heard Cam yell something indiscernible followed by a huge splash of water and a laugh.

Wait. Was that a twitch at the corner of his mouth? A fighting-a-smile twitch? It made her want to see if she could coax out an actual smile. "Sounds like he's having fun."

"Well, this bungalow is a very happening place," she teased. "What are you up to tonight?"

And just as quickly as he'd twitch-smiled, his mouth straightened again. Dang it. "Swimming," he said shortly. Then, without another word, he turned and went into his room.

She threw herself back on her mattress and stared at the ceiling. It wasn't like they needed to be friends or anything. She just didn't like the idea of someone not liking her.

Then you shouldn't have blackmailed him.

Well, fine then. Apparently, she and her conscience were at an impasse, because she needed this bungalow. But she also needed him to not hate her.

Cameron clattered out of the bathroom, and she met him in the hallway. His hair was wet, and he wore a huge smile—along with inside-out clothes, his signature style.

"Feel better?" She poked him in the side, in a place she knew he was ticklish, and he laughed. She kept reaching around to his ticklish ribs on each side as he squirmed and laughed. "You said you had to go to the bathroom. Not take a whole bath."

"Er!" Cam's face lit up.

She turned to see Asher coming out of his bedroom in that wet suit again. It hugged every muscle in his body—and boy, did he have a lot of muscles. And boy, did that fabric hug tight.

She turned away before she had to start fanning herself.

"Cameron!" They did their handshake, and it ended with a hug. Asher had his back to her, but she could feel the smile coming off of him, and tried not to be jealous of her brother for being able to win one. "I'm going to the beach," Asher said. "Want to walk with me?" He subtly pointed to Cameron's talker, where it hung from a strap around his shoulder.

Cameron pulled it up.

"You can say, yes, I want to go. Or no, I don't want to go." He pointed to where each button was as he said it.

Cameron said, "Yes. I want to go. Beach."

"Great job." Asher gave him knuckles, and the two of them walked out the bungalow door together. Asher was reminding him where the beach words were on his talker, and they were talking about the flamingos.

They looked adorable together—both so different. Asher was tall and broad with longish dark hair. Cameron was slim and had short blond hair, and the top of his head barely came to Asher's shoulder. With Cameron, Asher was—dared she say it?—friendly. Which proved that side of him did exist.

It didn't explain why she felt compelled to provoke him. Maybe because it was the only way to get him to acknowledge her at all.

"Sure, I'd love to come too," Eliana said to their backs. "Thanks for the kind invite."

Asher's long side-eye was the only indication that he'd heard her.

CHAPTER 8

ASHER

THE TURTLE ON HIS kitchen table chewed its lettuce with lazy, round jaw movements as it stared at Asher.

"I don't like animals," he informed it with a low voice.

The turtle seemed unfazed. If only Asher could be so calm.

Ever since Eliana showed up at his house almost two weeks ago with her suitcase in one hand and a turtle habitat in the other, his life had taken an unexpected twist. And an animal? She hadn't told him about that, or else he might have taken his chances with Mr. Richardson.

He finished closing the blinds Eliana had opened and leaned against the kitchen counter. She was going to arouse curiosity with the open blinds. Eliana unsettled him—and he hadn't even seen her yet today.

Chicken alfredo. That would do the trick.

In his desperation to avoid the bungalow, he hadn't cooked anything since Eliana moved in. He missed it, and not just the good food, but the process of making it—that time relaxing and creating he only experienced while cooking.

He didn't know where she'd gone tonight, but it was the first time in a while he had the bungalow to himself.

He opened the fridge to get the butter, Parmesan cheese, cream, and garlic cloves out. He debated using dried pasta, but a day like today called for homemade noodles. He set eggs and flour on the counter beside the other ingredients, already feeling more settled.

Something happened in the kitchen, with his fingers kneading dough or when chicken sizzled in the pan or in the rhythmic motion of cutting vegetables, where his mind finally calmed.

As he cooked, each tightly wound nerve unfurled. And when he plated his chicken alfredo and inhaled its buttery, garlicy scent, he didn't even mind as much that a turtle temporarily lived in his space.

These months would pass. Eliana would move out.

And then?

He couldn't think that far ahead. One hurdle at a time.

He sat on the couch where the turtle couldn't watch him, eating that first blissful bite, when Eliana blew into the bungalow like a fresh summer breeze. How did she do that?

She didn't see him at first. She hummed one of Aurelia Halifax's new songs as she kicked off her sandals, then muttered, "This is why I'm never getting married again."

"Again?"

She screamed and tripped over her shoes, landing against the door with a thud. Her gaze shot over to his with lightning speed as she realized she wasn't alone.

He cringed. "Sorry." Wait. Was he apologizing for being in his own house—well, his grandpa's house?

She laughed with a hand over her heart, as if to slow it down. "Uh, I'm sure that was quite a sight." She kicked her shoes farther from the door. "It smells incredible in here."

His stomach tightened as she breathed in his cooking—not an unpleasant feeling, but not a welcome one either. "You can't open all the blinds." There. Put her back at a distance. "Someone will notice."

She winced. "Oh. Sorry."

"This is a vacant house as far as everyone is concerned."

"Won't anyone who sees an open window just assume you're cleaning it out?"

He frowned. "No one minds their own business here. They'll want to see who's here while I'm at work, and it would only take one pushy step into the house to realize I'm actually living here." The Palms' residents were strong-willed and opinionated, and they had no qualms sharing—and in some cases enforcing—those strong wills and opinions. Especially when it came to someone a couple of generations younger than them.

He really liked the residents. He respected them. He was completely intimidated by several of them. And he could name at least seven who seemed extra curious about his life lately.

She dropped onto the couch beside him, and it suddenly felt much too small. "If I can't open the blinds, we need to at least start going through the boxes so more light can get through the space."

He grunted in acknowledgment. He'd get to the boxes. Eventually.

She looked at his full plate of chicken alfredo as her stomach growled.

He wanted to be petty.

He wanted to ignore her hunger.

He wanted to pretend she didn't exist and let his life go back to normal

"There's extra food on the stove," he said instead, because at his core, he was a decent person. And he could never deny anyone a plate of food—even if her actions roller-coastered his life upside down and sideways at breakneck speeds. "Plates are in the cupboard next to the microwave."

She raced to the kitchen with an excited smile that zinged all the way through him. He dug back into his food, savoring each bite, until she sat beside him again, closer this time. His food turned to sawdust.

"This is delicious," she said after her first bite. "Did you make this?"

He wasn't offended by her incredulous tone. Most people were surprised to learn he loved to cook and bake—something to do with the bike and the black clothes and long hair. First impressions were rarely correct.

"Yes. You might be more comfortable at the table," he hinted.

"No, this is fine." She bounced slightly on the springy couch. "This couch is more comfortable than I expected it to be the first time I saw it."

He took another bite and chewed slowly, trying to retrieve that zen feeling he usually got while eating a meal he'd created.

"We should get to know each other." Eliana licked sauce off her fork, and he blinked away from the sight with a heavy swallow. "Since we're living together and all."

"Not like that." He set his half-full plate on the coffee table.

"That's not what people would think …" She waggled her eyebrows.

He didn't know what expression his face held—something between absolute awareness of every single part of Eliana and horror, if he had to guess based on his feelings. She laughed, and his stomach twisted tighter than rotini, which happened to be his second-favorite type of pasta.

"I'm messing with you," she assured him. "I have taken a vow of singleness."

His shoulders relaxed. Of course she was teasing him. He'd seen the *Happily Single* video. He needed to unwind this spool of tension, or else the next couple of months would be torture. "A vow."

"Yep. I put it on the internet, which means it will live forever. Screenshots never forget."

"Life lesson number one." He drew a one in the air with his finger. He needed to ignore her. Glare. Brood.

But it was hard to brood with a stomach half full of homemade pasta and cream sauce and Eliana's sunny smile lighting up his depressingly dark bungalow.

She laughed, and the tension eased. Perhaps that was the key—keep her laughing. Too bad he wasn't particularly funny. Or good at conversation.

"What socials are you on? I'll look you up." She took her phone from her immaculately organized purse. All of Eliana was immaculate, from her pink painted nails to her hair carefully pulled back into a tight ponytail that swung back and forth every time she turned her head.

"I'm not on social media."

She set her phone down in dramatic slow motion. "Excuse me?"

"There's no one I care to follow."

"You don't want to watch dog or cat videos?" she asked.

"I'm not an animal person."

"Babies doing adorable things videos? People doing stunts videos? Soldiers surprising their child at school tearjerker videos?" She gestured wildly as she spoke. Everything about her was full of life—even her conversations.

He shrugged. "I spend most of my spare time in the ocean."

"You are superhuman." She narrowed her eyes. "How old are you?"

"Thirty."

She melted into the couch as if relieved. "Okay. For a moment there, I wondered if you were an eighty-year-old who had aged exceptionally well." He let out a surprised laugh, which made her sit up straight, her eyes lighting up, her expression victorious for some reason. "Your whole face changes when you smile."

Self-consciousness stole over him, and under the guise of rubbing at his beard, he covered his mouth. He hadn't had much occasion to smile lately.

Time to give his excuses and leave. His arms were exhausted from so many nights swimming, but it was his only escape. "I'm going to—"

"Let's play a game," she said eagerly.

It was so unexpected, he lost his train of thought. "Like cards?"

"Not that kind of game—though I do love cards." She paused as if considering, but then shook her head. "Another night. Let's do the question-answer game."

"What's that?"

"We take turns asking each other questions, and we have to answer them. Like truth or dare without the dare."

"What are the stakes?"

"Nothing."

"Then what's the point?"

"To have fun," she said. "I'll go first."

He grimaced. Answering personal questions about himself was not his idea of fun. He started to stand. "Actually, it's about time I—"

"Swim?" she finished. She lifted a brow and then looked at his plate, where half of his food remained. "Before you finish your delicious dinner?"

He lowered himself back to the couch. He needed to set some boundaries. They weren't friends. They weren't living together because they chose to do so. He liked quiet and sameness and sepia-toned things. Eliana was the opposite of those in every way.

"So, Asher Brooks." She leaned closer. "What's your story?"

"Nope." He'd play a few rounds of her pointless game, but he wasn't going to spend the entire night talking about himself. "That's too broad of a question. What specifically do you want to know?"

Her eyes glinted with amusement. "You're already catching on. Fine. Where were you born? How many siblings do you have? And why don't you like animals?"

What in the world had he gotten himself into? "I was born in Georgia. I don't have any siblings. And animals eventually die."

"Whoa, that got dark quick. Have you always felt this—"

He cut her off before she could finish. "My turn. Why did you make an internet vow of singleness?"

Her nose scrunched up in a cute way. She clearly didn't want to answer this, but she was the one who started the game. "Relationships aren't all they're cracked up to be."

"I'm going to need more than that." He looked at her expectantly.

"Fine." She huffed, the first hint she'd given that he might be able to get under her skin just like she did with him. "Short version: I got married too young to someone who wanted to control everything I did, and once I got free of him, I realized I like who I am alone better than who I am in a relationship."

"In what way?" He tried to imagine Eliana being stuffed inside of a too-tight box against her will, and he clenched his jaw.

She held up her finger in a no-no gesture. "My turn. Hmmmm." She looked around the room as if looking for inspiration. "Where are you going to go when you leave this place?"

He grabbed his plate and took another bite of his tasteless food to stall. Eliana waited patiently for him to finish chewing. Unfortunately, she also drew her finger across some of the remaining sauce on her plate, and her tongue poked out as she licked it off. All his brain synapses fried out at the sight. What in the world was this woman doing to him?

He was going to lose his mind—what was left of it, anyway—with her living here.

He cleared his throat and filled his fork with more noodles. "I don't know." The problem was, he couldn't imagine himself anywhere else. Once he cut his ties with The Palms, he'd be truly adrift in the world.

"Where's your family?"

"Uh-uh. My turn."

Her teeth bit down on her bottom lip to hide her smile. Why was he so obsessed with her mouth?

"In what way are you better alone?"

"I was hoping you'd forget." She sighed and stared at the closed blinds. In the silence, he heard ocean waves crash against the shore. One of the best sounds in the entire world. "For the two years we were married, I never relaxed. I always had to look perfect, act perfect, and be my best self. It was exhausting."

"And impossible. What would happen if you were less than perfect?"

She gave him the stink eye, but to his surprise, she answered. "His disapproval was palpable. Passive-aggressive comments. Side-eye. Suggesting I skip out on events. I'm a bit of a perfectionist, blended with some people-pleasing tendencies, and the combination was a cocktail for a self-esteem disaster."

He clenched his fists. He despised men like that. "It sounds like he deserved to lose you. And you deserve better."

"Maybe. Either way, I'm alone and have no one to answer to but myself, which feels good."

"Sure." He also had no one to answer to, and sometimes he found it so stifling, the only way he could breathe was to be outside. If anything happened to him on a Friday, no one would discover it until Monday when he didn't show up for work. He tried not to think about that fact too often, but it lingered in the back of his mind whenever a ladder wobbled under him, or he swallowed his drink wrong, or he hit a corner on his bike too hard.

"Don't think I didn't notice you cheated," she told him. "Can I have more pasta?"

"Is that your question?" he drawled.

"Your alfredo sauce is definitely worth giving up a question for."

His cold, dead heart warmed. He only cooked for himself these days and had almost forgotten how much he loved watching someone else enjoy his food. "Yes, you can. And I won't even count it as a question. Even though your first question was actually three."

"Oh yeah. I hoped you wouldn't notice that." She threw a sneaky smile over her shoulder as she got up to fill up her plate again. He also ate a little more, relieved to find it didn't taste like sand anymore.

When she came back, she had her plate in one hand and her turtle's box in the other. The turtle sized Asher up as she set it on the coffee table. Great.

He'd almost forgotten the turtle had existed, and now it was back in his orbit.

"Where's your family?"

Dang. He'd hoped she'd forget that one. It was definitely a conversation killer. "I don't have any."

"What? How is that possible? And yes, those are counting as my questions."

"My parents and my grandma died in an accident when I was in high school. I came to live with my grandpa, and he died last year. I'm the last living Brooks."

"That's really ... sad."

"Yeah. I'm kind of a downer at parties," he tried to joke. She only frowned, and he didn't get that same thrill as when she smiled. "What's your turtle's name?" *Crap.* He didn't want to know her turtle's name. He didn't want to know anything about it.

Her sunny smile peeked through the clouds he'd caused with his "little orphan Annie" sob story. "Her name is Louisa May Alcott."

He nearly choked on his drink when he inhaled it too fast with an unexpected laugh. She reached over to pat his back, which was unnecessary, but he might have coughed one or two extra times just to keep her close. "Why?" he finally asked.

"'Women, they have minds, and they have souls, as well as just hearts. And they've got ambition, and they've got talent, as well as just beauty. I'm so sick of people saying that love is all a woman is fit for.' Louisa May Alcott was ahead of her time. She was single and successful, and when Beth in *Little Women* died, I cried for a week." She leaned close. "I adore a tearjerker. Sometimes you need a good cry, you know?"

He did not know. He'd never understood the draw toward sad, depressing stories. He loved an underdog arc—the ragtag hockey team that wins against all odds, the detective no one believes in cracking the case. "Why a turtle?"

"Because they have a hard shell and a soft inside—and I'm a total sucker for that." She grinned at him like she wanted him to catch the double meaning. Asher had a hard shell *and* a dried-out husk for insides. "And when they trust you, they'll poke their cute little heads out and touch their noses against your hand. Louisa likes to follow me around, too, like my own little duckling." She put her hand in the box, and the turtle nestled its head against her finger as if giving her a butterfly kiss.

He would *not* be taken in by turtle butterfly kisses.

"What's your tattoo?" Eliana pulled a bottle of hand sanitizer from her purse and rubbed it into her hands.

"Which one?" he asked absently as he peered in her open purse. What else did she have in there?

"You have multiple?" Her eyes went wide and way, way too excited. "I meant the one on your arm, but now I want to know all of them. And where."

"That's too many questions," he said with mock regret. He was definitely not answering that. "I'm sorry. We can't be breaking rules willy-nilly, or else the game becomes meaningless."

"Willy-nilly?" Her eyes lit with pure delight, and he regretted his word choice instantly. "Are you sure you're thirty?"

"The Palms' residents ... their ways are contagious." His grandpa had said "willy-nilly" often. Asher started repeating it to mock him, and then one day, he realized he was using it for real, and there was no going back. He rolled the sleeve of his shirt up to reveal the red octopus hugging his bicep with its eight tentacles.

"Wait. A. Second. That's an animal," she said, accusingly.

"A technicality. They're one of the smartest animals on the planet, limited only by their tragically short life span."

"Which is?"

"Four years."

She gasped. "Louisa could live up to sixty years."

He whistled under his breath.

"I'm struggling to wrap my brain around the fact that you have an animal tattoo." She said it slowly, like she was trying to process it.

"They can also kill a person in seconds."

"Ah. That's more like it. For a minute there, I thought you were going soft or something."

None of those reasons were why he had an octopus on his arm, but she hadn't asked that question.

She twisted her smartwatch around to see the time. "One more question," she told him. "Then I've got to work on my book. I spent all afternoon on the wedding, and I'm behind on my daily goals."

He leaned back into the couch, alarmed as he realized he was disappointed. He wanted to ask her questions all night. There *was* one thing still tugging at him. "What happened today that made you declare you'd never get married again when you walked in the door?"

She rolled her eyes. "Oh, that. Julia's wedding is stressing me out. Did you know how many people are getting married this summer?" She paused. "*Everyone.* Everyone in Florida is getting married this summer. Which means there are no photographers, no venues, one low-rated florist available, and I called every single bakery within a two-hour radius of us, and no one can decorate her cake, so Logan's childhood babysitter who *thinks* she can do it is taking it on. I'm just *trying* to help my sister have the perfect wedding, and it shouldn't be this hard." She rested her elbows on her knees and grabbed her head. "I'm so ready for this to be over."

"You're a good sister." He didn't want to admit it. Didn't want to give her a compliment—after everything. But she was. With both Cameron and Julia. They were lucky to have her. And she was lucky to have them.

"Thanks," she said. "I try. And fail. Then try again." She stood with a groan. "I ate way too much, but I have no regrets. I'll do the dishes."

She held out her hand for his plate, but he waved her away. "I'll do them. You need to go work."

She saluted him. "Yes, sir." She walked down the hall but turned at the last minute before she went into the guest room. "Thanks for playing with me, Asher. Next time, you can pick the game."

Next time? He didn't hate the thought.

CHAPTER 9
ELIANA

"But, like all happiness, it did not last long ..." —Louisa May Alcott

"**B**OXES, BOXES, BOXES," ELIANA sang to a made-up tune as she carried a set of them one by one to the couch.

She was starting with the boxes in her bedroom, then she'd work toward the ones in the living room and kitchen. She hadn't seen the inside of Asher's bedroom to know if there were boxes in there too, but she couldn't imagine it had remained unscathed.

Playing the question-and-answer game with Asher last night had been fun. Relaxing. She hadn't realized how worked up the day had made her until all the stress was gone. All it had taken was good conversation, excellent food, and a laugh or two. With Asher of all people.

Or maybe *because* it was Asher. Having him hate her really weighed her down, and they'd made great inroads toward becoming friends.

And now that he'd agreed they needed to go through the boxes, he'd be even happier with her. See? Having her live with him was going to improve his life. She'd done him a favor by blackmailing him.

She kept the blinds closed even though the low lighting made her eyes ache with strain. He didn't have a backup plan for a place to live, but he couldn't live here forever. Her heart ached remembering his story. She couldn't imagine losing everyone she loved.

She couldn't fix his problems, but she could help him go through these boxes, because that would at least give him some options.

She worked on her book all morning and through lunch, and she had only written half a page. She tried to write about the non-monogamous birds, but the words weren't coming. She skipped to a different chapter and tried to write about the power of solo decision-making, but every word was like slogging through mud.

Asher had left a covered plate in the fridge, a sticky note with her name attached to it. She could definitely get used to this. Maybe Asher would continue to want a roommate once he moved out of his grandpa's bungalow?

He'd cook dinner for her when she was working late.

She'd make him play silly games when he got too serious.

It was a perfect arrangement.

Nothing was keeping her in Boston. Not really. She'd lived there with Corbin, and after the divorce, she'd stayed. Partly out of embarrassment, partly out of pride. She hadn't wanted to come crawling back home in failure. And Corbin had told her she was much too dependent on her family, and they on her. It was one of the things that used to drive him nuts.

She realized now Corbin's complaints about her family were one more way for him to control her life. She'd missed her family. She didn't want to live with them again—especially not in a two-bedroom apartment—but she wanted to have dinner with them, and take walks on the beach with them, and help with Cam's appointments, and be an active part of their lives.

She rolled her eyes at herself. One good meal, and she was ready to move back home and force a taciturn man who didn't even like her—or Louisa, yeah, she'd noticed—to be her roomie.

But he'd used *real cream*. And *butter*. And *garlic*.

No, Elly. This is only temporary.

She opened the first box. If the outside had been dusty, the inside was a miniature Sahara Desert. Her throat dried up, and she began coughing and waving the air in front of her to clear the dust particles.

What treasures were in this box?

She reached in and pulled out a handful of worn boxer shorts. Seriously? Nobody wanted these. She riffled through the rest of the box without pulling anything out. All used underwear and socks went straight to the trash pile.

The next box was bedding, so she put that into a giveaway pile.

The third box had been so heavy she'd had to drag it into the living room. When she opened it, she expected to find books. Instead, it was filled with mail.

Her heart skipped. Finally, something interesting. She grabbed as much as she could hold and set it on the coffee table to go through. She wouldn't read any of it without Asher's permission, but just to see handwritten cursive address labels and old stamps was exciting.

The first stack, though, was filled with pretty recent mail—all of it junk. Advertisements from lawyers, for life insurance policies, for windshield repairs, for credit card applications ... This went on and on, and she deflated with every piece of mail she threw into the trash pile.

She unpacked more and discovered what made the box so heavy. Magazines. Dozens of them, from celebrity gossip to political, all of them from the last couple of years.

She paused to take in all the boxes surrounding her. Would they all be bedding, underwear, and old magazines? No, she refused to believe it.

The act of sorting and organizing was relaxing, and she fell into a rhythm of separating things into three piles: one for giveaway, one for things that were very obviously trash, and one for Asher to go through and make a decision about.

She startled when the door opened and Asher walked in. Was it already the end of the workday? She glanced at her watch. She'd been at this for almost four hours and had accomplished so much more here than she had with her book this morning—especially since she'd made the decision to delete everything she'd written that day and start fresh tomorrow.

No one cared about the mating patterns of birds.

Asher stood frozen in the doorway.

"Hey," she said. "I know it looks like a mess, but there's a system, I promise."

His expression was as frozen as his body. She tried to take the room in from his point of view, and realized how disorganized it might appear from his perspective.

"Over here is the giveaway pile." She held her arms out to encompass the boxes she'd refilled by the television. "This is the—"

"What do you think you're doing?" His voice was low and growly.

She stilled. "Going through the boxes."

"Why are you doing this?" He bit off each word, like ice chipping from his frozen frame, leaving behind a hot core. An angry, hot core.

Confused, she turned on him with her hands on her hips. "You said I could."

"No. I didn't."

"Yes," she insisted. "Yesterday, I said we needed to start going through the boxes to help with the lighting, and you said yes."

"You mentioned I needed to clear the boxes, and I acknowledged that I heard you." His face was turning a bright shade of red, as if the heat was filling him up to the brim.

She thought back on their conversation, and she clearly remembered that he'd grunted in agreement. "I said *we*, and you made this sound." She mimicked his grunt.

"Exactly. I agree *I* need to do it sometime." He looked around the room, his jaw flexing. "It's one thing to move into my space, but another to go through my stuff."

"I'm trying to help you." Now it was her turn to clench her jaw. Couldn't he be grateful? She'd spent hours on this and hardly made a dent.

"I don't want your help! I don't want you here!"

His words cut her right to her core. Hurt flashed through her, but she covered it up quickly with anger. She turned on her heel and grabbed Louisa from the counter.

"Where are you going?"

"Not that it's any of your business, but we're going for a walk."

"You can't just leave this all—"

66

"You don't want my help, then fine. Do it yourself." She headed toward the front door, where she'd stashed the container she'd been using for Louisa's walks.

"Go out the back way—"

"I KNOW!" She set Louisa inside it, her hands shaking with anger.

She went out the back door, barely refraining from slamming it shut, and stomped all the way around to the front of the bungalow just to spite him. If the blinds had been open, he'd see her there.

They weren't open, of course, because he lived in a box-riddled cave filled with old underwear and magazines. And apparently that was how he liked it.

She stuck her tongue out at the house. It made her feel just a little bit better.

"What are you doing all the way down here?" Grandma Winnie called out.

Eliana whirled around to find Grandma, Nancy, and Rosa walking toward her. It took all of her self-discipline not to panic-glance at Asher's bungalow. Had they seen her leave? She was angry at Asher—the ungrateful ambiguous grunter that he was—but she didn't want him to get caught. "Taking Louisa for a walk," she said.

"Did you park at my place? I didn't see your car."

"I'm on the street." She waved in the vague direction of the neighborhood she'd been parking her car in, beside Asher's motorcycle.

"I'm glad we ran into you," Nancy said.

Grandma Winnie slid her arm through Eliana's. Could she tell Eliana was fuming? Was her skin as hot as it felt? Eliana led the women away from Asher's house.

Nancy opened her notes app on her phone. "We're organizing a family day fundraiser for sea turtles."

"Oh. Do you need a donation?"

"In a way. It's a week from Saturday. Everyone's kids and grandkids are invited. It'll be filled with games and activities, and we'd love to have you participate."

"What kind of games?"

"Outdoor games. We're still figuring it out," Nancy said.

"But they'll be really fun," Rosa interjected.

Eliana frowned. The fundraiser was in less than two weeks, and they didn't have the activities nailed down? "Do you need help planning?" she asked, despite her better judgment.

Luckily, Grandma Winnie shook her head and squeezed Eliana's arm closer. "You've got enough on your plate with work and Julia's wedding. We'll take care of it. We'd love for you to attend. I think you'll enjoy it."

"Of course I'll be there." Her anger lessened every moment she was in the presence of these ladies. How could it not? They were so filled with love and a clear desire to cheer her up, even though they had no idea what was pulling her down.

"Did you know sea turtles have an internal magnetic system that helps them navigate over hundreds of miles of ocean to migrate and then get back home again?" Nancy asked. She looked up from her phone. "And scientists estimate that only one in every ten thousand born survives to adulthood."

Nancy continued to read off facts while they walked, and Eliana's temper cooled. She thought through her conversation with Asher again. Maybe his grunt *hadn't* been a clear yes. And maybe she'd been out of line to go through his grandpa's personal belongings. She'd tried to push the issue, and he'd gotten upset. It had been more than anger, though—that had been raw grief.

She was going to have to apologize. She hated apologizing.

They went inside Grandma Winnie's bungalow to get drinks. While Grandma Winnie and her friends chatted about the fundraiser, Eliana perused her grandma's bookcase. Grandma Winnie had an extensive collection of self-help books. Perhaps one of them could help her navigate this situation.

A book on grief caught her eye, as well as a book about coping with the loss of a loved one. She snagged them off of the shelf, along with a book about healthy communication.

If she read these, maybe she could understand Asher better and not make such a huge mistake in the future. His grief clung to him in the same way his wet suit did, and that more than anything was going to give her the courage to apologize and repack those boxes.

She needed to focus on her book anyway instead of getting distracted by boxes and the lack of light—and especially by Asher Brooks.

CHAPTER 10

WINNIE

"**S**HE DIDN'T SUSPECT A thing?" Don asked, skeptical. They sat at their conference table at The Palms to brainstorm for their impromptu fundraiser.

"Not a thing," Nancy assured him.

Don had worried that planning a sea turtle fundraiser right after they learned about Eliana's love of turtles would be too on the nose. Then to add a game element to it, when they knew she loved games? It was obviously tailor made for Eliana.

"She doesn't know it's couples' games yet. Or that we're going to talk Asher into coming too," Nancy continued.

Rosa jumped in. "The idea of it really seemed to cheer her up," she said. "Didn't she look like she was about to cry when we bumped into her?"

Winnie nodded. "It's the stress of this book and the wedding. It's too much."

Winnie's phone buzzed with a text.

Horace: I'm not going to make it home for dinner.

Her heart sank. This was the third time this week.

"She's still writing that *I'm So Happy I'm Single* book?" Walt said. "I thought you were going to convince her not to."

"*Happily Single*," Nancy reminded him. "And Winnie's working on it."

Winnie tried to put her head back into matchmaking. The truth was, she'd been so focused on racing to finish Julia's wedding dress and the bridesmaid dresses that she hadn't had as much time as she would have liked to talk to Eliana about the beauty of a healthy relationship.

She had hoped that planning the wedding, and seeing Julia and Logan in love, would be a natural, organic way to convince her that she could be happy in a relationship too, but that seemed to be backfiring as well, as the stress of planning a last-minute wedding only seemed to be turning her off of marriage more.

Winnie's friends looked at her expectantly, and she realized they were waiting for her to report how the plan—the nonexistent plan—was going. "Well ..."

Her phone buzzed again. Eliana was going live on social media. Eliana had helped Winnie set up an account and notifications so she could follow Eliana's posts.

Social media. A light blinked on in her brain. "We need to speak her language."

They all nodded, though she knew they didn't quite understand her yet.

"By creating a social media page filled with our own stories about how we fell in love."

They erupted at the same time.

"What?"

"Wait."

"No."

"Ohh, fun!"

"I'm not against it."

"Brilliant," Nancy said loud enough to quiet everyone. "We'll all log in to take turns posting a picture of our wedding day—or as close as we can get, if you don't have a wedding picture—and talk about the moment you knew you were in love with your spouse."

"But how will that help?" Walt said. He still missed his wife, who had died several years ago. She didn't want this to be painful for him, but they'd had a beautiful love story.

"It will help her to believe in love again," Polly said. "I think it's a very romantic idea."

"What's the name of the app?" Harry placed his glasses on the tip of his nose and attempted to navigate his smartphone.

"Samantha can help us," Don declared. "I'll talk to her to get this set up."

"Thank you, Don," Winnie said, feeling relief. Not only had they liked her idea, but Samantha—the activities director at The Palms, and an unofficial member of the Secret Seven—was always a wonderful teacher and would help them get logged in and make a new group account.

"What should we call it?" Winnie asked.

"The Secret Seven!" Rosa gave everyone a fake innocent expression as their heads swiveled in her direction. "I kid, I kid."

"What about Wedded Bliss?" Walt said, his eyes suspiciously wet.

They all looked at one another, and Winnie felt their excitement rise.

CHAPTER 11

ASHER

A SHER SAT ON THE floor, snatched a handful of junk mail and an empty box, and shoved everything back where it should go.

The nerve of Eliana. Thinking she could go through his grandpa's belongings. Like they didn't mean anything. Like it was so easy to discard them.

He hardly glanced at the mail as he stuffed a box as full as he could, every movement jerky and heated. He snatched another box to continue with the magazines. Celebrity faces stared back at him, a blur of people he'd never really know, yet he had so much information about their lives right at his fingertips.

He paused at a cover with Aurelia Halifax on it. She held her guitar as if caught mid-song. *A Duo Made in Heaven*, the small text under the headline said. He heard enough gossip down at The Palms to know that Aurelia and Bo had not only broken up, but Bo had stolen an album's worth of songs from her.

The heat fueling Asher's rage dissolved, like steam escaping his pressure cooker. His spine went limp as he leaned against the legs of the couch and stared up at the ceiling.

What was he doing?

He didn't need to keep all this stuff. He didn't even *want* to keep it.

On some level, he knew his grandpa's memory wasn't found in celebrity gossip magazines or old bedding. He turned his head to the side and spotted the boxer shorts. He winced. Or old underwear.

He scrubbed his hands down his face, remembering Eliana's hurt expression.

She shouldn't have gone through the boxes. She shouldn't be here at all. But she wasn't wrong. Most of this was garbage. He boxed up the garbage and pushed it to the corner of the room. One glance at the giveaway pile, and he decided he didn't even want to go through it.

The final pile she'd set aside was the keep pile. It was small—so far there were only three things in it. A china tea set he remembered his grandma using on Sundays and special occasions. A framed picture of his grandparents from a cruise they'd gone on about twenty years ago. And a hemp friendship bracelet.

He pulled it from the pile, surprised to see it there. He hadn't thought about this bracelet in years. He'd made a matching set when he was ten or eleven and had given one to his grandpa, keeping the other for himself.

Asher had no idea where his bracelet was—probably thrown away in one of the many moves of his childhood. But Grandpa had kept his all this time.

Emotion clogged his chest, making it hard to breathe, hard to think beyond the rough fibers rubbing against his fingers and the memory of his grandpa's smile as he'd tied it around his wrist. This was why Asher didn't want to go through the boxes. This was why he'd put it off for so long.

He didn't even want to take the time to put on his wet suit before he fled toward the ocean. He slipped off his shoes and socks and stood in the water, letting the waves run over his pants, soaking his legs up to his knees.

He inhaled the salty air as deeply as his lungs would allow and then held the air inside. He repeated the action over and over until his hands stopped shaking and his heart stopped racing.

He clung to his grandpa's bracelet. Tiny clown-nose-red and sky-blue beads had been interwoven in the fibers. He couldn't recall why he'd chosen those specific colors, or if his bracelet had been an exact match.

A crater opened up inside of him, and it could not be closed again. On one side of the chasm, everything was safe. His life stayed the same as it always had been—a holding pattern or a limbo of sorts, where the future couldn't quite touch him. On the other side ... he didn't know what was on the other side of the chasm, and that disturbed him most. It was vast and unknown. It was untethered to his family.

Over there, what would keep him drifting away, like an unanchored boat at sea?

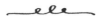

Asher successfully avoided Eliana for several days. So successfully, in fact, he was beginning to suspect that she was avoiding him too.

Which shouldn't bother him.

But the problem was, he wasn't sleeping well. Every time he closed his eyes, he pictured a flash of hurt crossing Eliana's face. He didn't know how to bridge the gap between them and get back to the tentative place of friendship they'd broached that night playing the question-answer game.

So he worked late, swam late, and slept—or, more accurately, tossed and turned—as late as he could. Avoidance always had been his problem-solving method of choice.

Grandpa had been the kind of person who addressed his issues with people head-on. In so many ways, Asher fell short of being like Grandpa. Was it so surprising that this was yet another way?

Asher needed to bake something delicious. He needed space for his mind to work out how to solve this problem. He imagined chocolate banana bread with a sugar-crumb crust on top. He'd picked up bananas nearly a week ago, and they were perfect for baking with.

He listened closely but couldn't hear Eliana. Most likely, she was holed up in her bedroom, working on her book. The scent of bread might draw her out to the kitchen, but he didn't know whether he wanted that or dreaded it.

He washed his hands in his bathroom and combed his hair back. It had been a minute since his last haircut or beard trim. Maybe it was time to get in with the barber.

Maybe it's time to stop hiding.

He left his bedroom and paused in front of Eliana's door, listening for the clacking of her keyboard. It was silent. Maybe she'd left. She seemed to have one family responsibility or another every day. He tried not to wonder too much what that might be like. Annoying, probably. But the good kind of annoying, where you rolled your eyes and groaned, but still smiled and felt good about helping.

He moved down the hall quickly, not seeing Eliana also rounding the corner into the hallway until too late.

"Oof!" He plowed into her, all six feet and three inches of him, and she flew into a stack of boxes right beside the hallway entrance. He snagged her arm to keep her from falling, but the damage was already done.

Like dominoes toppling one by one, the stacks of boxes fell.

"Louisa!" Eliana's eyes went wide with panic, and she raced into the dining room, where the boxes had fallen onto the kitchen table. "She was on here."

His stomach dropped, and he jumped over and stepped on boxes as he rushed toward the table, which was buried under a mound of boxes. "I'm so sorry," he said, out of breath, throwing boxes as far across the room as he could in order to get to the table. He might not like animals, but he never, ever wanted to see one hurt. Eliana's face was bone white.

None of these boxes were light, but Eliana managed to throw off as many as him, until they finally got to where he saw a corner of the turtle's habitat. The corners of the plastic box were scrunched down, and from this angle, he couldn't tell if a box had fallen into the habitat or not.

"It's here," he said. "I'll hold this box up, and you grab it."

She rushed to his side, her hair brushing against his arm as she reached around him and pulled out Louisa's habitat. The minute it was free, he dropped the box and took the habitat from her so she could reach in for Louisa.

"She's okay. She has to be okay," Eliana said over and over again as she held the turtle, still burrowed in her shell, up to her nose. Suddenly, she swayed. "I'm dizzy."

She shot out a hand and reached out for Asher's arm. He hadn't seen anything hit her head. Hopefully, it was just the adrenaline.

"Take Louisa. I don't want to drop her." She thrust the turtle into his. He held it, frozen. With Eliana hanging on one arm and the turtle in his free hand, he was afraid to move. They both felt impossibly fragile.

The turtle poked its head out from its shell and turned to look at Asher, blinking lazy eyes at him as if to ask if he knew what he was doing.

No, turtle. I don't.

"Let's go to the couch," he told Eliana. He looked at the massacre of boxes and then at Eliana. "How do you feel about a piggyback ride?"

She made a face. "Not great." But she looked out at the boxes and sighed. "Can you crouch or something? I can't hop that high."

He bent down, and she climbed onto his back, her arms coming around his neck, her fresh scent enveloping him.

"Do you still have Louisa?" she asked, her voice holding a hint of panic.

"Right here," he said as calmly as he could.

She rested her chin on his shoulder, and he knew she didn't intend to, but she breathed right into his ear, giving him shivers down his neck. "I'm only letting you carry me because this is your fault," she said. "And my heart is still racing thinking I lost Louisa."

Shame cut through him like a hot knife. What if the boxes had hurt Eliana's turtle? Or Eliana, when he'd accidentally knocked her into them? Or even Cameron, when he'd been here several days ago? Cameron wasn't always steady on his feet, and he might have been hurt too.

She tightened her grip around his neck, and her legs wound around his waist. He would *not* think about every part of her touching every part of him. He would *not* think about how she smelled like a piña colada, or how silky her hair felt as it rubbed against the side of his neck and his cheek. Especially since he needed to concentrate on navigating this mess.

He took his time, and when he got to the couch, he gently set Eliana down. He sat beside her and met eyes with her turtle. Its nose nudged his thumb as if in greeting.

"Hello, Louisa," he whispered.

Dang it. The first rule to not getting attached is to never touch it.

The second rule is to never say its name.

Eliana gave him a strange look he couldn't interpret.

"She seems fine." Nothing to see here. He handed Louisa—the turtle, he meant to say *the turtle*—back to Eliana, who held it close.

"Thank you," she said.

He hopped up to get them each a cold water bottle. When he brought them back, she had her purse open and was peering at herself in a tiny mirror. "Are you okay? Did your head get hit?"

"No." Her cheeks were pink. "I just realized I look a mess."

He lowered his eyebrows and took her in from head to foot. She looked entirely put together, as always. No one would know she'd nearly been avalanched just moments ago. "No, you don't. Are you sure you're okay?"

She pulled her hair into a low bun and set the mirror down. "We're fine. Aren't we, Louisa?" She looked over her shoulder into the dining hall. "But that room is not."

He didn't want to follow her gaze, so he looked at the side of her face instead. Her profile was made up of delicate lines and creamy skin. Had he noticed before now how crushingly beautiful she was?

Yes, of course he had. But he hadn't taken the time to really look. He didn't know how to talk to a woman like her, much less live with her.

She turned toward him, and he averted his gaze before she could catch him watching her.

"What are we going to do about this?" she asked. Did she mean the piles of boxes or the stalemate they were in over them?

"It's not safe," he said. "I'm going to have to go through them." It felt like declaring he was attempting to climb Everest. This task felt nearly as impossible. He cleared his throat. He had to ask, but it took humbling himself to the very depths of his soul. "Are you still willing to help?"

She stared at him carefully, and he braced himself for her to say no or storm off or give him a sarcastic remark about how he'd already turned her help down. Instead, she placed her hand on his, as if she had an inkling of how hard it was for him to ask, and simply said, "Yes."

CHAPTER 12
ELIANA

"Preserve your memories, keep them well, what you forget you can never retell." —Louisa May Alcott

E LIANA STRETCHED ACROSS HER air mattress as morning light flitted through the slats of the blinds. She lengthened every limb as far as she could and yawned. Her back ached from hitting the boxes last night, but she wasn't about to tell Asher that, not when he felt so guilty about knocking into her.

Louisa slept in her walking container—which would be her temporary habitat until Eliana could buy her a new one. Eliana had fallen asleep staring at Louisa, grateful that she was okay.

The scent of something divine wafted down the hallway. Chocolate and bananas and sugar. Three things she could always identify. Three things that always made her stomach growl extra loud.

She rolled out of bed and checked her watch as she headed down the hall. It was already eight a.m. Asher would be long gone for work by now. He must have gotten up extra early to make the bread. He'd wanted to start clearing up the boxes right away, but she'd convinced him they both needed a good night's sleep first.

Her books on grief helped her understand that Asher's grandpa's boxes were more than a checklist of items to go through and categorize. They represented his remaining connection to his grandpa. She hadn't been sensitive to that at all. It was no wonder he'd been upset.

This time, she'd wait until he got home from work, and they'd do it together. She'd offer moral support, but the pacing would be one hundred percent led by Asher.

She studied in her reflection in the bathroom mirror as she washed her hands. She'd been too worked up to do her intense bedtime routine last night, so this morning, her hair was wild and her mascara was rubbed under her still-sleepy eyes. She'd check out whatever smelled so good in the kitchen, shower, and then make another video today. She was feeling inspired to chat about the importance of having a pet in your happily single life.

She shuffled into the kitchen, her feet skidding to a halt at the sight of Asher's broad back at the stove. Like a bug careening helplessly toward the windshield, she remained frozen as he turned and saw her. Splat.

He smiled—smiled!—and said, "Are you hungry? I made banana bread."

She brought her hands to cover her face. Could a person die of mortification? Because that would be really convenient right now. "You were supposed to be at work," she said through her fingers. She took him in—blue plaid pajama pants and a tank top that made it possible for her to see the full image of the octopus hugging his thick biceps. In the deep armhole of his tank top, a tattoo peeked out from his ribs.

"I called in sick today so I can start cleaning the dining room." Confusion laced his voice. "Is everything okay?"

"No. You're not supposed to see me like this." She needed to stop covering her face—and she had to escape to her room—but her feet felt planted.

"Eliana. You look beautiful, as always."

His sincerity made her lungs hitch in her chest and emotion fly straight to her eyes. Corbin had never liked how she looked in the morning. His favorite phrase after she'd woken up had been, *It's lucky you clean up so nicely.* Worse, though, had been the look he'd sometimes give her. Like she was day-old, crusted egg yolk on a plate he was trying to scrub clean.

He never liked anything to be less than absolutely perfect. And he held compliments over her head like she was a dog, and kindness was a treat only to be meted out when she pleased him. She'd thought she'd managed to get past most of her impulses to meet his standards, but seeing Asher in the kitchen, looking so heart-poundingly hot, it all came flooding back.

She'd had to learn to give herself her own compliments—which was going to be one of the chapters in her book—and to hear Asher call her beautiful? It felt disconcertingly nice. People commented on her appearance all the time on her social media posts, but to have Asher say it in that low, grumbly voice so soon after waking up?

Whoa, butterflies.

See? Disconcerting.

She mumbled something incoherent and fled to the bathroom to take a shower, refresh her makeup, and blow-dry and curl her hair.

When she went back into the kitchen thirty minutes later, she found, to her disappointment, that Asher had gotten dressed as well. He wore basketball shorts and an Orlando Magic T-shirt, and he had cleared enough space on the dining room floor to sit amid the boxes. A plate with two thick slices of banana bread sat on the counter beside a steaming mug.

"There's butter next to the toaster," Asher said. He looked like a kid at Christmas gone very wrong with all those boxes around him.

She spread butter on her slices of banana bread and took a huge bite. It was moist and chocolaty and just as delicious as the alfredo had been. "How in the world did you learn to cook so well?" she asked. "This is seriously divine."

"I enjoy cooking. It's relaxing."

"Not for me. If I want to relax, I'll read a book or watch a show."

The air was still a little awkward between them. Normally, she didn't have a hard time figuring out what to say to someone. But also normally, she didn't accidentally emotionally destroy someone, followed by them almost killing her turtle. They'd had a busy few days, to say the least.

"I didn't peg you as the kind of person to call in fake sick."

"Really? You look at me and think 'rule follower'?" His eyebrow rose.

She snorted. "Despite all of this"—she waved her hand at his long hair and tattooed arm—"yes. But mostly, I can tell you love your patients and wouldn't want to let them down."

"I see most of them a couple times a week, so if I have to miss, it's not a big deal. For the others, I'll work late a few days next week to make up for it."

She appreciated his dependability. Her heart warmed, knowing he'd been shaken enough about what had almost happened to Louisa that he was willing to call in sick to get this taken care of. "So how do you want to do this?" she asked, her tone businesslike to hide how much she wanted to give him a big old bear hug. "Do you have a plan on where to start, or just dive in?"

His mouth straightened to a grim line. She'd been too panicked about how she looked this morning to appreciate the smile he'd given her when he'd first seen her this morning. She wanted to rewind time and sit in that moment.

"You had a good plan. Let's keep the three piles system: give away, keep, and toss out." He cut open a box and peered inside with a hesitant expression.

"Do you care if I start over here?" She wanted to be near the banana bread, but if he needed her close, she'd save her second slice for later.

"I know you need to work." He rubbed his beard, leaving behind some of the dust from the box, making him look like he had a handful of gray hairs. This was going to get messy.

"I'll do it this afternoon." Sitting in her bedroom and writing had almost no appeal to her right now.

"I don't want to pull you from stuff you need to do," he said, but he sounded too relieved for her to fully believe him.

"I'm writing an easy chapter today." She snagged the scissors from him to open a box. It would have been helpful if Asher's grandpa had labeled them. If there was a rhyme or reason to his methods, she didn't have a clue what it was.

"What's your chapter on?" He pulled out a bag of tangled yarn and held it up for her to see. "What do you think?"

Her nose wrinkled. "I'm tempted to trash it. That looks unsalvageable."

He threw it into the corner and started their official trash pile.

"I'm writing a chapter on the mental benefits of having a pet."

He snorted.

"It's true!" She tossed a single rolled-up sock from her box at him. It hit him in the side of his head, and he looked up with a puzzled expression before his lips quirked to the side. Almost a smile, but not quite.

This box was filled with odds and ends—worn-out hand towels, a yellowed lacy pillowcase, multiple unmatched socks, and several tote bags with grocery store labeling on them.

"Studies show that pet owners live longer. Also, petting a dog or cat releases endorphins and can help with depression and anxiety." She riffled through the box to see if any of it was worth keeping. Nope. She cut into the next box.

"What about petting a turtle?" He pulled items out of his box one by one and studied each from every angle. His appeared to be filled with half-completed craft projects and crusty art supplies.

"Studies are still ongoing in this field," she said. This box was filled with mostly-new towels. She set them aside in a keep pile. "I haven't found anything specific to turtles yet, but most of the studies use the wording of 'pets' or 'animals,' and they *do* fall into that category."

"What about the adverse effects of losing an animal?"

Her heart thumped in sadness. There was that grief again. He wasn't looking at her, instead studying what appeared to be a doll with half of its hair ripped out. He'd definitely picked the short straw when it came to boxes. "It's devastating," she said, "and no one but you can decide if the benefits of having a loving pet can outweigh that part of it."

His phone buzzed several times, but he ignored it.

"Aren't you curious who's messaging you?" she finally asked.

"There's no one I care to hear from."

It buzzed several more times, and her curiosity spiked. "Someone really wants to get a hold of you."

He sighed and held out his hand. She grabbed his phone from the counter and leaned over as far as she could, until their hands touched, and he grabbed the phone.

"Don, Harry, Smitty, Walt, and your grandma are all asking if I feel okay."

"Oh. That's super sweet."

"It is." Another text came in, and he frowned. "Your grandma wants my address so she can bring by some soup."

"Soup is one of Grandma Winnie's love languages."

"What do I tell her?"

"Ummm. I don't know. Ignoring it sounds good."

He snorted. "See how persistent they are? It's amazing I've gone this long, and you're the only person who's noticed I live here."

"Well, maybe if you'd towed one of their cars, they would have followed you and found out as well."

"Ha ha."

They worked side by side in silence, getting into a good rhythm. Eliana forced herself to slow down and give careful thought to every single box, and even still, she was going through them at a rate of three boxes for every one he went through.

They paused at one point to reorganize their piles and bag up the trash. "We're going to need to use my car for this," she said. "I don't think your motorcycle can handle it."

He sighed. "Maybe at night. So no one sees."

"Are you ashamed of me?" she teased, putting a hand over her heart.

He gave her some hard side-eyeing, which made her laugh. Why in the world was it so rewarding to get a reaction out of him? "Or else someone might offer to help," he said. "If they come inside ..."

"It's clear you're living here," she finished.

They took a break for lunch—Eliana insisted it was her turn to make a meal, and she put together two pretty good-looking turkey sandwiches—and dove back in for more work. Part of Eliana knew she needed to step away and work on her book. Her deadline loomed, and nothing but time in front of the computer was going to get this book done.

But they'd talked about her chapter. That was basically writing. She worried if she left Asher, he might get mired in his sadness. As it was, when they got quiet for a time, she'd look up and see him frowning again. She liked that she was able to distract him and help him do this. It made her feel like less of a bad person for forcing him to let her live with him.

She could feel herself spiraling into stress and needed to get her mind off of it. "I saw another tattoo on your ribs."

He merely hmmmed as he flipped through dozens of cassette tapes. He held one up for her to see. "Bruce Springsteen."

"Nice." She dragged another box toward her. This one had been at the bottom of the stack, in the corner of the room. It was heavier than any of the others. *It's probably filled with leftover bricks from an old landscaping job. Or half-empty cartons of paint.* Asher's grandpa had been a borderline hoarder. "About that tattoo ..."

"Celine Dion," he said, holding up another one. "I don't even know how you could play a cassette tape anymore."

"Some older cars still have players. What's your tattoo?"

He bit his lower lip but didn't look up from the tapes. "Why do you want to know?"

She huffed. "I just do." Hadn't he ever heard of getting to know someone?

He grunted. Fine. She didn't care that much anyway. Despite how much her brain kept flying back to that sliver of golden skin at his ribs.

She cut open her box with a little more gusto than required and opened it up with a cough as the dust puffed up. This one had a plastic file bin inside of it, one like what her parents used to keep important papers and bills in.

She shimmied it out of the box and pulled off the lid to look inside. Her brows furrowed as she slid her finger over each of the file folder labels.

They were all names of people who lived in The Palms. There had to be dozens of files in here. She opened one, and her brows furrowed as she read. Her heart racing, she pulled out another and another. "Asher, come look at this right now."

CHAPTER 13

ASHER

AT THE URGENCY IN Eliana's voice, Asher looked up from the Billy Joel cassette tape. "What's wrong?" He moved closer to Eliana. They'd cleared up enough boxes for there to be a path between them.

"Your grandpa has dirt on almost everyone in The Palms."

"No way." It wasn't that he didn't believe her, but she must have been misinterpreting something. Why in the world would his grandpa have dirt on people?

"Seriously. Look at this." She handed him a folder labeled Harry. "Was your grandpa a private investigator or something?"

"No. He was retired military." He flipped through the file folder and found several typed papers along with a couple photographs. One of them was of an old vinyl record cover. It had a picture of a younger-looking Harry, wearing a cowboy hat and holding a guitar.

"Harry has a country album." Eliana leaned against his arm to take one of the papers from him. He tried to focus, but between trying to wrap his mind around what all of this meant and feeling Eliana's soft skin pressed against his arm, his brain had gone to mush. "Listen to this: 'Harry made a one-time country album in 1968. His song "My Heart Ratatats for You" only got playtime on his local radio station for six months. He performed three times at the county fair.'"

She pulled out another file, this one for Troy Rogers. It contained copies of bank statements and a ledger. "It says Troy embezzled upwards of seven hundred thousand dollars from his company over the ten years he worked there. When the owner discovered it, he offered early retirement and swept it under the rug to avoid scandal." She looked up with dread. "Do you think this is true?"

He thumbed through the files, disturbed to recognize so many names on the tabs as residents of The Palms—mostly from the bungalow side, but a few from memory care and assisted living.

Eliana set down the Troy folder and pulled out one labeled "Winnie."

"I don't know if this is a good idea—" he started, but it only held one small piece of paper on it that said "In progress."

"What do you think that means?" She stared at him like he might have an answer.

"I don't know." Unease settled over him.

She found Horace's folder next.

"This is people's private business—"

But she'd already read it. "This one's true. It's about Grandpa Horace and Smitty. It details their business feud from so many years ago."

He recalled the details of their business dealings coming out last year after Smitty and his wife, Lydia, had moved to The Palms. Before that, no one had known about their friendship-turned-rivalry.

"And if this is true, that means ..."

"The rest of them might be true," he finished. The file burned his hands as if he'd pulled a pan from the oven without hot pads.

Eliana pushed the box away from her. "Was your grandpa the nosy type?"

"This goes beyond nosy and straight to creepy," Asher said, feeling disloyal even as he said it. "But my grandpa wasn't nosy or creepy. He hated secrets, though. He believed they tore relationships apart and made the world worse."

"Maybe he was on a vigilante crusade to reveal everyone's secrets. Or ..." Her mouth turned downward.

"What?" he asked with dread.

She whispered, "Do you think he was blackmailing people? Troy would probably pay to keep people from knowing he'd embezzled money from his work."

"Not everyone blackmails people to solve their problems," he said sharply.

Boom. His words dropped like a bomb in the middle of the room, and their easy rapport from earlier was blown to bits. He waited for her to say something cutting and rush out of the room. But she only swallowed hard and then turned toward him with a blank expression. "That's fair."

He rubbed his temples. He didn't want to get into a fight with her again, not when she'd been so helpful all morning. "No, I'm sorry. We don't know why he had this, and we can't rule out anything."

"I'm sure he wasn't a blackmailer, not if he was anything like you," she continued, sounding contrite.

He lifted his brow. "Oh, so blackmailers are only young, intelligent influencers now?"

"Yes." She sat primly with her hands in her lap, but then relaxed against the wall with her legs crossed. Did she realize her knee was pressed against the outside of his thigh? Was she as aware of every single movement of his body as he was of hers?

Her phone buzzed, and she pulled it out of her pocket while Asher stuffed all the folders back into the bin. This felt a whole lot like Pandora's box, and though in the fable hope remained, a whole lot of destruction wreaked havoc on people's lives first.

"My grandma just texted to see if I could bring you soup. She says she's waiting to hear from you with your address." She peered over her phone at him.

"She's making you deliver it?"

"She doesn't like to drive anymore," Eliana said. "What are you going to tell her?"

He opened up his text messages and debated. This was the thing he both loved and hated about The Palms. Everyone was in his business—but also, he had people who cared enough about him to be in his business. Definitely a double-edged sword. "If I fess up that I'm not really sick, will she turn me in?"

"Grandma Winnie isn't a snitch. She's covered for me loads of times."

"For what?" he asked. He could see a younger Eliana getting into all kinds of scrapes. She had that impulsivity that was both exciting and nerve-racking.

"I'll tell you, if you tell me what your tattoo is."

He leveled her with a bemused glare. He didn't actually care if she knew what his tattoo was, but it intrigued him how curious she seemed to be about it. It made him want to continue teasing her. So instead of answering, he called up Winnie to confess that he'd faked sick.

Eliana silently groaned and pretended to fall back against the wall, like he'd devastated her. He covered his mouth before she could see his amusement. No use in encouraging her, or she might endlessly provoke him.

"Well," Winnie said, "I already made the soup. I'll have Eliana bring it by anyway."

He put Winnie on speaker so Eliana could hear. She sat up and scooted even closer, and all his thoughts scattered.

"Uhhh ..." Winnie. Soup. "You don't have to do that."

"I want to. You're in Diamond Cove, right?"

"I am, but I'm cleaning my grandpa's bungalow today."

"Oh," Winnie said, sounding surprised. "I'll have her bring it there."

"That works. I'll keep an eye out for her." Did he sound too relieved? "Thank you."

"You're very welcome." Winnie paused. "You know, Eliana is a very nice girl."

Oh. My. Gosh, Eliana mouthed, clamping her hand down on his arm.

"She is," Asher agreed. *What?* he mouthed back.

Winnie continued, "And so pretty."

"I agree." He shrugged at Eliana, who was low-key, silently freaking out with exaggerated pained expressions.

"She's had a tough few years," Winnie said, "but she's strong. Always manages to get back on her feet. I just want her to be happy."

Eliana ran her hands down her cheeks like she was in a horror movie, and he gave her a questioning look.

"She seems really happy to me." Was he saying the right thing? Eliana nodded wildly, like he was.

"Maybe." Winnie sighed. "You're a therapist. Could you talk to her?"

"I'm a speech therapist."

"Oh, I know, hon. It would mean a lot to me."

"I'm really not that kind of thera—"

"She's so easy to talk to. I think you two would have a lot to say to each other. I'd better call her so she can get over there." Winnie hung up before he could respond.

The second his phone went dark, Eliana screamed.

He blinked and took her in. She was clearly distressed. "What is going on?" he asked.

She got up on her knees to be eye to eye with him. "My grandma. Is trying. To set us up."

"No way." There was no world in which any grandma wanted their granddaughter to be in a relationship with him. He was too scruffy and grumbly and literally homeless—though Winnie didn't know about that part.

In a falsetto voice he assumed was meant to imitate Winnie, she said, "She's so smart and pretty and you should talk to her."

"Grandparents tell me those things about their grandkids all the time," he assured her. "Every therapy session is half work, half bragging about their kids and grandkids. Trust me. It's normal."

She gave him an unconvinced look. "I know my grandma."

"So do I, and I don't think she meant it like that. Besides, even if she was trying to set us up, it's not like she can force us into a relationship."

She laughed and patted his arm as if consoling a child. Why did every casual touch shoot fireworks through his veins? "Oh, sweet, innocent Asher. You'd better sip her soup carefully, because it might be laced with a love potion."

His stomach flipped.

Eliana's phone rang, and she answered it. "What a surprise, Grandma," she said, sounding too surprised as she crossed her eyes at Asher and bumped her shoulder against his—and then left them pressed together. "I've got nothing going on this afternoon. Why?"

For the millionth time that day, his mind drifted back to when she'd walked into the kitchen that morning, still sleep-tumbled and drowsy. He'd been punched right in the lungs and couldn't get any air in. Winnie was completely justified in wanting to brag about Eliana. She had everything going for her, yet here she was, sitting on the floor at his grandpa's bungalow, spending hours going through boxes with him.

"Sure, I'll drop soup off to Asher. I'll be there in about fifteen minutes ... Yes, he *is* quite handsome." She rolled her eyes at Asher and mouthed, *See?*

His cheeks heated. He knew she was just playing along with her grandma, and he needed to get busy before she saw how she was affecting him, so he stood to break down empty boxes.

"I *have* always like men with facial hair," Eliana continued, her tone teasing. "Too bad I'm not looking for a relationship ... Oh, you're just making a statement, not trying to hint at anything. Okay, cool. Love you too." She hung up the phone and smirked. "Still think she doesn't have any ulterior motives?"

"I don't," he said, honestly.

She snickered. "You shall see."

She held her hand up and out, and he realized she was waiting for him to take it and help her up. Her soft hand slid into his, their palms gliding against one another in a way that nearly made him groan.

She, of course, was completely unaffected. "See you soon. With soup. Love potion soup," she sang as she slid her sandals on and left, taking all the sunlight with her. The bungalow seemed extra gloomier, dustier, and boxier without her presence.

Yeah, he was a sap. Maybe Winnie had already slipped him some love potion soup when they'd had their lunch together.

He picked up the secrets box and dropped it in the trash pile. This was a bomb waiting to go off, and he worried it could take all of Diamond Cove down with it.

CHAPTER 14

ELIANA

"Let us be elegant or die." —Louisa May Alcott

K ARMA. IT WAS THE only explanation.

In a fair world, Asher would be the one feeling like his stomach wouldn't be satisfied until it turned itself completely inside out, not Eliana. Since *he* was the one who faked being sick and all. She was completely innocent in all this.

Men were always dodging karmic consequences, leaving unsuspecting women to get smacked right in the face with them. She was adding a chapter about this to her book. No, a whole section.

She groaned as her stomach cramped, and she rolled over on her air mattress. It dipped dangerously closed to the ground. She'd been feeling too awful this morning to refill it, so it was half deflated. Everything was too much effort. Eating. Drinking. Showering. Watching videos. Making her bed comfortable.

If she could crawl out to the couch, then maybe she could manage to fall asleep out there. Sleep meant oblivion. That was her life goal now. Forget books and social media—those things were lost to her.

Her mom had always accused her of being a dramatic sick person. *Mom.* Eliana whimpered—what she wouldn't give to have her mom here to help her. But even in her sick state, she knew better than to give up her location and risk Asher getting found out.

The bed deflated even more, and her elbow dug into the flooring. Ugh. She'd been feeling a little under the weather over the weekend but had attributed it to stress and dust. She and Asher had managed to go through several more boxes but hadn't found anything quite as exciting as the box of secrets. Mostly more junk-drawer-adjacent belongings with the occasional keepsake for Asher. But this morning, she'd awoken with her entire body aching and her stomach twisting.

This did not feel like stress and dust ... this felt like a stomach bug. She reached for her phone and saw that it was almost five in the afternoon. She'd spent all day in bed.

Grandma had given her a quilt for her "new apartment," and Eliana wrapped it burrito-style around her body as she stumbled down the hallway.

Nope. Not going to make it.

She pivoted into the bathroom, and her stomach expelled everything she'd eaten since coming to Diamond Cove. Forget the couch. She was going to lie right here on this bathroom mat.

A tap sounded on the open bathroom door, and she tilted her head up to see Asher standing there. Yep, that tracked. Looking terrible? Of course Asher would be there to see it.

He crouched down beside her, and his cool hand pressed to her forehead. "You're on fire."

"You know it," she joked weakly, her voice raspy. "Did you hear me throw up?"

His eyes slid to the side. "Let me get you some water," he said, which was answer enough. He slipped out of the bathroom.

Get up, Eliana. Don't lie here on the bathroom floor, looking pathetic.

Oh no. Had she flushed the toilet after she'd thrown up? She pulled herself up onto her elbow with effort and flushed the toilet just in case.

Then she curled up on the bathroom mat. Whatever. So what if she was pathetic? Asher was destined to see her at her worst. At least Louisa loved her no matter what.

Asher returned with a cold water bottle and a straw. "Can you sit up?"

The bathroom felt impossibly small with him in it. She forced herself to sit, though her stomach pitched and rolled like a ship on a stormy sea, and she sipped from the straw.

"Want help back to bed?" he asked.

"I'm going to lie here for a bit." She threw her hand over her mouth, and like the wise man he was, he left the bathroom.

"Your bed is completely flat," he called from down the hall.

"It's only half flat," she replied. "I've got to pump it up. No biggie." She sipped more water and mentally geared herself up to move. The couch was out of the question now that Asher was home.

She very slowly got to her feet, holding on to the wall the entire time. Her stomach cramped, but she persevered, especially when she thought of Asher finding her still on the bathroom floor. Nothing like a little potential embarrassment to get you moving. Though he'd pretty much already seen her—and heard her—at her worst.

She looked in the mirror, and part of her died inside. Her face was pale except for two bright red spots on her cheeks, her lips were chapped, and her hair sprouted from her braid like wild potato eyes.

She snagged the water bottle and shuffled toward her bedroom, but when she got there, her bed was gone. She blinked. Yep, still gone. "Where'd it go, Louisa?"

Louisa very unhelpfully went back into her shell, so Eliana unceremoniously dropped to the floor. She should have brought the padded bath mat with her.

"Oh, I was going to help you." Asher appeared in the doorway. He held out his hand, but she waved him away.

"I'm fine. You can go."

He bit back a smile. "Go where? This is my home."

"I don't know," she said, irritated. "Swimming or something."

"I'm not going anywhere."

"I look horrible." She pulled her quilt up around her head like a hood so she wouldn't have to see his handsome face. "Just go away."

"You look sick, but even sick, you're pretty. And it's not like I'm winning any awards in the looks department."

"Lies," she whispered. Did he really think he wasn't handsome? No, he was just trying to make her feel better.

A chill racked her body, and the glint of humor in his eyes disappeared. "Up and at 'em, Elly," he said softly, wrapping his arm around her and hefting her up to her feet. He smelled good. Like salty ocean and fresh air. He held her tight against his muscular side as he led her down the hall.

"Um, where are we going?"

"My room."

Even sick, even *deliriously* happily single—heavy on the delirious, apparently—her stomach swooped. "Oh." She swallowed. "Why?"

He led her to the king-sized bed and helped her sit on the edge of it. "Because you're sick and your air mattress is garbage. You can sleep in here until you feel better."

"You don't have to do that," she said, but she was already sinking back into the soft-as-a-cloud mattress. It had been weeks since she'd slept on a real mattress, and she'd forgotten how heavenly it could be. He'd even moved her pillow onto his bed.

Her stomach swooped again. *Stop that,* she ordered it. Her stomach had enough problems today.

"I want to," he said. "I didn't realize your bed was so bad."

"It's not that bad." But enveloped in this bed? Yeah, the air mattress suddenly seemed much worse than she'd realized. "I don't want to get my germs all over everything."

"I'm not worried about it." He leaned across her to grab her pillow and tuck it under her head. She breathed him in again, even as it became harder with him so close.

His concentration seemed to be fully on making sure she was comfortable, and his pulse definitely didn't seem like it was racing unnaturally fast. He tucked her quilt around her and made sure the water bottle was within reach.

"Try to drink," he said, with a frown. He sat on the edge of the bed near her legs. "You don't want to get even more dehydrated."

"Thank you for letting me take your bed." She sipped some water.

"Who says you're taking my bed?" His gaze flicked to the extra space on the other side of the mattress. "There's room for both of us."

She choked on the water in her mouth. If her pulse had been racing before, it was winning world records now.

Asher laughed, and it wasn't just his eyes that lit up but his entire face. "Are you okay?"

Wait. He was teasing her. She didn't realize he had it in him. She liked this side of him. A lot.

She finally caught her breath. "I'll try not to breathe in your face," she croaked.

"Such a gem." He stood. "My bathroom is through that door, and there's a huge tub in there you can use if you want. I plugged your phone in next to the water bottle and put my phone number on a sticky note on the screen, so text me if you need anything."

He'd thought of everything. "Okay. Are you sure, Asher?" When she'd blackmailed him, she'd never intended that he'd have to take care of her.

"Don't worry about me. I've slept on a lot worse than a couch."

He left the bedroom, and she thought she'd fall asleep right away. But it took much longer than she wanted to acknowledge for her heart to stop racing. With Asher's inviting scent in every corner of this bed, and the imprint of his smile behind her eyelids, it felt like he was still in here with her, holding her close.

And it wasn't a bad feeling at all.

CHAPTER 15

ASHER

"**A**LRIGHT, I HAVE THE delivery scheduled for tomorrow after-noon. Can I get your payment information?" the voice on the other end of the line asked Asher.

"Sure." He rattled off his credit card number to the florist, and then he hung up and leaned back in his office chair at The Palms' clinic with a yawn. His grandpa's couch was not made for a man over six feet tall to recline comfortably on.

But he felt less comfortable with the idea of Eliana sleeping on it—or worse, on that air mattress that was little more than a floor covering. Especially when she looked so miserable. She'd been sick for two straight days, but he'd heard her up and moving around in his bedroom this morning, so hopefully that meant she'd turned a corner.

In that time, he'd managed to finish clearing out the dining room and the hallway. It hadn't been as difficult as he'd thought it would be to give away his grandpa's belongings. In fact, in some surprising ways, it felt good to know someone else might get some use out of his things.

The trash was taken care of, too, including the bin of people's private information. Why had his grandpa had that? He would never know, and Asher was more than happy to put it in the garbage and never think about it again.

He checked his watch and headed out of his office for his next appoint-ment. He had a full afternoon, which he liked. Keeping busy gave his mind less time to wander to thoughts of a certain pretty blond.

"How are you this afternoon, Mary?" Asher said to the octogenarian waiting to see him in one of the kitchenette rooms in the clinic. Her husband, Claude, sat beside her. He'd cared for Mary since her stroke, and the man loved to talk.

"We're quite well," Claude responded. "Have you heard the news?"

"I don't know. What's going on?" He turned to the kitchenette to prepare a few different types of food to try. Mary had suffered a stroke two months previous, and they'd been working on her swallowing. She and Claude lived in the bungalows, but he knew they were on a waiting list to get into the assisted-living portion of The Palms, where Asher would come straight to their apartment to do these therapies.

Claude lowered his voice, even though the door was closed. "Lorin Smith isn't sixty-five, like he's been claiming. He's *seventy*-five."

"Hmmm," Asher said, noncommittally. He opened a carton of vanilla yogurt and applesauce.

"He's shaved ten years off his age." Claude shook his head. "I've known the man for five years, and he never gave any hint that we were the same age."

"People lie about their age all the time," Mary said. Her words ran together, but she was speaking so much clearer than she had when they'd first started meeting.

"Maybe so. But *ten years*." Claude paused. "That means he married someone twenty years younger than him."

"Unless she lied too," Mary pointed out.

"True." Claude retrieved a clean handkerchief from his pocket and placed it on Mary's lap to protect her pants from any falling food. Asher saw small moments like this every day that made him long for a relationship like theirs, while also realizing the risk they took in loving each other so deeply and carefully. No one lived forever.

All afternoon, people buzzed about poor Lorin Smith and his newly revealed age. It turned out that his wife *hadn't* lied about her age, and he had in fact married someone twenty years younger than him.

"Perhaps that's why he lied," Fran Miller said to him as he stood beside her husband's bed in the memory care center, conducting a swallow study. "He was embarrassed to admit he'd married someone so young."

Asher wanted to tip his head back and let out the exasperated sigh he'd been holding in all afternoon. He couldn't care less how old someone was, or claimed to be, or what reasons they had for lying. He knew for a fact that several of his patients lied about their ages. He could name at least three people—from seeing their birth dates in their chart—who claimed they were younger. They didn't generally subtract an entire decade, but again, what did it matter?

"Did you see Sweetie's outfit today?" he asked to change the subject. His phone buzzed in his pocket three times in a row, but he didn't check it when he was with patients.

It worked. "Oh, yes. Ariel. It was quite creative."

He finished his appointments and went back to the clinic to do his charting. Usually, he liked to stay here as long as possible and take his time, but today, he was impatient to get back to the bungalow and check on Eliana.

He paused. She'd be mortified to learn he was this eager to see her. She was Eliana Peters—a gorgeous, witty influencer, who'd made a vow of singleness, by the way. And he was Asher Brooks—a long-haired, unconnected speech therapist without a home.

Yep, he was a *real* catch.

He shook his head. He wasn't trying to be caught. He was merely worried about her after how sick she'd been. Like any decent human being would be. At least he had that going for him.

He shut down his computer and headed for the parking lot. Bear left his vigil by the fountain and bounded over, eternally hopeful to get a belly rub from Asher. But Asher had his walls firmly up. You open the door a crack, and all the animals came pouring in. He dodged Bear and Sweetie, who were immediately enveloped in love by someone's visiting great-grandchildren, and he was quickly forgotten by the dog and alligator duo.

"Asher! Wait!" Winnie waved at him from the office hallway before speed-walking in his direction.

"No rush!" He took long strides to meet her halfway. The last thing he needed was Eliana's grandma taking a fall while trying to wave him down.

When he approached her, Winnie was out of breath and had a sheen of sweat on her face. He frowned. He'd seen her medical chart, along with her blood pressure, and knew she needed to be careful.

"I just spoke with Eliana, and she's sick." Worry creased her brow.

"Oh no." Asher had never been a good actor, so he tried to keep his wooden reaction to a minimum as he directed her to a chair.

Winnie sat with a grateful smile. "I know you're a busy man, but could you be a dear and bring her some bread I made? She always loves to nibble on bread when she's not feeling well, and I'm technically not supposed to drive. Horace, of course, is nowhere to be found." She said his name with an unexpectedly sour twist.

He sat beside her. "Are you okay, Winnie?"

"I'm going a little stir-crazy being stuck here so often," she admitted.

"I'd offer to drive you around, but all I have is my motorcycle."

"That sounds exciting," she said, looking a lot like Eliana when she got an idea. Her eyes lit up, and he regretted his words. He imagined hitting a bump in the road too hard and accidentally flinging Eliana's grandma off the back of his motorcycle. Yeah, a ride was not happening.

"So, what were you saying about bread?" he prompted.

"Oh, yes. Can you take some to Eliana? I'm just waiting for her to message me her address."

"Sure." He had no idea how Eliana was going to get out of this one, and he felt almost bad for her. Winnie was a force, especially when it came to taking care of her loved ones. "Just message me," he said.

She pulled him into a tight side hug. "Thank you, Asher. Oh, there's Nancy. I've been trying to get a hold of her for the turtle fundraiser. Don't go anywhere," she ordered as she bustled after Nancy.

He pulled out his phone to check the time, and he saw he had three messages from a number he didn't recognize. He'd completely forgotten about the texts from earlier.

Eliana: MAYDAY. MAYDAY.

Eliana: My grandma is trying to set us up again.

Eliana: With BREAD this time. DO NOT AGREE TO BRING IT TO ME.

Uh-oh. Well, that ship had sailed.
He saved Eliana's number into his phone and sent her a text back.

Asher: Too late. She caught me before I saw your texts.

Eliana: AAAAAAASHER.

He smiled. He could hear the groan in her voice as if she were right there, saying it to him.

Eliana: What have you done? We'll be married before Julia and Logan at this rate.

He snorted out a laugh that made both Nancy and Winnie stop their conversation to look at him with questioning glances. He felt his cheeks turn pink but went back to his phone.

Asher: Would that be so bad? We already live together.

He wasn't used to banter like this—and a tiny part of him worried she might think he was low-key proposing—but something about Eliana brought this side out of him. He liked making her laugh. Liked surprising her.
Relief rolled through him when her next text came in.

Eliana: I plan on becoming a crazy turtle lady in my old age, FYI. So you marry me, and you marry the whole bale.

Asher: Bale?

Eliana: That's what a group of turtles is called.

Asher: Ah. All named after single women?

"What are you smiling about?"

He nearly dropped his phone as Winnie popped up on one side of him and Nancy on the other. He hurriedly made his screen go black just as it buzzed through with another message.

Eliana: You know me so well.

Nancy took one of his arms while Winnie took the other, and they led him in the direction of the dining room. He resisted the urge to stare longingly toward the parking lot. He'd been so close.

"We have a question for you," Nancy said. "What are you doing on Saturday?"

This felt like a trick question. "Cleaning out my grandpa's bungalow."

"That can wait," Winnie said.

"Mr. Richardson would disagree."

"Winnie and I will take care of him," Nancy said. "We need your help."

Despite himself, his curiosity piqued. And he didn't hate the idea of Winnie and Nancy taking care of Mr. Richardson, whatever that might look like. If anyone could distract the man from his mission to clean out the bungalow, it would be those two. "What's going on?"

"You're coming to the fundraiser on Saturday, right?"

He hadn't planned on it, but with the way the two hopeful, upturned faces looking at him, he couldn't say no. "Sure. I don't know the details, though."

"There have been fliers all over," Nancy admonished him. "But never mind that. It's a fundraiser to save the sea turtles. We'll be playing games, and it should be a lot of fun."

"What do you need help with?"

"We need someone strong to help us set up the games."

"I can do that." The tension eased out of him. He didn't know what he'd expected them to say, but with Nancy, you never knew. She had a lot more confidence in people's abilities than warranted.

"Of course you can," Winnie said. "Meet us on The Palms' beach at seven on Saturday morning." Winnie's phone jingled, and she swiped the screen open. "It's Eliana." She frowned. "She says she feels all the way better and is on her way to my house to get the bread herself." She huffed, her expression an exact replica of Eliana's when she was annoyed. He bit back a smile. "I'd better grab my dinner to go and get home before she arrives. See you Saturday, Asher."

"And wear your swim trunks," Nancy added, as she followed Winnie toward the dining hall. "You're going to get wet."

CHAPTER 16

WINNIE

"**L**OOK AT THIS." WINNIE held her phone out to Horace, who sat beside her on the couch, flipping through one of his golf magazines. The man didn't get enough of actually golfing? He had to read about it too?

More than once, recently, she'd debated hiding his golf clubs, or getting rid of them altogether. But were the golf clubs the problem, or was it—

"Smitty has Instagram." He took her phone and scrolled through the Secret Seven account she'd made. Most of the Secret Seven had posted a picture of them with their spouse and had shared the story of how they met. "He says it's a good way to keep up with the grandkids."

She gritted her teeth and prayed for patience. "I've also been saying that for years. It's a good way to stay up to date on Eliana, especially."

"Smitty showed me a bunch of golf accounts with different golfing hacks, they're called," he said as if she hadn't said anything at all. "A hack is where—"

"I know what a hack is." Eliana had those on her Instagram as well. She called them life hacks, and they usually involved doing something that was just common sense, but for some reason young people overcomplicated tasks and needed to be told a simpler way of doing it.

She let out a short breath. Okay, that wasn't fair. The hack about using dental floss to cut cinnamon rolls was quite useful. She was letting her jealousy of Smitty get to her and make her bitter about anything he touched.

But really, could Horace not go one evening without talking about the man? Sometimes she missed the good old days when they were enemies.

"Hey, it's us," he said, flipping the phone back around so she could see the picture of them from their wedding day. She'd worn a lacy veil that trailed all the way to the ground behind her. Her mother had thought it was very impractical, but Winnie hadn't cared. She'd felt beautiful in it. "You're still just as gorgeous. And I love you even more," he said, and her heart softened to absolute mush. Horace had never been a charmer, which meant that every word he said was absolute truth. His genuineness was one of the things she loved most about him.

He angled the phone back toward him and read aloud what she'd written. "'I was working in a soda shop when a group of rowdy summer boys came in for a drink. They were loud and raucous and ordered me about as if I were their servant girl. All except for one. He politely asked for a cherry cola, and when I gave it to him, he grinned. I was a goner. He came back every day that week—and spent a good chunk of his savings on soda.'" Horace cut in then with his own commentary. "And I don't even like colas."

She laughed like she always did at the thought of young Horace coming in every day to flirt with her. "Then why didn't you order something different?" she asked, even though she knew the answer. She loved this story.

"I couldn't think whenever you got close, so I ordered the first word I saw behind you: Coke." They shared a secret smile, and then he continued to read. "'He eventually got up the courage to ask me to the new picture in town, *Spartacus*.'" He glanced up with a puzzled expression. "We saw *Swiss Family Robinson*."

She shook her head. "I distinctly remember the sign over the marquee. It was all lit up for the first time in months."

"I remember the marquee. But I saw that picture with Joelle." His baby sister. "And I don't remember any lights."

Irritation poked at her. How could he forget? The memory was so clear to her. The chill in the winter night air, how she'd pulled her jacket closer around her shoulders. No, wait. It had been summer.

"I'm sure you're right." He handed her phone back to her. "The best decision I ever made was following those guys into the soda shop."

She blinked and the memory dissolved. She exited the app, unsettled for reasons she didn't want to think about. "I'm putting this together for Eliana. I'm hoping our stories will convince her to believe in love again."

His eyes lit up. "Oh, maybe Smitty and I can help. We did a good job with Julia and Logan."

She gaped. "You two nearly ruined everything." Were he and Smitty rewriting history now?

"But then we fixed it. Who are you trying to set Eliana up with?"

She didn't want to tell him and risk him "helping" the same way he had last time. "Well," she hedged, "the first step is to help her out of this 'happily single' mindset."

He rubbed his hands together like an evil genius. "So we're making her miserable."

"No, of course not."

He dropped his hands. "Yeah, as the words came out of my mouth, they felt wrong."

"We're trying to show her how a beautiful partnership can enhance your life, if you're with the right person."

"Like salt," Horace said. "Just the right amount can bring out the best flavors of any dish."

"That's really insightful, Horace."

"It's something Smitty said once."

Of course it was. She glanced at her watch. They'd gone almost a full minute without talking about Smitty, so it was long past overdue to bring him up again.

Horace continued, "He was talking about my golf swing technique, but I think the salt analogy applies here." His phone rang, and he pulled it out of his front shirt pocket. "Oh, speaking of—Smitty!" He stood and headed to the office to talk.

She banged the back of her head against the couch a few times. Perhaps Smitty and Horace should share the story of when *they'd* first met. Or Horace and his golf clubs—the real love story. She took a screenshot of her Instagram page, just how Samantha had showed her, and texted it to Eliana.

Horace's laugh drifted down the hallway, leaving her feeling on the outside looking in. She had a meeting with the Secret Seven anyway. The turtle fundraiser games were on Saturday, and they still had a lot to plan.

When she arrived at the clubhouse, everyone was abuzz about hair colors.

"Have you heard?" Polly took her by the arm and whispered as they walked down the hall to the conference room.

"No." She really hoped that Don had baked something delicious for them to eat, because she was hungry.

"Margie is not a natural redhead."

Seeing as how Margie was in her eighties, that was not difficult to believe. "I've seen her get her hair dyed at the salon."

"I know." Polly's voice dropped even lower. "But before she went white, her natural hair color was light brown."

She stared at Winnie, waiting for it to settle in. Margie loved to talk about how she had bright red hair growing up, and she couldn't bear to part with it. Many of her stories involved how long and luxurious it had been, and how it had been the first feature her late husband had fallen in love with.

Winnie scrunched her nose. "Why would anyone start a rumor like that? She had red hair."

"No. She didn't." Polly showed Winnie a picture of a young mother with light-brown hair on her phone. She looked a lot like Margie, but it didn't necessarily mean it was her. But Polly swiped her screen to another picture, this one clearly Margie with light-brown hair.

"Maybe she dyed it light brown when she was younger," Winnie said. But Margie claimed that dye had never touched her hair until she went completely white. "Where did you get these pictures?"

"Someone pinned them to the socials bulletin board." The socials bulletin board was where all the activities for the week were posted.

"Who would do that?"

"No one knows. Samantha took them down, but I got a picture first."

"Why would someone target her?" Winnie asked.

"It's not just her." She swiped again to reveal a picture of a printed list of at least ten names, along with natural hair colors beside it. "My name is on there," Polly said. "But I don't care if everyone knows I dye my hair black."

Winnie studied the list, not surprised by any of the names. At least half the women at The Palms dyed their hair. Some liked to pretend it was their natural color, but it was like one of those well-known secrets. Of course, their hair wasn't naturally platinum blond, but what was the harm in pretending?

"Weird," Winnie said.

"Right?" Polly chuckled. "It makes you wonder what other secrets people are keeping."

"Are you talking about the list?" Rosa sidled up to them. "I just heard about it. And this after the whole age thing."

"What age thing?"

Both women looked at Winnie incredulously. "Lorin lying about his age? Being twenty years older than his wife?" Polly said.

"News to me." Wedding sewing and matchmaking had kept her extremely busy these days.

"It makes me wonder who's spilling all the coffee," Rosa said.

"It's tea," Polly corrected.

"But I don't like tea," Rosa argued.

"Yes, but the phrase the kids say is spilling the *tea*."

Rosa let out an irritated huff. "Whatever people are spilling, I wonder if there's more."

"And who's next." Polly squeezed her arm before they went into the conference room, Winnie frozen in place.

CHAPTER 17
ELIANA

"Nothing is impossible to a determined woman." —Louisa May Alcott

THE SUN WAS OUT in full force the morning of the Save the Turtles Fundraiser Game Day. Eliana had stopped by Julia's house to eat a really early breakfast with her family, and then they'd all driven over to The Palms to save the turtles together. Even Logan was there, holding hands with Julia in the very back seat of the SUV.

Eliana scrolled through her social media feed, stopping on Grandma Winnie's adorable story of her and Grandpa Horace. She shared it to her feed along with about a hundred hearts. She wished she could have found a love like theirs first, instead of marrying Corbin. Maybe then she wouldn't be so committed to staying single.

Her grandparents and parents had always been great examples of what it could be like to have a real partner in a relationship. It was probably the only reason she'd eventually seen how unhealthy her marriage to Corbin had been. She rubbed at her chest, wishing it still didn't hurt—all the things he'd said to her, how awful he'd made her feel. How much time needed to pass before those memories were obliterated?

She didn't want heavy feelings today—not on this momentous day of saving the turtles!—so she pivoted to a tried-and-true method of getting out of her own head. Teasing. She turned to Logan and Julia with a finger raised in schoolteacher fashion as they pulled into the parking lot of The Palms. "You'd better not be kissing back there."

Her dad found a parking spot up front on his first circle of the lot—without having to take a reserved space. Of all the luck.

"We've been kissing the whole time," Julia said, making loud smacking noises with her lips. "You're such a good kisser, Logan."

"If I was actually kissing you, you wouldn't be able to breathe, much less speak," he said with in a low tone. Julia giggled and whispered something too quiet for Eliana to hear, but it made Logan growl. And then they were actually kissing. She flopped around in her seat. Great. That plan backfired.

The tiniest bit of jealousy pinged in Eliana. A part of her wanted someone to say something like that to her. And mean it. Not that she was getting soft on relationships. But it wore on her to be constantly around a couple in love.

"I'm kissing too," she said to ease the weight on her chest. She made kissy faces at Cameron. He laughed, gave Eliana a kiss on her cheek, and then rested his head on her shoulder for a long hug. Okay, maybe teasing wasn't the right distraction today. Maybe it was soaking in all the Cameron hugs she could get.

"Us too," Mom said. Dad finished making sure he'd parked perfectly, and he and Mom gave each other a pretty hot and heavy kiss.

"Ew! Stop!" Julia and Eliana yelled. Eliana threw an old gum wrapper at them while Cameron laughed at all the commotion.

Their dad winked at them. "Should we go save the turtles?"

"Yes!" they all yelled, and they headed toward the beach, where they could hear loud rap music playing—one punctuated with a ton of curse words.

"This music choice is unexpected," Logan said.

"Is it, though?" Julia shared a knowing smirk with him, and Eliana felt that twist in her stomach again. They clearly had an inside joke here. She had plenty of inside jokes with plenty of people—in fact, Cameron's burp was now an inside joke for everyone who had seen the livestream with it—but there was something intimate about the inside joke for two.

"Good morning!" Polly, wearing a zebra-print sun shirt and a wide-brimmed hat, motioned for them to join her at the end of the table. "It's a flat rate to come and play—and all the proceeds go to the turtles. We have beach volleyball, flag football, three-legged races, an obstacle course, cornhole, chicken fights—which is not actual chicken fighting, I've been informed—and a lightning round of games that take around a minute a piece. Sign up for the ones you're interested in doing."

Eliana jumped from foot to foot with excitement. Here was the thing about her: she loved games. And she not only loved games—she loved winning. When she was in high school, she'd played every sport she could, and she was always happiest when she was spiking a ball over the net or running down the court or leaping over hurdles. But there weren't many opportunities for adults who weren't pro-level accomplished to play sports, so she'd started playing the kinds of games that didn't take much skill—those icebreaker, put-your-chairs-in-a-circle games that people always groaned about, but then ended up participating in and laughing through and finding people to connect with.

When she'd decided to start her social media pages and videos, that was how it'd begun: Let's Play a Game. To her surprise, people loved it. Over time, and as she'd gotten to know so many people, she'd realized how many of their problems stemmed from romantic relationships. Believing you loved someone was complicated and messy, and almost no one seemed happy.

When she'd played two truths and a lie, and one of her truths was that she was happily single, almost everyone called that out as a lie. (The lie was, in fact, that she'd always dreamed of owning a dog. Pshaw. #Turtles4Life.)

From there, she'd started a new channel, this one called Happily Single, and that's when her popularity really soared. She was able to quit her office job and devote all of her time to creating online content.

Sometimes she missed the simple days of coming up with fun games for her followers to play with her, but she loved reaching more people with a message she really believed in.

Sure, she occasionally—daily—got angry messages calling her all sorts of names for daring to suggest she was happy *and* single. So many people treated the words like oxymorons—like silent scream or deafening silence. Happily single.

Why it was so threatening to them, she'd never understand. Wasn't it a good thing for people to be happy in whatever state they were in? Wasn't it even better for people to take the necessary actions in their life to make themselves happy if they weren't already?

If being in a relationship brought you joy, great. It sure hadn't for her, and based on all those get-to-know-you comments, she wasn't alone.

"You're signing up for all of them?" Julia asked. "That's going to be all day, and we only want to stay until lunch."

"I'll get a ride home." Her plan was to close the place out and walk back to Asher's bungalow tired enough to drop straight into bed. His bed. Because he still refused to let her go back to her old room. Which meant she was sleeping surrounded by his scent and with the knowledge that he'd also been in that bed … and she needed to be completely exhausted in order to actually fall asleep.

Grandma Winnie bustled over, Asher's arm firmly in her grip. He gave Eliana one of his sideways grins that made her heart skip.

Grandma dropped Asher's arm to hug everyone. "I didn't expect to see you here," she said to Logan and Julia. "Don't you have full schedules with the wedding?"

They exchanged an exhausted look. "We need a break from all the planning," Logan said. "I had no idea so much went into a wedding."

Julia deflated a little. "We're supposed to pick out the food for catering …"

Eliana tuned them out, even though she knew she should listen and offer input for their perfect wedding. Instead, she sidled up beside Asher. He wore sky-blue swim trunks with a white swim shirt that contrasted deeply with his tan skin. "What did you sign up for?" she asked.

"Nothing. Winnie asked me to ref."

"Oooh, a man with power. Did she give you a whistle?"

Making him chuckle was as heady as winning a game. "A whistle *and* a flag," he said.

She fanned herself. "Be still, my heart." Cameron wandered close to them, so she linked her arm through his and pulled him close. "Me and Cam are going to win all the games, aren't we?"

"Yeah!" Cam yelled out with all the enthusiasm Eliana could dream of in a partner. Asher grinned. It was rare to see him so unguarded and happy.

"Asher! I've been looking for you all week!" Lydia, Smitty's wife, unsteadily walked toward them through the sand.

Asher lunged forward to take her arm before she stumbled or fell. "Where's your walker?" he asked, his voice low enough so only Eliana and Cameron could hear him.

She waved toward the sidewalk where it stood in the sun. "Over there. You sound just like Logan. I'm fine for a few feet."

Asher's smile was gone, a concerned frown replacing it. But she liked this expression too. It wasn't the grumpy frown he had when he'd towed her car or when she'd blackmailed him or when he'd learned she was sleeping on a crummy air mattress or ... Man, she saw that grumpy frown a lot. But this frown meant his brain was whirring, solving a problem, trying to figure out how to help someone. And this time, it meant steering Lydia in the direction of her walker. Grandma Winnie said the walker was a new addition for the proud Italian woman, and she was not adjusting well to it.

"I wanted to thank you for the flowers on my birthday," Lydia said.

The tips of his cheeks turned even pinker. "Oh, it was nothing—"

"Not to me," she interrupted to say. Her bottom lip trembled like she might cry, but she straightened her back and the action seemed to tuck the emotion away. "With the wedding stress and Smitty being so busy lately ... you were the only person who remembered."

Eliana's heart sank. She knew Grandma was Lydia's friend, but she'd been swamped with wedding too.

"You share a birthday with my grandma," he replied.

She placed her hand on his cheek. "I didn't know your grandma, but she must have been a lovely person to have a grandson such as you."

"Let's get you back to your walker," he said.

"Must we?" she said, but she allowed him to lead her slowly back toward it.

A month ago, this conversation might have shocked Eliana, but not anymore. In the time she'd known Asher, she'd learned he cared deeply and showed that care in quiet but meaningful ways. Her heart squeezed as she watched him help Lydia get settled with her walker and remained to chat with her.

Logan hustled over as well to give his grandma a hug. He threw a grateful look at Asher over Lydia's shoulder as he led her deeper into the shade, to a set of empty chairs near Julia and Cameron.

A shrill whistle broke her out of her reverie, and she turned to find Don standing on a platform, lowering his fingers from his mouth. "Volleyball starts in five minutes," he barked. "Head to the net if you signed up to play."

Eliana made her way over, the image of Asher picking out flowers for Lydia on her mind. She did a few stretches and met her team, which was mostly made up of grandkids from other Palms residents, but Don and Walt jumped in to play as well.

"Did you see a new sign was posted?" Polly whispered to Rosa from the sidelines. Eliana's ears perked up, and she listened.

"No. What did this one say?" Rosa paused. "Do I even want to know?"

Polly lowered her voice even further, and Eliana had to strain to hear. "Harry had a country album."

Rosa's head whipped in her direction, shock written on her face.

"I'm not kidding. There's a picture and everything."

The ground felt unsteady beneath Eliana's feet. She'd read about that in Asher's grandpa's secret files, but Asher had thrown them away while she was sick.

The women's whispers got low enough that unless she made herself more obvious, she couldn't hear them. She pulled sunscreen out of her bag and slathered it over her face and arms. What if ...? No. It had to be a coincidence.

Polly split all the players into two teams. "Paxton, Sean, Aaron, Avery, Essie, and Eliana, you're all on Team A. Don, Cameron, Walt, Kate, Ty, Cocoa, and Chad, you're on Team B. All seven can be on the sand at the same time. We'll play until fifteen points, best of three." She looked hard at them. "Play nice."

Sean, who Grandma whispered was a Navy SEAL, folded his muscular arms. "Why did you look at me when you said that? Gramps is the one you have to watch out for."

"Me?" Don linked arms with Cameron. "I've got my buddy Cam to keep me in line." But the gleam in his eye said he loved a good challenge. Cam grinned up at Don adoringly.

"No one can keep Don in line," Avery said under her breath. "I'm Walt's granddaughter," she told Eliana. "You must be Winnie's."

"I am." Eliana rubbed her hands together, already excited as she took in her team. They could definitely sweep this match.

Asher tossed a volleyball in and stepped to the side to ref. "Team A, you get first serve."

The sun beat down on them, and Eliana quickly had a layer of sweat over her sunscreen as she pulled her hand back to serve the ball over the net. It flew right past Walt, and Don dove to hit it but missed. She didn't hold back her satisfied smile as her team all came close to give her high fives.

"Game on!" Sean whooped.

It didn't take long to get into the zone of playing and forget everything but the game. Bump, set, spike. Her team got into a good rhythm, and she loved to be right by the net, spiking the ball into the sand on the other side. She also loved the friendly banter between everyone. Paxton loved teasing his grandma Polly, their self-appointed coach, by pretending he didn't know where to stand. Sean put equal energy into flirting with the grandmas as he did playing—and still managed to make almost half their teams points.

Don helped Cam serve the ball, and everyone cheered for him. Eliana lunged to the ground to hit it, sliding into the sand, but missed it. Cam cheered loudest of all as she rolled onto her back. Sean held out a hand to help her stand.

"Thanks," she said, brushing sand from her clothes.

"Your brother has a mean serve," Sean said, his grin spreading across his face.

"He'll tell you he's a man of mystery." She walked back to her position, catching glances with Asher, who was watching her closely. Her stomach swooped as their gazes met, but she hurriedly looked away. *Keep your head in the game.*

Aaron and Cocoa were maybe the cutest couple she'd ever met—and that wasn't something she noticed as a rule. They were the kindest players of the whole bunch, both of them encouraging their teams and each other. She hadn't had this much fun playing a game in ... she couldn't even remember. Everyone at The Palms was so friendly, and they included her as if they'd known her forever.

Halfway through the first set, Mom collected Cameron to make him drink water and sit in the shade, but he cheered the loudest of all for everyone who got a point, everyone who fell, and everyone who looked his way. Eliana found herself looking his way often, feeling the uncontainable grin on her face.

Her team won their two sets—more than won, they crushed the other team. She high-fived her teammates and went to grab her day pack. Asher approached her with an amused raise to his brow.

"What?" she asked. She pulled her tank top away from her stomach to fan some air in next to her skin.

"I didn't realize I was rooming with someone who is so competitive." He leaned close enough for his words to blow against her ear. Despite the heat, shivers rolled down her arms.

"I just gave it my all."

"I especially liked when you trash-talked Don, and when you spiked the ball so hard on him he tripped over himself trying to get it."

She rolled her eyes playfully. "Don can take it. After I called him 'old man,' he upped his game and it finally got good out there."

He barked out a laugh.

Don came over to give her a high five, out of breath. He used the towel around his neck to swipe at his sweat. "Good game," he said. "I want you on my team next time."

"Same," she said. "Your serve was the best one out there by far."

Don smirked. "Are you doing the obstacle course?"

"Sure am. See you there?"

"Wouldn't miss it. Bring your A-game," he ordered.

"You too." She shook her head as she turned back to Asher, who had watched the exchange with folded arms. "What?" she asked, self-conscious. "He knows I'm teasing. He likes it."

"I know." Asher headed toward the pool, Eliana beside him. "A lot of people here treat the residents like they're children. They talk to them in a different tone of voice and can be really condescending."

"I've seen it," Eliana said. For the most part, all the workers at The Palms were respectful and lovely, but several spoke to her grandma like she was a three-year-old, and honestly, it was insulting.

"I like that you don't. If you could refrain from hurting the octogenarians, though, I'd appreciate it."

She cut her gaze to him and bumped her bare shoulder into his sun-warmed arm with a laugh.

CHAPTER 18

ASHER

A SHER APPROACHED ELIANA'S FAMILY'S table with a pitcher of ice-cold lemonade that Winnie pushed into his hands to deliver.

"Thank you!" everyone called out as they refilled their empty glasses.

Eliana scooted over on the bench and patted the seat beside her. "Come sit before Grandma sees that you're free. She's had you working nonstop all morning." After refereeing the volleyball game, he'd also reffed the basketball game and had been tapped in to participate in the three-legged race. He would love nothing more than to jump into the pool, but the idea of playing chicken with one of the residents wasn't appealing, so he'd volunteered to ref again.

"Thanks."

Julia grabbed an empty glass and filled it with lemonade for him, and he gratefully took it.

Eliana slid half of her sandwich toward him, along with her uneaten chips. "Do you like turkey?" she asked.

"Yes, but I can get my own."

"No. You can't. She'll see you, and next thing you know, you'll be setting up the obstacle course for this afternoon."

He nodded in acknowledgment as his stomach growled. He was pretty hungry. He took a bite of her sandwich. Eating from someone else's plate was an almost intimate activity.

The Peters family members were all givers. They gave without thought, and even more, they often seemed to notice when someone needed something before it was even asked. They were also a touchy bunch—always hugging and linking arms and sitting right beside one another. For them, it was like second nature, but he—who could go weeks without touching someone—always noticed it.

For a moment, he allowed himself to imagine what life might be like if he had a family like theirs. But that thought path was too raw to travel, so he took another huge bite of the sandwich. Bruno had *not* made this—it tasted like a grocery store special.

Cameron rested his head on the table with a groan. Though the sun was covered by a huge, striped umbrella above them, the heat of the day had firmly set in.

"What's wrong?" Eliana scratched his back and shared a concerned look with Asher. The morning had sped by with a game of basketball in the pool—which Eliana had dominated, of course—and a three-legged race that had left Cameron red-faced and panting.

Eliana's mom placed her hand on Cameron's forehead. "He's burning up. Are you feeling sick, Cam?"

Cameron groaned in response. He'd been losing energy all morning, but Asher had assumed it was the sun and exertion getting to him. Now Asher wished he'd kept a better eye on him.

Eliana rested her head on Cameron's shoulder. "I was sick with a bug last week that was pretty bad. I hope he didn't catch it." Eliana worried her lip between her teeth.

Asher caught himself just before he confirmed how bad it had been. Her family would wonder how he knew that. As it was, he kept getting glances from her family, and he knew they were burning with questions.

"I hope so too." Eliana's mom frowned and turned to her husband. "I think we need to call it a day. He needs to shower and rest."

"Sounds good to me." Her dad stood, followed quickly by Julia and Logan.

"We should go too," Julia said, concern pulling her brows low. "If something's going around, I want to get as much done as I can before I get sick."

Eliana stood to give her family all a hug. Her dad and Logan patted Asher on the shoulder as they walked past him, and Julia gave him a quick side hug, even though they'd only met a few times. Then it was just him and Eliana, shoulder to shoulder at an empty table, sharing a plate of food.

"Hey, before I forget, I need to ask you something," Eliana said.

"Sure." He tried not to let his mind grow fuzzy when she leaned into him. He smelled her sunscreen and the floral mousse she'd come out of the bedroom this morning scrunching into her wavy hair.

The sight of her exiting his bedroom so casually had his mind in a fog for pretty much the rest of the morning. His throat had been so tight, he hadn't even managed to tell her he'd made her breakfast, but had instead shoved the plate with whole-grain avocado toast topped with crispy bacon, fresh arugula, and a drizzle of his homemade balsamic reduction glaze at her like she was an irritating diner in his restaurant.

It hadn't fazed her, so maybe she was getting used to his weirdness. She'd tucked into her food like it was the best thing she'd ever eaten, and watching her appreciate the food he'd made was extremely rewarding.

"You threw away that box of secrets, right?"

He blinked away the image of her from that morning. "Yes."

"Okay." She rested her hands on the bench behind her and leaned back. She didn't seem to notice that her entire right side was pressed against him and that her hair tickled his neck. But he noticed. He noticed everything about her.

She turned to him, and their faces were inches apart, but she didn't move away, so he didn't either. "But *how* did you throw it away?"

When had breathing become so tricky? "Umm ... I put it on the back of my bike when I went into work and dropped it into the trash."

"Which trash? The big dumpster in the parking lot?"

He nodded, trying to think through the haze of her closeness. "Yeah, I took most of the boxes there."

"Most of them?" she pressed.

"The trash can was so full, I had to put one in the trash at the clinic."

"Which box did you bring into the office?" Her eyes were wide.

"I don't know. All the boxes were the same, and I wasn't thinking about it." He wished he could remember exactly which box he'd put where, but she'd been sick, and he hadn't slept well on the couch. "Why? What's wrong?"

"Nothing. I just ..." She paused. "I heard something that reminded me of one of the secrets your grandpa unearthed."

"It made it into the trash," he assured her. "Some of those secrets might not be as secret as we think they are. Just because we don't know about them doesn't mean everyone doesn't know."

"True. I'm overthinking it." She rested her head on his shoulder, and he stopped breathing. For her, this touch was casual; it didn't mean anything. For him? His entire chest expanded like a helium balloon about to send him into the atmosphere.

"How are you feeling?" he asked, his voice a little too gruff.

She yawned. "Good enough to beat every person here at all the games this afternoon."

"I don't doubt it." Had the affection he was feeling for her come out in his voice? He shook his head. If anyone was overthinking things, it was him.

True to her word, Eliana dominated every game. He loved that she didn't let people win just to make them feel good—instead, she had a way of bringing out the competitive nature in everyone else around her until they all tried their best and had a blast. She had the kind of enthusiasm for playing that was infectious, and she was always the first to jump in and encourage a teammate or poke good-naturedly at her opponents. He hadn't seen the residents of The Palms move so quickly and consistently as he had today.

"Last game!" Nancy called into a megaphone she'd acquired at some point. "Obstacle course time. Find a partner!"

Eliana turned to Don, but Don was already partnered with Samantha. Winnie, Polly, and Rosa were sitting this one out, and Walt was with his granddaughter, Avery.

"We don't need you as a judge for this round," Nancy said to Asher. "Go find a partner."

"Do you want to do it with me?" he asked Nancy.

She took in the blow-up obstacle course stretched several feet across the beach. "That thing is a broken hip waiting to happen. I can't believe Walt and Don are attempting it."

"I believe it."

Nancy let out an exasperated sigh. "You're right. Those two are never ones to let a challenge pass them by—even when they should. I'm just glad Harry's not here."

"Where is he?"

Nancy shrugged. "I hope he's not embarrassed about the country album nonsense." She ran her hand over her face. "I'll bet he's out at the flea markets today."

A jolt shot through Asher. The country album? There was only a one-in-four chance the secrets box had made it to the inside trash can. And the thought that anyone would see it and go through it ... wasn't that hard to believe, actually. He'd been in such a hurry, and it was too big to fit all the way into the trash bin. Someone might have thought it was a giveaway box.

There's no way that had happened.

Except he could picture it in his mind—someone opening the box, realizing what it was, taking it home, and then revealing people's secrets. But why? Why would someone do that?

From the corner of his eye, he saw Eliana put her hands on her hips and scan the crowd. Asher felt the moment her gaze landed on him. It was like warm sunshine escaping a patch of clouds. "Asher! Partners?" she yelled over all the people between them.

For some reason—whether it was the twist in his stomach, the increased beat of his heart, or the certainty that he would never get enough of Eliana Peters—he hesitated.

Nancy nudged him. "Go on. Don't leave her waiting."

Eliana waited, her eyebrows raised, her perfectly pink lips curled into a smile just for him.

Nancy nudged him again—really, it was more of a shove between his shoulder blades—knocking him out of his stupor, and he jogged in her direction.

"Yay!" She took his arm when he got close.

"We may have a problem," he murmured.

"What?" she asked.

"You may be right about the box of secrets."

"That someone found it?"

He nodded grimly.

"What are we going to do if it's out there?" she whispered.

"I don't know. I should have been more careful with it."

"You couldn't have guessed someone would go dumpster diving." She moved her arm around his waist and pulled him into a friendly side hug. "There's nothing we can do about it now."

"I guess you're right."

"So let's focus on the fact that we're so going to win this."

"Maybe," he said as carelessly as he could pull off. At her outrage, he could hardly hold his disinterested expression.

"If I have to *drag* you through that thing, we will beat every last one of them."

"That might be fun, seeing as how I'm about double your weight." When had teasing her become one of his favorite things to do?

"Don't underestimate my determination."

The devil on his shoulder convinced him to lean close enough to her ear that when he whispered, his words caused her little hairs to move. "I never underestimate you."

He felt gratified when she inhaled a sharp breath. Then he shook himself. What was he doing? He hadn't felt playful like this since before his grandpa died. But with Eliana, it was more than playfulness that spurred him on. It was something more intoxicating than that.

"Good. That's really ... good," she said, her cheeks flushed.

A whistle sounded. "Obstacle course racers: to your marks!" Nancy yelled.

"Come on," Eliana said, her brows cut into a determined line. She slipped her hand into his and tugged him to the starting line. Her hand was so soft, so delicate, it made his mouth dry.

He took his shirt off and tossed it on top of their towels near the judges' table.

"We've got to come up with a strategy before we ..." Her voice drifted off. He turned around to her to see why she'd stopped talking. Her train of thought had been derailed by the sight of his abs, based on the direction of her eyes. He bit back a pleased grin. Maybe it wasn't just him.

She paused on his tattoos, first the octopus and then the one on his ribs. She looked up at him with a question in her eyes, but he didn't want to talk about it right now. Not when they were having so much fun.

"Ready?" she asked, a competitive glint in her eye that relaxed his shoulders.

"You're not the only person who likes to win," he said. "We've got this."

"There are two prizes for the obstacle course!" Nancy yelled. "One is a surprise, but it's good. Trust me. The second one is that you'll get to name the sea turtle we've adopted through the Southern Florida Wildlife Conservation Center. It was rescued last week after a shark attack, and most of the proceeds will go toward caring for it and other turtles that come through the SFWCC."

"I have the perfect name," Asher said, rubbing his hands together.

Her gaze flicked down to his bare chest again, then back up as if it was an effort not to stare at his skin. He didn't hate her reaction at all—it just surprised him. He was attracted to her—how could he not be?—but he'd never had any indication that she was attracted to him too. Until now.

"What is it?" She blinked a few times as if trying to focus.

He gave her a determined smile. "We'll have to win if you want to find out."

Everyone would go through the course separately, and their times would be taken at the end. The winner would be whoever had the fastest time. They watched as the people went before them, noting what things they got hung up on and where they excelled until it was their turn.

"On your mark. Get set. Go!" Nancy yelled.

Asher and Eliana took off toward the inflatable obstacle course. At the first ridge, he made a step out of his hand for Eliana to use to reach up for a pull-up bar and hoist herself up the seven-foot-high ledge. He then jumped to grab the bar, and pulled himself up after her. They jumped over huge inflatable balls, and he'd observed that the less thinking you did—and the faster you went over them—the better off you were. Neither of them fell, so they moved on to the next obstacle, which was climbing side by side up a wide ladder to get to a slide that would dunk them into an ice-cold pool.

He lost his breath as he landed in the water, every part of him burning like he'd jumped into a fire, but he pushed himself up and toward the platform. Eliana was already waiting for him, and she reached out a hand to help him up when his legs didn't want to work.

He shook the chill out of his brain, and they raced to a set of monkey bars that were extra hard because their hands were wet, but they both made it across on their first try.

After that, they had to balance on an unstable foam platform that would drop them into another ice-water bath if they mis-stepped. Both of them made it through to the very last challenge: another inflatable slide, this one taller than the last.

They clambered up the ladder as fast as they could, but near the top, Eliana slipped. His heart dropped in his chest as she glided down to the pad at the bottom. He reached toward her and snagged her hand in his, jerking his shoulder and almost losing his hold. She scrambled back up the ladder and got her footing.

"Thanks," she said, breathless, as they hurried to the top. Once there, she took his hand, and together, they flew down the slide into a pool of foamy water.

As they emerged, Nancy yelled, "Time!"

The next contestants went while he and Eliana stepped to the side. She was shivering, so he wrapped his arm around her waist and tugged her into his side. He tended to run warm, and even an ice bath couldn't lower his temp for long.

She tucked herself into him, her chilled skin pressed against his warm chest. Could she feel his heart thudding? Want thrummed through him as she snuggled even closer, and her hair brushed against his mouth. "I could have sworn I had our towels right here," she said.

He didn't care where their towels were, if it meant they could stand like this for the rest of the afternoon.

"I don't think we won," Eliana said. "I lost us time when I slipped."

"Not that much time," he murmured against her temple. She shivered, and he didn't know if it was from the cold or his closeness, but he definitely wanted to find out.

"But enough, maybe."

"We have a winner!" Nancy announced too soon.

They held their breath.

"Eliana and Asher! Come claim your prize!"

They looked at each in shock, and then Eliana jumped and cheered. "What did we win?" she asked Nancy.

"Salsa and salsa," Nancy said. "Bruno is going to teach you to make four different kinds of salsa, and we have a dance instructor who'll teach you to dance the salsa."

"Wow. That sounds fun! Are you up for that?" She gave Asher a brilliant smile.

He was such a goner. She could have asked if he was up for swimming with the sharks that had attacked the rescue turtle, and he'd have said yes. But this was even better. Or worse, depending on how you looked at it. At least with the sharks, he'd have a distraction from the girl who was determined to remain single. But with salsa lessons, they'd spend more time together. Close. Touching.

"Yes, definitely," he told her, swallowing. He was in so much trouble.

"And we get to name the turtle?" Eliana asked.

"You do. Do you already have a name picked out?"

"Asher does. And since he saved me from falling, I think he should get to name her." She nudged her hip against his. "So what'll it be?"

"Miss Havisham," he said.

It took a beat for her to connect the dots, and when she turned to him with wide eyes and an outraged expression, he could hardly hold back his grin. "No."

"You said I got to name her. And I know you like naming turtles after single people in literature."

Looking like she was trying to hold back a laugh, she leveled him with a stern expression. "Miss Havisham was crazy."

"I like her. She's interesting."

"Oh my gosh." She ran her hands over her face, and a tiny snort escaped, making him feel very satisfied. "I can't believe you right now."

"So ... Miss Havisham?" Nancy said, furrowing her blond brow.

Asher nodded. "It's a good name," he insisted to Eliana. "You should post about her on your social media."

"Stop." Eliana laughed and pushed at his shoulder playfully. Was it normal to crave every touch? "Fine. You win. Miss Havisham."

"Alright. If you insist." Nancy wrote it down and then picked up her megaphone, nearly blasting out their ears as she yelled her thanks for a wonderful day.

Eliana and Asher moved out of the sound blast, still laughing. Eliana raised her fingers to Asher's mouth to touch his smile. He stilled completely, except for the blood rushing through his body like a high-speed train.

"You're different today. Happier." She brought her hand down as if just realizing she'd touched his lips. He missed the soft touch as soon as it was gone. "I like this smile."

"It was a fun day." His voice sounded like he had rocks in his throat. "I'm glad you were here."

And it was in that moment, as she looked up at him with pure laughter and happiness in her eyes, that he realized he had two big problems. First, he had to find out if his grandpa's box had been taken and someone was revealing the secrets. And second, he'd completely fallen for a woman who was so off the market, the market might as well not exist.

CHAPTER 19
ELIANA

"She'll go and fall in love, and there's an end of peace and fun, and cozy times together." —Louisa May Alcott

FOR THE FIRST TIME, words in *Happily Single* were coming easily. She didn't even need to peek through the kitchen blinds every ten seconds or have a snack every other page to keep her going. The words flowed.

Maybe it was because the chapter she was writing was so easy for her to write about. Friendship. Part of being happily single was making sure you had good friends. Having good friends was an essential part of life, no matter your relationship status.

When she'd been married to Corbin, she'd let her friends drift away, something she regretted. She valued her friendships—the old ones, her influencer friends, her family who were her best friends, and her new friends. Like Asher. She had so much fun playing the games last week with him. He wasn't afraid to tease her, but in the end, she sensed he wanted to win just as much as she had.

Her gaze drifted to where he sat on the living room floor, going through boxes like a man on a mission. The tear of tape, the pulling back of the cardboard, and the sound of a lifetime of belongings thunking to the floor were the soundtrack to this writing session. She knew how difficult it was for him to do this, and her chest expanded at the thought of him facing something so hard.

Meeting Asher and becoming friends with him was one of the best things to come out of this trip. And not just because it gave her a quiet place to work, write, and continue making content.

He was a distraction, but in a good way. The kind of way that made her just a little bit happier, especially when she recalled curling into his warm, hard-as-a-rock chest. Maybe her other friends didn't distract her in *quite* the same way, but she refused to overthink it. She and Asher had that elusive friendship click, like two interlocking pieces snapping together just right, and with all the stress of planning the wedding and writing this book, she needed that.

She finished summarizing a study done on happiness and friendship and stretched out her back with a yawn. Out of habit, she pulled up her social media to check the stats on her latest videos and posts.

To her shock, she saw that the post she'd shared from Grandma's page—the one about how she'd met Grandpa—had gone viral. People loved it. There were over ten thousand comments, most of them some variation of "AW!" and "I want something like this someday" and "Reminds me of how I met my partner."

She texted Grandma Winnie.

Eliana: You went viral!!

Grandma: What? No, I'm feeling fine. Are you sick again? How's Cameron?

Eliana: I'm fine and Cam is feeling a lot better, but Dad is sick now.

Eliana: But that's not what I meant. Viral means that a social media post got a lot of views and shares. The post you made of you and Grandpa is SUPER popular. Everyone is reading it and loving it.

Grandma: Wow. That's something.

Eliana: Congrats, Grandma! You achieved something many people aspire to and work toward for years.

Grandma: Leave it to me to do it accidentally.

Grandma: And not be one hundred percent sure of what you're talking about.

Grandma: *GIF of a confused person walking into walls*

Eliana laughed. When had her grandma learned how to use GIFs? She'd have to go over later and show Grandma what it meant for a post to go viral. It was a surprise that the local news hadn't reached out to her for an interview yet, but probably for the best. Grandma Winnie would hate the attention.

Boxes clattered to the ground, followed by Asher cursing under his breath. She grinned and turned to Louisa, who she'd propped on the table beside her. "It sounds like he's struggling. Should I go help him?" she whispered.

Louisa's head moved in what could have been a nod of agreement or an attempt to reach another part of her lettuce snack.

"You're right. He needs help." It was a good time for a break anyway. She popped out of her seat and headed to the living room to find boxes strewn everywhere. This wasn't an organized attempt to systematically go through all the boxes, but rather like someone bursting a confetti tube all over the room, Asher in the middle of the mess.

"What are you doing?" She took him in. Dust from the boxes and belongings coated his hair and beard like snow. A pile of notebooks sat in his lap.

A smile creased his face as he saw her. She'd never get used to that—or how wrong she'd been about him. He'd seemed so grumpy, so unapproachable when she'd first met him. But underneath that protective layer of stay-away, he was a huge softie. "That box of secrets is really bugging me."

"What about it?" She cleared off a spot to sit by him. The space was so limited that as they sat cross-legged facing each other, her knees pressed against his.

Her mind was drawn to the games last weekend, how it had felt when he'd whispered teasingly into her ear, his lips just grazing her skin. Hot. The room was suddenly very hot. She fanned her shirt away from her body to get some fresh air circulating.

"Why he'd be so invasive." His expression was perplexed as he rested his elbows on a box behind him. "He must have spent so much time investigating everyone and pulling these files together."

"What are you looking for? I'll help." Her looming deadline nagged at her, but she couldn't leave Asher to go through this pile of emotional wreckage alone.

"He kept a journal, and I have this Hail Mary hope that he wrote an entire confessional about why and how he did it," he said wryly.

"That would be convenient." She reached across to him and took half of the notebooks from his lap, attempting, but not quite succeeding, to ignore how her fingers brushed against his hard stomach as she did.

Of course she was aware of him; they were in a very small space together. And he was an extremely handsome man. She'd taken an internet vow of singleness, not of never noticing a hot guy and/or his tight line of abs again in her life. She was only human, after all. It was fine. Completely, totally fine.

Her phone buzzed recklessly in her back pocket with messages, but she ignored it in favor of combing through old notebooks filled with everything from grocery lists to calendar reminders. Asher finished going through the notebooks on his lap and moved on to a stack of mail—nearly all of which was junk.

She grabbed another box—staying far away from the abs this time. Car warranty renewal notices, grocery store deals, credit card applications ... A handwritten envelope caught her eye, and she slipped it from the pile. It was addressed to someone named Michael, but it wasn't stamped, and it looked like the envelope had never been sealed. She pulled the lined notebook paper out and noted the date in the corner. Ten years ago. The handwriting was messy and angular, but she was able to make out most of it.

Michael—

I've gotten settled into Diamond Cove. My research is progressing, and I'll keep you updated as I go along. My grandson is coming into town for Christmas next week, so you won't hear from me until next month. I'll email as you suggested—

The letter was cut off at that point, and nothing else had been written. "Asher, did your grandpa write this?"

She handed it to him, and his eyes scanned the page, his brows furrowing the further he read. He turned the paper over to check out the back, but it was blank. "It's his handwriting."

"It looks like he never sent it," she said.

"He would have written this right after he moved here," Asher said. "I was just finishing my undergrad."

"Are we *sure* your grandpa wasn't an undercover cop?"

Asher ran a worried hand over his beard. "He was military until he retired."

"I'm sure there's an explanation that makes sense."

"Or the one person I thought I knew best in this world was really a stranger to me."

132

She grabbed his hand. "He loved you, Asher. We know that for sure."

"I don't know anything for sure anymore." He stood, dropping her hand and the letter. "I need to cook."

He moved into the kitchen, and something told her to give him some space. It couldn't be easy to learn a secret like this about your grandparent. Thankfully, her grandparents were open books. If only she had more answers for Asher.

Her phone was still buzzing, so she pulled it out of her pocket to check her messages.

Her agent. Her publisher. Giselle. Her sister. Logan. Whoa.

She opened up her agent's text first. *Heads up, the publisher wants to pull up your release date. They'll need a first draft in three weeks. I told them you were almost done.*

Her stomach sank. She had only fifty pages written, and she wasn't convinced they were any good.

She opened up the text from her publisher next: *Great news! We were able to squeeze your book into a prime release spot with better sales opportunities. This means we'll need a finished manuscript much sooner than anticipated. Your agent assures us you're on track to finish early. We've attached the updated contract with the abbreviated timeline.*

Eliana broke into a cold sweat. Did she even want to open the rest?

Giselle: Did you get the updated contract from Big House Publishing? Florida looks divine.

She opened Julia's next, needing something good. Something happy to get her mind off the dumpster fire that was her career.

Julia: Hey.

Julia: Want to come see Miss Havisham today?

Julia: She's adorable.

Julia: Did Logan just text you?

Julia: I'm totally fine, for the record. No worries. You just keep working.

Julia: It's alllllll good.

Uh-oh. That was a lot of Ls on that all. She opened up Logan's text next.

Logan: There's been a slight issue with the wedding and Julia is freaking out.

Logan: Do you have a minute to come to the Wildlife Center? She doesn't want to bother you because you're under a deadline, but I convinced her you could come see Miss Havisham.

Everyone in her world was imploding at the exact same time. A bright red warning light flashed in the back of her mind, indicating that she might be next. She sent a thumbs-up text to both her agent and her editor—the only communication she could muster—and let Logan know she was on her way. She desperately needed a distraction.

She stood, slipped on her sandals, and went into the kitchen to tell Asher she was heading to the conservation center, but she came to an abrupt halt.

Asher stood at the counter, staring blankly at a bunch of unrelated, unappetizing ingredients. She was no chef, but she didn't know how coconut flour, baking soda, chocolate chips, a block of Parmesan cheese, a can of sardines, orange juice concentrate, and red wine vinegar were going to pair together into anything delicious.

She took a soft step closer. "Whatcha making?"

He blinked at her, looking lost. Her problems jumped into the trunk of her mind, while his took the passenger seat. "Garbage."

"Hmm," she said, lightly placing her hand on his forearm. "As interesting as that sounds, do you want to come with me to visit our baby instead?"

He rubbed the back of his neck, surprise winking light back into his gaze. *Gotcha.* "We have a baby together?"

"Wow." She straightened her mouth in mock disappointment. "Did our sea turtle adoption mean nothing to you?"

Her silliness broke him out of his moroseness, just as she'd hoped, though his expression was still a long ways off from any semblance of a smile. "I didn't realize Miss Havisham was a baby—ours or otherwise. My apologies."

"We eviscerated the octogenarian competition for that win."

"I remember. Don may never be the same."

"He'll get over it." She leaned closer and whispered, "Besides, I think he faked missing that last monkey bar and falling."

"Don would never let anyone win. Especially someone younger than him."

Don had flown through the obstacle course, and his time would be faster than theirs, but she could have sworn he'd glanced at her briefly before he'd overshot the next monkey bar and fallen. "Maybe he didn't want the responsibility of another child," she said.

That earned her a lip twitch. Asher took in the messy living room and kitchen. "I shouldn't leave all of this."

"It'll be here when we get back. Come with me. Please?" She slid her hand down his forearm, gliding her fingers across every raised vein and tendon, until she got to his hand. Goose bumps erupted on his arms in the wake of her touch, and she caught her breath. He wrapped his hand around hers, holding her in place. She could feel him looking at her, but she refused to look up at him, afraid of what she might or might not see.

He slid his fingers through hers in a gentle caress, so slowly she had plenty of time to pull away. But she didn't. Why didn't she? Fire raced through her veins, and the heat of it burned all the way from the tips of her ears to the tips of her toes.

Her throat went dry. They didn't move, and she knew he was waiting for her to meet his gaze. When she did, she was shocked to see that fire blazed fiercely in his eyes. Something in her expression banked it. He loosened his grip on her hand, though he kept their fingers intertwined loosely. Casually.

Yet nothing about this felt casual at all.

"Want to take the motorcycle?" he asked, his voice low and rumbly.

"It's about time you asked."

CHAPTER 20

ASHER

F OR SOMEONE WHO DIDN'T like animals, Asher was acquiring them at a fast rate. First a live-in turtle, then an adopted rescue turtle. He lowered his voice to speak to Logan, who stood beside him in the indoor aquarium portion of the conservation center. "This adoption is in name only, right?"

Miss Havisham rested on a fake beach beside a small body of water. Lamps meant to simulate the heat and light from outside were set around the habitat. She hadn't moved once since they'd arrived, and he had to take Logan's word for it that she was alive and well.

"Yes." Logan turned toward him, leaning his side against the rail. "Our goal is to rehabilitate and return to the wild when possible. When it's not possible, we still want to keep them in as natural environment as possible." He grinned. "Think of yourself as the parent to a new adult."

"One who has my credit card memorized?" he grumbled.

"And really expensive taste."

As it turned out, winning a turtle adoption came with a Pinocchio-load of strings attached. Financial strings, mostly, though he felt the unwelcome tug of emotional strings too. He rubbed at his chest. Luckily, Asher was in a position where he could support the food and care of this sea turtle beyond the money the fundraiser brought in.

And doubly lucky, he had a cold, dead heart when it came to animals. The pain in his chest better be heartburn and not any sort of thawing.

No wonder Don had thrown his game and let them win. He was the only smart one.

But then Asher remembered Eliana's radiant face when they'd won, and how she'd thrown her arms around him, and he knew he'd adopt a thousand sea turtles if she asked him to.

When they'd arrived, Julia had taken one look at Eliana and burst into tears. Eliana had ushered her sister into the nearest bathroom, leaving Logan and Asher alone together.

There had been a beat of awkwardness between the two of them in the wake of that bathroom door closing, cutting off the sound of Julia's sobs. Asher didn't have a lot of friends. Really, he didn't have any friends who weren't also patients or former patients or friends of his grandpa that he'd sort of taken on as his own. It wasn't that he didn't like people, but he didn't see the point. It was better to go through life alone, without getting attached to people, missing them, and realizing they were always strangers anyway.

Yikes. That was a bitter thought. When had he become this way? After his grandpa died? After his parents and grandma died? He'd curled up in his shell and snapped at anyone who tried to reach out to him, until everyone gave him a wide berth. Except for Eliana. Being friends with her was nice.

He flexed the hand she'd been holding earlier. More than nice. Filling in a way food never could be.

Winnie had been not-so-subtly encouraging him to go to therapy for the last year. And he'd been not-so-subtly pretending he didn't know what she was talking about. Perhaps it was time for him to actually call the person on the card she'd given him.

"Do you think they need help?" Asher asked Logan, indicating the bathroom.

Worry creased Logan's brow. The awkwardness from earlier had dissipated, and the two men leaned side by side on the railing, their backs to Miss Havisham, as they stared at the bathroom door. "No. Eliana's got this."

"What's going on? If you don't mind talking about it," he hurried to add.

Logan let out a long sigh. "The fabric Winnie ordered for the bridesmaid dresses arrived stained. The company refunded Julia, but they can't get more material shipped out here in time for Winnie to make the dresses."

"Oh." He paused. "Are there no fabric stores near Diamond Cove?"

"I don't know, man. Maybe?"

Asher pulled out his phone and searched out fabric stores. Seven popped up within a thirty-minute drive, and if they were willing to drive up to two hours away, they got that number up to nineteen. He tipped his phone to Logan to show him the map. "One of these has to have something appropriate, right?"

"I hope so. I hate when she's sad. Sometimes I wonder if we shouldn't have just eloped."

"Why didn't you?"

"Julia has the softest heart of any person I've ever met, and she worried her family would feel bad about missing her wedding." His own eyes softened as he talked about her, his love palpable. Asher tapped at his chest. This heartburn business was going to be the death of him. "I'm glad she has Eliana, who is determined to make this a perfect wedding."

The phrasing "perfect wedding" set off an alarm bell in his head. "No wedding is going to be perfect." Asher had attended enough weddings at The Palms—many of them second or third marriages after a spouse died—to know that things happened. Seagulls descended on the cake, or the resident flamingos stole the show, or Sweetie set off a chain reaction of screaming and scrambling when the out-of-towners saw her.

"I know. But the Peters women are perfectionists, and they'll do everything in their power to make it as perfect as they can."

That sounded really stressful to Asher. And impossible.

The bathroom door opened, and Julia came out, her face red and streaked with tears, but she smiled at Asher warmly when she saw him. "How are you?" she asked, so heartfelt he knew she meant it. She was in crisis mode but still reaching out to the people around her. Logan slipped his arm around her waist and pulled her close to his side.

What Asher wouldn't give to do the same with Eliana.

The lines around Eliana's eyes and mouth were deep, and her expression strained. She didn't look like she'd been crying, but close.

"Asher found a bunch of fabric stores we can drive around to and check out for more dress fabric," Logan said.

Julia's lips trembled. "I can't. We don't have time to drive around everywhere. We have a meeting with the caterer later this afternoon, and I've got a book signing tonight."

"We can go," Asher said, surprising himself. And everyone else, apparently, by the way they gaped at him. "I mean, I can go. I don't know what Eliana's plans are ..." he stammered.

"I don't have anything going on today," Eliana said.

"But your book," Julia protested.

Eliana waved her hand like it was nothing, though those lines deepened even more. "This is more important. Besides, Asher has no idea what kind of fabric to get, do you?" She looked at him inquisitively.

"I don't," he admitted. He knew about pretty much every different kind of butter and how it could affect the taste of a pastry, but fabrics were an entirely different world.

"Silk," Julia said. She took in a shuddering breath and swiped at her cheeks. "Blue or purple. Any shade at this point, though if given an option, I prefer pastel."

"Got it. I'll send you pictures before I purchase."

"No need. I trust you." Julia pulled Eliana into a hug, and then she surprised Asher by wrapping her arms around his waist in a super-tight hug. He left one of his arms hanging awkwardly at his side but brought the other one around to give her a bro-pat on the back. Would he ever get used to this family's affectionate nature?

He didn't hate it, but he never expected it.

"Thank you." Julia beamed up at him, her eyes the exact same shade and shape as Eliana's. He glanced at Eliana, whose soft expression did wildly acrobatic things to his stomach. Julia pulled away and then tucked herself back into Logan's side. He kissed the top of her head, and it was clear the two of them belonged together. To each other.

Eliana waved at Miss Havisham. "Bye, cutie! Don't plan any weird weddings without us." She turned to Asher with a wry smile. "We'd better go. But first, let's pick up my car. I'm not riding on the back of a motorcycle with a bolt of fabric in my lap."

CHAPTER 21
ELIANA

"Some people seemed to get all sunshine, and some all shadow ..." —Louisa May Alcott

W HY COULDN'T ANYTHING GO right with this wedding?

Eliana drove into the parking lot of the eighth fabric shop she and Asher had visited. Her phone continued to buzz, and she continued to ignore it, knowing that it was most likely her agent and editor, needing more communication than a thumbs-up.

If she ignored it, it was like it didn't exist, right? She inwardly rolled her eyes. *Sure, that's mentally healthy.*

"This is the place. I feel it," she said to Asher as they walked through the muggy heat into the blessedly cool fabric store.

"Me too," he said. "I mean it helps that we called first."

"Luck favors the prepared!"

Once they'd exhausted all the local fabric stores, which didn't have enough fabric to make three dresses, they'd called ahead before driving the forty-five minutes to this one, to see if they had the fabric they were looking for. The woman they'd spoken to assured them they did, and they'd raced into the store for it.

"Let's head straight to customer service," she said. The woman on the phone said she was going to pull the fabric for her to look at.

A young woman in her twenties stood at the counter with a bored expression on her face.

"Hi. I called you earlier about the silk."

The girl nodded and, moving at the pace of a snail, turned and grabbed a bolt of fabric from a pile behind her.

Eliana's smile faded. Grandma wanted twenty-one yards, and there was no way that bolt had more than ten. "Is this all you have?" she asked.

"In the lavender. We have more in sky blue and sage green." She grabbed those from the counter behind her as well, but they had even less fabric than the purple one.

Her mind went blank as she looked at them, like her brain had stopped working. "You said on the phone there was enough," she said, sounding desperate to her own ears.

The woman smacked her gum. "There is, combined."

"I didn't mean combined." She spoke through her teeth as her body's temperature increased. It was too late to make it to any other store, which meant they wouldn't get the fabric to Winnie tonight, which meant another delay in getting these dresses done, which meant one more strike against her planning the perfect wedding.

"Well, you should have been more specific," the girl defended. "You asked if I had twenty-one yards of silk in green, blue, or purple. And I do."

"*Or*," she said, knowing she was being too loud. But if steam could come out of a person's ears, it would be coming out of hers. "I said *or*. Not *and*."

The girl shrugged like she couldn't care less. And Eliana's phone buzzed in her pocket, nearly sending her over the edge of her sanity and over the counter as she gripped the ledge in front of her.

"I am trying to plan the perfect wedding in a limited amount of time, and you just cost us an entire night of work."

The girl blinked. "So these ones aren't going to work for you?"

"No!" Eliana let out a frustrated yell, and then she turned on her heel and stormed out of the store. She didn't remember that Asher was with her until he got into the car beside her, shutting his door considerably less hard than she had.

She closed her eyes and tipped her head back against the headrest, her face tilted toward the car roof. "I'm sorry."

"Why?" Asher asked. His tone wasn't judgmental, just curious.

"For losing my cool. For making you drive with me all the way out here. For wasting your time."

She peeked out of the side of her eye at him when he didn't respond. He was on his phone, and she peered over to see that he was looking up other fabric stores.

"You're not wasting my time. I chose to come, and I like spending time with you." He shook his head. "Besides, I don't blame you for losing your cool. That was a frustrating experience overall."

"Right?" she said, feeling justified. But then she deflated again. "Still. What if someone had caught that on camera and tagged me in it? It would be that easy to lose my career. One wrong video, and I'm done." She thought about Sienna and her caffeinated beverage. She'd completely disappeared from social media since.

"That seems like a lot of pressure. To never make a mistake in public."

"It can be. I'm not complaining, though. I love my job and my platform, and getting to make videos that reach people and help them, you know? I'm pretty lucky." She groaned. "I should have been nicer. It's just this wedding. It's getting to me."

"Why are you so stressed about making your sister's wedding perfect?"

"Because I love her."

"Does Julia expect a flawless wedding?"

Flawless. He hit on the exact right word, arrow to bullseye. The thing she'd chased her entire marriage. Corbin had wanted her to be flawless—her appearance, her behavior, everyone's perception of her. It had proved to be an impossible task, one she found herself clinging to many years later. It seemed so pointless sometimes, and yet the thought of letting go of attempting perfection made her feel like she was riding on Asher's motorcycle without holding on.

Asher had seen her soaked, without makeup first thing in the morning, throwing up and lying on the bathroom floor, and now losing her cool in a fabric store. And he still hadn't written her off as a completely worthless mess, so maybe she could attempt to explain.

"My wedding was a disaster."

"What happened?"

"Nothing was good enough for my mother-in-law or my ex. I scheduled the flowers to be delivered too early, and they wilted. The shade of red I chose for the bridesmaid dresses clashed with my sister-in-law's skin. I picked out a chocolate cake when almond is the traditional wedding flavor. At the reception, I teased people I should have ignored and spoke too briefly with people I should have fawned over. And don't get me started on the hugging."

"What happened with the hugging?"

"My ex, Corbin, did not appreciate how many people I hugged that night. He thought so much physical affection with acquaintances was low class."

Asher's jaw tightened. "I love that your family are all huggers." His words warmed her more than they should. "It sounds like you planned the wedding you wanted, and not the wedding your mother-in-law wanted. And that your ex is a tool."

She let out a short, surprised laugh. "I think you're right. But sometimes I wonder, if we'd had the perfect wedding, maybe our first year of marriage wouldn't have been as hard as it was and ended like it did. It put a strain on our relationship right from the beginning, and I don't want that for Logan and Julia. I want it to be magical."

"Logan is nothing like Corbin." He took her hand in his, holding it like he didn't quite know what to do with it, but the effort was enough. "For them, their wedding is one day in a long line of days together."

She wanted to believe him, but whenever she thought about all the many, many things that could go wrong, her breath caught in her chest and she felt like she might pass out.

Her phone lit up wildly in the center console.

Those tears she thought she'd managed to hold back sprang to her eyes. She blinked wildly, not wanting to add "crying basket case" to imperfections Asher had witnessed.

"Is everything okay?" He indicated the phone and looked at her too closely.

"It's nothing. Just my agent and publisher moving my date up on my book."

He frowned. "Are you that close to finishing?"

"No?" She attempted to clear the emotion from her throat and speak with more confidence. "But I can be. I have to be."

"They won't honor the original date?"

"They might, but the new date is so much better." Her voice cracked, and she stopped speaking. *Keep it together.*

But compassion was her kryptonite. Asher squeezed her hand, and then, so slowly, so carefully she knew he was unsure about his actions, he pulled her into an awkward hug. The console squeezed between them, and he didn't seem to know what to do with his right arm, so he patted her on the shoulder. It made her laugh, but it also made her cry. All at once. A laughing, crying mess of a woman who had just yelled at some poor fabric store worker.

Appearing flawless to Asher was so impossible at this point, it wasn't even a worthwhile pursuit. If it ever had been.

She pressed her chin into the tight spot between his collarbone and neck, fitting there perfectly. "Do you ever feel like life is just happening to you, and you have no control?"

His awkward patting hand finally found a place at the back of her head. His fingers threaded into her hair and drew downward in a soothing motion. She let out a long, shuddering breath and almost made a joke about comforting the crying Peters sisters today being a full-time job. But she held back, wanting to soak in that comfort instead of teasing him about it.

He pulled back too soon, and she wished he would have stayed close, with his arms wrapped around her so she could keep breathing him in. His soap was so much more potent with her nose pressed against his neck than when she was wrapped in his blankets on his bed.

"What would help?" he asked. "Getting away from everything for a few hours, or going back to the house and working?"

She should go back to the house and work. It was the responsible thing to do. But a million buzzing bees hopped from flower to flower in her brain, and the thought of sitting down at her computer and putting words on the screen felt as futile as trying to control real bees. "I need to work. But I will probably die if I don't get a break."

"I mean, you're going to for sure die someday."

Again, she laughed, even though she was still crying. "Well, that's a pleasant thought, Asher."

"I'm not the sunshine in this duo," he said.

She put her hand to her chest, feeling more touched than she should. "Are you calling me sunshine?"

"Yes. You're bright and cheery and fiery and sometimes molten material shoots off of you—"

"So I'm hot," she supplied.

Instead of laughing, like she expected, he looked at her in a way that made her entire body feel like it was *filled* with molten material. "Yes, you're hot."

The car suddenly felt much too small as a tingle slid over the back of her neck and cheeks. His gaze darted to her lips, and they parted in response. Her breathing quickened. The silence was taut, strung between them by a growing desire she didn't want to face. *Couldn't* face. With effort, she tore her eyes away from his mouth. "So that break ..."

He paused for a beat, as if waiting for some cue from her, but she held completely still. He relaxed into his seat. "Let's go to the house and get our swimsuits. Tonight, we're supposed to have perfect boogie-boarding waves."

Eliana had been boogie boarding many times in her life. On this beach. In full sunlight!

But never with Asher.

It was the only explanation for why she could not ride a wave this time. Instead, she biffed it over and over again, the nose of the board diving into the sand and flipping her over the waves, and her falls causing her to swallow more sea water than was probably healthy. She pushed her stringy, wet hair away from her stinging eyes.

Asher stood to the side in his wet suit, watching her with a smirk. He'd offered to help her several times, but she insisted she could do it on her own. Pride. Today, it tasted like salt and was always her downfall.

"Fine!" She motioned him closer, then put her hands on her own wet-suit-clad hips. They'd rented one from Chad's surf shop just before it closed. "Will you please help me?"

"Yes." He rode on his board over to her and then stood up beside her in the waist-deep water. "It's your timing. You're jumping too soon, and the waves are rolling over you."

"How are you so good at this?" she asked him.

"I surf a lot."

That explained his muscular chest and arms. She knew he came out here with his wet suit nearly every evening, but she'd assumed he only swam.

"Okay, get ready, a good wave is coming. I'll tell you when to jump into it."

He stared at the wave, and she took the opportunity, unobserved, to look at his profile. He had a straight nose and firm brows. Was his beard as soft as it looked?

"Now!" he said.

She jumped in and took off, riding the top of the wave for the first time that evening. It was exhilarating and incredible, and it made her forget her stress for a moment. She slid onto the beach and then rested her head on the board while she held on to the amazing feeling.

"That was awesome!" she said to Asher, who had landed about ten feet beside her.

"Again?" His eyes sparkled with excitement.

If she was sunshine, he was the ocean with unexpected depths, a sparkling surface, and ... fun. He was really fun.

She raced after him into the ocean, and hours fell away while they rode wave after wave into the beach until her stomach was growling, and her leg muscles were shaking, and the sun had set in a brilliant peachy haze behind Diamond Cove.

"I'm done," she said to Asher, out of breath. She walked over to where their towels were laid out and started to remove her wet suit. She wanted to lie on her warm towel in her bathing suit and soak the warmth from the sand and sky into her skin.

She unzipped the front of her wet suit and rolled it down her shoulders. Asher came up beside her and made a strangled noise in the back of his throat as she bent to pull it over her waist and reveal her black swimsuit bottoms. He turned his back to her and expertly removed his own wet suit.

He lifted his arms above his head to stretch out his muscles—and oh boy, did he have muscles. She knew she should also turn around and give him the privacy he gave her—but she was completely frozen. The muscles in his back flexed, and she followed the crossing lines from one shoulder blade to another, then down his spine until a hint of black across his ribs caught her gaze. She could tell he hadn't wanted to talk about his rib tattoo at the games, which had only fed her curiosity.

"You can turn around," she said.

He swiveled toward her, taking her in fully for a split second, before his eyes landed on her own tattoo on her hip. "A turtle," he said, amused. "I could have guessed."

"Louisa," she corrected, running her fingers over the tattoo. His heated gaze followed every move of her hand as if he was the one touching her, and she dropped it from her hip like it was on fire. "Will you tell me about yours?"

He looked down at his ribs and then turned to the side, lifting his arm so she could see the rest of it. "An anchor. With my parents' names beneath it."

She peered closer. Sarah and Ryan Brooks. A rope from the top of the anchor wound around their names. A shiver ran through her. She couldn't imagine losing her parents when she was so young. Only a teenager. She relied on her parents so much—even when she went weeks without talking to them. Just knowing they were only a phone call or text away was enough.

Asher dropped down onto his towel and rested a hand over his eyes. She followed suit, more exhausted than she'd felt in a long time. She stretched out, closed her eyes, and listened to the ocean waves crash against the beach.

This was the best feeling. The exhilaration. The exhaustion. The complete release of all the stress she'd been carrying. And just having fun for no purpose. With no cameras or goals or appearances to worry about.

She stretched her arm out until her hand brushed against Asher's sandy arm. She drew her fingers down it until she reached his damp, gritty hand and intertwined her fingers through his. She squeezed it, and he tilted his head to look at her through the dim light of the dusky night sky.

"Thank you," she whispered, and he squeezed her hand back.

Chapter 22

Winnie

W INNIE HAD LESS THAN three weeks to finish these bridesmaid dresses before Julia's wedding. Not just finish the bridesmaid dresses—*start* them. She was going to need help. Eliana, Julia, and Cameron sat at her kitchen table, not a scrap of sewing ability between the three of them. Why hadn't she taught any of her grandchildren how to sew?

Better yet, why hadn't her daughter taught them? She used to work with Lisa every day after school to teach her to sew everything from curtains to a prom dress. Lisa had complained endlessly about it, so perhaps it was no wonder she hadn't taught her kids.

"Call your mom," Winnie told Eliana. "Tell her to drop everything and get over here."

Eliana saluted her. "Yes, ma'am."

"Julia, what do you want to do about the bridesmaid dresses?" Eliana had explained to them that no one within driving distance had enough fabric to make three dresses in the same color, but that one store had several bolts of different colors.

"Let's do three different colors. Four, if we can do the flower girl too," Julia said.

"Oh my gosh, that would be so cute!" Eliana gushed.

It took all of Winnie's restraint not to die on the spot. To just let her eyes roll back and her body collapse on the floor. "Another dress?" she squeaked out through her growing panic.

"Oh." Julia must have heard something in her tone, because she turned to Winnie. "That's too much, isn't it?"

"Not for Grandma!" Eliana answered with all the naive confidence of someone who'd never sewn a dress in her life. "On those sewing shows, they whip out runway dresses in, like, a day, and Grandma's just as good as them."

"A single day is a bit of a stretch ..." Winnie hedged. Julia frowned and studied Winnie's expression, and Winnie found she didn't have the heart to disappoint both of her granddaughters. "We'll see what we can do. Let's get the fabric just in case."

Julia squealed as if it was a done deal. "Thank you, Grandma! Eliana, want to come to the store with me?"

"No way." Eliana folded her arms. "I have no desire to see the girl I lost it in front of."

"It's a good opportunity to apologize ..." Julia dangled her keys in front of her like a treat.

"Or to get angry again," Eliana said in the same singsong tone. "Grandma needs my help, don't you?"

Winnie needed three experienced seamstresses. And it wouldn't hurt to have Horace here. He was always so good at helping her calm down when the panic was rising in her chest like this. Plus he was much better at managing expectations than she was. Without him, she couldn't stop saying yes to things.

He was off with Smitty again, doing who knew what. He hadn't offered the information to her, and she hadn't asked. She'd hoped he'd notice she was being extra quiet, feeling extra stressed, but he was too excited about whatever new adventure those two were going on together.

"I'll find something for you to do," Winnie said. "Julia, take Cameron with you, and help him pick out some fabric for a bow tie." In for a penny, in for a pound.

"Oh, Cam, you're going to look so handsome in your suit," Eliana said.

Cameron laughed and rubbed his hand along the top of his head, his version of brushing the dust off your shoulders.

Winnie watched her grandchildren interact, teasing one another and laughing, and her heart ached a little less. She missed Horace, but she did have these wonderful kids visiting her almost every day. Not everyone had that. In fact, most people didn't.

Julia and Cameron left. Eliana called her mom—emphasizing just how dire the situation was, which was exactly what Winnie hoped she'd do. Julia, bless her heart, was too much like Winnie, and would downplay how much her help was needed. Eliana, though, knew all the right things to say to get her mom to take the rest of the afternoon off of work, grab her sewing machine, and promise to be there in an hour.

Eliana worked on cutting threads off the wedding dress while they waited for the fabric. Winnie'd had Julia try it on at least a dozen times. After the epically small dress at the Watermelon Festival last year, Winnie was paranoid. She'd never live that moment down, for the rest of her life, no matter how many times Logan reminded her how very much he appreciated that dress mix-up.

She called Nancy next. "Do you have time to help me make some brides-maid dresses?"

"I can't today, but I can come over tomorrow," Nancy said. "Want me to round up Rosa and Polly?" None of them were expert seamstresses, but they could follow directions and at least keep her from going crazy.

"Yes, that would be great."

Nancy paused. Winnie was so distracted pinning a portion of lace to the wedding dress, it took her a moment to click that she wasn't talking, which was unlike Nancy.

"Is everything okay?" Winnie asked. Eliana looked up from cutting the fabric to give her a questioning glance.

"Another secret was posted this morning."

Winnie's stomach dropped. "What was it this time?"

"That I ran for the city council when my kids were young, and I lost," Nancy said, sounding frustrated. "I don't care that people know. I mean, it's public record, but it feels violating to have it announced without my permission."

"I'm sorry," Winnie said. After she and Horace were first married, someone had broken into their apartment and stolen a few things. They hadn't lost anything of value—they didn't even have anything of value back then—but she'd still carried that icky, unsafe feeling of someone being in your space and riffling through your stuff for months afterward. How much worse was it when it was your personal business being posted for everyone to see? It made her shiver. What could this mysterious person post about her? That she used to sew lingerie? Maybe. Relief filled her at the thought. It was just salacious enough to keep people judging and whispering—but definitely not the biggest secret she had.

She hung up, and Eliana looked at her, her face sort of pale. "Was it another secret?" she asked.

"Yes, this one about Nancy." Winnie used the back of her hand to feel Eliana's forehead. "I'm going to make you a drink. Something with sugar in it." At least helping her granddaughter feel better was something she could control right now.

Julia and Cameron arrived with the fabric—"I call the lavender!" Eliana yelled—and soon after, Lisa came with her sewing supplies. The bungalow felt so much less lonely with everyone there. Winnie brought out the cookies she'd picked up from the store—who had time to bake with all these dresses to be made? But none of them seemed to care that they'd come from a package as they dug in. She watched them, love for each of them filling her. It almost choked her up.

Get it together, Winnie. We have too much to do to be blubbering about. Not only did they have the wedding, but she needed to do more to set up Eliana and Asher. They'd hit it off at the turtle fundraiser, but she'd dropped the ball since then.

"So who's your plus-one for the wedding, Eliana?" Winnie asked, going for subtle but missing the mark, if Eliana's stifled laugh was any indication.

"No one. I'm going alone."

"You can't."

"Sure, she can," Julia jumped in to say. "Dates aren't required."

"If they are, I call Cameron," Eliana said.

"Cameron is going with Shayla," their mom said absently as she set up her sewing machine.

"You have a date? Go, Cam!" Eliana and Julia high-fived him.

Winnie was happy for him, too, but she needed to stay focused. "That does mean you'll be the only person without a date."

Eliana snorted. "Way to make me sound pathetic, Grandma."

"It's not pathetic, dear. Just lonely." Her heart pinged with her own loneliness, but she soldiered on. "And think of all the questions you'll get."

"Everyone knows she has her Happily Single platform," Julia said around a mouthful of cookie. *Not helpful, Julia.*

"And I'm not interested in dating."

"Exactly. And everyone is going to be trying to set you up all night. It'll be exhausting," Grandma Winnie continued.

"Who would do that, Mom?" Lisa said. "Our family doesn't have big matchmaker energy."

Et tu, Brute? Winnie carried on despite her family's less-than-helpful comments. "Perhaps you could convince a young man to be your fake date for the wedding, just to avoid questions." She'd read that story trope in an Allegra Winters book recently, and the main characters had fallen madly in love. "But who could you ask? Oh, I know! Asher. He'd do it."

Eliana, Julia, and Lisa looked at her like she was nuts before all three broke into peals of laughter. Winnie felt indignant at first—fake dating was a great idea—but their laughter caught on, especially when Julia choked on the cookie she was eating and started yelling out she couldn't breathe, while clearly breathing.

"Oh, Mom, I thought you were serious for a minute there," Lisa said, between bouts of wheezing laughter. "Fake dating. You're hilarious."

"Fake dating is just about the only dating I'd agree to," Eliana quipped before dropping into giggles again. "Let me run it by Asher."

"Please, please ask him," Julia said, her hands in the prayer position. "Let us know what he says."

"It doesn't work if everyone knows it's fake," Winnie grumbled, wiping away her own tears of mirth. The doorbell rang, and Winnie went to answer it while everyone worked out who else Eliana could ask to be her fake date to the wedding.

So that idea had bombed, but that didn't mean she'd given up. If the Secret Seven could be deterred by one bad idea or one scheme gone wrong, they'd have given up a long time ago.

She opened the door distractedly, still half listening to the conversation when her eyes landed on the tall, handsome gentleman standing in the doorway. He wore light-gray slacks and a white shirt with the sleeves rolled up to his elbows, and he was holding a small bouquet of colorful daisies.

Her favorite. He remembered.

"Hi, Winnie." His voice sucked her back in time nearly sixty years, and it was like no time had passed at all.

"Gerard," she breathed. Oh, no. No, no, no.

It couldn't be.

Gerard Hammond was her first husband. The one no one, *not even Horace*, knew about.

She pushed him against the chest—his very muscular chest—and out the door before her daughter and grandkids could see him. "What are you doing here?" she hissed, feeling more flustered than she had in a long time. She ran a hand over her hair, hair that hadn't seen the inside of a salon in almost six weeks. She probably had roots for days.

What was she doing? She brought her hand down to her side and straightened her shoulders. She would *not* feel self-conscious in front of Gerard.

He held out his phone, and she saw Wedded Bliss, the social media page the Secret Seven had started. He'd pulled up the viral post of her and Horace. "I'm here to see you."

CHAPTER 23
ELIANA

"You are like a chestnut burr, prickly outside, but silky-soft within, and a sweet kernel, if one can only get at it. Love will make you show your heart someday, and then the rough burr will fall off." —Louisa May Alcott

E LIANA LAID HER CLOTHES on Asher's bed to decide what she should wear tonight for Salsa and Salsa. Was this the kind of activity that required dressing up? Or was it more casual? She threw the question out on social media, and immediately got answers that she needed to dress sexily in order to appropriately dance the salsa.

She frowned at her options. She could wear her jeans. Her jean shorts. Her swimsuit—she giggled, imagining Asher's face if that's what she wore. It was tempting for that reason alone, but she'd better not. Her swimsuit cover-up could work. It was a teal-green cotton sundress that hit her about mid-thigh and made her tan legs look pretty fantastic. She paired it with some dangling earrings and a pair of leather strappy sandals.

Asher said he'd meet her at The Palms' ballroom, so once she was ready, she sneaked around the back of the house and walked. The sun was just setting, and it was one of those gorgeous summer evenings where the humidity eased up enough to remind a person why they lived in Florida.

She waved at Don and Nancy, who walked together, talking intensely. They narrowed their eyes when they spotted her before quickly walking away. Okay.

She debated stopping by Grandma Winnie's house, but opted against doing so when she saw the time. Grandma had been acting weird since their sewing day. It felt almost like she'd been avoiding them, but that couldn't be right. She was probably tired. After her collapse last year, they'd all been on edge, worried that something like that might happen again.

Sweetie and Bear lounged by the fountain just outside of The Palms. Sweetie had one foot draped in the fountain, and Bear slept on his back with all four legs in the air. They weren't dressed in adorable outfits today. That was a first. Eliana had no fondness for the alligator, but it gave her an off feeling to see them without their playful costumes.

She walked inside, and instead of the usual friendly waves and smiles, she was met with silence. People milled about, not making eye contact with one another, like robots going from point A to point B. Something was definitely wrong.

She found Polly at the entrance to the ballroom.

"Bruno is inside waiting for you." Polly glanced behind Eliana. "Where's Asher? Is he not coming?"

"He'll be here," Eliana assured her. "What's going on, Polly? It seems like there's a huge cloud over The Palms today."

Polly sucked in her bottom lip, looked around, and then leaned close to whisper. "Whoever is revealing secrets posted five today. And some of them were pretty ... personal. And one of them illegal." She winced.

"Oh no." Eliana could guess. "Embezzlement?"

Polly nodded. "Did you see it?" Luckily, Polly didn't wait for an answer. "Until we know who it is, no one trusts anyone right now." Something must have shown on Eliana's expression, because Polly patted her hand. "Oh, we know it isn't you, dear. But everyone's on guard. It's not a good feeling to have your past mistakes dredged up for everyone to see."

Guilt dumped over Eliana like a bucket of ice water. She and Asher needed to figure out who was sharing these secrets ... and soon. Before all of Diamond Cove was torn apart.

In the endearingly gruff way that only Bruno could pull off, he informed Eliana that they couldn't wait any longer for Asher and needed to get started.

She sighed and checked her phone, but there was still no response to her message: *Are you coming?* He was only fifteen minutes late, but she knew him well enough to realize this was unusual for him.

He's fine, she told herself.

Bruno put her to work cutting up roasted tomatoes while he explained the importance of using a sharp knife. They slid the tomatoes into the food processor, and then he passed along the roasted peppers, onions, and garlic.

"Eyes on the knife!" Bruno barked as her knife slipped and she nearly cut her finger as she glanced at the doorway again.

"Sorry," she said, but she didn't complain when Bruno motioned for her to give him the knife and finished cutting the onions in a fraction of the time it would have taken her.

"Hey, sorry I'm late!"

Eliana's breath caught at the sight of Asher strolling in. He wore a white oxford that molded to his biceps and pecs, and the sleeves were rolled up to the elbow, showing off his toned forearms. She knew he was muscular. She'd seen him without a shirt, for Pete's sake. But something about the contrast of his dark, hard edges in this button-up was doing something for her. Something that made the room suddenly feel a bazillion degrees. Bazillion was a word, right? She couldn't even think straight.

He'd also gotten a haircut and beard trim. It was still him, just with clean lines from head to toe. She suddenly felt lightheaded and was very grateful Bruno'd had the foresight to take the knife from her.

Asher ran a hand over his hair self-consciously, and she realized she was staring. She blinked and tore her gaze away with effort. Monumental effort.

He came to stand beside her. That was worse. He smelled like sandalwood and fresh air, an intoxicating combination. She swiveled toward Bruno and focused on his rapid cutting skills.

It's just Asher. Your grumpy roomie.

Who was also an amazing chef. Who swam every day and had the arms and chest to prove it. Who was a study in contradictions with his octopus tattoo and resistance to loving all animals. Who ordered flowers for old women, but helped Eliana beat out everyone on an obstacle course no matter their age.

Who might be hard and gruff on the surface, but had an irresistible soft side.

"I got caught up at the barber, but I should have called," he continued, and she realized she hadn't said anything. But what could she say? Her throat was tight.

Shake it off, Elly.

She swallowed and faced him head-on, like the brave social media influencer she was. Looking at Asher was like diving into a cold pool. At first, it was shocking to the entire system—hard to breathe, hard to think, even. But after a short amount of time, you got used to the temperature and your body went back to baseline.

"It's fine," she thought she said. But instead, somehow, the breathy words that came out of her mouth were, "You look *really* good." Okay, so not back to baseline yet.

He looked away almost bashfully.

Stop it, Asher! Stop being so dang cute.

"Thanks." He cleared his throat. "It's been too long since my last haircut. I never intended for it to grow so long in the first place, but after ... everything, I stopped caring for a while."

"I'm glad you didn't cut it too short," she blurted. Why not just spill out every thought in her mind? "And that you kept the beard. Women dig a beard."

He lifted a brow. "All women?"

"All women," she said firmly, even though she knew that couldn't possibly be true. But safety in numbers, right? "I have it on good authority that Miss Havisham is particularly hot for men with beards."

Asher barked out a laugh. Bruno pretended not to hear them, though both of his brows winged upward.

Asher's shoulder bumped into hers as they watched Bruno make the salsa. "I'm mostly occupied by what Louisa May Alcott thinks."

The temperature in Eliana's body shot up. Forget a cold pool. She was in a sauna.

Bruno turned on the food processor and drowned out any further conversation. By the time Bruno stopped pulsing the salsa, Eliana had wrangled her body's temp back to normal, and everything was good again.

Bruno unceremoniously plopped a bowl of warm chips in front of them, and then he dumped the salsa into a gorgeous yellow serving dish. "Here. We're only doing one salsa. Your dance instructor will be here soon." With that, he turned on his heel and marched out.

"A friendly guy," she commented.

"The president of our outreach committee."

"Makes sense."

They dug into the chips and salsa, and Eliana was grateful for something to keep their mouths occupied. Every second that ticked by, she relaxed more into being with Asher.

"So my grandma approached me with an interesting idea."

"What's that?" He scooped salsa onto his chip and put the entire thing in his mouth.

"You should be my fake boyfriend at Julia's wedding."

Asher's eyes flew wide, and he choked on his chip. His face turned red as she filled a glass of water for him from the pitcher Bruno had left, and he guzzled it down between coughs.

"What?" he croaked out.

"It's no big deal," she said as casually as she could while she picked through the chips for a full-sized one. "I'm sure all the grandparents try to convince you to fake-date their granddaughters."

"Nope." He refilled his glass, and his voice sounded almost normal. "This is a first."

"But I'm *sure* she's just being a proud grandma when she suggested that I take you to my sister's wedding and pretend to be in love with you." There. The perfect chip. She dipped it into the salsa, getting just the right amount on it. Perfection.

"Okay. Fine." Asher held up his hands. "You win. It does seem like Winnie is trying to set us up."

"Thank you!" she crowed, but then her expression turned serious. "Do you want to be my fake, fake boyfriend for the wedding, or what? Let's make her day."

He gave her a skeptical eyebrow raise. "*Fake*, fake boyfriend?"

"Yes, pretend that you're pretending to date me. Lots of layers." She stacked her hands on top of one another.

"Too many layers. I'm more of a simple guy."

She put a hand on her chest and gasped in mock outrage. "You won't pretend to be in fake love with me? Rude."

He grinned and held up his hands. "What would be involved? Hugging? Holding hands?" His eyes twinkled mischievously. "Kissing?"

Her stomach felt weightless, like she was coasting over a wave on a boogie board. "Um ..."

"If we can drop two of those 'pretends,' I'm in."

Salsa dropped from her chip onto the floor.

The door flew open, echoing through the ballroom. "¡Hola! I am Alondro Sanchez." An older Latino man in a black tuxedo with a red vest and bow tie glided toward them as if on a conveyor belt. His hair was mostly black, except for the white patches at his temple, and his mahogany brown eyes sparkled with excitement. "You must be the lucky winners, Asher and Eliana! Are you ready to salsa?"

"Yes." Asher held out his hand to Eliana, his eyebrows rising in challenge. *Do you dare?*

Eliana always dared. She snatched Asher's hand and led him a little more forcefully than necessary onto the dance floor.

"Salsa is a fusion of many different dance styles, but heavily relies on Cuban and Puerto Rican influence." Alondro started to dance with an invisible partner, his feet moving forward and backward, his hips swaying, as he continued his explanation. "The salsa is about living in the moment and spicing things up."

He walked them through some basic steps, and it took most of Eliana's concentration to follow along. She'd never been a great dancer, but she loved learning new things. He counted their steps out and turned on some music.

"Very good," he said. "But the salsa is not about dancing alone. It is about being with your partner—expressing your desire for them through your movements."

Her cheeks pinked, and she refused to look at Asher.

"Asher, take Eliana by the hand, and I want you two to do the dance steps to my count before I turn the music on."

She reluctantly faced Asher, steeling herself for the sight of him. *Come on, brain. Acclimate already.* But nope. Still just as stupidly handsome as he was before. So inconsiderate.

"I wish I hadn't eaten the salsa," he said to her as they followed Alondro's count.

"Why?" she asked.

He gave her a wry smile and ticked off the answer on two fingers. "Garlic and onion."

She released an unexpected laugh. "Yeah, maybe we should have saved the salsa for after the close dancing."

"Probably would have been wise. Bruno did not have my back."

Maybe not. But he'd had hers.

They went through the steps woodenly as Alondro counted to eight.

"Feel the dance," Alondro said to them. "Right now, you're too worried about how the steps look. I want you to reach into how it feels."

They tried again, but Eliana kept stepping forward when she should have stepped back, or turning right when she should have turned left. She stared at her feet, trying to memorize the steps, frustrated at doing so poorly.

"Can I show you?" Alondro held out his hand, and when Eliana took it, he swiveled her into him. "Look at me, sweet Eliana, not at your feet. Don't let your eyes dictate the dance. Feel it."

She *felt* herself stepping all over his shiny black shoes.

"Close your eyes," Alondro said. "Let go of control. Let go of trying to do it right, and lean into the experience."

She closed her eyes, reluctantly, but it did force her to feel for the way his hand led her to the next dance move. They didn't dance to music, just the sound of their breathing and Alondro's lyrical counting.

Layer by layer, she dropped her expectations of herself—to be the best, to win at this, to be mistake free—and she just danced. She felt like a lazily flowing brook gliding peacefully over smooth stones, instead of the raging river trying to smash through rocks she usually channeled.

And it felt ... good. Freeing.

"Perfect!" Alondro announced as he pulled her to a gentle stop, and he spoke quietly, just for her to hear. "When you allow yourself to breathe in the movements and trust yourself, you finally become who you are meant to be. Salsa mimics life in this way. Now, for your partner."

She stepped back while Alondro spoke quietly with Asher. Alondro showed Asher how to lead with his hand high on her ribs, and then he said a few more things that had Asher darting glances in her direction. Asher nodded, and when he walked toward Eliana, it was with purposeful steps and a heated expression.

Her blood was a molten river racing through her veins. Acclimating to this version of Asher was impossible.

"Take your partner," Alondro instructed.

Asher stood in front of Eliana and held out his hand, waiting for her to take it. She hesitated, but of course she slid her fingers into his. How could she not?

His hand was large around her small, slender fingers. He brushed his thumb along the soft skin at the inside of her palm, sending a pleasant shiver through her.

Alondro pressed play on his phone, and the opening notes of a salsa song filled the ballroom via the Bluetooth speakers. "This song is about desire and longing, about endless days of separation spiraling toward passionate nights together—"

Asher's hand tightened almost imperceptibly on hers, and he led her in the steps they'd just learned. His body emanated heat as it moved tantalizingly close to hers, reeling her in with desire and flinging her away before the fulfillment of it.

One of her hands gripped his, while the other held his muscular shoulder. His firm deltoids under her hand led to a bulging bicep that begged for her to trail her fingers down it. What would he do if she pressed her lips to his neck? If she buried her hands in his hair?

His eyes darkened as if he could read her thoughts. He spun her out, and when he pulled her back in, she was much closer to him than before.

Energy pulsed between them, visceral and heady.

The music stopped, and it was just the two of them in the room, breathless with exertion. With passion. With possibility. Eliana was drawn to Asher like a magnetic force specific only to her, drawing her toward him no matter where he went, linking them in sensations she'd never felt before. Brick by brick, her walls crumbled around her, leaving her bare, exposed. But with Asher, she felt safe.

His gaze flickered to her mouth, and her lips parted as her eyes fluttered shut. She'd never wanted anything more than to be connected to Asher. To have his mouth pressed to hers. To kiss him until she couldn't think or talk or breathe, but just exist. His breath flitted against her lips. He was a mere whisper away.

"Great job!" Alondro clapped his hands, tearing her painfully from the spell. She blinked through the haze of desire, unsteady with that confused feeling she sometimes had after being awoken from a deep sleep. "You two are naturals. And your chemistry?" He did a chef's kiss.

Confusion buffeted Eliana like wave after endless wave attempting to drag her down.

"Thank you," Asher said to Alondro. His voice was thick, and he cleared his throat. "That was really fun."

"Fun," she said weakly. Was that the word she'd use? Enlightening? Intoxicating? Frightening?

They left the ballroom, the silence between them charged. When Eliana was a kid, she used to scuff her shoes against the carpet, never letting her feet break contact until after she touched Julia on the arm so she could shock her and make her sister shriek.

That's how she felt now. If she broke this moment, one of them would get hurt. She didn't know if it would be her or Asher, but either way, she didn't like it.

They arrived at the exit leading out of The Palms, and Asher tugged her to a stop. He rubbed his free hand along the back of his neck. "Eliana, I—"

"Asher!" Mr. Richardson approached them, panting, Polly at his heels. She threw them an apologetic grimace. "I have an interested party for your grandpa's bungalow."

"He's not ready yet—" Polly began, but Mr. Richardson cut her off.

"I've been more than generous with the time allotted," he said. "I need you to have the bungalow completely cleared out in two weeks. Anything that's not moved, I'll have disposed of at your expense."

Eliana hadn't realized how bright Asher's light had shone through him all evening, until Mr. Richardson reached out with his two fingers and snuffed it out. She wanted to set an alligator on him—and not one whose mouth was bound by a leather strap like Sweetie.

"But my sister's wedding is in two weeks," Eliana said. "And Asher is playing a huge role." That might be overstating things, but being her *fake*, fake boyfriend was serious business.

Mr. Richardson peered at her as if trying to place who she was. "Fine. I'll give you until the following Monday. Does that suit?" he asked sarcastically.

"Yes," Asher said. "I'll make sure everything is out by then."

"If you need to take a few days off of work to make it happen, I'm sure we can arrange for that."

Asher's jaw clenched. She gripped his hand as Mr. Richardson walked away with a spring to his step.

CHAPTER 24

ASHER

A SHER DID NOT TAKE Mr. Richardson up on his offer to let him take a few days off of work, and instead did the opposite—worked nonstop. His charting had never been more thorough. His schedule had never been fuller. And he offered to take every single new patient who called.

Busy was good. Busy meant he didn't have time or energy to think about the house or what he was going to do in two weeks when he couldn't live there anymore.

The only bright spot was Eliana Peters. Since their salsa lesson a few nights before, things had shifted between them. Some of their easy camaraderie was gone, and Eliana seemed more tentative around him. But she hadn't bolted, and Asher was taking that as a good sign.

Alondro's advice when he'd pulled Asher aside in the ballroom still rang through his mind. "She is a strong woman, and I love a strong woman. But you are letting her do all the leading, and it is making you both stumble. In dance, it is give and take. Small signals that direct where you go as a partnership. Be confident. Be bold. And see what happens."

What happened was that they'd almost kissed—and that moment had been hotter than any actual kiss he'd ever had in his life. Despite Alondro's presence. Despite Mr. Richardson soaking them with his rain cloud.

Even now, Asher pulled at the back collar of his scrubs to allow some airflow. What he wouldn't give to go back to that moment again. It was easy to be confident on the dance floor, with Alondro lending him a boost, when they were caught in the moment. It was quite another when they were surrounded by boxes that provided a constant reminder that he'd be without a home soon.

All morning, people had complimented him on his haircut and beard trim. He should have done this a long time ago. He'd never let it grow so long and messy before, but after Grandpa died, he'd stopped caring. The fog that had descended over Asher was finally lifting.

He'd regretted the trim the moment he'd done it, though. He'd stared in the mirror at the barber and realized he was laying most of his cards down on the table. Eliana was going to know he'd done this for her. But the stunned expression on her face had taken away every doubt he'd had. And the way her lips had so willingly parted as he'd leaned toward her after their dance ...

Why was it so dang hot in here?

He sat at his desk, playing around with some new software for augmentative communication devices, when someone knocked on his office door. "Come in."

Eliana opened the door. Tote bags hung from each of her shoulders, and she gripped a bulging paper bag. "Are you busy?"

He motioned her in. "Not for you."

She appeared almost flustered as she closed the door behind her and set everything on his desk. Her gaze caught on the shelf beside his desk, and she walked over to it to study the books and knickknacks he had there. She must have walked to his office from the bungalow, because her hair was stuck to her neck in sweaty tendrils and her cheeks were a bright, glistening pink. The sight of her was like getting slammed by a massive wave—both breathtaking and exhilarating.

It felt strangely intimate to have her studying the items he kept close to him.

"Are these your grandparents'?" She pointed to the salt-and-pepper shaker set Harry had helped him complete.

"Yep. Grandma loved those as much as she loved my grandpa." Which was why it had been so devastating when he'd shattered one of them. He loved seeing the set back together. It might not have been the exact one she'd used, but it still made him happy to see.

Eliana took a seat across from him. "I brought you lunch. A turkey sandwich with sprouts, tomatoes, lettuce, and avocado. Plus a bag of chips." She pulled them from a paper bag and plunked them down in front of him, along with a chilled bottle of water. Heaven.

He opened the bottle and drank half of it down with one breath. "You didn't have to do that."

She leveled him with a "come on" stare. "You're letting me live in your house and sleep in your bed and eat your food. The least I can do is bring you lunch. Especially since I accidentally killed the outlet and forgot to tell you." She winced.

He'd plugged his phone in to charge and hadn't realized that the outlet wasn't working until he'd woken up with only minutes to spare before his first appointment—and a dead phone. "It's fine. I was only ten minutes late, and I caught up pretty quick."

"Still." She pulled a homemade rice crispy treat from the bag. "Here's an apology treat. I made it this morning. I know it's not gourmet, but—"

"Thank you," he said. Emotion hit him unexpectedly, like a 2x4 to the side of the head. It was more than the food she brought, but that feeling of someone caring for him. Of *Eliana* caring for him. He dug into his turkey sandwich before he started to do something he couldn't come back from—like bawling like a baby or proposing. Either one would probably scare her off.

She riffled through one of the totes and pulled out a breathable container with Louisa May Alcott in it. "Louisa says hi," she told him. She opened the top and set it on his desk.

"Hi, Louisa," he replied, placing his finger close enough for Louisa to nudge her nose against it. He felt Eliana's happy smile all the way down to his toes. So what if he was talking to a turtle, losing his home in two weeks, and would be completely adrift? He'd made Eliana smile today.

"Also, I brought this," she said, her eyes alight with energy. From the other canvas tote bag, she lifted a black plastic rounded box that looked familiar. "I had a few minutes this morning to go through boxes—"

"Elly, you don't have to do that."

Was it just him, or did she settle even more comfortably into the chair at the sound of her nickname? It had just slipped out.

"I know," she said. "I want to. I filmed some content, but I needed a break. I tried to write, but it's like walking through tar today."

He hoped it was because she was feeling less committed to her vow of singleness.

She handed him the box, and he flipped it open to reveal alphabetized index cards with names and contact information written on them. "It's his Rolodex," he said.

"Flip to where I put the sticky note." She retrieved another rice crispy treat from the paper bag—how much food did she have in there?—and took a bite.

He navigated to the letter M, and then he saw it. Michael.

Eliana's voice was soft. "I know it's been bothering you, why your grandpa would have dug up so much dirt on everyone."

"Should I call him?" he asked. Seeing his grandpa's familiar cursive made him feel shaky and unable to think clearly.

"I think you should," she said.

No time like the present. He pulled out his cell phone and dialed the number into it.

"This is Mike," the no-nonsense voice answered.

"Hi, this is Asher. Asher Brooks. I'm Mason Brooks's grandson." Eliana smiled encouragingly, and he continued. "He died. Last year. And while cleaning out his things, I found a strange box—and a letter to you." He stumbled through the words, not sure how to explain, what information to give, if this was even the right Michael.

There was a pause, followed by a heavy sigh. "I wondered when this day would come."

Asher straightened. "You know what I'm talking about?"

"I do. But this conversation would be better in person. Where are you?"

"In Diamond Cove."

"I'm in Orlando. Let's meet for dinner next week." They determined a time and place, and Michael hung up.

Eliana came around his desk and stood between his legs to give him a hug. He rested his head against her chest, barely hearing her heartbeat over the sound of the blood rushing through his ears.

Her hand ran a steady rhythm at the back of his head, and he breathed her in. He shouldn't let himself feel this way. Eliana was just one more person for him to lose. But at this point, it was too late. It was going to hurt whether or not he leaned into this, and being with Eliana made every risk seem worth it.

Her fingers scratched at the back of his neck, and he was nearly undone. "Eliana," he growled. Begging. For what? Space? No space at all?

Then, so slowly she could pull away at any moment, he tugged her into his lap. Her arms wrapped around his neck like they were always meant to be there. The tug between them was unstoppable, and she must have felt it as strongly as he did as she stared into his eyes.

"So intensely green," she murmured, and he recalled their first conversation. They'd come so far since then. "There's no way people can focus on speech therapy when you look at them like this."

"I don't look at anyone else like this."

"Lucky me." Her eyelids fluttered shut, and her soft lips pressed against his. That was all it took for him. He wrapped his arms even tighter around her waist and kissed her back. All the problems dragging him down like an insurmountable riptide released him with one touch, one breath.

Kissing Eliana was better than he'd ever imagined, and yet somehow as earth-shattering as he thought it might be. Fire raced through his veins as she dug her fingers into his hair and deepened their kiss, just as drawn in by him as he was by her. That would never cease to amaze him.

She pulled away slowly but kept her forehead pressed to Asher's as they both breathed hard. He threaded his fingers through hers and brought them to his lips to kiss every knuckle and then her palm. She gave a short intake of breath as he gently bit the tip of her thumb.

They sat, suspended in that moment, until she scrambled off of his lap and several feet away. Her chest rose and fell rapidly, and her cheeks were even pinker than they'd been when she'd arrived.

She straightened out her shirt and put a hand to her hair, which was mussed from him running his fingers through it. Her lips were slightly swollen and raw from kissing. She licked them, and he nearly groaned.

"Well, that was ... good practice. For the pretending to pretend thing. For the wedding. Good kissing practice." Her hand went to her mouth, maybe to feel her lips, maybe to stop herself from rambling.

He leaned back in his chair, satisfied to realize he could throw her off just as easily as she could him.

She continued to talk as she gathered her things. "The fake, fake pretend stuff, you know. Kissing, holding hands, all that. To make Grandma happy and keep my family from trying to set me up, though I don't think they'd do that—other than Grandma, of course, who is like a matchmaking wrecking ball." She pantomimed a wrecking ball smashing into a building.

He bit back his smile as she put his half-eaten sandwich into the tote with the Rolodex, followed by her sticky rice crispy treat.

She hopped to her feet and headed toward the door. "Okay, then. I'm leaving. You're busy and—"

"Elly."

She turned to him with an expression that was trying so hard to go for nonchalance.

"You're forgetting something."

"Hm?"

He came around his desk carrying Louisa May Alcott in her container. She must be really in her head to almost leave her turtle behind.

"Oh. Thank you." She reached out to take it.

Asher held on to his end of the container and leaned forward close enough to breathe her in. "Eliana? I'm not pretending."

Her eyes widened. He let go of Louisa May Alcott's container as she tugged, and then she swiveled around and fled from the room.

CHAPTER 25

WINNIE

COULD PEOPLE FROM WINNIE's past *please* stop coming to Diamond Cove?

Retirement was supposed to be easy. Relaxing. Not filled with rivals and ex-husbands and romantic posts going viral and granddaughters writing books convincing people to stay single.

She needed one thing in her life to go right. Just one.

As if her thoughts had tempted fate, the bridesmaid dress she'd been running through the sewing machine snagged, and an entire thread bunched up under the runner, running down the length of the fabric and ruining it. That's it. That was the last straw. She was going to die right then or ...

She stood and released a chest-deep scream. The kind of scream she might let out if a murderer was in her master closet, one that made her throat hurt and would give Horace a heart attack *if* he was actually home to hear it. The sound died out.

Whoa. That felt good.

So she did it again. And again, until her voice gave way and her head swam with dizziness. Why hadn't anyone told her that screaming could be so amazing? Free therapy. And people were hoarding this secret? She'd spent so much of her life being quiet, sitting back, playing nice, not saying anything—and it felt amazing to actually hear her own voice for once.

She collapsed into her chair and looked at the dress. The top was salvageable, but the entire skirt needed to be cut off. She didn't have enough fabric for a whole new skirt, which meant she either had a mismatching skirt, or ...

She groaned. No. She'd promised herself she'd never make another short dress again. But she didn't have any other option. At least Eliana had inherited her long legs.

Her phone buzzed and buzzed, but she ignored it to finish the dress, until finally a knock at the door pulled her from her sewing haze. She opened it with trepidation, half expecting to find Gerard, but luckily, she hadn't seen him since he'd come to the house. After he'd arrived so unexpectedly, she'd insisted he leave before her family saw him, promising to talk soon, but had avoided him ever since.

Rosa stood there, an annoyed expression on her face. "Vamos. The meeting is about to start."

"What meeting?" Winnie asked.

Rosa's eyes narrowed. "Are you sick? Your voice is hoarse. I'll make you some honey tea later, but we need to go." She tugged on Winnie's arm, and Winnie—no match for Rosa on a mission—followed her out.

When they arrived at the conference room at The Palms, everyone was already there, but they weren't casually chatting like usual. Instead, they glanced warily at one another, or stared at their phones like they always complained their grandchildren did.

"Winnie and Rosa are here," Nancy said. "Let's get started. First, an update, Winnie." She looked at her expectantly.

"Oh, right." What update could she give? That she'd been too busy to come up with more matchmaking schemes? "I think we need to take a hiatus until the wedding."

She expected an argument. A reminder that Eliana was going home after the wedding. For someone to offer to step in and help, or come up with a brilliant wedding-matchmaking plan that would clinch the deal between those two.

Instead, she got five murmurs of agreement, and from Polly, one half-hearted statement. "Alondro said they looked pretty cozy at salsa and salsa, though Bruno said they were incompetent and he's never doing that again."

They all knew Bruno didn't mean it. He'd be running another cooking class by the end of summer, but he liked complaining as much as he liked cooking.

"Okay, well, that's settled," Don said. "We'll meet again after the wedding."

"Meeting adjourned," Nancy said.

Everyone filed out, except for Winnie, who sat in stunned silence. Polly was the last to leave, so Winnie grabbed her by the belt loop and held her back. Polly always loved a good gossip session.

"What's going on?" Winnie asked.

"You don't know?" Polly asked.

It took all of Winnie's willpower not to motion with her hands for Polly to hurry it up.

Polly lowered her voice, even though it was just the two of them in the room. "No one trusts anyone anymore. Who is keeping secrets from everyone? And more importantly, who is revealing all these secrets?"

Winnie felt like she'd swallowed one of her huge pills wrong.

"In the Secret Seven, only Don, Rosa, and Walt haven't had anything revealed about them yet. Harry has that country record, Nancy with the election, I dye my hair black, and you and Horace with the Smitty rivalry."

Winnie's relief nearly overwhelmed her.

"Everyone's thinking the culprit must be someone who won't reveal any secrets about themselves, so it's just a process of elimination, but there are still at least a hundred people who haven't had secrets revealed about them yet. Don, Rosa, and Walt swear it's not them—and you know it's not me. I can't even remember how old I am half the time, much less everyone's pasts—but since there's a possibility, everyone's wary."

Winnie nodded, seeing what she meant. "Then add the fact that we're learning things about our friends that they never told us."

"It's hurtful to realize they don't trust us enough to tell us these things."

"But everyone has things they'd rather stay in their past," Winnie defended. "It's not about trust but moving on."

"I agree," Polly said. "So how do we get the rest of them on board?"

"I don't know." Winnie rested her chin in her hand.

"In the meantime," Polly said, "you probably haven't heard about the silver fox, either." She shimmied her shoulders.

"No." Winnie could use a good story. She rubbed at a knot in her shoulder, wishing Horace could really work it out for her.

"He's moving into Mason Brooks's old place, which is a shame, but he is not hard on the eyes at all. His name is Gerard ..." She continued to talk, but Winnie's brain got caught on the name like an old record on a scratch.

"I have to go." She cut Polly off in the middle of explaining what kind of work he'd done in Washington D.C. She raced out of the room, looking everywhere for Gerard. She'd been avoiding him so effectively, she didn't know where to find him now.

And he might not even be here. He hadn't moved in yet. Her heart lightened. She still had time to stop this. To get him to see reason. To convince him to go home and leave her alone.

She was so engaged in her hopeful thoughts that she didn't see Lydia and nearly bowled her over as she raced out of the dining hall. Lydia appeared much older than she had a year ago when they'd moved here. A mild stroke had affected her ability to walk, and she now used a walker. For so many years, Lydia had been a sassy, fast-talking woman who Winnie wished she could be more like, and it was difficult to see her looking so vulnerable.

"Hi, Lydia," she said. Part of her wanted to keep rushing about, looking for Gerard, but one look in Lydia's sad eyes and she knew she needed to stop and talk to her friend. "Let's find a seat."

They did, and for an hour the two women talked about their grandchildren and the wedding, until the topic of conversation circled around to their husbands.

"Smitty is gone all the time," Lydia said. "And it's not as easy for me to get out and about as it used to be."

"I'm sorry." Winnie placed her hand over Lydia's. "Let's have a standing lunch date. Every Monday. Does that work for you?"

"You don't have to do that. You have your friends and your life." Lydia pulled her hand away. She looked past Winnie's shoulder, and Winnie turned to find Gerard standing ten feet away, waiting patiently to talk to her. She pretended not to see.

"I want to, Lydia. We used to be the best of friends, and I miss that."

"Me too. I think someone is trying to get your attention."

Winnie frowned. She turned, and sure enough, Gerard had moved to being only five feet away. "Do you have a moment?" he asked.

She gave Lydia a hug and walked away quickly. They needed to chat away from public hearing. Once they entered the empty conference room, she rounded on him. "You're moving here?"

"It's a nice place."

"There are other nice places," she said through her teeth. She'd help him find them, if she needed to.

"Not with you there." He took her hand. "I've missed you, Winnie. You're still a very beautiful woman."

She didn't know what to do with that compliment. Part of her loved hearing it, but another part of her pulled back hard. It felt disloyal to Horace to be in this room with him, much less listening to compliments. She tugged her hand away. "You can't say that," she told him.

"Why not? It's true. I know your husband doesn't appreciate you. That he's gone all the time. That you took him to the same movie we went to when we first met."

Her face drain of blood. Oh no. She remembered it now. The movie she'd recalled going to with Horace. She'd gone with Gerard. How could she have gotten the two of them mixed up?

She'd so desperately wanted to forget her first marriage. What would Horace think if he knew she'd been married before and never told him? Revealed secrets were tearing the Secret Seven apart. What about her marriage? After her divorce, she'd been so young, so embarrassed, she'd wanted to put it all behind her. Her parents had been more than happy to pretend her first marriage had never happened. "I love Horace, Gerard. What you and I had was a mistake, and it was so long ago."

"Meet me for lunch," he said, as if she hadn't spoken at all.

"I can't. Please, Gerard. Please leave."

"And I can't do that," he said with a determined glint in his eyes she hadn't forgotten, even after all these years. Gerard had never been a bad man, but he had run over her desires like a truck tire over a daisy. Never willing to compromise or give in. It had been exciting being with the most popular boy in school, until she'd felt suffocated under the force of him and started to lose who she was.

Luckily, he'd divorced her. He'd always been a flirt—he had a way of making you feel like you were the most amazing person in the world—and though he never said, she suspected he'd grown bored of her as she'd shrunk to almost nothing in their marriage. It had been the worst thing that had ever happened to her—and also the best. If he hadn't left her, she never would have met Horace. And she never would have had this incredible life with him. With *all* the people she loved with her entire soul.

Gerard kissed her gently on the cheek, then turned and walked away—Gerard always had to have the last word—and Winnie watched him go. Someone in Diamond Cove was spilling everyone's biggest secrets ... and her biggest secret ever was moving right into her backyard.

CHAPTER 26

ELIANA

"I want to do something splendid ... something heroic or won-derful that won't be forgotten after I'm dead. I don't know what, but I'm on the watch for it and mean to astonish you all someday." —*Louisa May Alcott*

T HE WEEKS LEADING UP to the wedding were a complete whirl of finalizing the cake, setting up appointments for hair and makeup, and following up with catering, and now they were deciding if they should set up the flower archway facing the ocean or facing the beach.

"Think about how amazing the pictures will be with the ocean behind us," Julia said. Hot wind whipped through their hair, pushing it into their eyes and mouth. Hopefully the wind would be much less intense during the wedding. It was still too early to check the weather forecast, but Julia said that same day had been sunny and clear for the last six years.

But seven years ago, it had stormed so bad all of Diamond Cove had lost power.

"They would look good," Eliana agreed. Which was why she'd made that very point twenty minutes ago. But Julia wanted to walk through all the scenarios.

"But I'd love to look out and see all of my friends and family with the ocean behind them. That would be lovely too." She sighed and faced the other direction, her eyes half closed as if trying to picture it.

Eliana's phone buzzed, and she pulled up a notification on a new town home in Diamond Cove that was up for rent. She'd set up alerts, hoping something perfect for Asher would pop up. This one seemed really nice, except for the amount they were asking for rent. Maybe too nice. But she didn't know how much money speech therapists made, so she starred it to show him later.

"Whatcha doin'?" Julia peered over her shoulder. Her eyes lit up when she saw the house listing, and she excitedly grabbed Eliana's arm. "Are you moving home?"

Eliana started to tell her she was helping a friend, but then paused. Why not move home? What was keeping her in Boston? She could work from anywhere, and she'd missed having her family so close. "I'm thinking about it," she said.

Julia squealed. "I'd love that so much. I've been really worried about being gone for four months, and I'd feel so much better if you were here to help out."

"Plus I'd be here when you start having all your babies," Eliana said, mostly to freak Julia out, because things were getting a little too real.

Rather than being scared off, Julia's entire being lit up. "I didn't even think of that! You'll be the best aunt." Julia hugged her tight, as if it was already a done deal. And maybe it was. She'd been gone long enough. Plus, she *would* be a stellar aunt.

And maybe a certain handsome man was a draw as well.

She couldn't think about Asher without tingles dancing along her skin like soda bubbles popping on her tongue. They were pretending the kiss had never happened.

Well, *she* was pretending the kiss had never happened.

Asher caught her watching him sometimes. He'd smirk like he knew exactly what she was thinking about, and her whole body would ignite, and it would take all of her self-discipline not to launch like an Olympic hurdler over the boxes they were sorting through and drag him into another kiss. Not that she thought she had to drag him. He'd given her plenty of appreciative looks as well—and those were even harder to resist.

"Did you still want to do your livestream?"

"I do. Have you figured out the archway?"

Julia cringed.

"What?" Eliana asked, already dreading what her sister might say.

"What if—" She paused, and then seemed to inhale for courage and tried again. "What if I don't want to get married here?"

"Here? As in Florida?" Eliana's voice rose in panic.

"No. Here as in the beach," she said, sounding miserable.

"Why wouldn't you? It's gorgeous! The archway would be absolutely perfect with the ocean behind it."

"I know, which is why everyone thought we should get married here, and I didn't want to say no." Julia had always struggled with significant people-pleasing tendencies. It was hard for her to say no—even when it came to the location of her wedding, apparently.

Eliana linked her arm with Julia's and strolled down the beach with her. "Where would you do it? If it could be anywhere?" Keeping in mind they wouldn't be able to book anything at all this close to the wedding. She decided not to say that part out loud.

"The conservation center," Julia said.

Eliana blinked. She hadn't expected that. "It smells like animals there."

Julia let out a short, amused laugh. "It does. But is it weird that I wish Lulu and Adia could be there for the wedding? They were there when Logan proposed, and I know they don't understand, but I can't help but think they're missing out."

"You want the elephants to be guests at your wedding," Eliana deadpanned.

"Yes?" She sounded so unsure of herself it made Eliana want to move heaven and earth to give this to her sister. Which she might have to do.

"Say it with confidence. 'Yes, Elly. I want elephants at my wedding, so don't be a jerk about it.'"

Julia laughed. "You're not a jerk."

"Sometimes I am." She elbowed her sister teasingly. "Hey, I didn't get *anything* I wanted at my wedding," she said softly. "It was all about what

Corbin and his mom wanted, and I still regret not standing up for myself. Maybe if I had, I would've seen Corbin's true colors earlier and saved myself a lot of pain. Does Logan know you want to get married at the conservation center?"

Julia stared out at the calm waves. "The beach was decided on so quickly that my head was still spinning from being engaged, and I didn't think to say anything. And then I didn't want to disappoint anyone."

"Will Logan be angry you don't want to get married here?"

"No," she said with the confidence she'd lacked earlier. "Never. He just wants me to be happy."

That's exactly what Eliana wanted too. Which meant seeing if Julia and Logan's wedding could be moved to the conservation center. "It's a good thing we have a connection," she said with a smile as she called up Logan.

"Elly—no! We can't change the venue at this point. The invitations are already sent out."

"Then we'll send texts with an update. And make sure someone is here to direct people to the new location. It'll all work out."

Julia bit her lip and looked very unsure of herself.

"Hey, Eliana," Logan said. "What's up?"

Eliana covered the phone with her hand. "Is this what you want, Julia? Really want?"

Julia's eyes welled with tears. "Yes. But I don't want to put anyone out."

That was all Eliana needed to hear. "Logan, how would you feel about moving the wedding to the conservation center? Is that a possibility?"

Logan got off the phone to talk to his boss. Eliana respected that he was a man who was willing to get things done for her sister. All it took was hearing that Julia wanted to have the wedding there, and he was determined to figure it out.

If anyone could pull this off for Julia, it would be Logan.

"Thank you!" Julia hugged her. "Do you want to do your video now, or do you need to make more people's dreams come true?"

"If only people's dreams were as easy to fulfill as yours, Julia." And if only everyone was as good as her sister.

But Eliana really did need to do a live video, since she had to put a video out today, and hadn't had time to record or edit anything. Normally, she'd be stressed, but her normal had gone out the window this summer, and her regular schedule was all out of sync.

She stuck her phone on a selfie stick, pulled a small mic out of her pocket to clip to her top, and started her livestream. She had a few things she wanted to talk to her followers about, a few assumptions people had made about her that she needed to get off her chest. But she wanted to do it in a lighthearted, casual way, rather than scripted and edited in front of her computer.

"Hi, everyone! I'm out here in Florida, where I grew up, helping my sister plan her wedding that's happening this weekend. All this wedding planning has me thinking lately—especially since this is the Happily Single channel. I know me talking about weddings might be difficult for some of you, and if you need to mute my channel for the next week, please take care of yourself and do that.

"I've talked a little bit about my own wedding and marriage on here before. You can go watch episodes 21 and 45, where I go into more details about my wedding and my divorce, but I want to bring up something I haven't spoken about yet, and which may surprise you.

"I don't hate relationships. I don't hate love. And I don't hate weddings." She leaned closer to the camera as if telling them a secret. "In fact, I love them. I really, really love them. The tiered cakes and the cascading flower arrangements and the flowing wedding dresses. I can't wait to watch my future brother-in-law see my sister walk down the aisle toward him. I envy what my grandparents have—being married for six decades. They still hold hands, guys. It's the cutest thing you've ever seen.

"Some people assume I don't think anyone should be in a relationship, ever, because I spread a message about being happily single. It's offensive to people that I'm so happy—and I've been called all kinds of names for it. Names I won't repeat here.

"But what I'm really advocating for is this: find happiness. Period. If you're not happy, what can you do to BE happy? I see so many people who feel like they can't be happy if they're not in a relationship, but I'm telling you that you can. I'm writing an entire book about it, even!"

She was glad she couldn't see the comments scrolling through on her phone. The sun was too bright, and she was wearing her sunglasses, which made it nearly impossible to see more than her outline on her screen. A weight was lifted from her shoulders as she spoke.

"I'm setting the record straight. I'm not a bitter woman who hates love, despite what some angry commenters think. I am happy, I'm fulfilled, I have wonderful friends, I am planning on remaining—"

"Eliana, look out!"

Something sharp jammed against the back of her leg. She screamed and nearly dropped her phone in her haste to get away from ... the flamingos?

The four flamingos circled her as if herding her somewhere, and she had no way to escape them. If she tried to edge away, they'd peck at her leg hard enough to draw a scratch. Great. The last thing she needed was a pair of bruised and scratched legs right before the wedding. Especially since Grandma Winnie had warned her that she'd be showing a lot more leg than she'd originally planned. Julia had only smirked and said it was Eliana's turn to wear one of Grandma's shorty dresses out in public.

"Do they bite?" Eliana yelled to Julia, holding as still as she could, as they shuffled agitatedly around her.

"I don't know!" Julia stepped farther back. *Traitor.* "I'll look it up."

Eliana remembered then that this was all live. Of course it was. She had to stop doing livestreams, period. Never. Again.

"Well, friends, I have a situation here." She giggled nervously and tipped her screen down to show the flamingos to her viewers. "It seems I'm being kidnapped by what may or may not be killer flamingos. My sister is looking it up."

"They peck!"

"I know! They've been pecking at me. Can you help?"

Julia hesitated. "I can't mess anything up. The wedding ... Let me call Logan and see if he has any ideas."

"My future brother-in-law, Logan, is a vet who works with exotic animals," she said to the camera. She didn't know if flamingos were on that list or not, but at this point, she'd take anyone.

Julia held her phone to her ear. "Logan says they eat shrimp, not people!"

Eliana lifted her face toward the sky to plead for patience, before she put her attention back on the camera. "I don't remember what I was saying anymore, because I'm in the weirdest situation I've ever been in, in my entire life. On live. I don't know if I should close this or continue recording, but since I'm too afraid to do any big movements, you guys get to watch for a while."

"Logan says he doesn't know of any reports where a person has been seriously hurt or killed by flamingos, and that you should follow them and see where they're taking you. Also ..." She paused, listening. "He says a group of flamingos is called a flamboyance. Isn't that fun?"

"Julia, trivia isn't going to help me."

"Right, sorry." She bit her lip, but then her face broke into a wide grin. "We can have the wedding at the conservation center near the elephants! We'll just have to do it after five, when they close."

She knew Logan could make it happen! "That's amazing!" A particularly hard nip at the back of Eliana's leg caused her to jump. "I come in peace!" she yelled at the flamingos, but they only fluttered their wings even more at her proclamation.

"Logan says they like Beatles songs. Try singing one."

"All flamingos like the Beatles?"

"No! Just these ones. They're named after the Beatles."

She racked her brain for a Beatles song she knew the lyrics to, and came up with "Here Comes the Sun." No reaction from the flamingos. And she was still on live. Singing. Heaven help her. Maybe they liked ballads better. She moved on to "Hey Jude."

"Logan's on his way. He'll be here in twenty minutes to help."

Twenty more minutes of being attacked by flamingos while singing through her limited knowledge of Beatles songs? Nope. "I'm done with this," she said under her breath.

Eliana took a few more steps, and endured another sharp peck on the back of her leg, before she made her decision.

"Run!" she yelled. Then she took off, feeling two more hard pecks on her calves, and ran as fast as she could toward Julia. Julia squealed as Eliana took her by the hand and ran alongside her, leaving the stunned flamingos in the background. They ran all the way to Asher's house and crashed through his door, still screaming and laughing, tripping over boxes and landing on the floor in a heap. At some point in the melee, Eliana had dropped off the livestream, thank goodness.

They lay on the carpet and laughed until they could finally breathe again.

"That was so weird," Julia said.

"You're telling me," Eliana said through choppy breaths. She hadn't run that fast in a long time. "What was their goal?"

"You're wearing a pink shirt and shorts. Maybe they thought you were one of them." They dissolved into giggles again. "We need to clean your legs up before they get infected."

"Wait." Eliana laid a hand on Julia's arm. "My stomach hurts too much from laughing to get up. I need a minute."

"Whose house did we break into?" Julia propped herself up on her elbows to look around.

Oh. Crap.

"Asher's grandpa's house," Eliana said as casually as possible. "I've been helping him clean it out."

"Huh," Julia said, and if that wasn't a loaded *huh*, Eliana would go join that flamboyance of flamingos and rename herself Yoko Ono.

"What?"

"Nothing. It's just ... you seem different."

"Different how?"

Julia laughed. "Stop sounding so suspicious. You're more relaxed. Open. Happy."

"I've been happy," she said, maybe a little too defensively.

"Yes, you have. Happy is the wrong word. More at peace."

Okay, Eliana could give her that.

"Usually, you're so made up, you're almost intimidating. Lately—I mean, you did a live in an oversized T-shirt, and you didn't refresh your makeup beforehand."

Julia didn't have to explain what she meant by that. Eliana didn't like to be seen by anyone without perfect makeup, perfect outfit, perfect surroundings. But all that perfection seemed ... exhausting lately.

"I like it," Julia said. "It's more real. It reminds me of how you were before—" She cut herself off, but Eliana finished the sentence in her head. Before Corbin.

"It's being here in Diamond Cove with you guys." And Asher. She hadn't changed for him—she'd never do something like that again. It was more that she felt comfortable being her real self in front of him, and it had been a long time since that had happened.

She was falling for him.

There. She admitted it. She was falling for Asher Brooks.

But remembering Sienna made her feel sick to her stomach. She'd gotten canceled for someone taking a picture of her holding a caffeinated beverage. If Eliana—writing a book on being happily single—fell in love? She could lose everything she'd worked so hard for.

"What's wrong?" Julia sat up, and Eliana followed suit. They sat with their legs crossed, facing each other, still in the entryway of Asher's house. Could she tell her sister? If not Julia, then who else?

"I'm attracted to Asher. Like, *really* attracted."

"Okay, that's normal," her sister said encouragingly. "He's a handsome guy."

"I mean ..." She lowered her voice. "I can't stop thinking about him. And me. Together. As more than friends." She brought her palms together for a visual that definitely wasn't necessary.

Julia's eyes widened, but to her credit, she didn't gasp or clutch her pretend pearls or accuse her of hypocrisy, or any of the other reactions Eliana had been afraid of. She saw the moment the dilemma of Eliana's situation dawned on Julia.

Julia's gaze softened. "You need to figure out what you really want. Not what anyone else wants for you. Or expects from you. But what you really want." She laughed self-deprecatingly. "I know that's rich coming from me, but I speak from experience. You've lived a lot of your life trying to live up to other people's expectations."

"I don't know what I want." She did know. She wanted Asher. And she wanted her book deal and her social media following and to be able to keep making videos for a living. She wanted both. But both was impossible.

"You'll figure it out," Julia said. "You're one of the smartest people I know."

If she was so smart, how had she let herself get into a mess like this?

Chapter 27

Asher

ASHER'S STOMACH WAS TOO heavy to want to eat while he waited for Michael to arrive. He sipped his soda and watched the door of the tiny Diamond Cove café, while his fingers tapped the table in a nervous rhythm.

The door opened, and a man wearing loose jeans and a polo shirt walked in. He looked around the café and paused when his gaze landed on Asher. This must be him. Asher sat up straighter as Michael approached the table and sat across from him. He was younger than Asher expected him to be—maybe in his fifties. His hair was mostly brown, with some generous gray sprinkled through it. A cell phone poked out of the top of the front pocket of his polo shirt.

"Asher. Nice to meet you."

Asher inclined his head, trying to get his footing. "Michael."

"Call me Mike." He waved down the waitress and put in his own drink order, along with a grilled cheese sandwich and a side of fries. "Want anything to eat? It's on me."

Asher shook his head, wanting to get this over with. He didn't know if he wanted Mike to have answers for him or not. What if the answer to why his grandpa had gathered all those secrets was worse than the mystery of it?

"Sorry I didn't introduce myself at the funeral. I loved Mason like a dad, but I didn't want to accidentally open a can of worms. But it's open now, I suppose," Mike said.

Open and uncontained. "How did you meet my grandpa?"

"I was in the military with him. Mason was much older than me and took me under his wing when I was an unlovable tool," he said fondly. "Then when I retired, I went into private sector investigating, and we stayed in touch. He always told the best stories."

Asher recalled his grandpa's military stories. They weren't just interesting stories; his grandpa had that storytelling skill of timing—he knew exactly how to pace his stories to keep them all wanting more. And he could drop a punch line with the sleekness of a missile.

The waitress delivered Mike's drink and refilled Asher's soda. He hadn't even realized he'd already drunk the first one down. Mike shared a few of his favorite Mason Brooks stories, and Asher was relieved he'd heard them all before. Maybe Grandpa wasn't as much of a stranger to him as he thought.

Mike tucked into his food when it arrived, and Asher took the break in conversation to ask the question burning in the back of his throat for weeks. "Why did he have all that information about people in The Palms?"

Mike finished chewing his mouthful of food and took a long drink from his straw, looking carefully at Asher the entire time. "What do you know about your great-grandfather?"

Asher blinked, not expecting that. "Nothing. I don't even know his name." Asher remembered his dad going to the funeral when Asher was maybe five years old, but he and his mom had stayed home. Grandpa had never talked about his dad, and Asher had never asked.

"Mason didn't talk about his childhood much, but sometimes, when he had a little too much to drink, he'd tell us about his father. On the surface, his father appeared to be a good man. He went to church on Sunday. He would chat with the neighbors. He worked to support his family. His shirts were pressed nicely. His wife always had a smile. That kind of guy, you know?"

Asher pictured a *Leave It to Beaver* father based on the description, but those words "on the surface" made him pause. "What was he really like?"

"Mean. He knew how to keep the bruises hidden on his wife and son. He would withhold food from his wife to control her. He once smashed a model plane Mason had built over an entire month of evenings, just to destroy something that had brought your grandpa happiness. He was only seven at the time. It's one of his earliest memories."

Asher was glad he hadn't ordered any food now that a block of ice had formed in his stomach, spreading a chill to his veins. Sometimes actions like his great-grandfather's could be generational, but Grandpa had always been loving. They hadn't been a touchy family, but he had other ways of showing his affection. After everyone died and it was just the two of them, not a day went by when his grandpa hadn't told him he loved him. Life was too short to keep things unsaid.

Mike continued. "Because his father was so good at keeping the secret of who he really was, no one knew what Mason and his mom went through at home. Once Mason was old enough to join the military, he left home, but he was never allowed to see his mom again."

Asher wished he could reach out and take a hold of Eliana's hand, feel the warmth and comfort of her pressed against the coldness cementing him to this bench.

"He was paranoid after that. Didn't trust anyone for a long time—and not until he saw them in situations that revealed their true self. I was a mess when I met him—and everyone knew it. My dad was done with my garbage, so he shipped me off to boot camp. Mason straightened me up and gave me a reason to believe in myself.

"After your grandma died, he started to believe most people were living a double life, like his dad had. I think it was his grief—I did a lot of research on it. People grieve in all different ways, and his brought up a lot of unprocessed childhood trauma. He called me up, oh, about ten years ago, and asked me to investigate some people. At first he told me he was looking for something, but about a year into pushing him for details, he confessed that he was looking for liars. People he could call out and expose as hypocrites, the way he wished someone would have done to his father."

The sun sank, illuminating dust particles in the air above the table. The waitress must have noticed it as well, because she leaned across their table to shut the blinds. "Sorry, hon. That sun blasts right in on this table."

"Can I get an ice cream sundae? One for my friend too," Mike said. He took another bite of his sandwich.

"Sure thing."

Asher heard them speaking, but he felt removed from the conversation as he watched a dust speck fly in the one pinprick beam of light that remained. He tried to blink away the sensation that he was standing on one side of the glass, and all of this was happening on the other.

"My grandpa didn't tell me any of this," he said once the waitress left.

"I'm not surprised." Mike flipped a sugar packet through his fingers. "He hated talking about it."

A flash of anger flared through Asher. "Didn't Grandpa see the irony? He was keeping his past from me, while he was digging up everyone else's history." His anger cooled just as quickly as it had come. He'd been reading parts of the books on grief that Eliana had subtly placed around the house—some with sticky notes marking chapters. He'd seen how his own actions weren't always logical. He was illegally living in his grandpa's house, keeping his boxes like a dusty shrine—not moving, not living, remaining as stagnant as those fake, plastic flamingos that made their way to everyone's lawns.

He pinched the bridge of his nose between his thumb and forefinger.

Their vanilla sundaes came heaped with whipped cream, hot fudge, caramel, and a cherry on top. Asher's stomach growled. Okay, maybe he *could* eat.

"Why did he come to you for help?" Asher asked.

"After the military, I worked for the police department as a detective. When I retired, I went into private investigating, mostly as an independent contractor specializing in insurance fraud and small business embezzlement. I know how to dig up dirt. And I did. Some of it illegal, but most of it just embarrassing. He wanted all of it. I tried to convince him to stop, but I also felt obligated to help, after everything he'd done for me when I was a kid.

"Then one day, years after he moved to Diamond Cove, he told me to stop."

"Why?" Asher asked.

"Because you were moving to Diamond Cove and had gotten a job at The Palms. Plus, enough time had passed that some of his grief demons were fading. We'd turned in one person to the police, after we had collected evidence of identity theft, but for everyone else, he just sat on the information. Our lunches became less about picking apart everyone's secrets, and more about him giving me updates on your life. He was so proud of you. It meant a lot to him that you'd move to Diamond Cove after you finished school."

"Grandpa was my only family."

"Yes, but he'd lost *all* of his family in one way or another. He figured it was only a matter of time before he lost you too. But then you came back and stayed."

It was such a small thing, it broke Asher's heart. It had never crossed his mind *not* to come back.

"He was worried about you. He said he'd pushed too many people away, afraid of the secrets they had and never fully trusting anyone, and sometimes he saw the same instinct in you—something he was sure he'd taught you. He knew he'd be leaving you all alone once he was gone. But he also knew you'd be all right. He used to say you were the best version of a Brooks that could be made. And man, he loved you."

Asher's eyes stung. He stared down at the chipped laminate table, allowing his gaze to absently follow one deep groove scratched into the surface. He'd loved his grandpa too. And to learn all of this? It was a lot to take in.

Asher didn't recall how their conversation ended, only that he rode his motorcycle home in a daze. He didn't go through his usual careful song and dance of parking in the trees and making the long walk to the bungalow. He pulled right into the driveway and sat there for a long time.

If only Grandpa was still here. Asher could assuage his worries. Yes, he had walls up. Yes, it was hard for him to trust, and his grief had made him push people away. But Grandpa had taught him how to love. How to apologize and change and be there for someone when they were going through the most devastating thing of their life.

Asher would never want to be the center of attention, or be in a large crowd of people, or become an Eliana-like ray of sunshine. But he didn't want to be alone either. Not anymore. But how did someone go from being so alone to ... not?

CHAPTER 28

ELIANA

*"I've got the key to my castle in the air, but whether I can unlock
the door remains to be seen." —Louisa May Alcott*

ELIANA, GRANDPA HORACE, AND Cameron strolled along the beach
in order to give Grandma Winnie and Julia some space for her final
dress fitting. Logan and his best friend, Kai, were down the beach observing the flamingos, which seemed to have less aggressive energy today. Much
to Logan's disappointment and Eliana's relief.

"I haven't seen you much this summer," Eliana said to Grandpa. She
linked her arm with his and gave him a side hug.

"I know." He patted her hand. "I've been out with Smitty and trying to
stay out of everyone's way while you all plan this wedding."

Cameron found a spot in the sand and dropped his towel down decisively. Cameron wasn't much for wanting to walk along the beach—he'd
much rather sit and watch the waves or wade into the ocean.

Today, none of them had their swimsuits on, so they all sat—Grandpa
in a chair, Eliana and Cameron on a beach blanket, until they got the
go-ahead to come back into the house. She'd offered to stay and help,
and tried not to be offended at the nose-scrunching reluctance in their
expressions. You accidentally cut one tiny hole in the hem while trying to
trim loose threads, and no one lets you near the dress again.

She checked her phone, hoping to see a text from Asher—but nothing so far. He met with Mike today, and she was dying to hear how it went.

"I watched your video," Grandpa said. "I've never liked those flamingos."

"Why not?" she asked, surprised.

"Too pink."

She burst out laughing. "What do you have against the color pink?"

"I prefer green animals." He winked at her, and her heart warmed. He'd been sweet to Louisa from the beginning.

"Me too," she said.

Cameron was focused on burying his feet in the sand and didn't join in their conversation. They chatted about Grandpa's golf statistics, which she assumed was just as interesting a topic for her as hearing about her social media statistics was for him. But they talked about it anyway, and they listened anyway. These kinds of conversations were one of the things she loved about her grandpa. With him, she didn't have to try to be interesting or marketable or wise or witty. She could be boring and analytical, and he loved her and kept coming back for more.

After her incident with the flamingos, her social media had exploded ... both the good kind and the bad kind.

Another viral video: Yay!

People mostly making fun of her? Boo.

People resonating with her happiness message? Yay!

People determined to misread her every word and label her a hypocrite? Boo.

Social media was definitely a mixed bag.

"Eliana!" Logan called out. The flamingos had moved closer, but were still far enough away that Eliana didn't have to flee. What was a fear of flamingos called? If she was developing it, she'd need to look it up.

"What?" she yelled back.

"Come help us! We can't recreate it," he called.

"We'll buy you dinner!" Kai offered. "Bait for bait!"

Logan smacked Kai on the chest with the back of his hand, and they whispered furiously at each other.

"I was joking, of course," Kai said.

She crinkled her nose. No, he wasn't. "No way! I have enough bruises on my legs already." She stared mournfully at her blue-and-black legs. There was no way they'd heal in time for the wedding, which meant she'd have these stylish polka-dotted legs in pictures for the rest of time—unless she could convince Logan's sister to trade dresses with her. They were about the same size. "Logan, can I get Willow's number? I need to call her."

He pulled out his phone, and a moment later, her phone pinged with a text from him.

"Thank you!" If she trusted anyone enough to keep her from getting hurt as she was acting as live bait, it was Logan. But that didn't mean she was going to do it.

Eliana: Hi Willow! This is Eliana, Julia's sister. Would you be willing to trade bridesmaid dresses with me? I had a run-in with some flamingos.

Willow: I saw the video! Are you okay?

Eliana: Yes, but my legs really bruised.

Willow: Your dress was the short one, right?

Eliana: It is. And you would totally rock it.

Willow: *eye roll emoji* Yes, all anyone wants to see is the legs of a mom of two.

Eliana: Please, I'm desperate. (For the record, you can totally pull this dress off—mom or not.)

Eliana: For the double record ... if you're uncomfortable, I'll make it work. My grandma says she has nylons I can borrow. *Shudder.*

Willow: No, gosh. Say no more. I can trade you.

Eliana: THANK YOU!! You have saved my life and my reputation.

Willow: Anytime.

Relief rolled through her. At least one problem was solved. Now if only Willow could finish writing her book for her and face the internet meanies and figure out what to do about a certain speech therapist she couldn't get out of her mind.

Grandpa chatted about his plans for after the wedding—most of them with his friend Smitty—when movement caught her eye.

Asher. Walking straight out of the bungalow without any subtlety, he wore his wet suit and held a surfboard. Most people knew he was cleaning up the boxes, but still, he was generally so cautious about people seeing him come in and out.

Maybe with his eviction date coming up so soon, he'd stopped caring. Or the meeting had gone badly enough he wasn't thinking straight. Either way, it worried her.

"So, Asher, huh?" She glanced over at Grandpa, who waggled his eyebrows exaggeratedly.

She groaned. "Oh no. Not you too. Did Grandma put you up to this?"

His expression turned confused, and then, for the briefest of moments, hurt. But perhaps it was her imagination, because when she stared more closely at him, he looked normal. "No. Is Grandma playing matchmaker?"

"Yes," she said. Asher walked into the ocean without a sideways glance toward them, clearly lost in his own world. He got deep enough to sit on his board and paddle out a little farther. She knew enough about surfing to see that the waves tonight weren't good for it—and most of the surfers came in the morning. And when he just sat on his board and floated, she realized he had no intention of surfing. Just being.

"And is it working?" he asked.

"Is what working?" she asked, distractedly.

"Are you falling for Asher?"

She whipped her head toward him. He sat with his hands folded over his stomach, a way-too-satisfied smile on his face. "No," she said. Maybe a little too vehemently. Especially because her gaze dragged itself back to Asher floating on the water, staring out at the horizon. "He just had a hard afternoon. I'm worried about him." And a little hurt he hadn't called her to tell her how things went. She could admit that.

She hadn't told him to call her, but she thought he would.

"You care about him, then?"

"Yes, I do. That's not wrong. That doesn't mean I'm in love with him."

Grandpa shrugged, which rose her hackles. She knew that shrug—it was his "I'm just humoring you" shrug.

"I'm serious, Grandpa. I have an entire platform dedicated to being single. I can't fall for him."

"Falling in love is rarely convenient," he said.

She let out a frustrated groan. "You are impossible."

"Elly," he said softly. He waited until she tilted her head and looked up at him. "Don't let one bad marriage keep you from ever trusting or falling in love again. Especially with someone as good as Asher. You have too much love to give." He nodded his head in Asher's direction. "And that one would never intentionally hurt you."

She pushed herself up on her elbows and stared out at him. He looked adrift. Lost at sea. He was used to navigating life alone, to losing all his people, and she hated that for him.

He shouldn't have to be alone anymore. But was she the person he should be with?

Chapter 29

Asher

ASHER FINISHED HIS SHOWER, got dressed, and stepped into the hallway to find Eliana there with her arms folded. "Hey." He tried to skirt past her, but she wasn't having it. She stepped in front of him to block his path again.

He let out a long, weary sigh. It had been quite a day, and he was ready to heat up some leftovers for dinner and crash on the couch.

"How did it go?" Eliana asked.

"Let me get some food, and I'll tell you about it." His stomach had been churning too much after meeting with Mike to eat anything, but he'd worked up an appetite after swimming around.

She followed him into the kitchen, watching as he heated up last night's leftover enchiladas. He'd slid an extra enchilada onto his plate and grabbed two forks as he made his way over to the couch for what had become their nightly ritual of eating dinner together, going through several boxes each, and watching something on television. It reminded him so much of his grandparents that the thought of it made him ache. Especially tonight.

They'd gone through at least three-quarters of the boxes, and his grandpa's bungalow looked empty in a way that was reflected in his chest.

They ate in silence, not turning on the television tonight, and he appreciated Eliana giving him some space to gather his thoughts. What could he even say about everything he'd learned? He finished his dinner and drank the rest of his water before he began.

"There were a lot of things about my grandpa I didn't know." He attempted to swallow down the emotion choking the back of his throat.

It must have still shown, because she scooted close and took his hand. He stared at their interlocked fingers, at her delicate pink-painted fingernails and lightly freckled skin, as he told her what Mike had revealed about his grandpa's past. It was hard to say the words, to tell her about the abuse, but at the same time, it felt right to say it out loud, like he was shedding light on something hidden in darkness for too long.

He swiped at the tears pricking his eyes. "I just wish he would have told me, but I also get why he didn't. It had to have been painful to even think about, much less talk about. He was so good to me, especially after my parents died. Even with all his family trauma, he found a way to love." He'd taken Asher in. Never made him feel like a burden. Always had encouragement when he called. Praised his successes and gently corrected his mistakes. When Asher looked at his grandpa's actions, he could see his love as clearly as the sun rising steadily over the ocean each morning.

"It makes sense why he'd want to know everyone's secrets." Eliana absently stroked her thumb over the back of his hand. "His motivation wasn't to expose his friends. It was to help people who were being hurt."

"But he's given fuel to someone who isn't trying to help and *wants* everyone to hurt."

Eliana rested her head against his arm, and he breathed in the fresh, citrusy scent of her. "When I was going through my divorce with Corbin, things got pretty ugly between us. Corbin didn't like that I was setting boundaries, and he said some hurtful things—and since he knew me so well, he knew right where to strike to make the deepest cut."

His jaw clenched at the thought of how Eliana had been mistreated by someone she'd once trusted. Anyone who could be hurtful on purpose was someone he could never understand, but to hurt Eliana? To think someone tried to make her feel small and unworthy and less-than? It was enough to make him feel torn between tackling his most complicated, intricate recipe and painting over every ugly word Eliana had been told by listing the amazing things about her. They'd be there a long time if he chose that option. Forever.

She pulled back to look at him, her gaze softening as she took in his anger on her behalf. She ran a light finger over his jaw, and it loosened under her touch. "My grandma said something to me that helped me understand him a little more. She said, 'Hurt people hurt people.'"

Asher let those words sit in his mind. Because of their own hurt, they lashed out and hurt someone else. And maybe that's what the person revealing the secrets was doing ... trying to release their own hurt by hurting others. "That doesn't make it right."

"No, it doesn't," she agreed.

He slid his hand behind her head, threading his fingers into the back of her loose, silky hair. She caught her breath as she stared at him, but she didn't pull away. "You're pretty smart," he said.

"Asher ..." she whispered.

He waited. He didn't want to push her into something she didn't want or wasn't ready for, though every part of him ached to be closer to her. But when her eyes fluttered shut and she leaned into him, he met her halfway, pressing his lips to hers in a kiss so emotional, so comforting, it almost brought him to tears again.

The pressure against their lips was gentle and soft, but his heart raced as if he were swimming against the tide with all of his energy. Her hand rested against his chest and had to feel how hard it pounded.

She pulled back just a breath, and her eyes studied his, confusion swirling in them. "What are we doing?" she breathed.

He gathered her close to him in a hug, relieved when her arms circled his waist tightly, and she pressed her head to his chest.

They remained like that long enough for Eliana's breathing to even out. Her question sat between them long after she'd fallen asleep cuddled into him on the couch.

What were they doing?

"I'm falling in love with you," he whispered in answer as he dropped a feather-light kiss onto her hair.

He didn't know if she felt the same way, or if she could give up her entire career for these feelings, or if he could even ever allow himself to ask her to do something like that. All he knew was that holding Eliana in his arms—her head curled into his chest, her hand splayed across his stomach—was the best feeling he'd ever had.

He relaxed into the couch, and despite the emotional turmoil of the day, he fell into the most peaceful sleep he'd had in a long time.

Chapter 30

Eliana

"You are the gull, Jo, strong and wild, fond of the storm and the wind, flying far out to sea, and happy all alone." —Louisa May Alcott

E LIANA PULLED UP TO the Southern Florida Wildlife Conservation Center for Julia's wedding rehearsal. The wind blew wildly, which broke up the sweltering heat they'd been experiencing all week, thank goodness.

She understood the timing of her sister wanting to get married so quickly, but did it have to be in the middle of summer? The wind also blew the scent of all the animals toward the parking lot. Yep. It definitely smelled like animal refuse. But if this was what Julia wanted, this was what they were going to give her, dang it.

And if this last-minute change kept Eliana so busy it distracted her from things Asher had confessed when he'd thought she was sleeping? That he was *falling in love with her*?

Maybe he'd been talking about Louisa May Alcott. *Right, Eliana. He was confessing his love to your tortoise.*

Eliana got out of her car with a single-minded determination to put any and all confessions of love—regardless of the subject of said confession—out of her mind, and make this the best wedding rehearsal in the history of wedding rehearsals. Her parents pulled into the parking lot beside her, and they got out, followed by Cameron, who wore his yellow swim trunks. They were all casual today—Eliana in jean cutoffs and a peach tank top—but Cameron had goggles slung around his neck and held a beach towel.

She glanced at her parents questioningly.

"We usually go swimming on Fridays," her mom explained. "And he's not happy we're here instead—since we usually come here on Tuesdays."

"Ah." Eliana nodded in understanding. Cameron thrived on routine and didn't always do well when their schedule changed. But since life couldn't always be predictable—like moving a wedding location the week of, for example—he sometimes had to roll with the punches.

Even if his willingness to roll was about the same as a square wheel's.

She took Cameron's free hand in hers—she was one of the few people he'd still hold hands with, which made her feel unaccountably happy and superior, she'd admit—and walked with him into the conservation center. "We're going to do the wedding rehearsal, and then I'll take you swimming tonight at The Palms." She glanced up at the sky with a frown. Was a storm coming in?

No. Only good thoughts.

"Pool," he said.

"Yep, we'll go to the pool. After this."

He scowled, clearly not happy with her answer, and yanked his hand away from her, then went to go stand by Kai, Logan's best man. He leaned against the railing in the exact same pose as Kai, who gave him a nod in hello.

"Don't take it personal," Dad said as he walked past her. "Kai's just cooler than you."

"Rude," she said with a laugh.

"He's cooler than all of us," Mom said. "Do the kids say 'cool' anymore?" she asked Eliana. "I heard 'on fleek' on the radio the other day."

Dad shook his head. "That show we were watching, they kept saying 'slay.' 'That dress slays.'"

"Oh right." Mom turned to Eliana. "Kai slays."

"Yeah, he does," said Leo, Logan's nephew, as he, his sister, and his mom approached them.

Logan's sister, Willow, was gorgeous, as always. She didn't look like she was working full-time as a nurse while raising two kids on her own, but rather like she'd walked straight off the runway and into the elephant enclosure. Eliana might be tempted to be insanely jealous of her, but she was so nice and down to earth, it was impossible to do anything but really like her. At least in the few times Eliana had met her.

Kai lit up when he saw them and walked toward their group. Eliana took the opportunity to escape and find Julia. She and Logan were talking to someone on speakerphone, and Eliana slowed down as she approached, but Julia waved her close.

"No, we're at the Southern Florida Wildlife Conservation Center. Not the zoo," Logan bit off. "You went thirty minutes in the wrong direction."

"The officiator went to the wrong place," Julia whispered to Eliana. "At least he did it today and not tomorrow."

True, but dread settled in the pit of Eliana's stomach. She'd never seen Logan look so stressed.

"Plus Logan hasn't eaten anything today," Julia said. "And I think it's finally hitting him that he won't be working with these elephants for a few months."

Eliana knew how much Logan loved Lulu and Adia, and she imagined that leaving for so long was bittersweet.

"We want to get started soon." Julia twisted her hands together as she looked out at everyone staring at them expectantly.

Logan ended the call, frustration evident in the tight lines around his mouth. "Let's get this over with."

Julia frowned. "Seriously? This is our wedding, and you just want to get it over with?"

He scrubbed a hand over his face. "I didn't mean it like that."

"Then how did you mean it?"

"Never mind. I'm just tired."

"Okay. The sooner we get started, the better." Julia blew out a quick breath. "Elly, can you stand in as the officiator?"

"Sure," she said at the same time Logan said, "No. Kai can do it."

"What does it matter?" Julia snapped.

Eliana's eyebrows shot up. She rarely heard her sister lose her patience like this.

"Eliana needs to walk with Cam down the aisle," Logan said.

"And Kai needs to walk with your sister."

Eliana cut in, her heart picking up speed and her hands starting to sweat—and not just from the oppressive heat of the afternoon. "Guys, this isn't worth fighting over—"

"We're not fighting," Julia said, too cheerily to be anything but fake. "And you're right. It's not worth fighting over. Which is why you're going to stand up there and officiate."

Eliana hustled to where Julia pointed, not making eye contact with Logan as she did.

Though she couldn't hear them, they continued to bicker for another moment as they figured out the best way to get this thing started. Panic rose in Eliana as they snipped at each other. A couple as perfect as them shouldn't fight.

A part of her realized that this was a no-big-deal argument. That he was hungry and Julia was stressed, and that couples sometimes lost their cool. They weren't being mean or horrible, just snappy. And it was a good sign that Julia was standing firm in her opinion. But scrolling on an endless loop through her mind was the thought that their marriage was headed for disaster unless everything went perfectly tomorrow.

Eliana ended up blowing a whistle between her fingers that silenced everyone. "Let's start," she said. "If you're in the wedding party, line up!"

Everyone listened—except for Cam, who refused to stand unless they were heading straight to the pool. They rushed through walking down the aisle, and Eliana did a pretty good impersonation of the priest from *The Princess Bride* that made everyone but Julia and Logan laugh.

The couple gave each other a perfunctory kiss, and then the night was over, everyone was heading home, and Eliana was driving Cameron to the pool, like she'd promised. He swam until he was so exhausted he kept yawning, and then she took him home. Her mom convinced her to stay for brownies, and she didn't beg off—not ready to face Asher yet.

She came back to The Palms, parked her car next to Asher's motorcycle, and walked slowly to his bungalow. It was late, and she unlocked the door as quietly as she could. The first thing she saw in the dim glow of the moon was Asher's sleeping form sprawled out on the too-small-for-him couch. His chest rose and fell with his steady breathing, and in sleep, his face looked completely open and relaxed.

She knew she shouldn't move closer—was it creepy to watch someone sleep?—but she did it anyway, unable to resist some time to really watch him unobserved.

I'm falling in love with you.

She'd been mostly asleep, and not quite sure she'd heard him say those exact words, or if it was a dream, but she'd felt the light press of a kiss on her head, and a wild group of butterflies—Logan could probably tell her what a group of butterflies was called—erupted in her stomach.

She'd wanted to sleepily pull his face down to meet hers and kiss him until her head was dizzy and her mouth raw, and he was as completely senseless as she was. She loved kissing Asher. Craved the feel of his lips pressed to hers, or to her jaw, or to her neck. Just the thought of it sent delicious shivers across her skin.

That wasn't the part that scared her and was making her avoid him.

Nope.

Kissing Asher was fun and exciting and a really great way to pass the time.

But what freaked her out was in that moment when she'd been mostly asleep, she'd almost told him she was falling in love with him too. Which was not okay, because she was happily single. Even if she'd never had to remind herself of that fact so often before.

Asher brought his muscular arm up over his eyes, giving her a different angle of his octopus tattoo, this one mostly tentacles. He'd never told her why he'd chosen that image. She imagined the conversation, her trailing her fingers over each line while he caught his breath with each dip of her finger and told her the story.

She liked the image so much, it made her eyes sting with tears of longing. She could do it. Cuddle up right next to him on this couch. She knew with full confidence that he'd open up his arms and tug her into his chest. That he'd sleepily whisper something sweet against the shell of her ear and hold her like he'd never let her go. That they'd fall asleep like that, and she could wake him up tomorrow by kissing the underside of his jaw and beg him to tell her the story of his tattoo.

The yearning she felt shook her enough to make her step away from him before she did something she couldn't take back. She wanted Asher in a way she'd never wanted anyone else, but she would be giving up too much to be with him. Not just her career, but her freedom, and maybe even her happiness eventually. Because wasn't that what happened with most relationships? Look at Julia and Logan. Even they were fighting, and they hadn't even gotten married yet.

No. It was better for her to keep her distance from Asher, no matter how much she longed to do the opposite.

CHAPTER 31

ASHER

I T WAS STILL DARK outside when Asher woke up, but Eliana was already gone. The only indication that she'd come home at all last night was that a plate and cup were in the sink.

The wedding had been stressing her out more and more as it drew closer, and he'd been seeing less of her as she worked nonstop. He missed watching a show with her every evening. It was his favorite part of the day, even as he tried to hold his heart back from falling too hard so it wouldn't hurt as much to lose her. But it was too late.

He'd been waking up extra early to hide out at The Palms' clubhouse in an attempt to catch whoever was posting the secrets. Asher needed to undo what his grandpa had inadvertently started. His grandpa never would have wanted this to happen.

Sunlight peeked over the horizon as he walked straight to The Palms. It was too early for anyone to catch him leaving his grandpa's bungalow. Besides, what was the point in hiding anymore? He had to be out of there by Monday. And he still had no idea where he was going to live. He didn't even have a car to sleep in.

He'd been looking at apartments, but some part of him kept hoping that something would change. That Mr. Richardson would change his mind about the new tenant, or forget he was there—though he knew that would never happen.

But the sooner Asher left, the sooner he lost that last piece of his grandpa—and the sooner Eliana moved on, whether that was back to Boston or back into her parents' house since the plumbing issues had been resolved this week. Either way, it wasn't with him.

Today, he wanted to focus on Eliana and the wedding, and figure out who was spreading the secrets. He didn't know if the person would come in through the front or back door of The Palms, and he'd been alternating days in hopes of catching them. This time, he went to the back door, the one that led out to the pool, and found a chair to sit in that was shadowed enough that no one would see him unless they stumbled right on him.

And he waited.

Surfers trickled out to the beach to catch the amazing waves. Since he'd been coming out here to The Palms to try to catch whoever was revealing the secrets, he'd been missing surfing—and it was during the best time of year to be out there.

He was so distracted watching the surfers, he almost missed the person walking into the clubhouse. There was a slight scuffle of noise, and then the door opened. He stood and followed quietly but closely. He didn't want to scare someone who was just there for an early breakfast or quiet reading time.

As the person walked slowly to the bulletin board, she looked around cautiously, and then pulled a folded paper from her purse.

His heart raced, and he tried to calm it. It could be an advertisement for a class. Or an invitation to a tea party. Or a flier for another fundraiser.

But why would she look around so furtively if that was the case?

He stepped as close as he dared. It was a list of secrets, more than on any other day.

The woman turned around and gasped when she saw him, one hand to her heart, the other gripping the handle of her walker.

"Lydia?" His shocked gaze darted from her to the board. "Why?"

She sighed long and hard, and slumped onto the seat of her walker. "Well, it's about time."

Asher sat across from Lydia at an outside table at a breakfast café on the pier in Diamond Cove. He'd driven Smitty's car to bring them here, away from anyone who might overhear their conversation. A light breeze came off of the ocean, and it was still early enough for it to be somewhat cool outside. Much cooler than it was going to be for the wedding.

Lydia tore tiny pieces off of her chocolate-filled croissant but didn't seem to be eating any of them.

Why had she done this? Messed with so many people's lives? Caused so many problems and violated people's privacy? As he watched her, concern warred with frustration over what she'd been doing, but in the end, concern won over.

Hurt people hurt people.

She looked so impossibly small in her chair. More than just physically small, but as if she had shrunk emotionally as well. He let out a long, deep breath and picked up his fork. Staring at her expectantly wasn't helping her feel comfortable enough to open up, so he might as well eat his fresh-berry-and-powdered-sugar-topped French toast, cheesy scrambled eggs, and bacon.

Her shoulders relaxed when he took his focus off of her, and she stopped massacring her croissant and instead sipped at her steaming tea. "This should be one of the happiest days of my life." Lydia gazed out over the water wistfully. "My grandson is getting married to a wonderful woman, and yet I'm unforgivably miserable."

Something he'd learned from Eliana over the last couple of months was that a simple touch could often go a long way. He reached across the table to give her fragile hand the gentlest of squeezes, just to let her know he was listening, before he pulled back and continued to eat.

She started to blink rapidly. Crap. He hadn't meant to make her cry. He was definitely doing this wrong—perhaps he should leave the hand-touching to the experts. "I'm sorry—"

She cut him off with a wave and a self-deprecating laugh. "This happened after I turned sixty," she said, indicating her tears. "I went decades without crying, and now I cry for everything. Don't get old," she joked—an often-given warning to him from his patients.

He smiled, knowing that getting old was much better than the alternative, but also knowing when to keep his mouth shut. He'd learned the value

211

of silence in his job, and especially how hard people will often work to fill it.

She swiped the tears off of her cheeks and straightened her shoulders. "I miss my daughter. I feel like I'm losing my grandson. We moved all the way out here to be near him, and now he's leaving. I know he's only going to be gone for four months, but it feels like the beginning of the end. I miss my husband. He's wrapped up in Horace and rekindling their friendship. And Winnie and I used to be so close, but she has her own tight-knit group of friends who are always meeting and texting and planning events together, and I feel like I have ..."

"No one," Asher finished for her quietly. He felt the punch to his gut with every phrase. He understood exactly what it felt like to be left behind, forgotten, alone. After his grandpa died, he'd been left with no one, and for more than a year, he'd lived on the fringes of other families and friend groups and the people at his work, never belonging, never really fitting in.

Until Eliana came into his life, like a Fourth of July firework exploding across a dark night, illuminating everything in color and vibrancy and giving him enough light to see that he wasn't alone.

"No one," she repeated. This time she patted his hand, and it made him feel a little choked up too. Perhaps they were both bad at this.

"The day I found the box, Smitty missed a lunch date with me. I sat and waited for him for almost an hour before he texted to say he wouldn't make it. He never texted me in his life until we moved here, and now it's the only way we ever communicate.

"I took a walk, unable to bear going back to the bungalow alone, and that's when I saw it. I thought it might be giveaway items, sitting there in the hallway, and I was desperate for a distraction—even if it was some awful hen-shaped wall-hangings or cookbooks from 1987.

"As it turns out, it was a lot more interesting. I got one of the boys in the dining hall to carry it home for me, and I spent the afternoon reading through a box of secrets. I didn't gather them myself; someone else did, and I don't know why, but I'm sure they were never intended to be found. I kept expecting Smitty to come home and ask me what I was doing, and I could show him, and we'd get rid of it together.

"But dinner passed, and then the time when we usually go to bed, and he didn't come home. And I continued to read." She exhaled and pulled off another chunk of her croissant. "He was out late with Horace and lost track of time, and by the time he got home, I'd hidden the box. I'd also learned that all these perfect people with all these friends weren't so perfect after all."

She sighed and shook her head. "But it isn't Smitty's fault. It's mine. I saw those secrets about Winnie's friends, and I saw a way to make them feel as bad as I felt. And then it kept spiraling, until I was posting everyone's secrets. And suddenly, instead of everyone being friends, they were fighting and ignoring each other, and—I'm not proud of this, Asher—but it was satisfying to know that I wasn't the only lonely one anymore."

She stopped to drink her tea, and he almost spoke, but something made him pause—maybe the crinkle of a frown by her mouth or the shaking of her fingers as she set her teacup down.

"And I didn't know how to stop it once I got going. To see you this morning was a relief in a lot of ways."

This time, when she slumped back in her chair, he knew she was done. This was more than just the physical exhaustion that came from being up so early and navigating the world with a walker; this was a soul-deep exhaustion that came from regret and sadness.

"That box was my grandfather's," Asher said.

Lydia touched her throat with trembling hands. "I never met him, so I didn't recognize his handwriting."

"He grew up with a father who looked and acted one way on the outside, but was a completely different—horrible—person in private. After my grandma died, we believe his grief reignited his childhood trauma, and he dealt with it by wanting to expose anyone else who was living a double life. So he began to investigate everyone in The Palms and compiled all the information you read in that box."

Lydia's trembling breaths filled the space between them. "I don't know what to say."

The weight of the situation crashed down on Asher. Both his grandpa's role in it, and then his own careless role in allowing those things to get out.

Lydia pressed her face into her hands, and her shoulders shook with crying. He slid his chair next to her and put his arm around her shoulders. Who was he? Initiating a hug with someone to comfort them.

The waitress came toward them, but he shook his head subtly, and she turned on her heel and went back into the bakery. Lydia felt impossibly small, and it was hard to believe someone so frail could wreak such havoc on their community.

But her spirit wasn't frail. The Lydia he'd first met had been fiery and hadn't let anyone walk all over her. She'd always had a mischievous smile for him, and had sent over her family's top-secret marinara recipe when she'd learned he loved to cook homemade pasta. She'd also critiqued it when he'd brought her some, and told him he needed to stop being stingy with the olive oil.

But the last year had been filled with blows—especially her stroke and learning to walk with a walker—to her spirit, and he found he couldn't be angry with her for what she'd done.

"We'll fix this," he said with conviction.

She pulled her hands away from her face, looking at least ten years older than she had when they'd sat down to breakfast. "I'm going to confess, Asher. No more secrets."

His breakfast churned in his gut. Would confessing really help everyone? It would certainly give them all a single person to heap blame and anger on—but it wouldn't take away the secrets that were already out there.

"I think you should wait." His mind whirled, trying to come up with a plan and failing.

"I know you mean well, but we've learned how damaging secrets can be."

"And we've also learned how damaging it can be for some secrets to come out," he replied with raised eyebrows. "And I don't mean the kind where someone is getting hurt and needs help. I mean the private things that people don't always want to share."

"I hurt a lot of people," she argued. "And it's only right I apologize."

"But what if they alienate you even more?" He fisted his hands under the table at the thought of what could happen to her and let out a heated breath.

"Then that's the consequence for my actions," she shot back, sounding like her fiery self.

Asher fought a weary smile. His morning had taken a strange turn. "I'm not going to lie; when I set out to catch you, I didn't think I'd be here trying to convince you not to tell anyone."

She chuckled and actually stuck one of those tiny croissant pieces in her mouth. He moved back to his side of the table to finish eating his breakfast. "Yes, well, I didn't expect I'd be arguing my need to confess, either," she said sardonically.

They ate in companionable silence as the sun rose fully over the Atlantic Ocean. "Wait until after the wedding," Asher finally said. "There's got to be a way to do this that keeps everyone from turning on you."

Her smile drooped. "I'll wait until next week," she promised wearily.

There had to be a way to help her—not only to confess, which he still wasn't convinced was the right idea, but to help the people of The Palms trust again.

CHAPTER 32

WINNIE

W INNIE FOUND HER ELVIS Presley CD and turned the volume up to listen while she got ready for the wedding. She'd finished the flower girl's dress late last night, in just the nick of time, and it was adorable. She couldn't wait to see it on Amelia, Willow's little girl.

She'd also sewed bow ties for all the groomsmen and Willow's son Leo, the ring bearer, which had been a surprise for Julia. She hadn't wanted to promise anything until she knew she could get it done, but all the coordinating, bright summer colors were going to be perfect for this bright, sunny day.

Now, if only the people could be bright and sunny for the wedding.

She checked her phone, sad to see that it had been over a week since her last text message from anyone in the Secret Seven. She usually had at least one text a day from them, but since the secrets started coming out, her phone was unusually silent.

Someone had to reach out first, though, and it might as well be her.

Winnie: Are you coming to the wedding?

She set her phone down so she could work on her makeup, and after only a few minutes, it lit up with messages.

Don: Yep.

Rosa: Of course!

Walt: Wouldn't miss it.

Nancy: Planning on it.

Harry: Me and Virginia will be there.

Polly: Me! Oh, and I'm bringing a new friend.

Rosa: A romantic friend?

Polly: Oh, heavens no.

Polly: I like to keep my romance to my books.

Don: Amen.

Polly: Have you read Allegra Winters's latest romance yet?

Don: Yes, the day it came out.

Winnie: Same! I love a fake-romance trope.

Don: It's not my favorite, but I like it better than the secret baby trope.

Polly: That one is the worst.

Rosa: Don't spoil it! I haven't read it yet.

Nancy: Hey, not to be rude, but could you take your message to a separate thread so my phone doesn't keep going off?

Winnie's heart, which had warmed with each incoming message, turned cold when she got to Nancy's. They talked about Allegra Winters's books all the time, but they'd never been asked to start a separate text thread before. Was everyone annoyed at them, all this time?

Winnie: Sorry. Yes, we can do that.

Don: Are we matchmaking tonight?

Walt: We should keep the night about Logan and Julia.

Rosa: But weddings are the perfect time for a little romance!

Polly: Walt has a point.

Polly: But so does Rosa.

Nancy: Any updates, Winnie? Are Eliana and Asher making any progress, or do we need to call it and move on to someone else? Harry's up next.

Harry: Maybe we need to take a break and regroup.

Walt: That's not a bad idea, Harry.

Panic crawled up her chest. They couldn't move on yet. They hadn't given this relationship enough of their time and effort.

She waited for someone to call Harry and Walt out, tell them what a terrible idea it was to take a break. But the line remained quiet.

She set her phone down and wound the hot curler through her hair. Maybe things would never be back to normal. Maybe the entire Secret

Seven would disband, and Horace would be off with Smitty, and Winnie would be entirely alone.

Well, if no one was going to help her, she'd do it herself. She didn't need them anyway. After all this time, she'd learned what worked and what didn't. She'd convinced Eliana to bring Asher to the wedding, so that was something.

She twisted the curling iron into a chunk of her hair as Horace got dressed behind her. He looked so handsome in his pressed white shirt and gray suit he'd gotten just for this wedding. She'd made him a bow tie too—and Smitty as well, though she'd done that one somewhat reluctantly.

"I have a question," Horace said pensively. He stood beside her at the mirror to comb his hair. "About a conversation I had with Elly a few days ago."

Something about his tone made her nervous. Eliana didn't know about Gerard, so it couldn't be that, but Horace sounded so serious.

"She mentioned that you were trying to set her up with Asher. I thought we were just convincing her that she could fall in love again."

"I am, but we're also setting her up with Asher," she said slowly, not sure where he was going with this.

"We. Meaning you and the rest of your friends?"

She nodded and stared at him through the mirror. He was very carefully not looking at her, but instead focusing on getting his part just right.

"I thought I'd be helping this time."

Oh no. She knew him well enough to recognize that he felt hurt for not being included. But to be fair, it wasn't like he was ever around anymore. "And when would you have helped, Horace? You're with Smitty all the time."

He scowled. "That's not true."

"Yes, it is. You're with him more than you're with me. You didn't even make it to the rehearsal last night because you two were so busy together. So yes, I had my friends help me matchmake Eliana. Maybe if you were here more, you could have helped too."

His face clouded with frustration. "You purposely left me out, and I had to find out from her this weekend."

"Huh. I wonder what it feels like to be left out—" She smelled something burning and realized she'd been holding the curling iron for too long against her hair. She pulled it away, along with a burnt-off chunk of hair.

Both she and Horace stared at it in horror. Her eyes filled with tears that she blinked back as rapidly as she could, and she threw the curling iron down onto the counter.

"Winnie—"

She held out her hand. "Don't say a word. I just did my makeup, and I can't cry."

"But—"

"Not. One. Word," she hissed. She pivoted away from him and went into the closet to get dressed. When she returned to the bathroom, Horace was gone. She stared at her reflection, and at the huge, burnt chunk of hair near the front of her face. It smelled bad too.

She tried to pin it back, but it wouldn't stay. She dropped the pin with a thunk and allowed that piece of hair to stick up on the side of her head. She stormed to the kitchen and grabbed her purse.

Horace watched her with wide eyes. "Aren't you going to—"

"Nope." One of these days, she was going to let him speak again, but it wasn't going to be today. "Let's go."

They left the house, not talking, the distance between them growing greater by the second. She didn't want to show up at Julia's wedding walking six feet away from her scowling husband, but she had no desire to be any closer to him either.

The car ride was frostier than a northern winter, and she felt nothing but relief as they pulled into the conservation center parking lot. She got out of the car and bustled toward the entrance. Every time the wind shifted, she got another whiff of her burnt hair. But she threw her shoulders back and walked faster.

Horace huffed in his attempt to keep up with her.

They turned the corner into the elephant enclosure, around the copse of trees that would provide a background for the guests. Rows of white chairs draped in white linen had been set up in front of a metal archway being decorated with a gorgeous array of flowers. A white rug ran down the center aisle for the bride and groom to walk down. The decorations were minimal, but not much was needed with the natural background of lush trees and bushes surrounding them.

They drew closer to the small crowd, and Winnie gasped. Because sitting beside Polly in the back row of white chairs was none other than Gerard. As if he sensed her arrival, he turned and spotted her, his eyes lighting up when they landed on her. He waved, but she grabbed a surprised Horace by the arm and redirected him away from Gerard.

"I think that man's waving at us. Do we know him?"

"Nope," she said abruptly. She approached Eliana and gave her a tight hug, then pulled her away as if she had something very important to talk about.

Eliana wore a pair of jean shorts and a white, dirt-streaked T-shirt. Her hair was in a messy bun, and she didn't have makeup on yet.

"Is everything okay, Grandma?" Eliana eyed her burnt hair with a frown. "Can I help you with this?" She tried to tuck it under some other hair, but Winnie pushed her hand away, irritated.

"I like it," she said petulantly. "Do you need help with *your* hair?" She looked pointedly at Eliana's messy do.

Eliana's eyebrows shot up. "I'm good. Heading over to get it fixed up right now." She paused, still looking concerned. "Do you remember where you're supposed to sit?"

Oh, great. Now Eliana thought she was losing her mind. Any minute now, she'd be talking to her like she was a toddler.

"Yes, I remember," she snapped. "I wanted to see if the flowers were delivered yet."

"They just arrived. In fact, I'd better make sure they're getting wound into the archway."

From the corner of her eye, she saw Gerard pause at the edges of the group separating them. "I'll help." She nearly dragged Eliana toward the archway by the elephants. Lulu was standing close to the fence, watching all of them in rapt attention. Horace found his seat.

Winnie peered over her shoulder to find that Gerard had been waylaid by Harry and Virginia. Relief whooshed through her—followed by the realization that she was going to have to avoid Gerard all night. Her chest tightened.

It'll be fine, Winnie. It'll be just fine.

CHAPTER 33

ELIANA

"Well, if I can't be happy, I can be useful, perhaps." —Louisa May Alcott

ELIANA CAME TO AN abrupt stop at the flower archway set up right in front of Adia and Lulu's enclosure. "What are these?" Eliana asked in a shrill voice. She pulled her hands into fists at her side as her stomach sank. Grandma Winnie tightened her grip on Eliana's arm.

The teenager who had woven most of the flowers through the archway blinked and pulled an invoice from his back pocket. "Um, let's see. Roses and lilies."

"No."

"No?" he repeated, confused. They both stared at the arch, where the roses and lilies were clearly displayed.

"We specifically didn't order those flowers."

"Well—" He looked around him as if hoping someone—anyone but him—would save him from the crazy lady yelling at him.

"Where's your boss?" she asked.

"Back at the store." He perked up. "Want to call her?"

She hadn't come? It was a wedding. She was supposed to help weave the flowers into the archway. "Yes. I do."

Grandma gave her a questioning look, her piece of burnt hair standing up nearly straight. But before Eliana could explain why she was freaking out, the florist answered the phone. "Flowers and More. This is Carrie."

"This is Eliana, with the Kent/Peters wedding."

"Oh yes," Carrie answered, sounding way too delighted. "What can I help you with? I sent my son, Trent, down there with the flowers. Is he there yet?"

"Yes," she said through her teeth. "But he brought the wrong flowers."

"Oh dear." Eliana heard rustling and clicking. "Can you put me on speakerphone?" Eliana held the phone up between her and Trent. "Which flowers did you grab, Trent?"

"The blue bin. The one with the roses and the lilies," he said.

"That's the right one," she said. "And I sent the green bin with Troy to take to the funeral."

"What was in the green bin?" Eliana knew what the answer would be before Carrie even said it.

"Hmmm, let's see. White gardenias and jasmine."

"That was *our* order!"

"No, I have it clearly written here. Order for the Kent/Peters wedding ..." Her voice trailed off. "Oh my."

"We need those other flowers," Eliana said desperately.

"I wish we could help, but the funeral already started. And I made the wedding bouquets and boutonnieres with the roses and lilies. Even if I could get the other flowers, I wouldn't have enough time to do a wedding arrangement." She paused, and when she spoke again, her voice brightened. "But roses and lilies are so much prettier for a wedding anyway—"

"My sister is allergic."

Trent looked up from where he was crouched on the cement, finishing the flower arrangement. He really had done a wonderful job—if not for the fact that it was all the wrong flowers.

"Well, the wedding is outside, right?" Carrie continued. "Hopefully it will disperse the scent—"

Eliana ended the call, the first time she'd ever hung up on anyone in her life. This was a disaster. She lightly banged her fist against her head as she groaned.

"Maybe she's right." Grandma pulled her hand down. "We don't have any other options."

Without the flowers, the arch was just rusted wrought iron. With them, it was gorgeous and lush, but not what she had planned.

She let out a frustrated huff. "I guess there's nothing we can do about it now."

"I may go sit down." Grandma looked a little pale.

Eliana immediately took her grandma by the arm and walked her to her seat in the front row. Grandpa chatted with Uncle Dave and her cousin Eric. Uncle Dave gave her a hug first, and then Eric, who was her favorite cousin and the one closest in age to her. "How long has it been?" she asked him.

"At least two years, which is about two years too long," he said. "How are you? I saw the video." They both cringed.

"I'm forever going to be known as the Flamingo Girl."

"It's a meme now. I should know." He shook his head regretfully. "I made it."

She laughed, something she hadn't thought she'd be able to do just moments ago. "You would."

He nodded toward the elephants behind her. "Is this the famous Lulu from Julia's book?"

"It is," Eliana said. Julia had written a series of books about animals, and her latest, *Loving Lulu*, had hit the bestseller list. It was part of why she was taking a break from teaching to write full time—the other part, of course, being that she didn't want to be away from Logan for four months.

"Elephants were my favorite animal growing up."

"I remember," she said. "You couldn't pronounce elephant for a long time."

"My parents didn't want to correct me, because it was cute." He chuckled and gave a self-deprecating eye roll. "Super cute when you're in sixth grade and everyone's mocking you."

"I was Team Don't Correct Him!" she teased. She checked her watch. The wedding was starting in less than an hour. She'd been running around all afternoon and hadn't had time to even think about getting ready. "I'd better go finish all this."

"Okay." He leaned closer before she could leave, and lowered his voice. "Is Grandma okay?" He indicated the very obviously burnt hair.

"I don't know. She's off tonight."

He frowned, but nodded, sliding his gaze back to Grandma. Confident that Eric would help Grandma if needed, she ran to the conference area they'd set up as a wedding dressing area, completely out of breath when she got there.

Before she could open the door, her mom grabbed her by the arm and yanked her toward the tiny staff kitchen. "We have a problem," Mom said.

Of course we do. "What's wrong?"

Mom just shook her head. "Follow me." She opened the kitchen door, and Eliana gripped the doorframe to keep from falling over in shock.

"What happened to the cake?" she squeaked out. The three-tiered almond cake had sunk into itself, creating something that looked more like a recreation of an atom bomb drop than the gorgeous wedding cake she and Julia had picked out.

"Logan's old babysitter delivered it this way. All we can figure is she left it outside for too long," she said, tightly.

"That can't be fixed." Eliana choked back her tears. How could so many things go wrong?

"There's not enough time to make a new cake, but your dad and Don are at the store right now, getting whatever they can."

Eliana's stomach dropped. "Don and Dad?"

"Don likes to bake. He swears he can help fix this." Mom looked way too hopeful for how skeptical Eliana felt. "We'll make it work. I promise."

"The wedding starts soon."

"They'll be back in time," Mom said with more confidence than Eliana thought was warranted. They hugged tightly. "It's going to work out," she said with feeling. "The caterers are here already, and the rest of the food looks amazing."

Eliana didn't have time to argue. Time was ticking down, and Julia had sent her at least three texts telling her the makeup artist and hairstylist needed to leave soon for another event, so she needed to get there ASAP.

Her phone buzzed with a text.

Asher: I just got here. Is there anything I can help with?

Eliana: Convince my sister to have a Christmas wedding?

Asher: It may be a little too late for that.

Asher: Are you okay?

Eliana started to write out everything that was going wrong when her phone rang. Logan.

"Hey," Logan said in a cagey way that made Eliana's heart completely stop.

"What's wrong?" she asked.

"Well ... Kai and I went over to the zoo this morning—"

"The wedding is at the wildlife conservation center!" Was the world losing its mind today?

"I know. We had a meeting set up with a flamingo specialist over there to talk about what happened to you. Julia knew about it."

Eliana pinched the bridge of her nose. This couldn't wait? But Julia knew who she was marrying. "Okay? What did you find out?"

"Oh, it was really interesting. We showed him your video, and he spotted—"

"Hey, maybe we can circle back to this after the wedding," Kai cut in to say, his voice sounding more than a little strained in the background.

"Oh, yeah." Logan cleared his throat. "We got a flat tire on our way to the wedding."

She made a noise that was somewhere between a choke and a scream.

"We're putting the spare on right now," he rushed to say. "But we probably won't get there until right before the wedding starts. So if you could stall—"

Something clattered in the background, and Kai swore.

"I've got to help," Logan said. "Tell Julia I love her and I can't wait to get married to her."

He hung up, and Eliana stared at her phone. Her stressed-out heart was going to burst into a thousand tiny pieces and litter the hallway like confetti.

She pulled up her text to Asher and stared at it, and then deleted the entire thing before sending. She didn't want to get used to him helping her all the time. Besides, hadn't he seen her look messy enough?

She took a deep breath. "It's fine, Eliana. You've got this." She forced a smile onto her face.

She opened the door to the makeshift bridal suite to find her sister with swollen eyes, a bright red nose, and piles of used, makeup-tinted tissues surrounding her.

And a gorgeous rose-and-lily bouquet at her feet.

Julia sneezed, and a piece of her perfectly done hair fell out of its updo onto to her cheek. "Hey, Elly," she said in a nasally voice. "The makeup artist had to go to her next appointment, so we're on our own."

Forget confetti. Eliana's heart exploded into millions of pieces of glitter they'd never be able to get out of the carpet.

Time to call in reinforcements.

CHAPTER 34
ELIANA

"Love is the only thing that we can carry with us when we go, and it makes the end so easy." —Louisa May Alcott

E LIANA HAD NEVER BEEN so happy to see a group of elderly people in her life. Grandma's friend, Nancy, assessed the situation in the conference room and immediately took charge.

Before Eliana could blink, Rosa was doing her makeup while Polly fixed Julia's hair. Harry and his wife, Virginia, were driving to the closest grocery store to buy out their fresh flower section—avoiding carnations, lilies, and roses. Walt and his two granddaughters were meeting up with Kai and Logan to trade cars—and they'd take the car to the tire shop to get fixed, which meant they'd miss the wedding, but they swore they didn't mind. Mom, Uncle Dave, and Eric were in charge of removing every last flower from the conference room. Grandpa was meeting Dad and Don at the grocery store to figure out the cake situation.

And Winnie was put in charge of cheering up the bride and maid of honor—since when everyone had arrived, they'd both been crying. Grandma sat in front of Eliana and Julia and took a hand from each of them to hold.

The tightness in Eliana's chest eased as everyone rushed off to fulfill their assignments.

"Your friends are amazing, Grandma." She squeezed her grandma's hand.

"They really are." Grandma exchanged an appreciative smile with Polly and Rosa, who were each proving to be a wiz at getting them ready for the wedding.

Eliana had a new life goal: Make friends as amazing as Grandma's. She wanted people who would drop everything to help her out when she needed them.

"This is ridiculous," Julia said with a teary laugh. "How could so much go wrong? Hopefully it's not an omen."

Eliana's stomach twisted. She knew Julia was teasing, but that really was her worry—what if this was a bad start to a bad marriage? What if Julia ended up going through the same pain she'd gone through with Corbin? Julia was so much sweeter and kinder than Eliana, and it killed her to think of her getting hurt.

Julia must have seen something in Eliana's expression, because her brows furrowed. "What's wrong?"

"Everything," Eliana said. "I wanted you to have the perfect wedding, and instead, this has been one disaster after another. First the rehearsal was a mess, and you and Logan are fighting, the flowers are wrong, the cake is wrong, our hair and makeup is wrong—"

"Whoa," Julia said. "It's okay."

"It's not okay," Eliana said vehemently. Rosa stepped back from drawing eyeliner around her eyes as Eliana blinked rapidly to hold back her tears. "You deserve to have the best, Julia. And I tried so hard."

"I know you did, Elly," Julia said. "But things happen."

"What if it *is* a sign?" she said passionately. "What if this is just the beginning of being miserable together and having your spirit chipped away at day by day until you hardly know who you are anymore?"

She couldn't look anyone in the eye as silence filled the room.

"Is that how you felt with Corbin?" Grandma asked quietly.

She hadn't wanted to make this about herself. She suddenly felt like she couldn't breathe, and Polly waved a stack of papers to fan her face. Grandma opened an ice-cold water bottle for her and held it out until she took it and sipped it, then twisted the cap back on and held it to the back of her neck. Embarrassment swept over her as she realized that all the women in the room had their gazes on her.

Julia put her hands on Eliana's shoulders. "Logan isn't like Corbin—you deserved so much better than him. The wedding wasn't the problem. It was the person."

Eliana gave up on blinking back tears and allowed them to stream down her face.

"Logan and I aren't fighting. If you're talking about yesterday, we were stressed and snippy and hot and hungry—so we weren't our best selves. But we love each other and we treat each other well, and I cannot wait to marry him." Then Julia hugged her and said quietly into her ear, "The wedding is just one day. I'm preparing for an entire *lifetime* with Logan."

"Yes, but you've been stressed too!" Eliana said exasperated. "I know you want everyone to be happy all the time, but you can't act like everything is peachy now."

Julia pulled back, her eyes wet with tears. "Of course everything isn't peachy! I'm allergic to my flowers. My cake looks like something Lulu would throw up. This muggy weather is making my hair look like a mop and is going to melt my makeup. And my groom is missing!" Her voice rose, and her teary eyes were wild. "But I'm *trying* my best to be *positive*."

Eliana cut her gaze over to Grandma for help, but Grandma just mouthed, *You started this,* with a lifted eyebrow.

"You don't have to be positive all the time," Eliana said carefully.

"I know I don't, but it's my wedding day, and I'm trying to be happy!" She slumped into her seat, her chest heaving with heavy breaths, looking very decidedly unhappy.

"Maybe we should call it off," Eliana said gently.

"No." Julia looked at her with a determined set to her jaw, one that was rare to see on her. "I am marrying Logan today."

"So, even with all this—" Eliana waved her hand around the room to encompass the chaos. "You still want to get married? You don't think everything falling apart is a sign you should walk away before your heart gets even more involved?"

"My heart is one hundred percent involved already, Elly." Julia sat up straight, and she was quite a sight—makeup smeared, hair a mess, eyes swollen, and robe askew. But something inside of her glowed. "The entire sky could fall down on this wedding, and I'd still want to marry Logan."

"At this rate, the sky *will* fall," Eliana grumbled. "And you *don't* have to be positive or happy or people-pleasingly serene about it."

"And *you* don't have to take all the blame and put so much pressure on yourself to make everything perfect."

The two sisters gave each other knowing glances.

"This is a stupid fight," Julia said.

"We're both pretty flawed," Eliana replied in agreement.

"Major hot messes," Julia said with a sigh. "I'm sorry I lost my cool."

"I'm not," Eliana said with a laugh that felt like it lifted a ton of bricks off her chest. "It's the best thing that's happened all day. Besides, every bride is entitled to at least one bridezilla moment."

"Hey!" Julia threw one of the foam makeup sponges at her with faux outrage. "Did you see my cake? I get at least two."

"You can have a million," Eliana said. "And we'd still love you."

"And you can be imperfect and messy, and *we'd* still love *you*," Julia countered, her words a perfectly pitched, game-winning ball. They stared at each other in the mirror, both biting back their smiles. Yes, they were a mess. And yet, they loved each other and had people in their lives who loved them.

Eliana took in her sister's face and how happy she looked. Despite the flowers and the cake and the missing groom, she was absolutely glowing.

"You really are happy," Eliana said.

"Happier than I've ever been," Julia said. "I mean, I'll be even happier when Logan gets here and I'm actually married."

Eliana sat up straighter in her chair, her tears finally dried up. She turned to Polly, Rosa, and Grandma. "Okay, ladies. We look terrible—"

"Hey!" Julia said, indignantly.

"—and we need some miracle work here," Eliana continued as if Julia hadn't spoken. "Who's up for the task?"

"You've called the right women," Rosa said with complete confidence. "You'll be looking like models in no time."

"Thank you," Julia said.

"Let's get these two married." Eliana sat back in her chair, closed her eyes, and felt peace about this wedding for the very first time.

CHAPTER 35

ASHER

T HE SUN WAS FINALLY starting to set, offering relief from the heat of the day. Asher shifted uncomfortably in his seat and checked his watch. The wedding should have started twenty minutes ago, and people were getting restless. He checked his phone to see if Eliana had texted him back when he'd offered to help. So far, nothing.

Harry and Virginia, along with a teenager he'd never met, were filling an iron archway with a random assortment of flowers they pulled from grocery store bags. Don, Horace, and Eliana's dad had shown up with four sheet cakes just a few minutes before and hustled toward the building behind the elephant enclosure. Asher frowned. Something had definitely gone wrong.

He'd decided to go find Eliana when Logan ran into the enclosure, his face red—and was that a streak of grease on his face? Logan raced to the front and stood under the just-erected archway, out of breath. "Car trouble," he called out, and everyone chuckled, releasing the tension that had built with every minute that had ticked past the starting time. "We're ready. I can't wait one more minute to marry Julia."

Lydia stood with a handkerchief that she'd gotten wet with her water bottle, and everyone paused as she shuffled toward him to dab at the dirt on his cheek. He smiled sweetly down at her and then gave her a kiss on her cheek. Asher's shoulders relaxed at seeing the interaction. He'd been worried about Lydia since their conversation that morning, but it was a good reminder that she had people who loved her, even if she was going through some rough times.

The music began to play, and everyone straightened as the wedding party walked down the aisle. Logan's niece was the flower girl, followed by his nephew, who held the rings. Then Kai and Logan's sister walked down the aisle together, arm in arm.

Asher held his breath as Eliana came into sight with Cameron. Her long, blue dress brushed her ankles and hugged every curve. Her hair was curled around her shoulders, the strands woven through with sprigs of delicate white flowers.

But it was her expression that made him wonder if he'd ever be able to fully breathe again. She looked absolutely radiant. If he'd thought she was sunlight before, now she was a supernova. She looked happier than he'd ever seen her. And he knew with absolute surety that he was completely in love with her.

Eliana walked straight toward him when the wedding ended, her gaze locked on his in a way that made his heart skip. "Ready to be my fake, fake boyfriend?" she teased as she sidled up beside him.

He brought her knuckles to his lips. "You look beautiful."

She blinked in surprise, and her cheeks turned a bright pink. He'd clearly caught her off guard. "Thank you," she said, sounding as flustered as she looked.

"Are you needed right now?" He hoped to steal her away for a visit to Miss Havisham.

"Pictures," she said. "And then dinner. And the reception. And cleaning up." She looked as reluctant to leave him as he felt watching her go.

He sat beside her at the outside dinner, the stars twinkling on one by one as night overtook the day, but he couldn't even say what they ate. He was so wrapped in Eliana. The long curve of her neck as she tipped her head back to drink. Her full laughter that made her eyes shine. Her glowing smile as she watched Julia and Logan sneak kisses in between rushed bites of dinner and conversation, and soon dancing as they stood for their first dance as a married couple.

"What?" she asked, catching him staring at her.

"I can't take my eyes off of you," he said quietly.

"Stop," she told him with an eye roll and a shoulder push.

"I'm serious."

Logan and Julia finished their slow dance, and a fun, silly song played that enticed at least half of the guests to go out on the dance floor. Cameron and his date, Shayla, topped everyone for enthusiasm. Eliana tugged at Asher's hand, a ball of fiery energy that he couldn't keep up with as she danced in circles around him until she was breathless and her hair stuck in hot, humid tendrils to her neck and around her ears.

The DJ played another slow song, and Asher tugged Eliana close to his chest. "Dance with me?" he whispered.

She swallowed hard but nodded, and his breath caught as she wrapped both of her arms around his neck and rested her head on his chest as they swayed to the soft piano in the romantic song. He placed his hands on her hips, and then he slid them around her waist to hold her close to him like a hug.

She sighed against him. He could stay like this forever. If only she'd let him.

CHAPTER 36
WINNIE

W INNIE WATCHED ASHER DRAW Eliana closer to him while they danced, and she held her breath until Eliana sank into his arms as if she'd belonged there all along. Winnie knew Eliana had developed feelings for Asher. Her granddaughter was so caught up in what everyone else might think that she wasn't taking into account her own desires.

Winnie pulled out her phone to record them, catching a moment just as Eliana looked up at something Asher said and laughed. Her fingers twisted into the hair at his nape, and her eyes glowed as bright as her smile. Asher's adoration was written all over his face—clear for anyone who took a second look at them.

She pulled up the Secret Seven's Wedded Bliss account and uploaded the video, just as Eliana had taught her. Hopefully that would make someone else's night, just as it had made hers.

Since her phone was already out, she sent a thank-you text to the Secret Seven group chat. They couldn't have pulled off the wedding without them. Between the flowers and picking up the groom and even the wedding cake—which was plain sheet cakes from the grocery store stacked high with fake flowers—the night had come together into something beautiful.

She and her friends were being silly, letting these secrets come between them. You didn't live as long as any of them and not collect a few skeletons in your closet.

It was time to finally tell her own secrets. Horace deserved to know about Gerard. She'd been so upset that he'd been leaving her out to do so many things with Smitty, but she'd been leaving him out of her life for longer, hiding things from him. And why? Because of fear that he'd realize she was less than perfect? He knew that about her already.

He sat in the chair beside her, watching Logan and Julia with a soft smile on his face. For someone who had been so against them getting together, he'd made a complete one-eighty, and pride was written all over his face. Her love for Horace was so deep and full her heart ached with it.

It was time to tell him. Tonight, when they got home. And it was time for her to include him in her matchmaking plans, once and for all. If she gave a little, perhaps he would as well. She missed him—and not just spending time with him, but being emotionally close to him.

"Winnie, finally. You are a difficult woman to track down."

Winnie's spine stiffened as Gerard stepped into her view, blocking her granddaughters from sight.

"I haven't met you yet," Horace said, sounding friendly, at least as far as Winnie could hear through the blood rushing through her ears.

Gerard held out his hand. "Gerard. And you must be Horace, the lucky man who snagged the girl who got away."

Horace's brow furrowed, and it was like Winnie was across an ocean, trying to swim to them, trying to stop this conversation, but the waves kept pushing her back. "I'm sorry, I'm confused."

Gerard laughed as if this were a merry reunion and not as if they were watching her drown, no one coming to save her. "I'm Gerard Hammond," he said as if that name should ring a bell for Horace. "Winnie's first husband."

As if the DJ were playing an actual record, the music screeched to silence at Gerard's booming voice, and everyone's gaze shot toward them in shock.

Winnie opened her mouth like a fish, not sure if she should confirm the statement, deny it, or pretend to faint. All around them, people exclaimed and started talking, but she couldn't look away from Horace. Her throat too tight to speak, she confirmed what Gerard said with a nod.

And she watched as her husband's heart broke in two.

CHAPTER 37
ELIANA

*"Human minds are more full of mysteries than any written
book and more changeable than the cloud shapes in the air."*
—*Louisa May Alcott*

E LIANA'S BRAIN STRUGGLED TO catch up with what that man had
just revealed about Grandma Winnie. She'd been married before?
When? And why hadn't she told any of them?

She pulled herself from Asher's arms and ran to the table, but by the time
she got there, Grandma and Grandpa had slipped away, leaving behind a
confused-looking man.

Eric exchanged a surprised look with Eliana, then turned to encourage
the DJ to get the music going again. "It's the cupid shuffle!" the DJ announced, and Eric got Cameron to lead the dance with him, distracting
everyone from the drama.

"I thought he knew," the man said to Eliana as she approached, like
she might offer him absolution. But all she could see in her mind was
Grandma's panic and Grandpa's hurt—and it didn't make her feel like
offering any forgiveness, whether it was hers to give or not.

"Who are you?" she asked, sounding accusatory. A supportive hand
rested on her hip, and she knew without looking that it was Asher, and
that he was on her side, no matter what.

"Gerard." He stood and offered his hand to her, which she reluctantly took. His handshake was firm and businesslike. "I just bought one of the bungalows."

She narrowed her eyes. Asher's grip tightened at her side. It had to be *his* bungalow. She didn't need any more reasons to dislike Gerard, but he was just offering them up on a silver platter. "Why are you here? Are you trying to break up their marriage?"

"No." He ran a hand over his mouth and looked like he wished he could escape. "Of course not."

Anger rushed through Eliana. "What? So my grandma isn't good enough for you?" Wait. She was so angry she didn't even know what she was saying.

Gerard's mouth tightened. "She's *too* good for me. I often wonder how much better my life would be if I'd never left her." He paused. "It's Eliana, right?"

She glared but nodded.

"I didn't know she'd never told anyone about me. We married the summer after graduating high school." He shook his head with regret. "But I always liked Winnie. She had a way of making everything seem happier." His weary, downcast eyes made him appear even older.

"Then why come here and try to wreck her life?"

"That wasn't my intention," he said. "We had an ill-fated marriage—as were my next five marriages." He smiled, but it didn't reach his eyes. "I've lost everything important to me. And when I saw that viral video of Winnie, I needed to see her again. To remember better times."

Something about him reminded her of Corbin—maybe the way he'd only thought of himself in all of this, or assumed he was still a large part of Winnie's world, even though their relationship had ended decades ago.

"I only want to be her friend, but it seems my presence here has caused quite a bit of trouble."

"Yes, it has," Eliana said with an edge to her tone. She sat at the table, the shock of everything sinking in. Grandma had been married before. Why hadn't she told any of them? Especially Eliana. When Eliana had been going through her divorce, it would have been a huge comfort to know her grandma had been through something similar. Grandma had been there for her, more than anyone else, but it stung to realize she'd held back that part of her.

Eliana was so sick of secrets, she was starting to understand why Asher's grandpa might have done what he did. Gerard left, but Eliana remained frozen in place.

Julia and Logan seemed completely oblivious to the drama, lost in their own happy world. They cut the cake and danced some more—Cameron and Shayla stealing the show several times—and finally Logan and Julia left together holding hands, Julia's dress flowing behind her as if in a movie.

Eliana should feel happy. Ecstatic! The wedding had come off—with several hitches, but still successful. Yet she collapsed into a chair as the staff cleaned up after them and people streamed out to the parking lot, emotionally and physically exhausted. The sun had long set, and though the air was still sticky and warm, the night sky was poked through with shining stars, making it bearable. Almost pleasant.

"Are you okay?" Asher stood behind her and placed his hands on her shoulders. She tipped her head to rest her cheek on his fingers, grateful for his grounding touch.

"I will be," she said, believing it. She could hold both grief and joy in her heart at the same time.

"Are you ready to head home?"

Home. The word sent a flutter through her stomach. "Yes."

Eliana rinsed off the makeup, hairspray, sweat, and stress of the day in one of the longest showers of her life. She pulled on her oldest, comfiest sweats and twisted her hair into a still-dripping loose braid, then stared at herself in the steamy mirror.

Before being seen by anyone, she usually did her makeup. Brushed and blow-dried her hair. Wore her cute lounge clothes. Sometimes she wore glasses, or did a neutral makeup application, or pulled her hair into a loose bun so it might appear to her viewers she was being all natural, but her appearance was always very carefully curated.

With Asher, she didn't feel like she had to be "on" every second of the day. She could let her guard down and be human—be the person she usually only felt comfortable being when she was completely alone.

Still, her nerves were on high alert as she left the bedroom and drifted toward the scent of freshly baking cookies. With most of the boxes gone, the bungalow was easier to walk through. Yet it was bittersweet to see it all clean. A reminder of how little time she had left here. Asher had showered as well—in the hall bathroom and much, much quicker than her—and his damp hair was mostly dried and left loose around his shoulders.

His back was to her when she came into the kitchen in her bare feet, and he clearly hadn't heard her. He hummed the song they'd been dancing to together as he pulled the cookie sheet from the oven. She'd learned over the last two months that he always had frozen cookie dough, ready to pop into the oven for quick, homemade cookies.

When he'd learned white-chocolate macadamia-nut cookies were her favorite, he'd made a special batch just for her. As she smelled them now, and her heart filled all the way up with a feeling she couldn't describe, she followed the impulse to come up behind him after he closed the oven and wrap her arms around his waist, pressing her cheek to his back.

He didn't miss a beat putting the cookies onto a plate as she breathed in his clean, soapy scent mixed with the vanilla, sugar, and flour. Then he placed his hands over hers, where she clasped them at his stomach, and they stood there until she had time to realize how awkward she'd made things by hugging him like this.

When she went to pull away, he twisted to keep her in his arms. Her nose pressed to his neck in a way that should have intensified her awkwardness, but instead dispelled it completely, and she relaxed into him.

Asher had that effect on her. It was nearly impossible for her to feel uncomfortable with him. She didn't want to let go. This was their last night like this before everything changed—and they both moved out and returned to their normal lives.

When she had sat on his front porch, nearly giddy with glee that she had something to blackmail him with and solve all her problems, she never would have believed she'd find herself in this place, held tight in his embrace, never wanting to let go.

She pushed up on her toes to take his mouth in hers. He tasted like chocolate, salt, and the very best of everything she could imagine.

"I have something for you," she said, breathless, as she pulled away. "But you have to agree to take it before I tell you what it is."

He raised an eyebrow suggestively.

Her cheeks burned, and she rolled her eyes. "Not that. Say yes or no."

He lowered his lips to her ear, his breath brushing at her tiny hairs. "It's always yes with you, Eliana. Haven't you guessed that yet?"

Her stomach swooped at the low tone in his voice, and she swallowed. "Good," she said, attempting to get her brain back in thinking order, but that was proving to be a massive struggle with him so close. "Because you're moving into Julia's apartment until they get back from Logan's work trip, or until you find somewhere else to live."

He paused. "I thought you were going to live there."

"Nope. I'll move in with my parents until I figure out my plans."

"Any ideas about those plans?" His tone was casual, but the concerned lines around his mouth couldn't lie.

She pulled out of his arms and snagged a cookie. She didn't want to go back to Boston, not anymore. But she couldn't be here with him, either, and think she could continue writing a book about being happily single. "I'm not sure," she finally said, as honest as she could. What she wanted and the responsible thing to do were polar opposites.

He grabbed a cookie as well. "Then let's only worry about tonight."

They sat on the couch, and when he put his arm around the back of it, she took the invitation to snuggle into his side. They tried to watch a movie, but mostly kissed as if they might never kiss again.

Asher fell into an exhausted sleep sometime after two in the morning, his head tipped back as he steadily breathed. She took in his peaceful, open expression and wished things could be different. She drifted off curled up next to him, her cheek pressed to his chest, her arm thrown over his stomach, her new very favorite way to fall asleep.

Eliana awoke alone on the couch, a blanket spread over her. She stretched out her arms, missing the feel of Asher beside her. She heard him in the guest room, shuffling around in his socks. With a yawn and a stretch, she reached for her purse on the end table and pulled out her phone.

Hundreds of notifications. She pulled the blanket over her head and groaned. That's what she got for taking one day off for her sister's wedding.

Three missed calls from her grandma caught her eye, as well as one missed call from her agent. Was someone hurt?

She called her grandma back, but it went straight to voicemail. She went to her text messages. The one at the top was from her agent. *Why would you do this? Call me immediately.*

Do what?

She sat up quickly, the blanket falling to her feet as she read through her other texts.

Grandma: Call me when you get a minute.

Grandma: I'm so sorry. Your mom explained to me what I did.

Grandma: I love you.

Eliana grew more panicked as she read through each message, until finally, *finally*, she got to a message from her sister.

Julia: Have you seen this yet? *video link*

Eliana: Why are you on your phone on your honeymoon? Is Grandma okay?

Julia: I think she's okay. We're in the airport, waiting for our plane. Just watch the video, then message me.

It linked to Grandma Winnie's social media page. Eliana played the video, and her heart stopped when she realized it was her and Asher dancing together at the wedding. Asher looked so smitten with her, it almost hurt to look at. But that wasn't the bad part. No. It was that Eliana was staring up at Asher, so clearly, unmistakably, inarguably, in love.

Eliana: OH MY GOSH.

Julia: I know.

Eliana: I'M FREAKING OUT. Even if I have Grandma take it down, it's too late. People have seen it and downloaded it.

Julia: I know.

Julia: It's been on social media since last night.

Eliana's eyes stung with tears as she watched the video again, torn between mortification and longing to be in Asher's arms. Her agent called again, and she sent her straight to voicemail.

A video message from Giselle pinged in her notifications. Then one from Sienna. Her stomach lurched. She was going to be sick. She had to talk to her agent. She had to erase the video—go back in time and have it never happen. That's what she needed to do. Time travel! Easy peasy.

Julia: Listen. Maybe it's not so bad. I've never seen you look so happy before.

Eliana swiped the message away without responding to it. Her heart rate accelerated quicker than Asher's motorcycle, and she stood, turning one way and then the next, not sure where she was trying to go or what she'd do when she got there.

Asher, unfortunately, chose that moment to walk into the room, his hair tousled with sleep in a way that was irresistible. Her chest tightened as panic clawed at her.

His brows pulled together. "What's wrong?"

"Everything." She grabbed her purse and stuffed her phone into it. "We can't do this, Asher. We never should have started. It was a mistake. A horrible mistake."

He flinched with every anxious word as though she was striking him, but he took a slow, gentle step toward her. She threw herself away from him, banging her shins on the coffee table.

"Eliana—"

"Stop, I need—" She didn't even know how to finish that sentence. She felt like a trapped animal, and thankfully, Asher didn't come any closer. The pain in his eyes physically hurt her. She couldn't hear what he had to say and think she could still walk away. "We can't see each other anymore."

Tears spilled from her eyes as she fled this amazing man, needing to escape before she took everything back. She flung the front door open, her vision blurry as she raced out, straight into the broad chest of Gerard, a bemused Mr. Richardson beside him.

Chapter 38

Eliana

"I wish I had no heart, it aches so ..." —Louisa May Alcott

GERARD KEPT HIS HANDS on her arms until she was steady on her feet, and when he stepped back, she noticed that he positioned himself halfway between her and Mr. Richardson. "Is everything alright?" he asked quietly.

She swiped at her cheeks, mortified. "I'm fine. Yes. We pulled an all-nighter to finish packing the boxes." It would be clear to anyone that she'd just woken up. She stood there in her pajamas, her hair a mess, crying, and she wasn't even wearing shoes, for heaven's sake.

Gerard nodded like she made perfect sense. "That was very kind of you."

"And who are you?" Mr. Richardson asked, anger lacing his tone. "Did you *sleep* here?"

"This is Winnie Rees's granddaughter," Gerard said, his tone smooth and soothing. "It's my understanding that she's been helping clean out the house in preparation for my moving in."

"That's correct." She held her shoulders straight. Dang it. Gerard was making it really difficult to hate him like she wanted.

"Listen, young lady," Mr. Richardson said, clearly not buying what they were selling.

Asher's hand grabbed the door's edge, and he opened it wider. It was very clear he'd also just woken up. His eyes held the kind of resolution that filled her with foreboding.

"Don't," she said to Asher firmly.

Mr. Richardson looked back and forth between them, his face turning red with anger as he put two and two together—and came up with fifteen. "Our bungalows are not love shacks."

The words shocked the tears right out of Eliana. *Love shacks?*

He continued, spit flying out more generously with every word. "You have taken my generous gesture of letting you have time to clean out your grandpa's bungalow and abused it by turning it into a den of fornication."

"That's not what—" Asher began, but Eliana's own anger bubbled over like a hot pot, and she couldn't hold her words back.

"Excuse me," Eliana said. Mr. Richardson was making Asher sound like some sort of lawless predator. *She* was the one who had pushed herself into Asher's bungalow. *She* was the one who had kissed him first. And *she* was the one who got them caught. "Asher is not the kind of person you're making him sound like—"

"It's okay, Eliana." Asher placed a gentle hand on her arm, resigned. "It's time."

"No," she snapped. They had not hidden his secret this long, and gone to so much effort to do so, for it to all come out now, right at the end.

Mr. Richardson scoffed derisively. "I should call the police for trespassing."

Gerard placed a firm hand on Mr. Richardson's shoulder. "That seems unnecessary to me. The kids were cleaning up, and they fell asleep. It happens. I fall asleep mid-project more than I'd care to admit." He flashed a charming smile at Mr. Richardson that took some of the hot wind from his bloated sails. "I have another meeting soon, and I'd still like to discuss my donation to The Palms' memory care center."

She saw the wrestle Mr. Richardson had over railing them about whatever he thought they were doing in there, and the potential of getting money from Gerard. Money won, as well as a not-so-gentle leading down the stairs Gerard did with his hand on Mr. Richardson's shoulder. When

Gerard glanced back at them, she mouthed, *Thank you,* and he winked before returning to his conversation with Mr. Richardson.

Now not only did she kind of like the home-wrecking Gerard; she owed him.

"You should have let me tell him." Asher ran a frustrated hand through his hair.

"Why? So they could press charges against you?" she shot back.

"Because secrets haven't done us any favors so far," he said, his jaw tight.

"Maybe not. But the truth hasn't either."

He laughed without humor. "You aren't willing to even face the truth, Eliana. Not when it's staring you in the face. Not when it's one of the best things to ever happen." A charged beat passed.

"I just ... can't." She yanked her gaze away, backed up, turned, and took off in a run. She half-expected him to call after her. To follow her. To stop her.

She didn't want that—so why was she so disappointed when he didn't do those things?

She needed advice. Someone who could tell her why she was thinking this way and what to do. Grandma Winnie would know the best way out of this situation. She may have posted the video that started this whole mess, but Eliana was the one who'd gone and fallen for Asher. She didn't believe for a second that Grandma'd had any notion of what she was setting in motion when she'd posted that video—though Eliana was going to teach her what she could and couldn't post, as soon as she figured it out herself.

Besides, Eliana still didn't have shoes on, and she wasn't going back for them, so her options for places to go were very limited.

She ran on the beach side to avoid Mr. Richardson and Gerard, and banged on Grandma and Grandpa's bungalow door. Grandpa answered it after a minute, the wrinkles on his face deeper than she'd ever seen them.

"Is Grandma here?" she asked, breathless.

He motioned for her to follow him into the house, moving slower than Louisa May Alcott. She wanted to snap her fingers at him to get him moving quicker. Her life was crumbling apart, and every second that passed was another piece of cliff that crashed into the ocean.

They arrived at the kitchen, where she sat at the table, and Grandpa sat across from her.

"Where's Grandma?" she asked, sounding as impatient as she felt.

"She's at your parents' house. Telling your mom about her first husband." He swallowed as though he'd eaten something sour. "I guess your mom missed all the excitement last night."

"Lucky her," Eliana muttered.

"Can I help you with something?" Grandpa sat across from her in his usual chair, his hands clasped in front of him. His hair looked like he hadn't combed it yet today, and his wrinkled shirt was his dress shirt from the wedding. He looked as miserable as she felt.

"We're a pair, aren't we?"

Grandpa barked out a laugh. "I guess we are. We both know why I'm a mess. Why are you?"

Eliana frowned. She hated seeing her grandparents unhappy. She needed them to work through this—needed that stability in her life. "I know why Grandma kept the secret from you for so long," she said.

Grandpa lifted a brow. "Is that what you came here to tell your grandma?"

"No. I came here to complain about my life and have her solve all my problems and tell me what to do."

"Oh. She is good at that." Grandpa bit down on his lip—was that *almost* a smile? No way was he trying not to laugh at her. He paused, then gestured for her to keep talking. "So why didn't she tell me after all these years?"

"I don't want to tell you anymore," she said petulantly. "I think I'd rather tell you all my problems and see how good *you* do solving them."

He winced. "Unless the answer is a rousing round of golf with a good friend, I'm afraid I don't have any good advice for you."

She snorted. "Rousing. Oh, Grandpa." Then, to her horror, her eyes filled with tears. What was she going to do?

Grandpa reached out his hands and enfolded hers in his larger ones.

She stared at their clasped hands, following the blue veins and familiar brown age spots along his skin. "Grandma probably didn't tell you about Gerard because she's been happy. You make her happy. And when you're

happy, you don't want to think about your mistakes or your past relationships or your regrets."

"She could tell me anything. She should know that."

"She does know that." Eliana stared at him now, and knew she was saying
the truth. "But she didn't *want* to tell you this. And not because of you.
Because of *her*. I think she needed a fresh start—one where no one knew
she was rejected by someone she'd loved, or where people treated her like
she'd failed—one where she could forget he existed and have the life she'd
always wanted."

Grandpa stared at her closely. Too closely. She felt like she'd laid herself
bare on this table for examination and didn't like it one bit.

"But you did the opposite," he said.

"In a way, but I still grabbed the narrative and spun it the way I needed
it to be for me to keep going through the hurt." She swallowed. "And I
let it define my life. I've dedicated nearly every moment since Corbin left
to eradicating his memory—and part of that includes living single forever
because of his actions. Grandma did the opposite and tried to give it so little
meaning, it didn't exist for her anymore. She found love and happiness and
joy—and so she could let it all go."

Grandpa sighed, long and heavy, weighted with every one of his years.
Weighted as though he hadn't woken up today anticipating being his
granddaughter's free therapist, especially while going through his own
problems. Yet here he was. Showing up, as he always did. And as she always
knew he would, even when he was hurt and upset with Grandma Winnie.

"I saw the video," he said, "on your grandma's social media. I was
scrolling through it last night like a sop, and I saw you dancing with Asher.
You looked happy."

"I was happy," she said, her voice rising to an unknown octave through
her sudden tears, knowing she sounded ridiculous.

"Then why are you crying?" he asked her, his voice warm but incredulous.

"Because—if I'm happy, then I'll lose everything."

"That makes no sense." Grandpa patted her hand. "And so what if you
lose everything?"

"No offense, Grandpa, but you're kind of bad at this advice thing." She sniffled. "I need you to tell me how I can have it all—the job and the man and the Happily Single platform and the money—and not have everyone mad at me."

He barked out a laugh, which made her scowl. "Oh, honey," he said softer but with his signature honesty, "you can't have everything. Your generation is always saying 'you can have it all,' but the truth is, it's impossible to get everything you want. You're going to have to choose."

That wasn't what she wanted to hear. She wanted Grandma to walk in, having overheard everything, and have a ten-step plan in hand on how Eliana could have all of those things at once.

Grandpa pulled one of his hands free to bop her wrinkled nose, something he'd done since she was a little girl. "Don't give me that disgruntled look, Elly. What's most important to you?"

"I don't know," she whined. "Can't you just tell me?"

"Sure," he said. "But that's about as satisfying as walking to the cup and dropping my golf ball straight into it. We value the things we work for."

She dropped her head onto the table with a groan.

He patted her hair and then stood. "Let me get you a soda while you think, but don't think too hard, okay? Trust your gut. Line up your club to the tee. Have confidence in your swing."

"Wait. Are we talking my life or golf?"

"One and the same." She heard the crack and hiss of a can of soda opening. "Sometimes when we're out there on the green, we get a hole in one, but most of the time it takes a few swings to get the ball exactly where we need it to be." She felt the cold soda at her elbow and looked up to see his satisfied smile, his eyes adrift, lost in his golf metaphor.

"I know, I know." She couldn't help the smile that crept across her face. Grandpa had always had the magic touch to pull her out of a funk. "Keep trying. Never give up. Never surrender ..." She sipped the icy root beer—her favorite—feeling better despite herself.

"True. But also"—he rapped his knuckles lightly on the table—"you deserve all the happiness, love, and joy you can get. Whatever club or ball you choose, aim for that." He peeked over the side of the table, where she wiggled the toes of her bare feet. "But first, why don't you go into our closet and borrow some shoes from Grandma? Everything seems better with a good pair of shoes."

CHAPTER 39

WINNIE

W INNIE SAT IN A corner of the dining hall, wearing large, dark sunglasses and a floppy sun hat, hoping no one would notice her—most notably a certain ex-husband she hoped to never see again. Her life was in shambles, thanks to Gerard.

No, she thought, *thanks to me.* She was the one who had kept this secret for so long from Horace. She had no one to blame but herself. Lisa had taken the news about Winnie's first marriage surprisingly well, but she'd let Winnie know what a problem her video last night could pose for Eliana.

So not only had Winnie ruined her own life; she'd ruined Eliana's as well. How would she ever face her granddaughter again? She'd thought posting the video of Eliana and Asher dancing would be something cute and fun for her followers to see. Instead it had gone viral again—darn it all!—and suddenly she was reading all these terribly mean comments about what a hypocrite Eliana was and how she was only pretending to be single to earn money.

Her stomach pitched and rolled like it was a boat on a stormy sea. How could she have gotten so many things wrong?

Polly slid into the seat beside her but didn't say anything, just opened her library book and read. Winnie wanted to tell her that she needed to be alone, but she didn't have the energy to even speak. Besides, Polly was being quiet for once, so what did it matter if she sat there and read her book?

A moment later, Walt sat on the other side of her. He didn't say anything either, just perused his daily newspaper. Winnie let out a long, shuddering breath.

Nancy sat down next and pulled a half-done crocheted potholder from her purse. Less than a minute later, Don plopped an extra chair between Walt and Nancy and sat on it backward while scrolling through his phone, like a teenager in a movie. Rosa bustled over and squeezed in beside Polly, a fan in one hand and a frosted glass of iced tea in the other, her cheeks pink as if she'd just come in from being outside. Winnie wasn't surprised when Harry showed up last with a puzzle box under his arm that he opened and dumped onto the empty table.

They all quietly worked on their things. Each minute they were there ruined Winnie's pity party more and more. She wanted to sit in a dark corner and stew and feel bad for herself. Alone. Was that too much to ask?

"What are you all doing here?" she finally asked them, irritated.

"Escaping the heat," Rosa said.

The rest of them nodded but kept their focus on their work.

Irritation spiked in Winnie. "Y'all—I don't know what this is, but—"

"I had a baby in high school," Nancy said casually.

"What?" Winnie's eyes widened, as did everyone else's.

"My first. We got married really quick and were very happy together, but you know how people were back then." Nancy cut her yarn and pulled out a ball of a different color.

Winnie blinked. "Why are you telling me this?"

"Because we've all been idiots," Don said. He set his phone down on the table, and she realized he'd been reading an article about his grandson. "Getting mad at each other for keeping secrets, and suspecting each other of telling our secrets."

Rosa placed her bookmark in her book and closed it. "Being at the wedding reminded me of what brought us all together in the first place. Amor."

"And not just helping our grandchildren find love," Polly added. "Our love for them. And for each other. I've missed you all."

"Life has certainly been boring without our meetings and our match-makings," Walt said.

"And Rosa just finished the newest Allegra Winters novel, but we can't talk about it without you," Polly said to Winnie.

"I'll read it too," Nancy announced, and they gasped, because she was on record disliking historical romances. "I'm sorry I got angry on our text about it."

"You don't have to read it," Don said. "We accept your apology."

"Speak for yourself, Don," Polly said, a twinkle in her eye. "I only conditionally accept her apology until she reads it." She'd been trying to get Nancy to read them for years.

Winnie chuckled despite herself.

Harry leaned forward. "We're too old to hold grudges and not work things out. I've learned that the hard way once, and I'm not a big enough knucklehead to have to learn it again."

Winnie pulled off her sunglasses and swiped at her tears. "You guys are all nuts."

"I call pecans," Harry said.

"Hazelnuts," Rosa said, raising her hand. "My daughter puts them in mole … and it is divine."

"I don't really like nuts," Walt said. "Can I be a legume?"

Winnie sniffled and took in a deep, shuddering breath as all of her friends laughed and playfully argued over what kind of nuts they were. If only Horace could forgive her as easily. He hadn't come to bed last night, and she'd been too afraid to see if he was sleeping on the couch or in the guest bed, or if he'd left their bungalow completely at some point.

Polly noticed her fallen expression and took her hand. "We've got a plan, Winnie. We came up with it last night after the wedding."

"A plan?" For her and Horace? Her heart lifted.

"Yes." Don rubbed his hands together. "All it's going to take is a little duct tape, a blindfold, and brushing aside any aversions to kidnapping you might have, and we'll have those two together in no time."

Those two. Eliana and Asher. Of course. She focused on the matchmaking task at hand, and tried to ignore her heart squeezing every time she recalled how betrayed Horace had looked at the wedding.

"We agreed we wouldn't use duct tape," Nancy said to Don firmly.

"Oh, right, right," Don said shiftily—a twinkle in his eye—and he unfolded the plan for Winnie, Nancy jumping in every now and then to explain certain aspects in more detail. It was good. Really good. If it worked.

"We'll meet at my bungalow, at sunset." Harry tipped his pageboy cap. "That should give everyone enough time to do their part. Do you all understand your assignments?"

The Secret Seven nodded in agreement.

"Then let's go." Don mimicked unrolling a piece of duct tape and ripping it off—to Nancy's glare—as they all went their separate ways.

Maybe if Winnie could give her granddaughter her happily ever after, she'd forgive her. And then she could figure out Horace, somehow.

CHAPTER 40

ASHER

"I'M DOING IT TONIGHT. I just wanted you to know," Lydia said over the phone to Asher as he pulled a length of duct tape from the roll and ripped it off. He placed it on one of the final boxes for giveaway, and then sat on the ground.

"Lydia ..." He didn't know what to say. He'd promised to help her find a way to tell everyone, but he didn't know what he was doing. He'd planned on talking to Eliana about it, but now they weren't talking at all. He hadn't seen her since she'd stormed out of the house that morning, calling everything off between them, looking more closed off than he'd ever seen her.

Since then, he'd had no less than ten patients send him the video of the two of them dancing together at the wedding, wanting to know all the details. He was torn between watching the video on a loop that continually ripped his chest in two, or ignoring it completely and feeling like he was being buried alive. Two really great options.

"I'm ready to do this," Lydia continued, bringing him back to the conversation. "I don't want to keep it secret anymore, Asher. I'm losing sleep over it."

He understood that. He pulled his hair back from his face with dusty hands. Hadn't he wanted to confess everything to Mr. Richardson just that morning?

Besides, how could he help anyone else clean up their own life when his was such a mess? Look at how well falling in love had gone for him. He was worse off than before he'd met Eliana—because now he knew what he was missing.

No, he didn't actually believe that. He was glad Eliana had crash-landed into his life with her blackmail and zest for going through boxes without asking and propensity to leave windows open that should be closed. He hadn't realized his life had gotten so cloudy until Eliana came in with her sunshine. Even Louisa May Alcott, who had been staring at him all day like he was her favorite reality television show, had grown on him. At least he knew Eliana would return at some point to get her turtle. She'd never leave Louisa behind, and on some level, he felt good knowing that Eliana trusted him to take care of Louisa.

Plus, when she hadn't answered any of his calls or texts, he'd had to carefully pack her things up as well. He'd drop them off at her grandparents' house on his way out of The Palms, including Louisa. It surprised him to feel a pang at the thought.

"When are you going to tell everyone?" He wanted to be there so she'd have at least one friend when this went public. He tucked the phone between his cheek and shoulder as he picked up the box and set it by the front door.

"There's a Palms Association meeting tonight at the clubhouse at seven-thirty. I'll do it then," she said with confidence, but her sigh at the end was a dead giveaway that she was nervous.

In front of everyone? Nearly all of The Palms' residents went to those meetings to make their concerns about the community known. He'd attended last month and heard complaints about the hot tub's too-warm temperature, a request for the library to update their catalog with more spicy romances, and—most notably because of the uproar it caused—a heated argument over whether Bruno's chicken gravy had too much pepper in it or not, which resulted in Bruno refusing to make chicken gravy for six long months.

There were legitimate concerns and Palms business issues covered in these meetings, but that's not why people went. They went for the drama. "You'd probably like it, Louisa," he told the turtle once he hung up with Lydia. "My life is boring compared to those meetings."

After Eliana had fled Asher like Joseph running from Potiphar's wife, Asher had rented a truck and finished packing the rest of the house. He left Louisa on the table, but he took the last box to the truck and placed it in the bed. Then he went back inside the house to look around one last time.

It was strange, being here without all the things that had made up his grandpa's life. The house looked bigger, but empty like a discarded conch shell. He opened all the blinds for the first time since his grandpa died and let the light in.

Walking away from this house felt like leaving his grandpa behind. He knew his grandpa wasn't in this house; he was in Asher's memories, in most of the decisions he made, in his soul. But being in the bungalow had anchored Asher to his grandpa's life and memory. And with this bungalow gone, Asher felt adrift without a map.

He had no idea what his future held, but maybe that was okay. It was time to let go. To stop wishing for life to stand still. To stop paddling sideways on his board, avoiding every wave. Hard times were sure to come, because that was life, but his grandpa had taught him how to get back on his board when wave after wave knocked him down. To continue getting up every day and living life and to be the kind of person who never stopped trying.

Asher walked through every room to double-check that nothing had been left behind. But mostly to say goodbye. Emotion swelled in the back of his throat as he went from the master bedroom, where he used to sit on a chair next to Grandpa's bed when he was really sick and read to him, to the guest bedroom, where Asher slept when he'd come to visit. Down the hall to the front room, Asher had talked about his life, and he and his grandpa had laughed and forgotten about every hard thing when Asher came home on breaks and holidays. But it was also where they'd cried, on anniversaries and birthdays and in those moments when memories sideswiped them right off the road and into an emotional ditch.

Finally, he went into the kitchen, where he had a single cookie waiting on a napkin for him. Oatmeal raisin, his grandpa's favorite, something they'd joked endlessly about—arguing over whether it was the best cookie ever (his grandpa) or the worst cookie ever conceived (Asher). He took one bite of it and made a face. "Still the worst cookie ever." Asher held it out like he was toasting his grandpa. "Love you. Miss you. Thank you for everything."

He went to take another bite, when there was a knock at the door. His stomach lurched. Eliana? Whatever his future held, he wanted her in it.

He set the cookie on his napkin and went to open the door. He took a step back as he absorbed the sight in front of him. It was seven people wearing black from head to toe, including the bandannas covering their noses and mouths. They looked like an octogenarian set of bank robbers.

From the back of the group, he heard the distinct sound of duct tape being unrolled. Was that ... Don? He had a maniacal gleam in his eye.

Until someone—Nancy?—elbowed him hard in the ribs. "I *said* no duct tape."

"He might not come otherwise," Don muttered.

"Come where?" Asher asked, his eyes narrowed on each of them. Now that he wasn't so surprised at the unexpected sight, he recognized every single one of them. Including Winnie, who stood a bit off to the side. He gave her a quizzical glance, wishing they were alone and he could ask her about Eliana.

"To the association meeting, mijo," Rosa said.

"This is a kidnapping," Walt complained in Rosa's general direction. "We shouldn't use terms of endearment."

"Oh, sorry." Rosa turned back to Asher. "To the association meeting, you *blackguard.*"

Harry and Polly both stifled a laugh, which earned them a glare from Don. "Take this seriously."

Asher scrubbed an exhausted hand over his face. He didn't know what a blackguard was—and was pretty sure he didn't want to know. "I'm actually planning on heading over to the meeting right now."

"Oh. Well." That seemed to deflate Don. He stuck the duct tape into his backpack. Asher spotted rope in there too. He definitely didn't want to get on Don's bad side. Ever.

"That's a bit anticlimactic," Polly whispered loudly. "What do we do now?"

"I'll go with him and make sure he's not lying," Don said with narrowed eyes.

Asher frowned. "Why in the world would I lie—"

"The rest of you continue with Part B," Don said over him. "We'll reconvene in thirty minutes. Godspeed."

And with that, Don took him by the arm in a firm, no-nonsense grip and marched him down the stairs in a take-no-prisoners kind of way.

"What is going—"

"No questions," Don barked, and Asher clamped his mouth shut. *Okaaaay*. It wasn't like Asher had anywhere else to be or anything else to do; he didn't even know where he was going to live, since he'd never gotten Julia's keys from Eliana. This was what his life had come to—being bullied around by retirees—and he didn't hate it.

Even though Don hadn't used the blindfold, or the ropes, or the duct tape, and Asher could *probably* take him in a fight, he followed along and felt very much like Don was a determined pirate walking Asher to the plank.

CHAPTER 41
ELIANA

"The emerging woman ... will be strong-minded, strong-heart-ed, strong-souled, and strong-bodied ... strength and beauty must go together." —Louisa May Alcott

ELIANA SAT IN HER car, parked next to Asher's motorcycle in his usual hidden spot, and pulled out her phone. Part of her hoped Asher would come out here and she'd get to see him again. She fully planned on ducking low, so he didn't see her, if that happened. But a girl could hope.

She'd attempted to take her grandpa's advice and tackle her problems at her parents' house, but it had been way too loud. It was amazing how much noise three people could make—plus driving around town, looking for the perfect hiding spot seemed like a really great idea.

But she couldn't stall anymore. She opened her email from her agent and read through it. It was exactly as she suspected—her book was being dropped unless she could offer a believable explanation for what that video showed.

She tried to think of an explanation—something, anything. She'd tripped and fallen into his arms and they'd mistaken her look of gratitude for adoration. He was her fake, fake boyfriend and she was a really good actor. Send her to Hollywood!

She groaned and opened her video messages. She clicked on Giselle's first. Her smiling face popped up on screen, looking as amazing and put together as ever. "Hey, I saw the VIDEO and heard about what happened with your BOOK."

Eliana paused the video. How had Giselle heard anything about the book? Eliana had just read the email a second ago. She frowned and pressed play again.

"I'm SO SORRY! I'm here for you if you need ANYTHING. If you want me to share your story so you don't have to, let me know. Also, WHO is the guy? I'm DYING to hear all about it. Message me back soon."

Giselle reveled in gossip, and now that Eliana was the subject of juicy news, it felt gross—both to have this happen to her and to listen to it happen to someone else.

She didn't reply, and instead opened her message from Sienna. The room was dark around her, and Sienna spoke in a hushed tone, close to the phone.

"Hey, I heard about what happened. I'm in a theater, waiting for the movie to start, but I saw the video and needed to message you right away, because I completely understand. Call me if you want to talk."

Eliana's eyes stung with tears, and she pulled up Sienna's phone number. She usually didn't call like this—but she was desperate.

The phone only rang once before Sienna answered. "Hey, Elly. I'm glad you called." They caught up for a few minutes before Sienna softly said, "Tell me what's going on."

Eliana groaned and dropped her head onto the steering wheel. There was only one way to explain this. "His name is Asher. And he's turned my world upside down."

"In a good way?"

"In the *best* way."

Sienna sighed, but it sounded ... happy? "That's what I thought. You can't fake that look you were giving him."

Eliana groaned. "What do I do? They've threatened to drop my book deal."

"Of course they did." Eliana heard the eye roll in Sienna's tone. "And they want the advance back?"

"Yep." Nausea clenched her stomach. "I don't know what to do."

Sienna paused. "I'm going to tell you something that no one else knows. This is just between you and me."

Eliana sat up straighter, intrigued. "I am a vault," she promised.

"I drank the caffeine in public on purpose."

"What?" That was definitely not what she expected Sienna to say.

"I went to the café on one of the busiest days and times of week—I looked it up online—and made sure to walk around with it for a bit until I saw someone take my picture."

"But why?"

"This is going to sound horrible and ungrateful, but I never wanted to be in the limelight. I happened to post something to my, like, two hundred followers that went viral, and suddenly I was the face of a movement. The pressure of living a public life was getting to me—to look and act a certain way, plus the criticisms and trolls—and I snapped. I met with a therapist, and I guess what I did could be considered self-sabotage, except I'm happier now."

"You are?" Eliana hadn't seen her update her socials all summer, and had assumed she was crying in a hole somewhere for everything she'd lost.

"Yep. I've been miserable and stressed for a while, but I was in too deep, you know? I didn't know how to get out, and so I finally did something extreme."

"I had no idea you felt that way," Eliana said. Some friend she was.

"No one did," Sienna assured her. "Except my mom. Every time I said yes to something else, she threatened to lock me up in her RV, drive me to Mexico, and hold me hostage there until I came to my senses."

"Why Mexico?" Eliana asked.

"The tacos. Plus they have great beaches with terrible cell service."

Eliana laughed and then covered her mouth. "I'm sorry."

"That was supposed to make you laugh," Sienna assured her. "But you're not me, Eliana. I know you love what you do."

"I really do love it," Eliana said. "But I don't think I can give Asher up either."

"All I know is that when I look at that picture of you two, it makes me ache deep inside with envy. Is that really something you want to give up for a book deal or followers?"

It made Eliana ache as well, which was why she couldn't stop watching the video. Maybe she was a self-saboteur too. Had she ever really wanted to be the Happily Single Girl, forever and always? Or had she just wanted to protect herself and grieve and help others who were in the same place as her?

"Social media has tried to put us both in a box," Sienna said. "And we let them. They made me the face of a movement, and you became the face of singleness, but we can be more than one thing, Elly. And you are more than just a vow you made on the Internet. You are a person, and people change."

"Set my own parameters," Eliana said.

"Exactly. And that may mean starting over. Or having people be mad at you. Or moving to Mexico for really great beaches and tacos. But make sure you're doing what's best for you and not everyone else."

"Thank you." Eliana took a really deep breath for the first time all day.

"Oh, before you go," Sienna said. "Asher doesn't happen to have a brother? Cousin? Cute, young uncle?"

Eliana laughed. "No, he doesn't. But maybe that'll be my next career step ... matchmaking. I think it runs in the family."

They hung up, and Eliana got out of her car, full of nervous energy. She had to figure out how to fix all of this.

A text from Grandma Winnie lit up her phone.

Winnie: Can you drop by my bungalow tonight? Soon?

Eliana: I can be there in ten minutes.

Winnie: Perfect. Thanks, dear.

Eliana: I love you, Grandma. It's all going to work out.

Winnie: I hope so.

Eliana hoped so too. She needed to see Asher really quick first. He might not want to see her at all, not with the way she'd stormed out earlier, but she needed to give him the key to Julia's apartment and grab Louisa May Alcott.

It was a testament to how upset she'd been earlier that she'd left without Louisa.

The bungalow was completely dark. The doors were locked. She peeked in the open windows and saw that everything had been cleaned out. Louisa May Alcott was on the table in her habitat, safely tucked in her shell.

Where had Asher gone? His motorcycle was still there, so he had to be somewhere close. Her heart dropped. He'd done all of this without her?

She pulled out her phone to call him, then chickened out in the last minute and texted instead:

Eliana: Where are you?

No answer came, so she put her phone back in her pocket.

She backed away from the bungalow and headed to Grandma's house, her mind full of Asher and what Sienna had said. Eliana didn't want out of the social media sphere completely. She loved creating content and meeting new people and giving advice on how to be happy.

She was so involved with her thoughts, she didn't notice the dark shadows surrounding her one by one as she approached the bungalow. In fact, it wasn't until one of them placed a hand on her arm—and she screamed—that she realized she was surrounded by six ninjas.

No. Grandma Winnie and her friends were wearing all black, including black bandannas.

"What—?"

"Come with us if you want to live," Walt interrupted in a low voice with a faint English accent. Then he whispered out of the corner of his mouth, "I've always wanted to say that."

Eliana bit back a smile. Count on Grandma and her friends to turn an epically horrible day into something interesting. "What if I don't want to go?" she asked, just to see what would happen. Because honestly, she was intrigued enough to go wherever they wanted. And besides, she had emails to avoid.

"I'm sorry about this, hon." Grandma Winnie didn't look sorry at all as she threw a linen-scented black pillowcase over her head and took her by the hands.

"It's a good thing Don's not here with his duct tape," one of the women whispered, and Eliana had to agree as she found herself blindly marched across the beach, left with no choice but to let them lead her wherever they wanted.

CHAPTER 42

ASHER

D ON SAT BESIDE ASHER, so close that if Asher were inclined to run—which he wasn't—Don could tackle him in half a second flat. The meeting was set to start in less than five minutes, and he'd had more people come to say hi to him than usual. Most of them were current or former patients, but there were a few other people he'd met through his grandpa as well.

Lydia walked in with Smitty, her shoulders back and her chin set to a resolute angle. She spotted Asher and sent him a wink. He was glad to see her in good spirits. His heart was racing enough for the both of them.

Claude turned in his seat to face Asher. "Mary planted the rosemary bush you dropped off last week. She'd love for you to come by and see it."

"That's great." He didn't know when he'd be able to come by, especially now that he wasn't living at The Palms. During lunch, maybe. Relief swept through him. For the first time in a while, he didn't have to worry about anyone finding out what he was up to. He hadn't realized what a weight that was until it was gone. "I'll definitely do that—"

His words choked off into a strangled sound as he spotted Winnie and her friends march into the room with Eliana, who had a black pillowcase over her head. They stood in the back and whipped it off. Her hair flew around her, caught with static electricity, and she blinked at the bright fluorescent lights of the large conference room. She hadn't spotted him yet. He would have thought his heart couldn't race any faster. He was wrong.

A WEDDING MISMATCH

She still wore the same sweats and oversized shirt she had on that morning, but she'd procured pink leather sandals at some point and had pulled her hair into a fluffy bun at the top of her head. He'd seen her disheveled like this before, but he knew no one else had. His temperature rose with the desire to be closer to her. He let out a slow breath as her gaze met his, and heat burned like the Florida sun between them.

"Let's get started." Mr. Richardson banged his gavel on the conference lectern.

"He never comes to these," Don said. "Usually, he has Samantha run them."

Foreboding twisted in Asher's gut.

"I have some proposals," Mr. Richardson said.

Samantha, sitting behind him, cleared her throat. "Announcements first."

"Right. Announcements." He paused, clearly at a loss, and motioned for Samantha to take over.

She rattled them off from memory, and then she sat, turning the meeting back over to Mr. Richardson. "Now we open up the floor for discussion," she prompted.

He glared at her but turned to everyone and repeated her words. "Does anyone have something they'd like to discuss?" His tone made it clear their answer should be no.

Don raised his hand and began to stand, but before he could get all the way up, Lydia spoke, her voice ringing through the room. "I have something to say!" She faced the crowd, her rapidly rising and falling chest the only indication of her nerves. "I'm the one who shared everyone's secrets. I found a box someone meant to throw away, and I abused the knowledge in it. I was lonely and miserable, and it's no excuse, but that's why I did it."

Asher held his breath as people gasped and whispered.

"Quiet!" Mr. Richardson banged his gavel several times until it was silent. "Any relevant *business* matters?" he asked pointedly.

"You went through someone's trash?" someone called out.

"That's no excuse!" another voice said.

"That was really embarrassing!"

"It was awful. Why would you do that?"

The calls continued, getting more and more angry as they rolled forward, and he saw Lydia's hands shake as she stood there, each angry accusation a dart, and Lydia the board they hit time and again.

Everyone ignored the gavel's pounding, and though it was too erratic to imitate a heartbeat, it still made him think of a hunting documentary he'd watched once ... the steady heartbeat that grew faster and faster until the prey was pounced upon. Lydia tried to speak, tried to answer their questions, but no one gave her any space to be heard.

Without thinking, Asher stood and called out over the yells. "I've been living in my grandpa's bungalow since he died."

The room fell silent as all heads swiveled away from Lydia and toward him.

Mr. Richardson's eyes looked as if they might bug straight out of his head. His face turned a shade of purplish red, and he yelled out, "I knew it! I knew something fishy was going on. I will be getting our lawyers involved—"

"I got pregnant in high school!" Nancy yelled out, and every head in the room turned from Mr. Richardson to her with a gasp. "I am not ashamed of it, but it's not something I tell everyone either."

"Horace is my second husband," Winnie announced, her voice strong despite the tiny tremble he could hear. He knew she hated speaking to large groups of people, and that this revelation was something she'd worked hard to keep hidden on top of it. "I was married to Gerard first." She pointed him out, and he gave the room a guilty smile as he waved. "Horace second." Her face fell when she looked around and realized he was nowhere to be found.

"I've had five wives and I have three sons, and not a one of them will talk to me," Gerard said into the silence. "My granddaughter is the only family member who will acknowledge me at all, and that's because she's too dang sweet to realize I'm a worthless old man."

Glen Stewart, another resident of The Palms, gave Gerard's shoulder a squeeze. It was well known that once he'd given his family their inheritance early, they hadn't visited since.

"You're not worthless," Winnie said, and several people followed that with a "here, here!" Gerard threw her a grateful nod.

Don pulled on Asher's arm and forced him to sit as one by one, the residents of The Palms stood and confessed one secret after another, things that hadn't even made it into Asher's grandfather's files. "This is the best meeting I've ever been to," Don said with a satisfied smile, as if he were the one who had orchestrated it in the first place.

"It's my turn!"

Asher whipped his head around so fast at the sound of Eliana's voice, he might as well have given himself whiplash.

She stood with a confident set to her shoulders. "I'm a content creator who vowed to always remain happily single, but my grandpa told me a very compelling golf metaphor today, and, well ..." She looked at Asher, and he nearly swallowed his tongue. "I'm madly in love with Asher Brooks."

White noise filled Asher's ears as he stared at Eliana, and she looked back at him. Had she just said what he thought she had?

"Go on. That's your cue." Don elbowed him just hard enough to cross the friendly-nudge line and border into bruising territory. But Asher didn't need to be told twice. He nearly knocked down his chair in his rush to make it over to Eliana.

He stopped a foot away from her, wondering if he'd heard her right. Did she *really* want to be with him? Maybe she loved him, but she also loved her job—and she had her book, and perhaps she just meant she loved him, sure, but that didn't mean she—

She stepped closer and pressed her lips to his, wiping out any other thoughts he had in his mind. He brought his arms around her waist and held her close, coming out of his haze only when he heard Winnie shout over the cheers: "And if anyone posts this on social media—"

Most of the faces stared back at her blankly, but there were a few people, including Walt, who brought their phones down.

Eliana laughed and tugged at her grandma's arm. "It's okay, Grandma. I want everyone to know."

"On *your* terms," Grandma said stubbornly. "There's been quite enough of people revealing other people's secrets to last a lifetime."

"Amen," Harry said under his breath.

Asher kept his arms wrapped around Eliana and pulled her close to him as Winnie continued to talk. He didn't think he could ever let Eliana go. Just one day without her was enough to convince him he wanted her in his life forever. And the idea that she might want him just as much? It was going to take some time to process this.

"On that note ..." Winnie continued. She stomped forward and grabbed the gavel out of Mr. Richardson's hands. He stepped back, just as shocked as Asher and everyone else. Winnie was never this forceful.

"Go, Grandma," Eliana said under her breath.

"We need to forgive Lydia. She's our friend, and we didn't see that she was miserable and hurting. I've known her a long time, and this is very out of character for her. Would you ever do something like this again, Lydia?"

Tears glistened in Lydia's eyes. "Never. I can't express how sorry I am that I hurt so many of you, and I will spend the rest of my life making it up to you."

"No, you won't," Winnie said. "Because we're all going to forgive you without prejudice. You can't spend the rest of your life feeling like you're indebted to all of us because of one mistake." She looked out at each of them, and even Asher felt himself pulling his shoulders back, wanting to live up to Winnie's standards the way she believed he could. "We're all going to be a lot kinder and more understanding toward each other. We know things about each other now that we can't un-know, and we're going to protect that knowledge, not exploit it." She looked at the gavel in her hand and then held it up. "All in favor, say aye."

"Aye!" everyone called out.

"Anyone opposed?"

The room was silent.

Winnie swung the gavel down and hit the lectern. "Then it's agreed. Lydia is forgiven, and we're all going to be kinder."

She handed the gavel to Mr. Richardson, who looked about like a cartoon character did before steam came out of their ears. "If that's all the business—"

"There is one more thing," Don said. As he stood, he held out a sheaf of papers he pulled from his backpack. "I hold in my hands the signatures of every single person in the room, agreeing to allow Asher to continue living in Mason Brooks's bungalow."

Sudden dizziness swept over Asher, and he held onto Eliana's shoulders. Her mouth was open in shock as she looked back at him. "How did you know?" he asked Nancy.

She patted him on the arm. "Oh, hon. We know everything that goes on in The Palms. We've been covering for you since your grandpa died."

He blinked, thinking about all the times they'd directed Mr. Richardson away from him or it appeared they hadn't seen him on the beach. As they added up in his mind, like dominoes falling down, it became clear to him that they'd known this whole time.

"Did they know about you living there?" he whispered in Eliana's ear. She shivered, and it filled him with a sense of happiness.

"I don't think so. Perhaps they don't know *everything* that happens here," she said.

Nancy leaned closer, coming into their cocoon. "We knew you'd moved in, too, Eliana. We're just trying to keep the revelations PG-rated today."

"Oh my gosh." Eliana's face turned pink. "It wasn't like that—"

But Nancy gave her mischievous smile and mimicked zipping her lips shut and throwing away the key.

"I guess they *do* know everything," she muttered to Asher, who instinctively knew he should hold back his snicker.

"Furthermore, the bylaws state—" Mr. Richardson started.

"The bylaws state that the bylaws can be superseded by a two-third majority vote of the residents," Samantha interrupted him, a very satisfied smile stretched across her face. Asher squinted. Did her dress have kissing turtles on it?

"I have nearly one hundred percent of the residents voting that he can remain in that bungalow," Don said.

"But I have a new resident lined up," Mr. Richardson sputtered.

"I respectfully withdraw my application," Gerard said.

"No, you can't! And Asher broke our bylaws. He can't be rewarded for that."

Again, the room swiveled to look at him. He took in their faces, realizing that every single one of them had voted to keep him here. Since his grandpa died, he'd felt so alone, but each of these people loved him in one way or another. They wanted him here. He was at a moment of decision.

He heard his grandpa's voice in his head. *Do you want to keep paddling sideways, or are you going to grab the next wave?*

"Thank you, everyone. The fact that you would do this for me ..." He had to clear the emotion from his throat before he could continue. Eliana squeezed his hand supportively. "I can't even say how much this means to me—literally, I can't." He cleared his throat again, and people chuckled, easing some of the tension. "I love you all for doing this, but it's time for me to move out and see what other adventures life has in store for me. Being here, being with you all, has gotten me through losing the last person I had left. And I'll never forget that." Dang it. A tear fell, and then another, and he swiped at his cheeks.

He heard some sniffles around him as a few other people tried to get their emotions under control as well.

"But it's not like I'm going too far." He wanted to lift the somber mood he'd brought into the room. "I still work here."

"About that," Mr. Richardson said. "I wouldn't be so sure."

Asher's stomach sank. He'd given up the bungalow, but he wasn't ready to give up his job. Of course there would be consequences, though. Mr. Richardson wouldn't let this go.

"If he gets fired, I'm moving," Winnie declared, looking every inch the warrior she'd been all night. Eliana looked at her with pride in her eyes.

"Me too," Claude said as he stood.

"And me." Marilyn Detrix, using her cane for leverage, stood as well.

And in one overwhelming act, everyone stood, declaring that they'd move if Asher was fired. Asher's knees went weak, and he thought he might have to sit.

"This is incredible," he whispered.

"You deserve this," Eliana said fiercely. "You are loved for a reason, Asher."

Mr. Richardson gaped at them all, then sputtered as he hit the gavel on the lectern and muttered, "Meeting adjourned," before he fled the room as if he'd become the prey.

The room exploded in conversation. Eliana tugged at his hand, pulling him from his daze as she led him quietly out of the room, around the corner, and into a dark hall.

"That was ... something," he said on a long breath. He leaned against the wall. "Eliana, I don't want you to give up anything for me."

She stepped in front of him, close enough that if he filled his lungs all the way, his chest would touch her. Unfortunately, having her this close made it extremely hard to breathe.

"I'm not." She tipped her head to the side. "Well, technically, I am giving up my book deal and I'll probably need to start over as a content creator, which means I have no money, and I just canceled my lease in Boston, so I have no house—"

"So what aren't you giving up?" he asked.

"The things that actually make me happy," she said seriously. "Being close to my family. Accepting all the parts of myself. You." She leaned even closer. "I may be giving up some things, but I'm gaining so much more."

He leaned down until his lips were a mere whisper from hers. "I'm gaining the most."

She licked her lips, nearly causing him to groan. "Oh, you don't want to go down that road. You know how competitive I can be."

"Yeah, I do. It's one of the things I love most about you."

Her eyes brightened in that sunshiny way that lit him to his core. She brushed her lips against the corner of his mouth. "Well one of the things I love most about *you* is your white-chocolate macadamia-nut cookies."

He held back with every ounce of self-discipline he had. "I knew you just wanted me for my cooking."

She kissed the other side of his mouth. "What can I say? I'm basic."

"You are anything but basic. Which happens to be another thing I love about you."

"Hmmm," she murmured, drawing her finger in a line down his chest. "Well, I love that you—"

And with that, his self-discipline was gone, and he took her tender mouth in his in a kiss that was only interrupted by the catcalls of people leaving the meeting.

"So immature," Eliana called out after them, her lips plump in a way that made him eager to kiss them again and never, ever let her go.

Something in his gaze must have alerted her to his feelings, because she wrapped her arms around him even tighter, and he knew she felt the exact same way.

CHAPTER 43

WINNIE

W INNIE WAS ONE OF the last people to leave the clubhouse after the meeting, dreading arriving home. She wasn't sure what would be worse—Horace being there or not. No, not being there was definitely worse. They needed to talk. They hadn't been married this long without hitting a few speed bumps in the road along the way. Admittedly, this was more of a half-wall than a speed bump.

She opened the door to their dark house, and her shoulders slumped. Not home, then. What if he never forgave her for not telling him about Gerard? She couldn't imagine her life without Horace. She'd been upset with him for spending so much time with Smitty because of how lonely it made her feel. But this? This was devastating.

She went to flip on the light when she noticed a flicker in the kitchen. She walked toward it, surprised to find a battery-powered candle lit in the middle of their kitchen table. It illuminated two of her best china plates, each with a generous wedge of black forest cake.

"What?" She turned around, confused, and saw Horace standing in the kitchen doorway, holding two goblets. Her heart raced at the sight of him, just as it had the first time he'd come to the counter where she'd worked and asked for a soda.

"Your friends are something else," he said with fondness. He set down the glasses and pulled a note from his back pocket. She recognized Walt's handwriting.

There are two slices of Bruno's chocolate cake in the fridge, along with some raspberry sparkling cider. We'll let you take it from here.

Then, in Nancy's handwriting, it said: *Don't disappoint us.*

"This was duct-taped to the door when I got home from fixing the bathroom sink at Eric's rental." Well, that explained where he'd been. Their grandson kept a rental home in Diamond Cove he occasionally asked them to help with.

"They must have sneaked it in while we were waiting for Eliana," Winnie said. She blinked back her sudden tears. Her friends were matchmaking her and Horace. And with much less dramatics than they'd done with Eliana and Asher. Minus the threat from Nancy, she supposed, but it had come from a place of love.

Horace stepped closer to her, and Winnie held her breath. She had so much to say, she didn't know where to start. But being silent was what had gotten her into this mess in the first place. The dim lighting of the single candle made it easier for her to share this part of her past she'd kept hidden for so long. It was time.

"I met Gerard when I was a teenager."

"You don't have to tell me this if you'd rather not," Horace said softly.

"I want to. I should have done this a long time ago." She swallowed and stared down at her hands. How different they looked now than they had when she was eighteen. "We had a whirlwind romance that ended in my heartbreak when he left, and I wanted to forget him. My parents suggested we act as if it had never happened, since they worried no one would ever marry me if they knew I had been married before."

She glanced up to see Horace's mouth straighten. He'd sometimes struggled with her parents' traditional ways of thinking that valued perception over reality.

"I can't blame them, though, Horace. I was old enough to know my own mind. And I'm sure they never intended for me to keep it a secret for the rest of my life. I just ..."

"You were happy," Horace said, his voice gruff.

"Yes. I was. I am," she corrected with a small, teary laugh. "I've been so ridiculously happy with you, Horace. I was on my guard for so many years, worried you might one day leave me too, but at some point—I can't even tell you when—I trusted fully you'd never leave."

"It was after you had Lisa," he said, his voice filled with surprised understanding, as if something he'd wondered about for years suddenly made sense. "I came home from work one day, and you and Lisa were both crying. You because the house was a mess, you hadn't showered in three days, and Lisa had just thrown up all over your only clean pair of clothes. And Lisa because she had colic, and all she did was cry in those days. Remember that?"

She didn't remember the exact day, but she did recall how miserable those months were, all blended together, like a picture taken with a smudged lens.

He continued. "I threw in a load of laundry, straightened up the kitchen, and took Lisa to my mom's house so you could get a bath all alone. And when we came back an hour later, I found you still sitting on the bed, wrapped in a towel with your hair dripping all over your shoulders, sobbing. I said your name, and you looked up at me, shocked. I think that's the thing that sticks with me the most—that look on your face. And you said you didn't think I was coming back."

Winnie's breath caught. She recalled always being worried in those early days that he'd wake up one day and realize this life she'd given him was too hard and he wanted out.

"I told you I'd never leave." Horace took another step closer to her and reached out for her hand. She looked at their fingers, entwined together, both with wrinkles and purple veins and age spots, developed together over the years of their marriage. Years where they'd grown up and experienced life together, where they'd fallen more deeply in love than she could have fathomed. Years she'd never change for anything.

"And I still mean it," he said, taking another step closer, bringing their clasped hands to his lips. "I'll never leave, Winnie. I love you, no matter how many exes show up here because they realize they were idiots for ever letting you go. And who can blame them? You're the best thing that could ever happen to anyone. Especially me."

She laughed weakly and tipped her head into his chest, breathing in his familiar scent. That scent, this chest, all of Horace ... that was home. "It's only the one ex. I swear."

His chest rumbled against her forehead with a chuckle.

"I love you too," she said.

"As long as we're apologizing, I need to tell you that I'm sorry for not realizing how much it was hurting you that I was spending so much time with Smitty. I don't know if you're aware of this characteristic of mine, but I sometimes get a one-track mind and go a little overboard with things ..."

Winnie looked up at him with wide eyes and placed a hand on her chest in mock surprise. "Really? I had no idea."

He tickled her side in the one spot that always made her squeal. "I'll do better," he said.

"Me too," she promised. Wasn't that all any of them could do? Promise to do better and be better? "I thought you'd like to know that your golf metaphor to Eliana saved the day."

He puffed out his chest. "Well, I like to think golf solves all problems ... except for the ones it causes." He paused. "So Asher and Eliana?"

"To quote Eliana, they're madly in love," she said, and he smiled with satisfaction.

"You and your friends are good at this."

"We couldn't have done it without you." She squeezed his hand.

"Yeah, you could have." He smiled teasingly. "And in Julia's case, it would have been easier."

She couldn't deny that. But everything was more fun with Horace. And they really did make a spectacular team.

She twisted her hand in his grasp so she held his in a handshake, and she gave him her most serious look. "You know who I've been thinking about a lot?"

"Eric?" he asked, a gleam in his eye.

"Exactly. What do you say we combine our forces and help him find the love of his life?"

"Winnie, there's nothing else I'd rather do. Except maybe eat that chocolate cake." He waggled his brows and pulled her in even closer, not leaving a breath between them, their handshake completely forgotten.

"That sounds perfect to me." She reached up on her tiptoes, he met her halfway with a tender kiss, and everything felt right in her world once again.

CHAPTER 44
ELIANA

"The power of finding beauty in the humblest things makes home happy and life lovely." —Louisa May Alcott

"**B**ALL!" CAMERON CALLED OUT before he launched himself into the pool at The Palms in one of his best cannonball showings to date. He'd gotten most of the bystanders completely soaked. That was good. Too good. Eliana narrowed her eyes.

He surfaced and gave Eliana a challenging glare, combined with punching his chest, something he must have seen on television. She fought a smile.

"You've got this!" Asher yelled from where he sat at the pool's edge, his legs dangling in.

For a moment, she was distracted by his bare chest. All those abs. Those glorious pecs. Perhaps she could put this off for just a second—no, better make that several minutes ... Asher met her gaze and gave her a knowing grin that just about combusted her on the spot.

"Elly!" Cam yelled, snapping her out of it.

"Right. Sorry." She blinked. Refocused. "Cannonball!" she yelled just as loud as Cameron had as she raced to the pool's edge, tucked her legs under her, and slammed into the water with all the force she could muster. She tipped her head back to get her hair out of her face as she rose to the surface, and then looked to the judges—their grandparents—for their results.

The water rocked around them as they each held their breath.

Grandma Winnie gave her an apologetic smile. *Dang it.* Eliana slapped the water.

"Cameron is the winner," Grandpa bellowed. "By a lot, Elly. You've got to work on your form."

"I'm new to this cannonball business," she defended.

"Yeah!" Cameron raised his hands over his head and cheered, then threw himself back into the water over and over again in his victory water dance.

Eliana laughed and splashed him, so he splashed back until it became an all-out splash war between the two of them, with a lot of casualties on the sidelines.

She'd win next time. Maybe. She'd keep trying, at least, because it turned out doing cannonballs into the pool was a lot of fun.

Asher jumped into the pool and joined in the splashing fray. "I'll save you!" he yelled, grabbing Eliana by the waist and dunking her in the water in his pretend efforts to get her away from Cameron, which made Cameron belly-laugh. It was one of her favorite sounds in the world.

Especially since Cam had been missing Julia since she and Logan left for Africa. They video-called all the time, but those two were really close. Eliana was getting closer to Cameron now that she lived with her parents, which was her favorite part of living at home. Probably her *only* favorite part.

How three people could be so loud was a mystery to her.

Plus, Cameron loved the camera, which was dangerous when it came to livestreams. Luckily, she'd curated her followers to people who were excited to follow her on her new adventures: Happily Me. Except for a handful of miserable people who still couldn't seem to leave her alone. "Hypocrite" was their favorite word of choice. But hey, that's what the block button was for.

Over the couple months since she and Asher had shaken the entire Palms community by confessing their love (okay, so it was everyone else's secrets that shook the community, but they'd contributed!), she had lost her book deal and had to borrow money from her parents to pay back her advance.

She'd also lost half of her followers and several of her advertising sponsors, but the followers who remained were supportive and lovely. Plus, just this week, a new sponsor had reached out to her. It wasn't what she'd had before, not yet, but she had hope that maybe she'd get there someday.

But she'd never been happier. Truly. Which had made her wonder ... What really makes someone happy? Is it something so specific as having a dream job? Or having the perfect wedding? Or being single?

So she'd pulled out her *Happily Single* book and realized that everything she'd mentioned that led to happiness had nothing to do with ... wait for it ... actually being single.

It was surrounding yourself with good friends and supportive family and loving yourself. It was watching Louisa May Alcott stare at Asher like he was her favorite person in the world—who could blame her? It was learning that Miss Havisham was an uncharacteristically social turtle and had charmed not only all the workers at the conservation center, but the other turtles too.

It was learning that a group of Beatles-named flamingos had attacked her because they were protecting an adorable baby flamingo no one had known about, and she'd gotten too close to it. The residents of The Palms had named it Jude.

It was seeing Grandma and Grandpa hold hands, and Cameron do flip jumps for the camera, and Asher come out of his shell and let more people into his life.

It was feeling this sense of pure joy, deep in her soul, that made it possible to have wet hair and streaking eyeliner in public, that allowed her to gracefully lose. It reminded her that she had inherent value and worth regardless of how she looked or what anyone else said, something she'd genuinely come to believe.

She ran her finger over Asher's octopus tattoo as he pulled her into his arms. She wasn't complaining one bit. "You never did tell me why you got this." He'd grown to love Louisa and Miss Havisham, but he was still on his guard with most animals, and she often wondered why he'd chosen this one.

He shrugged, but it felt affected. Like he was trying to play it off as no big deal. "After my parents died, I went to the ocean a lot to grieve. I did a lot of snorkeling, and one day, I met a tiny octopus."

"Did you name him?"

"Jules Verne," he said dryly.

She perked up. "Really?"

"No." He kissed her nose. "Maybe if I'd known you then, I would have. But we just followed each other around for weeks. It was something to look forward to when I had so little to be happy about. Then we moved, and next time I went back to the ocean, he was gone. But I never forgot him."

Her eyes stung with tears.

"Plus, I knew the eight tentacles would look really incredible against my biceps, so ..."

She laughed and smacked him on said bicep, allowing him to deflect the emotion away with a joke. This time. "You're not wrong."

"Of course I'm not." He kissed her quickly, leaving her wanting more.

"Round two!" Grandpa bellowed.

"That's my cue," Eliana said with a sigh, not wanting to leave Asher's arms.

"You coming over tonight?" Asher asked. He was living in Julia's apartment and loving her kitchen, which was apparently better equipped with appliances than the bungalow had been. "I'm making bacon-and-butternut-squash ravioli."

"Marry me now," she deadpanned.

"Elly!" Grandpa called out. "We're waiting!"

"Hmm. I like the sound of that. A lot." They kissed again as everyone groaned and splashed them. "We still on for October?"

"October seems so far away. How do you feel about September?" she said.

"I've got that work conference in September," he reminded her. "I can blow it off," he said hopefully.

"No, you'd better not."

Mr. Richardson had made himself scarce since the infamous meeting—the one Grandpa Horace said he'd always regret missing, especially since it was all anyone talked about for weeks. And Samantha, eager to continually improve their medical department, had advocated paying for Asher to fly out to a speech language pathologist conference in Seattle to learn some new techniques. He was really excited about it.

"But we are going to have to name our first child Louisa May Alcott, Junior," she teased.

"We're not even married, and you're naming our nonexistent children?"

She shrugged. "I like to think ahead."

"Elly!" Grandma, Grandpa, and Cameron all yelled together.

"Duty calls," she said, swimming away. "Future Junior's pride in her mom depends on me winning this cannonball competition."

"Oh boy," Asher said. "Then you'd better get practicing, because you have a long way to go."

She squealed and splashed him, then raced away when he growled and lunged after her, wrapping his arms around her tight.

"I love you," she whispered, her nose pressed against his.

"I love you too," he said.

"And I love you both," Grandpa said dryly from where he sat at the edge of the pool, only a foot away. Oops. "But can we get this show on the road? This boy is ready." He hooked his thumb back toward Cameron, who took that as his signal to go.

"Baaaaall!" he yelled as he threw himself over Eliana and Asher and into the pool with the most epic jump yet.

EPILOGUE
WINNIE

Winnie sat back in her chair in the conference room, a satisfied grin on her face. The Secret Seven had done it again. Not only were Asher and Eliana in love, but Eliana had never been happier. She'd finally let go of the demons in her past and was embracing what the future might hold.

And that future grandson-in-law of Winnie's? Asher Brooks was a delight in every way. She still chuckled to think how out of character it was for him to tow Eliana's car, and yet she was grateful he'd done it. Without that, would they have ever gotten together? She wouldn't say anything to Don, of course. She didn't want it to go to his head. But they were so good at matchmaking, they were matchmaking without even trying.

"Should we get started?" Walt asked. "It's getting late."

Nancy sat at the front of the table, in her usual spot, staring at her phone with a frown. "Oh, sure. Yes," she said, setting it down but still looking distracted.

"Are you okay?" Winnie asked.

Nancy forced a smile. "Yes. Please give your report, Winnie."

"And then it's my turn," Harry said, with an excited grin.

Winnie began. "Well, the lovebirds are as happy as can be. They're engaged now, and they think no one knows, but of course we know." They all exchanged proud grins. They were so good at their jobs. "Asher will never lack grandparent figures again, but he did mention to me he doesn't need any more housewarming plants, so let's put the word out on that."

"How's Lydia?" Polly asked.

Winnie still felt bad for how much they'd all failed Lydia after her stroke. "She's doing well. Thank you all for reaching out to her." They made sure to check on Lydia daily, and Winnie and Horace did more group activities with her and Smitty. It was a lot of fun spending so much time together. Going on group dates made Winnie almost feel like a teenager again.

"Thank you all for your help and your love." Her throat felt tight with emotion. What her friends had done for her could never be repaid, but she'd never forget that they'd been there for her when she needed them the most. "And with that, I'll pass things along to Harry."

"Wait!" Nancy hopped up from her seat, her phone still in her hand as she stared at the screen. "My granddaughter just texted that she's at my house."

"What?" Walt asked. "Did you know she was coming?"

"No," Nancy said. "I'm sorry, Harry, but this is our chance. We have to save her."

"Of course. My turn can wait," Harry assured her.

"Save her from what?" Winnie asked.

Nancy looked at them all gravely. "The biggest mistake of her life."

Read on in *A Royal Agenda* by Lucy McConnell

Continue reading for a Bonus Epilogue

BONUS EPILOGUE
ELIANA

"Keep good company, read good books, love good things and cultivate soul and body as faithfully as you can." —Louisa May Alcott

October

E LIANA LAY BACK ON her chaise lounge on the beach and checked the placement of the sun before closing her eyes against the brightness. She had absolutely no idea how to tell time based on the sun, but if she had to guess, her email would be going out to her family and friends right ... about ... now.

A shadow fell over her, and she opened her eyes to see a bare-chested Asher standing there, holding a piña colada in one hand and a plate with a heaping pile of tacos in the other.

Her stomach growled at the sight. "Marry me."

Asher grinned wickedly. "I already did."

"Yeah, you did." She smiled back at him and moved her legs so he could sit on the end of her chair. "Sienna was right. Mexico is great. Especially in October."

"Fantastic," he agreed.

"Pretty much my favorite place in the world," she said through a mouthful of taco.

The last thing Eliana had wanted was to plan another wedding, so she and Asher had eloped. That morning. In Mexico. Where she had all beach and tacos, and no cell service.

While they were in the airport at three in the morning, she'd drafted and scheduled an email to be sent out today to let everyone know that they were married. They'd have to deal with everyone's reactions when they returned home in a week, but for now, this was absolute bliss.

Grandma and Julia would understand. Mom would come around once it dawned on her that she didn't have to plan another wedding. Dad, who would be over the moon to not have to pay for two weddings in one year, would help. And Grandpa had already predicted it—based on the envelope of money he'd slipped into her purse last time she was at his bungalow, with a note that had nothing on it but a drawing of a golf club and a ball.

She sipped the cool, sweet drink and set it on the side table, then picked up her book—Allegra Winters's latest that Grandma had pushed into her hands last week. Generally, Eliana read nonfiction, but this historical romance was sucking her in. Plus she'd left off at a good part.

Asher rubbed her feet, and it was hard to concentrate with Asher's fingers running over her arches and then moving up to her ankles and calves. Really, really hard. This was a man who knew how to knead dough in the kitchen. Her muscles were putty in his hands.

As she went to set down her book and give Asher her full, undivided, delicious attention, her gaze caught on a word in the novel. In a scene with elephants, one of the children called it an elf-ant. She knew someone else who used to call it that ...

She gasped. She flipped to the author's bio and confirmed what she'd already guessed. Allegra Winters was a pen name. And she'd just figured out who Allegra Winters really was. Did anyone else know? Was Eliana the only person who had figured it out?

Oh, this was going to be *so* good.

"What's wrong?" Asher asked.

"Nothing. Everything is oh so right," she said, setting the book down, her brain completely full of what this could mean.

"Are you sure? You're kind of wide-eyed." He copied her expression, which made her laugh. She was always laughing with Asher. It was impossible to think that she could really be this happy.

She scooted closer and closer until she was sitting right in his lap, with her arms around his neck. There'd be more than enough time to tell him later and figure out what to do about Allegra Winters. For now, she was on her honeymoon with her brand new not-so-secret (according to the sun's timing) husband, and she wanted to relish every single second she could.

So that's exactly what she did.

Want to read Logan and Julia's love story? *A Summer Mismatch* by Kaylee Baldwin is out now!

Join Kaylee Baldwin's newsletter to receive a free book and keep up to date on her latest releases, sales, and other news.

ACKNOWLEDGMENTS

THIS BOOK HAS BEEN a journey to get into your hands! Thank you to:

Ranee S. Clark and Kate Watson for your amazing (and quick!) feedback and all your encouragement. You two are the BEST.

Ellie Thornton for your thorough reading (and for the baby flamingo...)

My daily Zoom group that keeps me on task and (and also off-task in the best way).

Mom for reading this so quickly and on such short notice.

All the Diamond Cove authors—Lucy, Ellie, Holly, Maria, Elodia, and Erica. You are incredible women and writers, and I'm thrilled to do this with you.

The Summer of Rom Com authors and readers. Your enthusiasm was invaluable while writing this. Seriously.

My family for supporting my many, many (many) hours at the computer this summer.

And my readers. I love hearing from you! Thank you from the bottom of my heart for being so wonderful.

About Kaylee Baldwin

K AYLEE BALDWIN'S LOVE OF all things books and reading led her to graduate from Arizona State University with a degree in English. She has ten published novels, one of which was a Whitney Award Finalist. Her most recent novel is *Me and Mr. Just Right* in the Enchanted series. She lives in Arizona with her family. Check out her website at for a free novel, and follow her on Instagram @kayleebaldwinbooks to learn more about her adventures and the books she's reading.

Also By Kaylee Baldwin

The Match Series:
A Summer Mismatch
A Wedding Mismatch

The Enchanted Series
Me & Mr. Just Right

The Take My Heart series:
Take My Heart (A Christmas Romance)
Take a Chance on Me (Read for free!)

Small-Town Billionaire Series:
Her Billionaire Heartthrob
Her Billionaire Rival (coming soon)

Making the Play
Hearts in Peril
Silver Linings
One Little Kiss
Six Days of Christmas
California Dreamin'

Made in the USA
Monee, IL
07 September 2023

42356084R00164